Aaron's Year *of* '77

A Story in Twelve Parts

J FRANCIS GRICE

 FriesenPress

Suite 300 - 990 Fort St
Victoria, BC, V8V 3K2
Canada

www.friesenpress.com

ISBN
978-1-5255-9776-3 (Hardcover)
978-1-5255-9775-6 (Paperback)
978-1-5255-9777-0 (eBook)

1. FICTION, EROTICA, LGBTQ+, GAY
2. FICTION, ROMANCE, LGBTQ+, GAY
3. FICTION, COMING OF AGES
4. FICTION, ROMANCE, CONTEMPORARY

Distributed to the trade by The Ingram Book Company

For you, Stephen

Just prior to the official release of this book, Grice's partner and husband of 40 years suddenly and unexpectedly passed away. As such, this novel will serve as a Memorial Tribute to the memory of a wonderful, vital man who was well-loved and will be deeply missed by so many.

Steve: I will always love you. Your spirit and soul will be forever immortalized within the pages of this book - a book that will stand as a tribute, both to you and to the marvelous and magical life we had together.

Rest in peace, my partner - both in life (and in crime!).

JFG

A *Very* Special Mention

I must thank my clever and extremely patient friend, Nicolas Marulli for keeping me relatively sane (...whatever that is...) during the final editing process for this book, and for being the absolute best critic and proof-reader any fledgling aspiring author could ever hope to have in his back pocket!

Thanks, 'Nico'!

JFG

Table of Contents

Preface

The seventies were a raucous, free and naive time of sexual awakening, coupled with uninhibited kink, fetishism and unprotected sexual exploration just before the suffering and stigma of AIDS in the early eighties. They were an exciting, brash and irreverent time during which to come out.

The Disco Era was in high-volume Studio 54 mode. "Love Hangover" by Diana Ross, "Everybody Dance" by Chic and "Disco Inferno" by The Trammps were some of the top chart singles on the radio. *Saturday Night Fever* and *Star Wars* premiered at the theatres. And television gave us *Dallas, The Jefferson's* and *Charlie's Angels*.

Amidst all the tacky glitter and overblown excitement of 1977, there were still those of us in small-towns and cities right across Canada—anxious, naive and scared—at the same time, curious and excited to get away to find ourselves.

Intro

This gay male erotic romance novel is set in two primary locales, Brockville, Ontario and Ottawa, Ontario beginning in the year 1977 and continuing into 1978. It is written from the naïve perspective of an inexperienced nineteen year old young gay man coming out and navigating life as he enters College and has his first serious relationship with a handsome, spirited and complex older man.

It is a unique story exhibiting passionate love, rare tolerance and acceptance during a time of rampant political and social anti-gay sentiment.

Establishment suppression and virulent homophobia as exemplified by frequent police raids on gay bars and male bathhouses still occurred. The RCMP persisted in harassing and subjecting the LGBTQ+ community with their vehement intolerance and pre-legalization era 'Fruit Machine' tactics and strong-arm practices.

Ottawa was a mecca for many young men frustrated and stifled in small towns and cities across Canada as they sought to find acceptance and a confident sense of self in which to thrive and hopefully, find purpose, value, fulfillment and ultimate happiness.

The Disco era was a unique, colourful and important historic period driving the author to record it for the future and is loosely based upon his own life and personal experiences at the time.

Gay life in the seventies was strikingly different from what todays' youth experience in their respective journeys to discover themselves and find their place in today's world. The gay bar scene and culture of unprotected sex, drugs and one-night stands was a sober harbinger of what was to come when AIDs first started to reveal it's ugly face in the early-eighties.

So many failed to foresee the tragic and horrific events yet to come.

But for a brief, glittery, shiny tinsel moment in time, the music, the drugs, the dancing, the sex and the hook-ups were the pulse and driving force of what it was like to come of age as a gay man in the late-seventies.

Against all odds, the two main characters, Aaron and Adam evolve and mature, learning to face their many challenges with courage and sometimes silly and lame teasing humor—both individually and as a committed, passionate, loving couple during this compelling, fast-paced twelve month period.

1 July

On a good day we can get maybe thirteen television channels on our cable TV box at home. And that's about the only way the outside world ever penetrates the shuttered life in which I live as a young, repressed, good little Catholic boy with a wildly overactive imagination and obsessive, gay teenage sexual fantasies and urges.

Brockville is a small, conservative, eastern Ontario border city just across the St. Lawrence River from Morristown in upstate New York. Some smart-ass years ago sarcastically coined the nickname *Brock Vegas* for the city.

I've yet to meet Ann Margret, Dean Martin or Sammy Davis Junior on King Street, however.

I just turned nineteen back last December and am still living at home with my parents until I head off to Algonquin College in Ottawa in a few months time. I'm still technically a virgin, albeit one with a vivid imagination and more than enough experience using my very talented right hand to jerk off as often as possible. That being said, I walk around half-hard obsessing about having sex all the time. There is one guy in particular I just can't stop thinking about. His name is Adam. He's so sexy and handsome. I doubt he'd even give me a second look. And in my naiveté and shyness, I'd never deliberately do or say anything to give him any impression that I thought he was a hunky guy and that I liked him.

Brock Vegas wasn't exactly *Sin City* after all.

"Aaron, I need you to go and pick up a prescription for me at Tonner's today. Mrs. Tonner called me to let me know that the balance of my Valium and Tofranil are finally in now. When you are downtown this afternoon would you please pop in there and speak with either her or Adam Blanchard? I've got to let them know you'll be going in for me. And they'll just charge it to my account with them. Will you do that for me, darling, please?"

"Uhm, sure, Mom. No problem."

Meanwhile, I'm thinking, *perfect! Another chance to check out Adam.* Adam Blanchard is the pharmacy assistant at Tonner's and just about the best-looking and sexiest guy I think I've ever seen in Brockville. He always manages to get me totally flustered. And I'm sure I always get five shades of red in the face whenever I go into Tonner's to just look around or to pick something up for Mom. He's the very first guy I've ever had any kind of a crush on in any serious way. And my hormones and testosterone keep me masturbating and fantasizing about him and what's in his pants at least twice a day.

I know he works late most nights at the store. I know a fair bit about Adam, actually. I doubt he knows anything about me though and probably barely notices me the times I come into the drug store.

As for me, well, what is there really to notice?

I'm just beginning to lose my baby fat and while still skinny to the point where I dread wearing my old Speedo bathing suit in public, I suppose I'm not totally ugly. I've been working out to develop my shoulders and chest and have been told that I have nice eyes. And at just a shade under 5'-10" I don't imagine I'll be having any more late-adolescent growth spurts from here on in.

I've been out of high school for a couple of years and am now working for my brother-in-law up at the Brockville Shopping Centre. Before that, I worked for Mr. and Mrs. Elasse in the toy and hobby basement section of Symington's Home Hardware on King Street for a year and a bit until my sister, Astrid asked me to come and help Geraint out at his Benjamin Moore, *Floor and Wall* paint store franchise.

Fortunately, my terminal acne has finally cleared up so I don't look like some pathetic high school geek anymore. I've let my hair grow out a bit over the past year to the point where it looks full and wavy—I'm not exactly a rock star or John Travolta though.

Compared to Adam, no one would ever give me a second glance. I'm absolutely sure of that.

Tonner's Pharmacy has been on the corner of King Street and Fulford Avenue at the bottom of the hill for more than sixty years. It's a hallowed and time-honored institution in Brockville. Going in through the plate-glass front door, the checkout and cash register are to the left, with the drug prescription counter all the way at the back of the store, That's where Adam is usually stationed, filling prescriptions and advising customers about remedies and treatments available over the counter to treat whatever their health questions and issues might be.

Today he's on a small step-stool reaching up to a top shelf to pull a bag down with pill bottles inside for the lady in front of me. That's really lucky timing because I get to stare at his sexy man-ass and how those pants he's wearing tightly ride right up the crack of his butt and fantasize about whether he's wearing underwear and what side his big penis and balls are hanging on today.

He looks up into the convex mirror hanging down from the ceiling that gives him a panoramic view of the store as he is stepping down. He sees me staring at his butt and smirks to himself.

"Here ya go, Mrs. Craig," he says, handing her the bag. "You can pay Mrs. Tonner at the front, along with the other stuff ya have in your basket there. I'll hold onto the prescription slip here at the counter though for your file. Is there anything else I'm able to help ya with today?"

"No, Adam. That's perfect Thanks very much."

Then he turns around with his back to me for a second and reaches down to adjust himself inside his pants before turning back to face me.

"Yeah, kid. OK. Whaddya want? What can I help ya with there?"

"Uhm, uhh, I'm here to pick up a prescription for Mrs. Christie over on Bethune Street. She said she called the store for me to come and get it for her." I'm mumbling and staring down at the counter to avoid making any eye contact. I'm just so nervous and bashful around him.

"My eyes are up here, kid. Now, who did ya say you were here for again?"

I'm blushing scarlet red and shyly look up at him repeating, "Mrs. Christie over on Bethune Street. I think she told me there were two prescriptions for her here to be picked up."

"Yep. She musta' been talking to Mrs. Tonner about 'em. Yep. Here they are."

Just then I hear my friend, Wendy Yaegar right behind me.

"Aaron! Hey! Glad I ran into you here. Wanna head up to the 401 Inn later with Cala? Rob can join us there, too. It's Friday and I wanna dance."

"Sure, OK, Wendy. I'll see you there after nine thirty."

Then Adam tells me to see Mrs. Tonner at the front as I'm leaving since she was the one my mother had spoken to about a pick up, and to initial the receipt for him to put them on Mrs. Christie's account. He hands me a pen and checks me out while I take it and sign the slip of paper in his hand.

Jeez, that look and cute thing he just did with the nose twitching there just started to give me a hard-on! I've just gotta get out of here, like, right now!

The 401 Inn on Stewart Boulevard in Brockville is just beside the King's Highway 401 which runs between Montreal and Toronto. Once you go inside, between the motel dining room and the front desk there are carpeted stairs going down to what used to be a wedding reception and business conference room in the basement. Now this part of the motel has a disco dance bar that boasts the best sound system in town and a really cool DJ, named Zakary, aka *Trick,* who moonlights as the radio announcer for the local FM radio station. The drinks are cheap and the music is always cranked up to full-volume in the evenings.

"Heya, Aaron. It's Cala here," the voice on the other end says when I pick up the ringing phone back at the house. "Figured I'd give you a phone call to see what you're doing tonight. I'm not working and I was thinking we could head up to the 401 and dance with Wendy and Rob. I'll give her a call once I hang up with you here. I wanna get out of the house away from Dad, and it being the weekend and all, well, let's go, OK?"

"Sure thing, Cala," I say. "I ran into Wendy already and told her I'd meet her up there later. I worked up at the shopping centre earlier this morning for Geraint and had lunch with Rob. I'll see you guys up there after nine-thirty."

When I finally make it up to the motel and start to scan the place to look for Cala and everyone, all I can hear is Donna Summer on the turntable moaning and singing "Love to Love Ya Baby". The bar is packed tonight with almost every chair taken and people standing at the bar and along the wall beside the dance floor.

Holy shit! Adam Blanchard is in here tonight! He like, never goes out to the bars in town! I can't help but stare over at him. He looks amazing out of that cheap, tacky gold pharmacy jacket he sometimes wears behind the counter over his good clothes in the drug store.

He's really something! I'm blushing with dirty thoughts of his big cock and sexy, fuzzy man-butt racing through my head. Then I gulp and quickly avert my eyes.

I think he may have picked up on my reaction and is now just standing there casually leaning against the wall in the corner of the room, posing in a stone-grey wool, vee-neck sweater with his thumb hooked into the front pocket of his tight-fitting, cream-coloured chinos and his fingers splayed out to direct attention to his bulging crotch—staring back at me and grinning that dumb, lopsided, grin of his whenever I tried to subtly cast sneaky, fervent glances over at him.

God! I wonder if he is circumcised like me or not? Somehow, I just don't think so.

Of course I've seen uncut cocks in gym class back in high school. But I never could figure out what went on with guy's foreskins whenever they got horny. *Does it get uncomfortable for them when they get hard sometimes inside their pants? Does their cock get really big and stretch out that extra skin? It must, I guess. Can you peel that skin back and lick and suck on it? Jeez, Aaron!*

I can't help looking over and staring at his crotch. I can clearly see the outline of his cock in those pants. I can't stop thinking about whether he is circumcised or not. Tasting his cock and burying my nose deep down inside those pants between his big balls and inner thighs is something I can't stop fixating over. *I'd love to unzip that fly and shove my hand down the front of them to feel just how big that thing is between his legs. I wonder if he jerks off a lot or whether he is banging some girl. She'd be really lucky to have that big thing of his inside her—and with him on top, for sure.*

He keeps stretching his fingers to cup his big bulge and after five minutes or so, I have to look away and bite my lower lip to take my mind off wondering what he smells like down there and how hairy he is. I don't see any bikini or jockey short lines and wonder if he is even wearing any underwear. *His ass is just perfect in those pants!*

His five o'clock shadow is hypnotic and I can just imagine how it would scratch and feel against my skin, along with his hot breath if he ever went down on me.

Fuck!

I can't believe he keeps looking over and of course now I can't get up from the chair here until my hard-on goes away! *I must be imagining it that he even notices me. He's got to be looking at someone else!*

Fuck!

"Hey, Aaron," says Wendy as we head back to our table after dancing. "C'mon outside with me and let's smoke a joint. We can do that over in the parking lot and no one should be able to smell it if we're careful and discreet."

"Let's hide out beside that old, silver grey car at the back of the lot. No one can see us over there because it's in the darkest part of the parking lot."

I recognize that car as the one parked behind Tonner's Drug Store most days on Fulford Avenue, I'm not a hundred-percent positive, but I think it's Adam's car. The passenger-side window is down almost all the way and it looks like he has some clothes bundled up there for either laundry or dry-cleaning. I recognise those trousers in the pile from when he was wearing them earlier in the day. There is also an old brown-and-tan coarse tweed necktie absent-mindedly tossed over the seatback.

"You go on back inside, Wendy. I have to pee like, really badly and am just going to do it out here behind this car. I'll be back in with you in a few minutes, OK?

When the evening ends, Adam drives home alone minus that necktie and pair of wrinkled dress pants he was planning to take in to the One Hour Cleaners beside Tonner's the next morning before his shift started at the pharmacy.

An hour and a half later, I'm home alone and lying naked on my bed in my room. I've got the crotch of those trousers where his big bulge would have been held up against the side of my face to see if I can imagine him wearing them. The inside lining where his big penis and scrotum would rub against is pilled, worn and faintly discoloured with savory sweat stains. It feels so sensual and tactile as I play with myself, slowly starting to rub one out inside the lining and feeling that rough, masculine-feeling fabric against my hard cock.

I guess now this one time anyway, I won't be having any wet dreams about him tonight and wake up having to change the sheets on my bed in the morning.

I felt so guilty and was sure there was something seriously wrong with me for the longest time when those wet dreams first started to happen. It was pleasurable, but I just knew somehow it was really weird and more than likely wrong somehow.

Then when Dad tried to talk to me about it after Mom probably forced him to, I was like, so embarrassed. I know that he was as well at the time. But having to hide those sheets from Mom every morning was getting to be really tough and I just didn't understand why I kept doing that in my sleep every night. When Dad told me it was perfectly natural and not to worry about it at my age because I'd eventually grow out of having it happen, I felt a little better.

Every couple of minutes I stare over at the picture I snuck of Adam while he was waiting on a customer in Tonner's months and months ago when his head was turned and he was distracted with waiting on them.

I'm fantasizing about just how big his cock gets when he's hard and whether he's bigger than me when he jacks off. The crotch of those pants of his is making me crazy.

Guess this is as close as I'm ever going to get to know what his cock is like.

Ten minutes later, groaning softly, I ejaculate for the third time that day and shove Adam's cum-stained trousers under my pillow. I keep rubbing the fabric back and forth to feel the texture and feel of it between my thumb and index finger until I fall asleep.

July 7th, 1977.

It's just another humid summer late night for me in Brock Vegas. I'm out trying to walk off some of my pent-up sexual frustration and am in front of the Brockville Restaurant when, gradually, I start to hear the hesitant protests and sounds of a poorly-tuned car slowly cruising up behind me.

To my surprise, it's Adam. I now realize that old grey car as being his after all. I'm shocked and feel a secret sense of guilty pleasure knowing he and I are alone on this deserted street, with no one else around at this early hour of the morning.

That car of his is really old, a real beater of a coupe—I'm surprised it's still on the road. He goes past me and I stop to look at him and his wheels closely. His old car idles roughly as though it's about to stall out on him at any minute. I recognize it to be an old, faded-silver grey, dinged and dented rusted-out '67 AMC Ambassador SST two door coupe that's seen better days. He turns right at a corner about six blocks ahead onto Perth Street and disappears.

A few minutes later I turn that corner and he's pulled over by the side of the street, partially concealed in the dark shadows created by the streetlight. He's trying to start his car. He's clearly stranded and has fortunately managed to muscle his vehicle off to the side of the street. It's not a good situation. I know Perth Street is a pretty bad area of town to have your car stall out or break down on you.

His starter whines and grinds away and cranks and cranks, but the old coupe just won't turn over for him. Bluish white toxic exhaust smoke spills out of both tailpipes each time he tries to start it. I can smell the gas fumes from his car from where I'm standing. Suddenly, he sees me in his rear-view mirror and lets up on his starter. He has such a look of focused, serious determination on his face. He stares back at me without blinking.

Twenty or thirty seconds pass with me standing there, frozen in place, wide-eyed and looking back at him. I have this tingling sensation at the base of my stomach. He tries to start his car again.

This time, the starter wails in protest and grinds away with a slow, tired rhythm. Then it coughs, backfires, and reluctantly stumbles to life. The engine idles roughly.

Adam rolls down the window on the passenger-side and I walk up to it. He leans over from his driver's seat and starts to talk to me.

"Sure as hell glad it was just you watchin' me just now and not someone else," he says. "What a damn fuckin' shitty place to stall out, eh? And at this time a night, too. Jeezus fuck! Ya know kid, ya really shouldn't be out walkin' the streets alone at this time a night yourself there. Never know what could happen to ya or whatcha might wind up walkin' into. C'mon, hop in with me. Let's go for a ride together. I could use some company. Let's just cruise around for a bit—just you and me, OK? It's been a real shitty day for me up to now. C'mon, let's go. C'mon, kid. It'll be fun for ya. You're gonna be safe with me. I'll make it fun—I promise ya that."

He's a bit taller than me, maybe 6'-3" and kind of beefy with a really well-developed upper body—especially his biceps and shoulders. I'm guessing he's in his mid to late-twenties. He looks a bit disheveled and a little scruffy at the end of his work shift. I can tell he's moderately hairy and toned all over. He has medium length, thick, dark hair. It's wavy and hangs down carelessly across his forehead and just above his ears and the back of his shirt collar. *It isn't really fashionable, but it does suit him*, I think. I can't stop looking at his mouth and lips. They look like they belong on a marble statue. *God, I want to bite that bottom lip of his.* He's wearing a cheap polyester, dotted-pattern, unbuttoned dress shirt with the cuffs rolled up just past his wrists. He's got a dark five o'clock shadow with coarse bristly beard stubble and is clearly in need of a shave. It almost looks like a moustache and beard on him. *Hmmm... he'd look really handsome with a beard and moustache,* I think while looking over, taking in the angles and contours of his beautiful face. He has that *tired-fed-up-and-heading-home* look about him. I can see curling, dark forearm hair and strong pecs with visible hard nipples straining through the outline of that wrinkled shirt. His strong left hand hangs casually over his steering wheel and his right hand rests down between his muscular long legs cupping his big bulge.

I'm guessing he must be heading home just now after closing up the pharmacy. I've spied on him there so many times when I've gone into the store for no reason other than to look at him furtively and pretend to shop for something for either me or Mom.

The navy blue wool sports jacket he wears when serving behind the counter is lying rumpled up on his passenger-side, front-seat beside him. I'm guessing this worn, old jacket is probably the only one he's got. It looks good on him though and fits him perfectly in all the right places. Also, it gives him a real air of masculine authority. He grabs it to make room for me up front and close beside him. Then, on sudden impulse, despite the humidity, shrugs it on.

He straightens up in his driver's seat and, with his arm stretched over the seatback, gives me an inviting, mischievous little smile. Still on the sidewalk, I look down at his loden-green wool trousers and realize he's trying to hide a bulging erection. Holy shit! It's straining at the seam of his crotch and causing a prominent tent that fights with the zipper of his pants. It's the hour of chance, opportunity, and fulfillment for those who lust and I'm sure as hell not going to pass up on this chance with him… no way.

He reaches over, pulls his door handle and the door creaks and opens for me. I climb in beside him. He smiles once again at me and then turns his attention back to his old car. He revs it a bit with a little smirk on his face. Then he puts it in DRIVE and it starts to move forward for him. I can feel the rough vibrations from his tired engine. He pulls into the parking lot behind Howison's Confectionary and Variety Store and backs slowly out onto Perth Street. Then he revs his car even more, eventually forcing his worn gas pedal down to the floor and turns right onto King Street to head west out of town. His left hand is cupping and subtly rubbing his prominent pube-package all the time he is doing this, too.

He's pretty good at maneuvering and driving his big old car with just his right arm and hand on the steering wheel.

"Thanks, kid. Didn't really wanna hafta head on home alone just now after I saw ya watchin' me. You know, I've seen ya in the store and then out by yourself around town sometimes when I've been drivin' around by myself. Let's cruise outta town and see where we wind up. Sound like a plan to you, kid?"

Uhm, I'm not a kid! I'm going to be twenty this year and will be starting College in the fall."

"I'll try to remember that," he says while trying to conceal an amused grin.

He has a distinctive masculine baritone voice and speaks with a characteristic colloquial slang. It labels him, along with many others in town as being a true Brockvillian native who demonstrates a certain kind of guileless, unaffected sincerity and naïve, innocent charm. Everything is *wanna, woulda, coulda, gonna, or dontcha* with him. The tonality and cadence of his voice is beautiful. It's gentle, yet gritty and self-assured.

"Sure. OK. I'd really like that."

He drives on with me beside him, murmuring curses and profanities to his car as it protests and stumbles on. We head out of town on the old number two highway steering west toward the 401 turn-off at Long Beach where it turns and meets up with the St. Lawrence River. He slouches down deep into his driver's seat and spreads his long legs wide to make himself more comfortable. When he adjusts himself, I can see how aroused he's getting. All the while, he keeps glancing at me sideways from the corner of his eye. *If he doesn't realize he's making me rock hard, then he's an absolute, complete and total idiot!*

He has one of those cheap gas station green pine tree air fresheners most blue-collar and working-class men have in their pick-up trucks and cars. It dangles from the eight track player beneath the dashboard beside his steering wheel and in front of his spreading crotch. It keeps fluttering back and forth so I can smell the scent, which keeps me conscious of and focused on his big, furry man-package at the same time. I wonder if that's why he hung it there with that intention in mind. I can intensely feel him beside me and keep glancing over at his face and what's teasing me down there between his legs, but he keeps his eyes forward, concentrating on keeping his old ride going.

After a few minutes, I reach over to turn on his radio to break the silence and it's then that he leans over and puts his right hand on my arm. An intense electrical shock goes through my entire body. "Ya maybe don't wanna do that. Might drain down the battery in my car and my alternator isn't working too damn good right now."

A couple of minutes pass between us in silence, save for the protests coming from under the hood of his old coupe. "Ya looking for some good music?" he eventually asks, while giving me a shy little grin. "I'm not exactly Barry White or Lou Rawls, but why dontcha tune in to me here for a bit and see what comes up for ya?"

With that, he grabs my hand and, with one swift, deliberate calculated motion, shoves it down into the bulge between his legs. I can feel his big cock responding immediately to my tentative grip.

"Play with it in my pants until it gets all hard and ready for ya. Then you can take it out 'cause it really wants to have some hot sexy fuck time alone with ya here in my front-seat!"

I slowly undo his worn, black leather belt and start to pull very slowly on the tab of the zipper on his wrinkled trousers. I am seduced by his hairy pleasure trail as I take in the sight of his half-hard, thick tool.

Christ almighty, I just knew it! He's like, not wearing any damned underwear! His uncut dick is sitting out there and gradually rising up to full standing attention right in front of my eyes. And all I can smell is his strong, male pheromone scent and the obnoxious, sickly pine smell from that damned stupid air freshener.

His overwhelming and assertive manly smell is intoxicating. It's strong and pungent—unforgettable and virile, just like him. His scent reeks of intimate sexual need and desire in the middle of the night between two horny, boned-up strangers needing some hot male action. He looks directly at me and then down at his big cock. His eyes tell me exactly what he wants. He doesn't need to say a word.

"I just have to know what sucking a really handsome, sexy, hot guy like you would be like." I tell him shyly. "And I'm really glad you're going to be the first guy I ever get to do it with."

He grins and with a gleam in his eye says teasingly to me, "So, ya think I'm handsome, do ya, eh? Well, get down there then and suck on it. I think it kinda likes ya."

Hmmm, he sure looks pretty pleased with himself after I told him I thought he was handsome. I start to focus on his big cock. I taste the precum on its head with my tongue. He shudders.

His old car shudders at the same time.

"Jeezus!" he mutters under his breath. "OK, gimme a sec' here to pull my old wheels over to the side of the road. If you really wanna do that to me as bad as I wantcha to, then I'm gonna hafta pull over here before we stall out in the middle of the goddamn road."

He squarely plants his scuffed and worn black oxford shoe on his brake. I can feel his leg muscles tense up as he presses down to stop his SST. His old car shudders again. It keeps idling rougher and rougher and stumbles one last time, then the engine coughs and dies.

"Jeezus!" he mutters angrily under his breath. "OK, since we're not goin' any further right now, you might as well finish what ya got started down there. It's been one fuckin' bitch of a shitty day. And this goddamn piece-a-shit old car of mine isn't helpin' it one damn little bit right about now. Oh. And yeah, before I get distracted any more with my fuckin' car and with my dong and you suckin' on it down there, and while I'm really thinkin' about it here, hafta say you're just about the cutest damned young guy I think I've ever seen in Brock Vegas."

I blush beet red at his compliment.

He notices and smiles to himself. "Go on, get down there and suck it. It wants ya, big time. And I do mean big." Then he takes his right hand and holds onto my head while gently guiding me down into his furry crotch. Then he lifts his right arm and shoulder back up to stretch fully across his seatback as I try to get comfortable down there between his legs.

I can feel the friction of his trousers on my face as he moves back and forth to make full body contact with my probing tongue and lips. The feeling of everything—his big, throbbing hard cock, his old car, the coarse wool fabric of his dress trousers, the humid summer heat—I can't believe he's really letting me do this to him.

"Jeezus fuck! Lemme undo the rest of the buttons on my shirt! You're about to learn what nipple play is all about. Help me out here! You're making me fuckin' crazy! I wantcha to take your hand and grab onto my nipple. Now twist and squeeze it. Keep suckin' my dong at the same time. Let's see how much you can make me squirm and what we can tease outta me to help ya get me off."

I'm obsessed with rubbing my hand back and forth across his hairy chest while every now and then tweaking and pinching his sensitized left nipple. Soft sighs and moans of pleasure escape from those tantalizing lips of his when I bury my face in his hot crotch and suck on his throbbing, rock-hard tool.

"Fuckin' hell! You sure are one sexy, fuckable piece of boy candy!"

He lifts my head up gently after a short while and murmurs softly, "Just stroke it for a bit. Ya kinda got my stick-shift just a little too excited down there. It needs to calm down for a bit. You do know what a hand-job is, dontcha, kid?"

"Don't call me kid!"

After a couple of minutes he sighs with intense pleasure and says to me, "OK, just a sec'. Let's see if we can get my ride started again. Maybe find a more private place to do this. I really wanna be in my back-seat alone with ya. Would ya like my crotch-rocket to blast off inside your hot little butt?"

Jeez! Did he really just say crotch-rocket?! Like, what the hell is that all about?

He moves his right leg and aggressively pumps his big worn gas pedal seven or eight times. He turns the key. It cranks for a few seconds but won't start. "Argh! C'mon ya fucker!" he whispers, "Turn over for me." He turns his key again, "Ugh! C'mon ya fuckin' sonofabitch."

He brutally pumps his gas pedal and cranks his car much longer this time, "C'mon ya bitch. Start for me!" He turns his key one more time. His starter cranks slower and slower. His battery is draining—slower and slower. One final fuck passes his sensual lips and he is silent. I lean up and look into his face. It's a mask of intense frustration.

"Why not just leave it alone for a while."

He looks down at me for a second and says, "Shh, just lemme do this. No one knows this car better than me! I know what I'm doin'. This fuckin' shitbox of mine has acted up and caused me enough goddamn trouble and attitude ever since I just left work. Practically almost drained the fuckin' battery down completely tryin' to get it to start, too. Jeezus! It almost wouldn't fuckin' start at all for me at the end of my goddamn shift just now behind the store. Was just tryin' to get home after a long crappy day. And my goddamn car wouldn't hardly fuckin' start for me. Like, fuck me man. Was horny, hot, tired and just wantin' to get outta these sweaty, stinkin' work clothes and jerk off. Just wantin' to hop into a scalding hot shower and rub one out and fall into bed. And my pathetic old SST stalls out and floods and then like, totally fuckin' craps out on me again tonight!"

He sighs and continues saying, "Ya know, this kinda bullshit has happened to me one time too many lately. The cum rag under my driver's seat has seen way too much action that way. It needs to find itself a new fuckin' boyfriend. And I need to get a real decent sleep in my own bed tonight. Havin' to sleep again, sprawled out in my front-seat here with my jacket for a pillow in this goddamn hot weather and all is doin' a real number on my back."

"You mean to tell me you actually sleep sometimes, right where I'm sitting now?"

"Well, baby, not through choice. That's for damn sure," he grumbles and then sighs heavily.

I try to lighten the mood by wiggling my butt back and forth and say to him with a grin, "Hmmm, too bad I'm not on top of you right now. That could be really fun, actually!"

He stops in mid-sentence, looks stunned and then stares at me for a few seconds. There is a glimmer in his eye. He tries to hide a grin and stifle a laugh and then says sternly to me, "Simmer down there! That's not really funny, ya know. I'm bein' dead serious here. And dontcha try to distract me any more than you already have since ya climbed into my wheels to cruise around in the dark with me."

Then he pauses and takes a long breath, shakes his head, comes back to reality and growls, "Just don't need this goddamn fuckin' drama from my pathetic crap excuse for a car tonight. And now, goddammit, it's not gonna stop me from what I wanna do with you on top of everything else."

Tense silence ensues as he grabs his ignition key and leans far forward, his left arm slung over his steering wheel. Dontcha dare conk out on me here now, ya motherfuckin' bastard! He raises his sexy man-ass up out of his seat and his car starts to shake and sputter. "That's it! C'mon, c'mon, c'mon, c'mon, baby, turn over for me! Ugh! C'mon, c'mon, ya fuckin' cunt! Ugh! Argh! Start! Start! Start! Argh! C'mon, baby! Dontcha crap out on me, bitch! Start for me!!"

And with that, his old car coughs and stumbles to life and I can feel his muscles slowly relax throughout his body. He keeps revving his engine and the front end lifts up and reacts with angry, growling, tortured backfires every time he forces his gas pedal to the floor. He lets up on it after a bit and slumps back down into his driver's seat as it idles roughly away. Then he takes a big breath and says softly to me, "OK. Get back down there and keep playin' with my dong. It wants some cute, young, sexy Brockville boy action tonight."

I start to give his balls a tongue bath, sniffing his man-scent, tasting and rolling them around in my mouth. They smell of his pungent sweat and are hot in response to my probing tongue. On a sudden impulse, I take my middle finger and start to play with his tight asshole, teasing it around the rim while sticking my finger in and out until his sphincter muscles tighten up firmly around it. He groans softly once more with intense pleasure and shifts his hips and lower body up to better feel my actions on him and give me full access to his inviting crotch.

"Yeahhh! That's the way! Do it! Do it now! Yeah! Oh Jeezus fuck! Just like that! Dontcha stop now!" He reaches up to jerk his gear lever to DRIVE. He stomps on his worn gas pedal and his old car backfires, coughs, and promptly conks out again.

"Well shit! Since we're not goin' nowhere for now, might as well sit back and enjoy the fuckin' goddamn view." He shrugs off his jacket and carelessly tosses it down onto the floor on the passenger-side right beside my feet. His wallet and keys to the store spill out of his inside pocket and land right between my legs. As I'm bending down to pick them up, he grabs onto my arm and says, "Leave it. I'll get 'em later. Keep on playin' with my dong. C'mon then. Keep it up! Play with my stick-shift and make me bust a load so somethin' good happens to me tonight."

I wrap my mouth around his beautiful mushroom-shaped cock-head and can feel it throbbing and pulsing. Each time I taste the tip of his cock, I can feel him squirm with intense pleasure. *This must be torture for him. He looks like he's either in pain or what people describe as ecstasy. Maybe both?*

After a few more minutes, he starts to forcibly ram his rock-hard cock with rapid, deep, fast rhythmic thrusts up into my mouth and then suddenly yells out, "Aww, fuck! Gonna cum! Gonna cum right now! Fuck me, man! Suck it! Yeah! Yeahhh! Jeezus fuck! Suck on that dick! Jeezus shit, I'm cumming now!" He yells louder and erupts, shooting his sticky, white spunk load.

Rope after thick rope of hot man-juice explodes deep in my mouth.

Well, I guess his crotch-rocket blasted off after all, I think and secretly smile. Once I've swallowed the last of his cum load, I feel like he's branded me inside with his thick jizz as the last bit of it slides down my throat.

"Ahh, Christ! Jeezus fuckin' shit! Fuckin' fantastic," he groans. "You're really somethin' else. What you may lack in experience, ya sure as hell make up for with enthusiasm. You're gonna be a quick learner, I'm thinkin'. Next time you're gonna get fucked real good. My dude-piston is tellin' me it wants ya. Now c'mon, zip my pants up and finish off what ya started down there."

I bend down to get one last heady scent of his crotch and smile to myself at him describing his beautiful big cock as a dude-piston. *Like where did he come up with that description? That's a new one on me. That's some mouth and vocabulary he has on him.*

23

Then I tuck his cock back inside his pants while simultaneously cupping his balls in my hand through that warm, moist fabric. I tug on the tab of his zipper and slowly pull on it to close up his fly—one last grope and caress of his big, hairy package and that hot inner thigh. Finally, he sighs with pleasure and smiles down at me saying, "Uhm, just gimme a sec' while I get out and take a piss after that. OK? Be right back."

I can smell his sweaty pube-forest and testicles on my fingers—*wish I could make his scent last all night long.*

Once back, he opens his creaking driver's side door and slides in beside me. The heat inside his old Ambassador goes up a hundred degrees the second he drops his hot man-ass down in his worn-down, old driver's seat just inches away from me. He turns his key in his ignition and tries to start his old ride. "C'mon, c'mon ya sonofabitch, turn over. Argh! Dontcha do this to me again tonight. C'mon, c'mon, c'mon, ahh, fuckin' shit. Ugh! C'mon, bitch!"

It just won't start. "Ya goddamn shitbox! Argh! Jeezus, man! Aww, c'mon, baby!"

He has the foulest mouth on him. It's kind of a turn-on for me and I think he senses it too and gets off on that. But right now, pissed-off is a mild term to describe how angry and frustrated he is.

"You're gonna need to slide yourself on over here into my seat. It's all warmed up from me and just waitin' for your cute, little boy-butt. I'm gonna hafta get out and lift up the hood to see if we can get my damned old, piece-a-shit car runnin' again. Just do what I tell ya, OK?" He walks to the front of his car and hoists the hood up. He yells across it at me.

"OK, pump it real good for me—crank the livin' shit out of it 'til I tell ya to let up on my starter for a bit."

I do and nothing happens. Just that weak, whining, cranking noise. I can't see him because his hood is jacked up. But I know he's out there—alone—pissed-off—frustrated. I keep turning his ignition key. Nothing, nothing, nothing.

"Keep it up with the pumpin' there! I can see the choke opening and closing on the carburetor. Jeezus! It's just gotta start, man!"

Thirty seconds later and I've drained the battery down completely. Click—click—click and then nothing but silence.

Fuck!

Finally he slams down the hood and stares back at me from the front of his car. "Well, that's enough goddamn fuckin' shit from you for one night," he says angrily to his old SST.

Slowly, he walks over to his driver's side door and squats down so his head is level with mine, and is mere inches away. He bends in to plant his lips full on mine with a deep, probing, demanding kiss that sends me into total, mindless shock. "Just wanted to see if I could taste some of that ball-juice I topped ya up with just now," he laughs, then teasingly musses up my hair. He smiles flirtatiously and then playfully traces the outline of my lips with his tongue before suddenly thrusting it into my mouth. He gives me one more deep-throat kiss and winks with those incredibly long eyelashes as he moves back to gauge my reaction.

"Mmmm, thanks, baby. Fuck this old piece-a-crap shitbox of mine right now. Bein' with you just now has been just about the best thing to happen to me in a long time. Next time is gonna be even better, I promise."

He leans in for one more lingering kiss. The feel of his rough, unshaven five o'clock shadow rubbing against my sensitive skin is so sensual and masculine. His kiss ends way too soon and leaves me wanting more from him. He takes a deep breath finally and sighs. Then he rubs his hand through his sweaty, tousled hair and asks me, "So, do I hafta call ya baby or babe all the time? Or does my cute-and-sexy little babe have a name?"

"Aaron Richard Christie. Errr, rather, just Aaron, that is."

He pauses for a long moment and then he says, "Yep! I know that name Christie. Hmmm, I know your mom. I ring up her prescriptions for her at the store. I shoulda figured that one out from when ya come in to pick 'em up for her. And your dad works with my mom at the Hospital, I think."

He pauses for a few more seconds. His eyes light up and he smiles to himself. Then he chuckles, snaps his fingers and says, "Now I get it! Of course! Two cute and sexy guys with the same letter A in their first names. It all makes sense now. *Canada Grade 'A' Beef, eh?* Of course! Fuckin' hilarious! What else?!" he says and starts to laugh. And I mean really laugh.

"Well, Aaron Richard Christie. I'm Adam Richard Blanchard, at your service. Aaand, it looks like I've got some unfinished business to take care of with your little friend down there." With that, he reaches down and grabs onto my stiff cock and fondles it inside my jeans.

"Just call me Adam though, OK?" he says conspiratorially, and gives me the biggest lop-sided grin and a wink. He pauses for another couple of seconds before adding, more seriously, "Ya know, while my damn car let me down again tonight, at least you're here. And that sure as hell makes up for this whole shitty day."

I look deep into his eyes. They're a rich, medium shade of hazel-brown—a honey-chestnut colour—so beautiful.

He brings me back from my thoughts then by saying, "Tell ya what. We're gonna hafta hike it back in to town now. And I'm gonna need to call old Gerry to come and tow my old shitbox in to Prentice ESSO before I hafta start work in the morning. Are you gonna be OK with that for now? I'll make this up to ya next time we're alone together. Can I see ya again soon, puhleeze, Aaron Richard Christie?"

He has the most mesmerizing smile on his face and bends in to give me one more tantalizing, deep kiss. As if he even needs to ask me. "Yes, of course. Whenever you want to. Anytime and anywhere you want to. Absolutely. Yes! For sure, yes! Yes please!"

He reaches into his car right beside me and takes his keys out of the ignition. "Tempted to leave 'em here to see if anyone can get this damn cock-suckin' old heap of mine started. But I don't think anyone would give this sorry piece a rusted-out crap a second look. Joy-riding and stealin' it's not gonna happen tonight, I don't think. Besides, it's seen enough sexy, hot, boned-up, sweaty man action between you and me, mister cute-and-sexy, Aaron Richard Christie just now anyway."

With that, he deliberately leans in past me so I can feel his dude-piston, crotch-rocket, stick-shift, big dong—and whatever the hell else he came up with to describe his beautiful cock earlier while seductively and subtly rubbing his big, fuzzy man-package against my thigh. He bends right over me and further on down to the passenger-side floor on the pretext of looking for his jacket. All the while, he is smirking and trying to look at me sideways with those long lashes to gauge my reaction. *What a smooth guy. He knows exactly how to work me.*

"Gonna need this tomorrow when I hafta look reasonable and half-ways decent to wait on customers. Here, hold onto it for me, willya, please? Let's start to head back in to town. You're my cute little, boned-up, horny sex boy now Aaron Rrrrrrr... ichard Christie."

A flash of white teeth, another wink and his grin seduce me. The masculine texture, smell and feel of his old jacket makes me so horny when I hold onto it next to my skin. It's like snuggling up to him and wrapping myself around his hard, taut body.

"Next time I'm gonna pick you up right after work and take ya straight on back to my place. What we didn't finish tonight we're gonna take care of then, I promise ya. You need some real good, long lessons on how to kiss a man properly. And I'm thinkin' your sexy, tight, little boy-butt there needs me to take care of it, too."

As we start walking back into town he wraps his arm around my shoulder and pulls me in tightly against him. He's a bit beefier than I am so I can lean in and bend my head down into the stained armpit of his shirt to feel the fading pheromone heat from the explosive cum session he just had minutes before.

"Thanks for tonight. Ya know, you're really someone very special," he says while his tongue teases my ear. He nibbles on my ear lobe and his tongue works its way slowly down onto my neck. I almost fall right over into his arms with the distraction.

"Adam," I ask intently, "when can we start the lessons? You can teach me a lot. I've never had a guy fuck me before. And I'm really glad it's going to be you. I want you to do it to me more than anyone and anything."

He laughs softly, smiles to himself and pulls me in even more tightly to him, "Patience my young little firefly. Wanna see ya flicker and light up just for me in the dark," he whispers, while nuzzling my cheek with his unshaven jaw.

"Soon please though? Promise me, please? You're really someone special, too. I really like you very, very much." Then I take a moment to debate whether I should confess this to him or not.

"You know, sometimes I come into Tonner's just to look at you and be really close and just, well, just to be around you because I like you so much. And you're so handsome. And, and, well, uhh, uhm, I think you're just about perfect."

He blushes deeply, hesitates for a long moment and gives me a steady, earnest and thoughtful look. Then he says very tenderly and shyly to me, "Ya know, outside of my mom, I think that's just about the nicest thing anyone's ever said to me. No one's ever perfect though. We all have our flaws. Hafta admit though, I kinda wondered about that store business. At first, I thought ya might be shopliftin' and I kept my eye on you. Then I thought, well, uhm, uhh, well just maybe and tried to give you a little of my *big-cock-and-hairy-man-ass-performance-bit* when I spotted ya looking at me and my big boner." Then he gives me another deep and demanding kiss.

"That's why I go commando sometimes when I'm workin' now because I'm always hopin' you might show up in the store. I was thinkin' you'd notice me free-ballin' and maybe like what I was showing ya between my legs 'cause my big dick sure as hell decided to like you and get hard on me whenever I saw ya looking back at it and me! Really had to laugh to myself one of the last times you were in the store though. I'm behind the cash and you dump a pair of tweezers, a box of Fix-o-Dent denture creme, a package of pink Lady Schick disposable razors, a Fisherman's Almanac magazine, an eyelash curler, a tube of Ben Gay ointment and a huge honkin' tube of KY onto the counter! Like, baby, do ya even know what most folks use that stuff for? Oh yeah, and the *Cover Girl Perky Purple Passion Persuasion* nail polish! I kept thinkin' to myself while I was ringin' that up at the cash register, like, what in the

29

fuck does he think he's gonna paint on himself with that? I was killin' myself laughin' after ya left the store. I think that's when I really finally kinda figured out you weren't just there to buy and pick up stuff."

"Uhm, uhh, well, I knew you were watching me and had to buy something that time. So I just grabbed whatever was on the shelf in front of me." Now I'm really embarrassed," I say to him.

"Aww, dontcha ever be embarrassed in front of me, baby. Am more likely to embarrass myself. Seems to be happenin' pretty goddamn regular to me, too, lately," he says and his voice trails off. "Uhm, did ya not see my big hard-on pokin' out atcha and sayin' hello behind the counter when I was bagging up your KY? And I was wearin' the same pants I've got on now. Like, do you have any idea how hard it is to hide a big, fuckin' hard-on while goin' commando in a pair of lightweight wool dress pants? Jeezus fuck, man! I hadta' go on break in the back to give my dong a chance to settle down after that!" More laughter from him and then he grabs onto one of my nipples and starts to squeeze.

"Well, I just thought you were really big that way all the time."

Three seconds later and he clues into what I just said. Then he starts to really laugh and says, "Ya really don't know what KY is mostly used for, do ya?"

"Uhm, no, uhh, nope, not really."

"Well bring it along with ya when you come on over to my place and I'll explain it all then and show ya, baby. It'll be show and tell time!" He keeps laughing and I really don't get the joke.

We keep on walking and he turns serious again and says to me, "But seriously now, you hafta know. You're a lot younger than me. I'm twenty-seven. And I fill your mom's prescriptions and see her in the store all the time when she comes in herself to pick 'em up. And with my mom workin' with your dad at the Hospital and all, well, you know, I just don't wanna start any trouble and complicate anything for anyone. Jeezus though! Am startin' to get another nice big, juicy hard-on here after hearin' that. Really needed to hear somethin' nice and sweet like that this evening. And hearin' it from you makes it just so much more extra special. Hmmm, sweet, just like an Oreo cookie. Yep! That's the right word for sure, alright. Thanks there, *Cookie-Boy.*"

He smiles and then gently says to me, "You're really somethin'. I wanna get to know ya better. And not just for sex either, if ya get what I mean. Don't get me wrong though. Sex with you is pretty fuckin' amazing and is only gonna get better with lots and lotsa practice. I'll be makin' damn sure that happens from here on in on a fairly regular basis, Cookie!" he says laughingly. Then he pauses for a moment and says, "Hmmm, baby, do ya like pizza? Would ya like to maybe go to El Paso's Restaurant on Buell Street with me for dinner when I'm off sometime? I'll hafta check, but I think I'm off on Thursday later on this week. Think you can make some time for me that night?"

"I'd like that. Sure OK! I'd really like to get to know you a lot better, too. I think you're someone really worth taking the time to get to know. You're really something, too, you know."

Another blush from him—God! He's even cuter and sexier when he blushes—if that's like, even possible.

"And Adam, just to let you know, I really got off riding around with you in your old car. And I liked it when you got all pissed-off and talked dirty to it, too."

He laughs and grabs my ass and says, "Well, let's see if my mechanic friend old Gerry at Prentice ESSO can get it running half-ways decent for me again and we'll take it out for another midnight cruise real soon. Wouldya like that? Hmmm, I might even letcha' drive the damn sonofabitch for a bit so it gets used to ya. Ya got your license yet? You do, right?"

I nod my head. "Well, uhm, uhh, kinda, sorta. Just my learner's permit for now."

"Well, then there's somethin' else I'm gonna hafta be teachin' ya! We're gonna be spendin' lotsa time together. I can see that now," he says with a big grin and then bends down to plant a big, sloppy wet kiss on my cheek while wrapping his left arm tightly around my shoulder. "You aughta know though. My car is real temperamental. You'll need to talk nice to it to get it to start up for ya. It's my special buddy. We have a love/hate relationship. My SST needs to be given a real hard time every now and then to keep it in line. It used to belong to my dad before he skipped out on my mom and me and left her with the payments on it. It was the only goddamn thing he left my mom, besides all his other debts when he took off to Alberta ten years ago and left her high and dry to take care of me. That old car has seen her and me through lotsa tough times. It's given me lots of 'em, too, come to think of it, like tonight. But at least this time, I didn't get stranded in the middle of fuckin' nowhere and have to sleep in it all night and hafta walk miles and miles to a pay phone to call my mom to come pick me up like the last time, a couple of months ago. Tonight, it sorta did me a real big favor and gave me a chance to finally meet ya. Should be kissin' its back bumper, I suppose. Somethin' sure as hell good and juicy came outta that with you and me for sure, just now."

I look thoughtfully up at him, remembering and storing away in my memory what he just confided to me about his mom and dad. I slowly nod my head.

"So, Aaron, Cookie-Boy, Christie, I'll teach ya how to drive my damned old shitbox excuse for a car. Only though, if it decides to like ya. And of course, only if you're extra special nice to me." He laughs suggestively.

"Uhm, uhh, OK. I really like sitting in your driver's seat because it's just like you. It's warm and feels safe and masculine and hugs my butt just right. It has your own special, sexy man smell, too. It gets me really horny and really makes me want to get-off with you. Sort of like what sitting on your big, errr, uhm, dong would be like, I'm thinking.

"Whoa! Hold on! Careful there now or I might just hafta throw ya down and fuck ya silly right here and now, if you keep talkin' to me that way."

We both laugh like we've just shared some private, secret dirty joke between us and keep on walking back in to town.

"I'm gonna walk ya all the way home 'cause it's late at night and dark and all, and I don't wanna risk someone tryin' to pick ya up and molest ya," Adam says. "Besides, my mom always taught me to walk my dates all the way home to their front door. And, baby, you're just about the nicest date I've had in, well… I don't know how long."

"Thanks, Adam," I say and ask if he has far to walk to his place after that.

"Nah, Cookie. Just up to Pearl Street West, not far from the train station. I got a little place there I rent from Mr. and Mrs. Nicholson. But I'll probably call for a cab at the twenty-four hour restaurant on King Street after I phone old Gerry and his tow truck to come and take care of my damn fuckin' car. Doesn't matter though. I'm here for ya now. It's all good, Aaron Richard Christie. Ohh, and yeah, there's one last thing I hafta say to ya, and I'm being dead serious about it, too. Once I finally get around to gettin' into your sexy, tight-fittin' jeans there, fella, dontcha be expecting me to call your little buddy down there, *the Cookie Monster*. Like that's just not gonna happen. Ya got that?"

"This is turning out to be one great summer!" I reply between laughs. He laughs too and kisses me again. Then he stops and asks me to put my hands in his pants pocket for a sec'. "Do ya feel my big, hard dong sayin' hi to ya? It's gonna be thinkin' of ya now 'til the next time we get together. Remember that."

He has such an indecent and dirty laugh on him at times. " I really like you, Adam Richard Blanchard."

"Kinda figured that one out all on my own, Cookie-Boy," he says while grabbing my butt and squeezing me one more time.

"Aaron, there's someone named Adam on the phone and he's asking to speak with you."

"It's OK, Mom. I'll take the phone upstairs here on the hall extension. Thanks!"

"Hiya, Adam!"

"Heya there, Cookie-Butt. I tracked your phone number down from your mom's prescription file. Thought I'd take a chance here and give ya a call to say thanks for last night. Ya know, I can still feel ya pokin' around in my pants down there! What a fuckin' hot time we had with each other, eh? Hope ya don't mind me callin' ya at home?"

"No, that's OK. I was thinking about you just now and I'm really glad you called."

"Aww, that's sweet. I was thinkin' about you too, and wanted to let ya know my mechanic guy, Gerry was able to get my old Ambassador runnin' again. He said somethin' about my carburetor air intake flap needin' some kind of adjustment and my fuel line needin' cleaning and then havin' to replace a spark plug cable and gap a couple of spark plugs, whatever the fuckin' hell that means. All I know is I'm now out a couple a hundred bucks. But hey, at least I got my wheels back again, eh?"

I tell him, yes, that's really good news. Then we talk about going to El Paso's on Thursday. Suddenly then, he says he knows it's only Tuesday, but would I like for him to come and pick me up after work tonight and go parking with him out at the Lyn Pit? The old quarry is filled with deep water and it's good for skinny-dipping. It's also private and very quiet at night.

"My dong's been thinkin' about your hot, little boy-butt," he says. "And it's getting hard now thinkin' about it again. It kinda seems like it's been doin' most of the thinkin' here for me since we were together. And, ya' know, the back-seat of my car has never been properly broken in. I think it's time it saw some action, outside of me jackin' off by myself back there. Whaddya say? Can I come and getcha after nine? Or wouldya maybe come and meet me behind the store?"

I'm smiling and starting to get aroused. "Sure! Absolutely! I miss your big cock and want to play with it! You said after nine, right? I'll meet you there."

"Sure did. I'm gonna wanna go back to my place and change first though. My clothes need a damn good dry-cleaning to get rid of the shot-spots and cock smell in the crotch of my pants. And I'd sure like ya to see me wearin' something else besides them and my birthday suit."

"Both suits work just fine for me. And I really get-off on how you smell, so don't worry about that at all."

He laughs the dirtiest laugh and then says, "You're one kinky little fella, aren't ya? The birthday suit you'll get to see later. But for tonight, a pair of dark jeans and a clean tee-shirt so I can be comfortable and give you somethin' to picture me in 'til ya get to see me. I clean up pretty nice, ya know."

"I'm sure you do, but no underwear. I like it when you go commando for me."

Three seconds of stunned silence from him over the phone and then he lets loose with a huge laugh and says, "Any more talk like that and I'm gonna hafta go into the back here on break to give my dude-piston a chance to settle down!"

He never locks his car, so he tells me just to hop into it and wait for him to close up shop. He says he'll leave his keys under the rubber floor mat and to remember to bring the tube of KY and my learner's permit because he'll want me to start the, quote, "Goddamn sonofabitch" to get it to idle smoothly and warm it up for him to jump into before we head out."

"I'll be there," I tell him. "Bye."

After hanging up the phone, I head downstairs, thinking about and wondering why he keeps talking about that dumb tube of KY.

"Who was that on the phone?" Mom asks.

"Adam Blanchard, from Tonner's Pharmacy. You remember him from behind the counter there, don't you?"

"Oh, yes, I do. I know him and his mother, Delphine. I'm not sure if she's still using the name Blanchard or her maiden name, Bogaert after the divorce. She's a very nice woman. She was so beautiful and young when she got married. I remember her from back then. She's done a good job with her son. He's a decent young man. I like them both. How did you ever come to meet him?"

I tell her that we started talking one day at the store, and that he was interested to hear about my College courses. I continue to tell her that later that same night I went for a walk and helped him out when his old car broke down on Perth Street and that he was calling to thank me for helping him. "He said he wanted to thank me properly by having me share a pizza with him sometime."

"He'd be in his late-twenties if I remember correctly," Mom says, giving me a long and thoughtful look.

"I think he told me he was twenty-seven."

"Your father and I know Delphine from the Hospital. She's Head of Housekeeping there and manages a staff of around twenty. She's done well for herself after her husband deserted her and little Adam years ago. That was a terrible time for her."

When I tell her Adam offered to help me with driving lessons and said I could practise with him in his car, she gives me another measured, thoughtful look. "Well, that was very nice of him to offer," she says, "But, you'll need to talk to your father about that first. I assume he has insurance on his car and that it's safe to drive. I'll leave that for your dad and Adam to sort out, though. Ask him when he's free for dinner and I'll do up a pot roast and a rhubarb pie. I'd like to talk to him outside of the drug store. And I'm sure your father would, as well."

"OK, Mom, I'll find out and let you know. And thanks. He's a really nice guy."

"Yes. He's had a tough life. He missed out on a good education when his father disappeared on him and Delphine. But, he's done well, all things considered. And he's always been respectful and polite to me whenever I see him in Tonner's."

After that, we talk about finalizing my design portfolio and my appointment with the Head of Applied Arts and Interior Design at Algonquin College in five weeks. A portfolio review is a mandatory requirement even though I've been accepted for full-time enrollment in early-September. Then she tells me my sister Astrid called and that her husband Geraint wants me to continue working for him part-time up at the shopping centre until I move to Ottawa. Seems that I'm popular with his customers and have made some good sales for him. He'll deal with the commercial painting contractors and inventory and I can wait on customers.

"I told her you'll need time off to find a place to rent close to the Campus. That will need to happen very soon, as well as getting you and me established with a joint-chequing account at the Bank of Nova Scotia on Elgin Street up there. I also told her that Geraint will have to pay you. That even though he is having money troubles right now with his lease and paying his creditors, you are not free labour and will need some extra spending money of your own, and of which you will have earned. And darling, just between you and me, she is envious of you going back to school, especially given the troubles she's having right now with Geraint and money. Siblings should support each other and your returning to school has nothing to do with her and Geraint. She decided to marry him at nineteen and it is his responsibility now to provide for her and their children. Be kind to her, Aaron—even if she isn't to you right now. Do you understand what I'm saying?"

"Yes, Mom."

The rest of the afternoon stretches on slowly with me unable to think of anything but being with Adam when his shift ends. Dinner is uneventful with Mom and Dad discussing his day at work, how old our dog, Blackjack is, and how he's starting to slow up with hip dysplasia.

After dinner, I go upstairs to my room to look for the fiftieth time through my portfolio to show the Design Head when I meet her on August 22nd. I remember what one Professor told me when I first went to Ottawa to check out the programme—Interior Design—so much more than just furniture and fabric, paint and wallpaper. It's not just decorating, and the programme deals with subjects like interior architecture, building structure and detailing, compliance with building, electrical, plumbing and fire codes, and encompasses a wide spectrum of disciplines, not unlike what an architecture student would study in their first year.

I was really intimidated with the prospect of having to deal with butch, masculine contractors and general labourers on job sites. But I knew this was something I had to go for.

From the time I learned the term gay and its connotation at age eleven, I've worried about my future. When I started to work for my sister's husband in the Brockville Shopping Centre, it all seemed to come together for me and I eventually thought, well, Aaron, if this is the life you're destined to live, you're going to turn it to your advantage and make money and become good at it. The decision to enroll in Interior Design at Algonquin was a done deal from that moment on.

It's around eight forty-five and I'm upstairs staring at myself in the full-length, three-way mirror in the hallway, just outside my bedroom. I've decided to wear my favourite red-and-black plaid shirt and a pair of twenty-eight-inch waist, white Howick label *Five Star* bell-bottom jeans with my light brown, three-inch platform-sole wedge shoes. *I sure hope Adam likes how I look when he sees me.*

Tonner's on the corner of King Street and Fulford Avenue isn't so far from my parents' house on Bethune Street. I can cover the distance in less than ten minutes. As I do, butterflies vibrate in the base of my stomach and shoot right down to my cock. I have to remind myself not to walk too fast or I'll wind up waiting for him alone beside his car. Then I remember he told me to wait for him inside it.

I start to get aroused with dirty thoughts about being in his old car alone with his sexy, cloying man-heat all around me and with his car just waiting for me. At the same time I'm thinking, *Jeez, Aaron, white jeans and a hard-on. You're turning into Adam here!*

I turn the corner at King and Fulford to start up the hill and then turn left into the driveway that leads to the parking lot behind Tonner's. His dented and rusting, old silver grey coupe sits in the shadows, waiting.

I never really looked at it all that closely before. It really is one big sucker of a car. The swooping trunk and tail lights give it a masculine stance. He must have replaced the leaf-springs on the back because it looks all raised and jacked-up. I stand there staring back at it and think, *I'll bet it was one flashy, shiny piece of rolling metal when it was brand new and sitting in the American Motors showroom at the corner of King and Kincaid Streets. Remember now, Aaron, Adam said you could sit in his driver's seat and start it up for him when you got here.*

I open his creaking driver's side door and stare down at the front-seat. It's one of those long, cushy, bench-style types with a fold-down centre armrest that can seat three across. The pale, turquoise-coloured fabric is threadbare, worn and soiled—a really fancy woven kind of upholstery fabric with vinyl embossed trim that was very popular in AMC vehicles in the sixties. The spot where he parks his hot, sexy man-butt is hypnotic and almost pornographic to me. His old driver's seat has a hollowed-out recess where his butt-cheeks have carved out two globe-like indentations in the foam padding. The fabric has a jagged, small rip in one place where his big cock and inner thighs would rub with friction against the tear. *Hmmm, I didn't notice that the other night.* His sagging seat is much more worn down on his side than the passenger-side.

I slide into his driver's seat and sink into the recess his butt has carved out—such an intimate, sensual experience. I can smell a faint aroma of Christian Dior's *Eau Sauvage* cologne mingling with his male musk and sweat and it makes me half crazy. I lean back and feel where his strong, muscular back has imprinted his shape into the seatback.

It feels like he just came up behind me and shoved his big man-bulge right into the crack of my butt. I take my time to feel the steering wheel that his strong hands grasp so confidently. I imagine him hopping into his old wheels early in the morning, wearing his sexy, navy blue sports jacket and scuffed dress shoes to head in to work.

Then I reach down to find his car keys under the floor mat—precisely where he told me they'd be. His keys dare me to start his old car up for him. His keychain has a red, blue, and yellow Superman logo on a metal tag dangling from it.

There's a story there, Aaron.

I shove his key into the ignition switch and turn his key to the ACC position. Then I pump his gas pedal ten or eleven times—just like I

41

saw Adam do that first night. Finally, I turn his key all the right to the START position.

His car starts to vibrate, shake and wail with a high-pitched, plaintive, whining rhythm. I can feel it protesting and vibrating as it cranks and tries to turn over for me.

All I can smell is gas—*like, what the hell?*

Hmmm, I can see now why Adam calls you his goddamn, sonofabitch piece-of-crap. I try one, two, three long crank sessions. I stomp on his worn gas pedal and lift my hips and butt up while distending myself in his driver's seat, stretched-out fully with my foot pressing his gas pedal right down to the floor—the same way I remember Adam had done to try to get it to start for him before.

All of a sudden, I hear a rap on the passenger-side window and turn to the right. There is Adam, staring back at me with a smirk and knowing eyes. He opens the creaking door and slides in beside me. He raises the armrest out of the way and moves over so I can feel his heat and take in that masculine smell I am beginning to recognize as being uniquely his alone. His left arm somehow finds its way around my shoulder as he bends in close and says very quietly, "Having car problems I see, are we, butt-boy?" with a dirty, wicked grin on his face. "Hmmm, well, why dontcha just slide that cute, tight, little boy-butt of yours over onto my lap while we change places? And I'll see if this damn sonofabitch will turn over for me then."

I shift over and start to sink into his crotch, only to feel his big cock poking my butt and demanding my attention. He laughs and wraps his arms around me, pulling me back into his chest and says, "Told ya my dong would be thinkin' of ya 'til the next time we got together. Now, seriously, just how many times did you pump my gas pedal tryin' to get this old thing to start up for ya?" He asks this while nuzzling my ear and groping my cock.

"You're distracting me and I can't remember right now."

"Distraction and pleasure were just what I had in mind. Now think—did ya pump it more than one or two times?"

"I think maybe eleven or twelve times, maybe more. I don't know. Just the way you did the other night."

"Then you've managed to flood the carburetor like, big time, baby. We're just gonna hafta sit here like this for a few minutes, 'til the gas evaporates, and then I'll see if I can get this cocksucker to turn over for me."

"But I did exactly what you did on Sunday with it."

He starts to kiss the nape of my neck and says, "Aaron, baby, it needed lotsa gas to start up for me that night. Normally, unless it's real cold, you only need to pump it a couple a times to get it to turn over. It's all good though. I think I kinda like having ya sit in my lap like this. And I think I'm gonna let your little buddy outta those sexy white jeans and play with him for a bit since we're all alone here waitin' for my damn car to start up for me in the dark and all. Kind of a reverse situation from the time we first did this, isn't it, baby? Am kinda likin' the way this all turned out here. I sure as fuckin' hell know my dong is enjoyin' the experience. Now raise your hot, little boy-butt up for a sec' and let's getcha outta those tight, white jeans. I'll work the zipper and have ya naked in my crotch-basket in ten seconds or less."

Less than five seconds later he says, "Actually, babe, lemme get more comfortable, too. I have an idea here. I'm gonna undo my pants and get my cock to slip right tight into your butt crack while I play with your little buddy. I'm gonna getcha just as revved up as this old shitbox of mine will be in a few minutes. And screw the goin'-home-to-change crap. We're headin' straight out to Lyn Pit just as soon as I can get this cocksucker runnin' for me and we start movin'."

Uhh, uhm… my little buddy isn't that little, Adam."

He chuckles and lifts me up to let me pull down my jeans for him. At the same time, he is pulling his trousers down to expose his half-aroused cock.

"Now… I wantcha to take my crotch-rocket and aim it to sit right tight inside your tight little ass-crack. Then I'm gonna unbutton your shirt and play with your little boy nipples while you lean back against me and let me lick and suck on your ear."

He spits a wad of saliva into the palm of his left hand and starts to work my dick. "This is just the beginning of what they call foreplay. Five minutes from now, you're gonna be squirmin' and my dong's gonna be throbbin'. And hopefully I'll be able to get this damn shitbox old car of mine started. Then we can head on out to where I want to fuck ya for the first time. It's gotta be special—and it will be, I promise."

Close to ten minutes pass and the now familiar routine to get his old car to start for him is about to commence. "Ugh, c'mon ya cocksucker, fuckin' start." His starter grinds and whines at a faster pace, and once he hears the faster rhythm, he forcefully rams his accelerator down to the floor. "Argh! C'mon, c'mon, c'mon, start for me, ya goddamn sono-fabitch." His car eventually stumbles and roars to life. He revs it two or three times, then lets up on it while stroking my cock at the same time.

"Slide offa me 'cause I think you're gonna play with my dong too while I drive us out to Lyn Pit. Can't say we're gonna make it out there before I hafta shoot my load. But we're sure as hell gonna give it our best shot. So hang on tight and let's just hope a cop doesn't see us drivin' this way or we'll get busted for sure."

"Uhm, Adam?"

"Yeah, baby, what?"

"Can we get rid of that dumb, smelly pine tree air freshener down there? I just want to smell you and your cock and not it when we're alone together in your car."

"Jeez! Ya really are a little bit kinda kinky there, aren't ya?"

"Nope. I just really get-off on the taste of your cock and the smell of your crotch in your car, that's all!"

"Yep! You're fuckin' kinky as hell, for sure! But I can live with that. No problem! Just toss it out the window once we get outta town."

Lyn Pit is about two miles up the old number two highway, just past the Brockville Country Club and then a right turn and four or five miles further north on the Lyn Road. He holds tight onto my cock, massaging and stroking it with his warm right hand while guiding his steering wheel with his left. We creep along in the pitch darkness with only his dim headlights lighting up the road ahead.

"This is the hottest and horniest thing I've ever done," I whisper to him as we drive under the CN Rail overpass and head up the hill, passing the shotgun rifle shooting range and getting closer and closer to the quarry.

"Me too, baby! Me too! And I'm tryin' real hard here not to bust a load 'til we get there!"

"Can I play with your nipples and chew on your ear when we're there, like what you're doing to me now?" I whisper as we make a wide turn to head down the gravel and dirt road into Lyn Pit.

"You can do whatever the fuckin' hell ya want to me once I find a dark place to park this damn sonofabitch," he moans hoarsely and wrestles with his steering wheel to manoeuvre his lumbering old car into a secluded spot off to the side of the unpaved road.

He pulls his car tight over to the right shoulder leading into the parking lot behind some tall bushes. "I fuckin Jeezus hope no cop or anyone else can see us here," he says, and turns off his car. "Well, we sure as fuckin' hell managed to get this far. So gimme some breathin' room for a sec' 'cause I wanna bury my tongue down your throat for the next two hours or so."

"Only if you *finally* explain to me what KY is supposed to be used for."

Another stunned look from him and a burst of laughter. Then he says, "You've really been wonderin' about that, haven't ya?"

"Uhm, uhh, yeah, I have, actually."

"Well, tell ya what. Hows about I show ya after we lock tongues together in my front-seat here for a bit? Is that gonna satisfy your curiosity?" His lips press down on mine and his tongue probes the deepest recesses of my mouth. "You constantly surprise me and make me laugh. You're really somethin' special. I wantcha to know that."

With that, he starts to work his way down to my nipples. And then when I think he can't arouse me any more than he already has, pinches them and follows up by sucking on them until he makes me moan with soft moans and groans of pleasure. His five o'clock shadow is intense, sweet torture against my soft skin.

I have no idea how he managed to get both my shirt and his off without my realizing it, but now his fingers are reaching around to feel the top of my butt crack. "This is fantastic," I say softly.

"Just gettin' started here, Cookie-Butt-boy. Your ass is gonna remember this night when I'm through with it. Now where's that KY? Did you remember to bring it with ya?"

"Oh, shit! I forgot it."

"Never mind. I kinda had a feeling and thought ya just might. Reach into my glove compartment and grab the tube I've got in there. Good thing I work in a pharmacy, eh?" Then he opens up his driver's door and steps out with his trousers down between his knees and ankles. His belt buckle is dangling and noisily scraping the side of the car door at the same time.

"You're wearing underwear tonight, I see."

"Well, I didn't exactly have much of a goddamn chance to go home and change for ya now, did I?"

I suddenly have a very dirty thought and ask him, "Uhm, Adam, can I have them to wear tomorrow so I'll smell like you and feel like you're inside my pants all day?"

Another shocked look from him. Then he forcibly drags me out of his car and with a look of pure lust on his face, starts to yank my jeans down. "You're makin' me fuckin' crazy! Now I wantcha to get your sexy, tight little ass into my back-seat. And you'll soon enough learn what big boys can do with KY!"

I struggle to pull his driver's seat back and scramble into his back-seat. I never noticed before that he has a pillow back there. He's right behind me with his pants in one hand and the tube of KY in the other.

"I don't wanna hurt ya, this being your first time gettin' fucked. So I'm gonna go as slow as I possibly can and if I hurt or scare ya, you let me know right away, babe, OK?"

"It's OK. I trust you."

"Well, OK then. Uhm, I put a pillow back here for you to lay your head on. I wantcha to lay down on your stomach and then bend your knees so your cute, sexy butt is up where I can rim it with my tongue. You're gonna really like how that feels," he says softly to me.

He starts to tease the rim of my asshole with his tongue. At first it feels like a strange ticklish kind of thing to do, but then I relax and realize it feels very sensual and exciting. His hands grasp my ass-cheeks. I can hear him breathing heavily and feel his head moving back and forth against my butt with a steady and determined rhythm.

"I'm thinkin' you're loosening up and relaxin' a bit now so I'm gonna take my finger and play with your asshole like what you did to me on Sunday. By the way, where in the goddamn hell did ya ever learn how to do that?"

"I read about it in a gay mens sex book I got from a bookstore on the Sparks Street Mall up in Ottawa when I was there with some friends a while back and just wanted to see if it worked."

"Well let's just thank the fuckin' lord you're literate and learned to read," he replies and laughs.

Then he takes the cap off the KY gel, breaks the seal with his teeth and squirts a glob of it onto his middle finger.

"I'd like to tell ya this is gonna hurt me more than you, but I'd be lyin'. It'll only hurt for a short bit though this first time and then you'll see, you're gonna want more than just my finger up your sexy, tight little ass there. So hold on now. I'll be as gentle as I can be."

His finger traces the outline of my butt and then starts to probe in and out until my sphincter muscles tighten around it. "Try and relax, baby. I'll go nice and slow. Let me know when it starts to feel good for you."

A couple of minutes later and I whisper to him, "Shit! I never knew I could feel so boned-up. Does it always feel this good?"

"If the man you choose to do this with is gentle and patient, it'll be fantastic every time for ya. And that's where I come into the picture."

"I'm so glad it's you I waited to do this with, Adam."

"I know, I know," he murmurs softly to me. "Now you're finally gonna learn what two men can do with some KY and a bit of imagination. Are ya ready for my big crotch-rocket to blast off inside ya, butt-boy?"

He chuckles to himself and pulls off his underwear to reveal his fully-aroused cock. Then he squeezes the tube of KY again and lubes up his penis right down to where the base of it meets his scrotum.

"I'm gonna go real slow here. I won't lie to ya, it's gonna feel weird and you're probably gonna tighten up and feel some pain at first. But dontcha be scared. I'm not gonna hurt ya. I'd never hurt ya, Cookie... ever."

"You're so big though. How will you fit that thing of yours in me without hurting?"

"Trust me. We've got all night to get this right."

"Last time I studied math, I learned that eight doesn't go into one," I say.

More laughter from him and then he says, "You've never heard of long-division then. And believe me, it doesn't get any longer than what I'm gonna divide your crack with before we're done here."

I couldn't help but laugh at that remark and the laughter helps make my sphincter muscles relax more. It still feels like he's trying to shove the wooden butt of a hammer handle up my ass with a strange, invasive fullness, like when I have to have a dump, but it doesn't hurt quite so much now and I'm getting used to the sensation of him inside me. His cock starts to inch it way up, bit by bit. Any time he feels my muscles tense, he lets up for a few seconds to give me a chance to focus and relax. Then he starts to thrust deeper and deeper into me.

"Uhm, Aaron, men have a sweet spot deep up inside them that's called a prostate gland. It's sorta like women's G spots. Most straight guys never know how strong an orgasm they can have when someone stimulates their prostate. With any luck, my cock's gonna find yours tonight. And with some skill and good timing, we're gonna blast off together at the same time in a few more minutes. Let's see if we can make this happen for us tonight. I really want this to be extra special for us both, this first time together."

"Well, Adam, if your big cock can't find it, I most likely don't have one."

More laughter from him, and then finally, he's all the way inside me. "Feels like you're a toasty, warm glove inside there keepin' my dong all hard and warm and juicy and throbbing. How are you doin'? Can I start to move in and outta ya without you feelin' discomfort?"

"Mmmm, yes, I think so."

With that, he starts to thrust his hips back and forth and his big penis starts to move inside me. I try to match his rhythm by moving my butt up and down. Each minute that passes, his pace picks up, gets faster and more determined.

"I think you found my prostate. It likes your big dick pounding it that way!"

An animal-sounding, guttural, deep grunt comes out of his mouth and he grabs onto me tightly and buries his head against the back of my neck. "No more funny talk for the moment! I need to blow my load real soon now. Do ya think you'll be able to get-off at the same time as me? I want for that to happen for ya this first time," he groans.

"I think if you keep banging my ass that way and stroking my cock, you'll make me cum soon. Shouldn't take much longer now."

Thirty seconds later and, "Adam! I'm gonna cum real soon! Like, any second now!"

"I can tell! I can tell! Me too, baby! Me too!"

And then, "Holy fuck! Ahhh, Jeezus, man! Fuck! Ah, fuck, Cookie! Jeezus fuck! I'm cumming. Gonna cum right now! Ah, ahh, ahhh... Jeezus goddamn fuck!"

He rolls off me to raise himself up, slowly drawing his spunk-covered, lubed-up cock out from my butt.

"What an *abso'fuckin'lutely* perfect orgasm," he murmurs, his chest still heaving. He's shot his cum load deep inside me and I've creamed all over the threadbare carpet floor in his back-seat. I'm a hundred-percent positive the back-seat of his old car has never experienced two guys moaning and moving together in perfect rhythm and harmony like we did just now.

"Adam, you really *are* perfect, you know," I whisper.

"Shhh, now. No one's ever perfect. Just be quiet for a while now and kiss me, OK?" His tongue parts my lips and invades my mouth once more. "Just wanna lie back here now and hold onto this moment with ya for as long as I can."

Minutes turn into a half-hour or so and all I can feel is his strong arm around me as I curl up tightly beside him.

"Uhm, Adam, can I have your jacket? It's getting cold, even with you generating a hundred-and-ten degrees of body heat next to me."

"Sure thing. Gimme a sec' first though. Gotta put my pants back on again before someone comes along and I get arrested for indecent exposure." He stretches and leans forward to hop out of the car. I watch him grab his pants and, with a few brusque movements, shove his legs into them and pull them up in one sweeping, hasty gesture.

"Gotta little present for ya, butt-boy," he says as he tosses his day-old briefs at me and laughs as I struggle to catch them.

"What's with the *Superman logo* on the front?" I ask with a smile and a direct stare down at his big, furry pube-package.

"If you hafta ask me that after I just fucked ya the way I did, then you disappoint me there."

He grabs his jacket from the floor of the back-seat where it somehow wound up—along with my shirt, his shirt, and his tie and casually tosses it back to me. He tells me to knock myself out with his sweaty clothes and chuckles, telling me this is kind of perverted, but he's cool with it. Then he says, "Uhm, uhh, I guess if I can drive out to Lyn Pit with you workin' my stick-shift all the way, I can't really judge ya when it comes to weird and kinky. I expect those Man of Steel briefs back though in a few days. Freshly-laundered and folded, too."

"OK, no problem. Did you say days or weeks, though?"

Big bursts of laughter spill out from both of us as he dives into the back-seat and tries to smother me with the pillow.

"Ten more minutes of this and I'm gonna hafta getcha home before your mom and dad send out a posse to track us down."

"That reminds me," I say. "Mom asked me about you when you called. She and your mom do know each other… you're right. And my dad does work with her at the Psychiatric Hospital. My dad is the Chief Attendant there and my mom says your mom is Head of Housekeeping."

"I didn't know if they worked together or not," he says.

"My mom works there too, on the midnight shift as a part-time Registered Nurse."

"Hmmm, I kinda wondered about that, given the medication list I fill for her at Tonner's. Is she a happy lady?"

"Let's not talk about her right now. It's just too weird to think about my mom after what we just did. I just want to snuggle next to you and have your arm around me and pretend that this night can go on and on." Meanwhile, I'm groping his cock through his pants and squeezing it to see if I can make him hard again.

"Consider it done. But you're gonna hafta let me put those sexy, tight, white jeans back on ya and do up the buttons on your shirt. Dressin' ya might be just as much fun as undressin' ya was."

"Any excuse to touch me, I'm guessing."

"Ya got that one right," he laughs, bending over to nuzzle my ear lobe again.

"Outta the back now while I zip ya up and then you're gonna drive us back on home to your house. Consider it your first driving lesson with me."

"Ohh, shit! I almost forgot! Mom says I have to get Dad to say yes for you to give me driving lessons. And she also said to ask you if you'd like to come over for dinner with her and Dad sometime soon."

He's silent for a good long five seconds before looking closely at me and asking, "Do you really want me to meet 'em?"

"Yup, I sure do. I already told you you're someone I want to get to know better and they're really good people. Mom said really nice things about your mom and you and told me she wanted to get to know you, now that you're grown up and all. She remembers when your dad left and you were still a kid with your mom. She said that you've turned out well and she would like to meet you outside of the store."

"Well, uhh, uhm, OK. I'll get back to you with when I can come over then. But I hafta say, your dad sorta intimidates me with his job and his bein' so religious and all. He wouldn't exactly be happy or approve of what we're doin' right now."

"Give him a chance, Adam. Let's see how this goes. Besides, all he needs to know for now is that you've offered to give me some driving lessons and I tried to help you get your car started the first night we really met. I told Mom you were asking me about my College courses coming up in first-semester and that's how we started talking in the store. That's all they need to know for now."

"Take it from me, moms know their kids better than they know themselves. I aughta know that well enough from my own mom. There's a thing they have called intuition. She'll figure out what's up with you and me in the first five minutes. That is, if she hasn't suspected already. Trust me on that one. The eyes always give a person away. Just the same as when you look at me with those beautiful dark brown ones of yours. They're like a chocolate river. I know what you're thinkin' sometimes without you even havin' to say a word. But if ya really want me to meet 'em, then sure, of course I will. Now get your cute little butt outta my back-seat so I can pretend to dress ya and then let's hop in the front for another ten minutes or so. My dong is startin' to tell me it wants ya to rub your hand along my hairy pleasure trail. Do ya know what that is?"

"Yes, sir, I sure do! That was in Chapter Two of the book."

"Hmmm, keep readin' that book there. Between it and my lessons, you're gonna be my sexy, little student for a long, long time, Cookie."

Amazing how fast he can move when he really wants to.

"Uhm, Adam, you didn't turn your car off completely when you parked here. The red GEN light is still on and the key is turned over to the right ACC position on your switch there. Look at your dashboard. Uhm, uhh, how long have we been here?"

He checks his watch and, with a worried look says, "Just over an hour and a half. I think my battery can hold up for that long though. Even so, we're gonna play it safe and just sit here for a while. That'll give it a chance to charge up a bit. And then we'll see if you can finally get my damned old SST started. Now gimme your hand. You're gonna stick it down the front of my pants that ya really seem to get-off on and rub my hairy pleasure trail. Wanna see if you can give me another big boner before we hafta head on outta here. Does that sound good to ya?"

"Yeah, it does. What you said to me the other night about liking how you taste—you were right on that one."

"You'll soon learn I'm right more times than wrong, baby."

Ten minutes later, Adam is beside me in the passenger-seat, his legs spread wide to expose a raging hard-on with wet spots starting to stain the moist, sweaty inside crotch of his good dress-trousers. "Christ!" he says. "Ya got me all juiced-up and ready to shoot again! That never happens to me so fast after I bust a load of my ball-juice." He reaches in and rubs the tip of his cock to gather up some of his thick, creamy jizz and holds his finger to my mouth. "Here, Cookie," he says. "Another little present for ya 'til Thursday. Will that hold you over 'til then?"

"I'll have to make do with that for now."

More laughter starts to spill out from us both—along with his tasty, creamy cock-juice.

"Now comes the moment of truth, baby. Hopefully, my battery is charged up enough by now. You're gonna learn how to start this fucker and drive the living piss out of it, just like I do. Think you can manage that for me now? Try it without pumping the gas pedal first. Let's see how it behaves without any gas in its carb. We sure as hell don't wanna flood it out again now, do we?"

"Uhm, nooo, not again," I say while casting an embarrassed look at him. He just smiles smugly with a raised eyebrow, showing off a super-cute nostril twitch and a highly amused look on his face. I turn the key all the way and his old Ambassador starts to wail. The first time it coughs, shudders, and promptly stalls out.

"I think it likes you more than me…"

"Nah. It just needs to warm up to ya first. Now, turn that key of mine one more time and dontcha let up on it 'til I tell ya to."

I do what he says and, suddenly, his old car sputters, coughs, and starts to idle roughly away for me.

"Yeahh, Cookie! I knew ya could handle my old shitbox! Now, keep your foot on the gas so it doesn't stall out on ya 'til it starts to idle a little better. Pretend you're grabbin' onto my dong there 'til you feel it settle down and start to purr nicely for ya." He starts to snort and chuckle. "Now, jerk that lever into DRIVE and let's give it some gas and head on back home."

He moves over tight next to me and starts to lick and bite my right ear lobe and tweak my left nipple, with his arm and hand casually draped over the back of his driver's seat behind me.

"Unless you want me to wind your car up in a ditch, you'd better not do that until I pull up in front of my parents' house."

"Mmmm, but dontcha forget, I've nicknamed ya Cookie. And with those deep, rich, dark-chocolate eyes and your cream-filled centre, well, ya know, I just can't help myself after the first taste of you—addictive, delicious and all—you really can't blame me now, can ya, baby?"

"Eyes on the road, hands in your pockets, and tongue back in your mouth, Mister Smarty-Pants!"

"Speakin' about pants and pockets there, baby, gonna have to drop these ones off at the one-hour dry cleaners beside Tonner's tomorrow first thing—along with my old jacket that ya seem so attached to. Another crusty day in 'em with a stiff dick, sweaty balls, and fuzzy ass and pits and they'll be walkin' around on their own just to get away from me, I'm thinkin'!" Adam laughs. "And as for those blue Superman briefs—gonna want 'em back sometime soon."

"All things are negotiable, Adam Richard Blanchard," I answer as we pull up in front of my parents' house.

He hops out on the passenger-side and comes around behind his old Ambassador to meet me. As he gets close, he reaches down, grabs my ass cheek, and says, "Your sexy boy-butt's all mine, baby from now on. I'll pick ya up right out here at seven on Thursday. Be hungry and horny and we'll see if we can make it through a medium combo pizza without rippin' each other's clothes off, OK?"

"Sounds like a plan to me."

He gets back into the car and wiggles his ass in his driver's seat. "Someone's been sittin' here and I can feel their cute, little boy-butt-cheeks makin' a dent in my seat," he says with a shit-faced grin.

"Well, since it's your butt now, I figured I'd give you something to remember it by until Thursday."

He laughs and says, "If you saw my cock strainin' against the zipper of my pants right now, you'd know I don't need much more than that to remember ya by 'til Thursday!"

With that, he gives his old car three quick revs and takes off into the darkness.

Hmmm, Thursday, just past hump day. Always liked that day of the week.

I smile and head up the steps to my parents' front door.

2   July / August

"Are you having dinner with your mother and me this evening?"

"Uhm, no, Dad, not tonight. My friend Adam is picking me up to go and have pizza with him to say thanks for helping him out with his old car last Sunday."

"That's Adam Blanchard, right?"

"Yes, Dad, that's right."

"Your mother and I were talking about that this morning. He's a good bit older than you, isn't he?"

"Uhm, yeah, I guess so. I got to talking with him in Tonner's Drug Store. He was asking me about Algonquin College and the Interior Design programme. He's a pretty nice guy."

"Yes, she mentioned that to me. He's offered to take you out for driving lessons so you'd be able to get your license before starting school in September—have I got that right?"

"Yes, Dad. Is that OK with you?"

"Does he have insurance and how old is his car?"

"I don't know."

"Well, when he comes to pick you up, I want to meet him to look at it and have a little talk with him."

"OK, Dad. He said he'd be here around seven to pick me up and then we're going to El Paso's on Buell Street."

Freshly-showered after work and with a fresh change of clean clothes on, Adam locks the front door of his apartment and energetically bounds down the outside stairs to where his old car is parked in the driveway, just in front of the Nicholson's garage doors. He opens the creaking driver's side door of his SST and hops in, bending over to shove his key into the ignition on his way heading over to pick up Aaron for pizza. Three tries and it stubbornly refuses to start. He pleads with it saying, "Ahhh, fuckin' c'mon, baby! Argh! Jeezus fuck! Ugh! Start for me, ya goddamn cocksucker!" One more try and it coughs and promptly stalls out. He sits there with a dejected, discouraged expression on his face.

Then he leans forward with his hands together, grasping the top of his steering wheel while he bends his forehead down onto them, shaking his head and thinking, *C'mon! Not tonight! I'm fuckin' horny and just gotta go see Aaron. You were runnin' ok earlier when I left work an hour ago. Don't let me down now. Like, c'mon! I'm already late and you're not gonna gimme a hard time, ya bastard! That's like, just not gonna happen. Now... turn over for me, ya fuckin' piece-a-crap! Start!*

He straightens up, stretches back, stomps on his gas pedal and pumps it seven or eight times, continuing to pump it while it continues to shake and vibrate, noisily squealing and whining away in protest. Finally, one final last long crank session and it coughs and starts to vibrate and idle roughly with noxious, blue-white smoke pouring out of it's tailpipes.

"Yeahhh, that's better, ya fuckin' cocksucker," he exclaims with a relieved look on his face. He heaves a big sigh, shakes his head, and runs his hand roughly through his hair while looking into his rear-view mirror to check himself out. Then he stomps on the gas several more times, revving it hard, buckles his seatbelt, shifts his old coupe into REVERSE and slowly heads over to Bethune Street.

It's a couple of minutes after seven and I can hear Adam's car idling roughly and noisily outside. He honks the horn and rolls down the window on the passenger-side while staring up at our front door.

"Go out there and tell Adam I have beer in the fridge and that I want to speak with him out back on the patio before you two head off for pizza," Dad says as he stares out the living room window at Adam's old car.

"But, Dad, I don't know if he made a reservation for dinner and it's already past seven now."

"I don't believe that was actually a question. Now, you go out there and do what I tell you, young man."

I look at him and start to get nervous about what he might say to Adam.

"Yes, Dad."

"And don't look all concerned there. I'm not going to bite his head off. I just want to find out what kind of insurance he has on that old car and how safe it is. Frankly, I'm fine if he wants to take you on and teach you how to drive. I don't think I want to have to go through that again after you backed my car into Mrs. Larocque's garbage cans when you attempted last time to back out onto Cedar Street without checking the rear-view mirror first. I had a lot of explaining to do to her after that little episode and had to promise her four new ones. If he has the patience to deal with you behind the wheel, it will save me having a stroke and going bankrupt when you are on the road."

"Gee, Dad. Thanks for the vote of confidence."

He laughs at me.

Just then Adam blows his horn two more times and Dad says, "Go out there and tell him to stop blowing his damned, blasted horn! This is a quiet street and the neighbours are nosy old busybodies. Besides, he'll wake up your mother and she has another midnight shift at the Hospital to get through tonight. I want to see him. He can turn his car off and come around to the back patio for a few minutes. I promise I won't give him the Spanish Inquisition."

"Yes, Dad."

As I approach his car and get close to the passenger-side window, Adam looks over at me and says, "Jeezus, babe, do ya always hafta take so long to get ready?!" Then he leans over to open up the passenger-side door. "Uhh, not so fast," I say. "Dad said to tell you he wants to talk to you about driving your car. He told me to tell you to stop blowing your horn and come around to the back patio to have a beer with him. He's waiting now for you and me. So turn off your car and let's go see him, OK?"

If there was ever a *deer-in-the-headlights* expression that could truly be conveyed in a photograph, the one Adam was giving me at that moment would have been the classic one to capture—*capture* being the perfect word.

"Uhh, OK, Cookie." He turns his old car off, grabs his keys from the ignition, and gets out the driver's side. Then he stands there, unsure of what's to happen next.

"And for God's sake, don't call me Cookie in front of him!"

"Gimme some credit here! That's just for when you and I get naked and are alone together and when I get to stick my big dude-piston up inside ya."

Oh, God!

I take a few seconds to get a good look at him. Freshly showered and shaven, with a nice-fitting pair of tight, dark-blue jeans— *God! That big bulge inside them. Fuck!...what a hot guy* —and what looks to be a brand-new, starched and ironed, dazzling white cotton, button-down shirt. He looks like he just stepped off the page of a Simpsons-Sears catalogue.

"Told ya I cleaned up pretty nice, didn't I? You look pretty cute and sexy yourself there."

"How did you know what I was thinking just now?"

"Told ya before—your eyes give you away every time—now, let's go meet your dad and get this over with."

I lead the way up the driveway beside the house and Blackjack, our Labrador Retriever is right there waiting for me to open the gate. Dad is sitting on one of the turquoise Adirondack chairs around the low table and I see three open bottles of Molson Canadian sitting out ready for whatever he is about to say to Adam and me.

"Adam Blanchard," Dad says standing up and holding out his hand to shake Adam's. "Last time I saw you, you were about fourteen years old and with your mother at the Hospital. Welcome. Nice to see you again. Give Delphine my best regards when you see her and come on over and have a beer."

"Hello, Mr. Christie. Good to meet you, sir. My mom says nice things about you and Mrs. Christie. You all work down at the psychiatric together." Adam bends down to pet Brock Vegas Blackjack, who is sniffing around his feet.

"That's right, Adam. Ahhh, I see Blackjack has warmed up to you already. Dogs are good judges of people and character. I trust Blackjack better than I do most folks I know. He was given to Aaron as a Christmas present by his sister, Astrid and her husband. How old were you, Aaron, when we got Blackjack?"

"Uhm, I think around seven or eight."

"He's slowing up these days and not as active as he used to be. Guess the same can be said for all of us," Dad says and then laughs. "I have a beer here with your name on it. Come and sit down for a few minutes. Do you have a reservation for dinner?"

"No, sir. El Paso's is pretty quiet on a weeknight. I figured we'd just take our chances and drop in on Louie there for a pizza. It shouldn't be a problem. I think he closes at nine though."

"Well, son, I won't be keeping you here until then. So have a seat and let's talk about these driving lessons. And, Aaron—just sit there and pretend to be a statue the way Sister St. Francesca made you do in that third-grade play. You have a way of making things all about you, and this one time you're going to be quiet and let me get to know Adam a bit better. You got that, young man?"

"Aww, Dad!"

Adam laughs at Dad's remark and my reaction. I think Dad is trying to put him at ease. He's actually pretty good at making people relax and feel good about themselves.

Dad laughs and says, "You didn't notice, but there's a third beer on the table here and it isn't for Blackjack. Since you turned legal drinking age last year, I figured it was high time to start offering you liquor legally instead of having you steal it from the locked box in the basement. I never could hide that padlock key where you wouldn't find it! I know you've watered down the scotch and your mom's tequila to make it look like the bottles weren't touched before. So, no more of that. Now, you just sit there and don't say a word until I finish with Adam here, understand?"

"Uhm, yes, Dad."

I try not to roll my eyes. Then I call Blackjack over to pet him in a valiant and ultimately futile attempt to distract my dad.

"So, Adam, this car of yours… Mrs. Christie tells me that Aaron had to help you on Sunday because it broke down on Perth Street?"

"Uhh, uhm, well, yes, sir. It's been givin' me some trouble lately. But I took it over to Gerry at Prentice Esso and he fixed it all up for me. It should be OK now, sir."

"You took it over or had it towed over?"

Adam is scarlet red in the face at this point and I can see him shifting uncomfortably in his chair. He takes a swig of beer and then says, "Well, sir, uhm, uhh, I had to have it towed."

"I see. You say you think it's safe now to drive though. Have I got that right?

"Yes, sir."

"I saw it outside when you pulled up and honked the horn. By the way, don't do that again with the horn honking—it's a quiet street here and everyone on this street minds everyone else's business but their own! From now on, you park it in the driveway and come right on up to the front door and feel free to come inside anytime. I'm sure your mother raised you better than that. You're not some long-haired hippie who has a van with burnt-orange shag carpet in the back, driving up and down King Street and roaming the countryside now, are you?"

Jeez! I can't believe my dad just said the word hippie.

"No, sir. I suppose I'm not, sir."

"I didn't think so. And it's going to be either Mister Christie or Richard and not sir from now on. You're making me feel like I'm interviewing you for a job. Now, relax and tell me just how good a condition this car of yours is really in and how many miles it has on it, and whether you have full insurance coverage to let Aaron drive it."

"Well, sir, errr, that is, Mr. Christie, it's a 1967 Ambassador SST my mom gave to me when she got her new car. It used to belong to my dad before, well... before he went out west."

"Yes, Adam. Mrs. Christie and I remember those unfortunate times with Delphine. But let's focus on your car for now, shall we? Continue, please."

"Last time I looked at the odometer it had around 81,700 miles on it. And I have a five-hundred dollar deductible with comprehensive coverage, personal liability, and property damage for me and any occasional driver I let drive it. Just so long as I'm with them in the car when they do."

"You're how old again, Adam?"

"I'm twenty-seven, Mr. Christie."

"Your insurance must be costing you around three-hundred-and-fifty dollars a year, given your age and the fact that you are a relatively young man. That's almost more than what I estimate the value of your car would be. Are you absolutely sure you want to take on the risk and let my boy here drive it?"

"Well, Mr. Christie, I think he's pretty responsible and I'll make sure he doesn't do anything reckless when I take him out. That is, if you'd be willing to let me teach him how to drive."

"That's exactly what I wanted to hear. Last time I took him out in my car, he managed to run over four aluminium garbage cans and we had to clean up the mess in front of Mrs. Larocque's house on Cedar Street. Cost me forty-seven dollars and a trip to Canadian Tire to get her some new ones!"

Adam lets loose with a huge laugh and my dad just looks over at me and smiles.

"OK, Adam, better you than me. Take him out anytime you like. Just bring him back in one piece, that's all I ask."

I couldn't be more embarrassed. And then Adam looks over and says to me, "Next time, Aaron, aim for the plastic garbage cans. They don't make as loud a noise when you hit 'em and won't dent the car so badly either."

Dad, taking a swig from his beer, starts to choke and convulse with laughter.

"Well, well. What's going on out here? Sounds like a party and someone forgot to invite me," my mom says as she stands in the kitchen door, surveying the scene.

"Ana, honey! I hope we didn't wake you just now. You remember little, well… not so little anymore, Adam Blanchard, don't you?"

"I do indeed. So nice to see you outside of Tonner's and away from that prescription counter, Adam. How are you? And how is your mother?" Mom says all this while assessing Adam from head to toe with an unblinking stare.

"She's doing just fine, Mrs. Christie. And things are good with me, too. Thanks for asking."

"I'm glad I caught you just now. Aaron sometimes has a selective memory and tends to forget things I want him to pass on. Did he tell you we were hoping to have you over for dinner here sometime soon when you have a day off from Tonner's?"

"Yes, ma'am, he did."

"Good, then. You check your schedule at the store for the next couple of weeks and get back to us with a couple of dates, please. I trust you like either red meat or chicken," Mom says, raising one eyebrow.

"Yes, ma'am, I'd like that. Thanks very much, Mrs. Christie."

"It's Ariane, Adam. But do feel free to call me Ana when you come over here."

"Uhh, yes, err, umm, Ana. I'll try to remember that."

Adam hops into his car, reaches over to grab the loose door handle on my side and motions for me to climb in beside him. Once settled, he heaves a sigh of relief. I'm beside him and see a few sweat beads on his forehead. "Well, you can't blame me this time for those sexy beads of sweat on your face. Can I lick them off you before we go into the restaurant?"

"Settle down there! I don't need to be gettin' a full, boned-up, hard-on erection sittin' right out here in front of your parents' house! So, do ya think I passed inspection back there?"

"I'm pretty sure Dad made his mind up to like you before you even came to pick me up tonight. He isn't really so intimidating now to you, is he?"

"Nope. He's a pretty decent guy. Your mom though, she's gonna take a bit of time to warm up to. And by the way, trust me, she already knows I'm bangin' her little boy. Like I told ya, moms always know these things. It's like they have *mom radar* or can smell it off us, or somethin'."

"Well whatever she thinks, she's just going to have to get used to being less protective and allowing me to have a life of my own—on my terms, too. She's always hovered over me and I know she thinks she's going to lose me when I start school. Maybe if you could spend some time over here and offer to help out with her back garden, she might come to see that while things are going to change soon, maybe some of those changes could be good for all of us."

"OK, sure thing, Cookie. I can do that, no problem. Now let's just hope this lousy, cock-suckin' shitbox of mine doesn't embarrass me and starts up without too much protest so we can still grab that pizza over at El Paso's. I'm fuckin' starving here. It felt like old Mrs. Tonner was grillin' me for a job interview just now. Hell, pressure like that makes me hungry and horny. First the food and then we'll see what pops up after that. OK, Cookie?"

"Adam, you look really nice this evening. I can't believe someone as good-looking as you likes me."

"Aww, you have no idea, do ya? If you could only see what I see. I really wantcha to take a good long look at yourself in a mirror. Outside of that cute little, crooked upper tooth ya got there, I'd say you're just about perfect! Was it always that way or, like, how in the hell did ya ever do that anyway?"

"Ohh, that! Well, uhm, when I was seven or eight, I was riding my bike down Georgina Street one day and wasn't paying attention and ran over a big pothole. I managed to hit my jaw on my handlebar and ended up with a crooked premolar. I suppose I should ask Mom and Dad to call Dr. Sandringham to have a look at it again before I move to Ottawa."

"Nope! Dontcha dare do that! It's as cute and sexy as hell. It makes ya extra special. And I don't think I could deal with you bein' a hundred and ten percent perfect! Besides, you're perfect enough to me just the way ya are."

"You're perfect, too, Adam."

"Yeah, I know!" he says. And then he laughs and says, "Remember what I told ya before. No one's ever perfect. We all have our flaws. Except of course for you! You make me laugh and surprise me all the time. And I get hard every time I'm close to ya. It's all I can do not to grab ya and rip your clothes off. We have what's called chemistry! And you can't buy that in any drug store I know of. And after all, I aughta know."

We're still out front sitting inside his rusty, old grey SST coupe. I smell his Dior cologne wafting over me as I get comfortable and turn to face him. He bends over his steering wheel and turns his key to try to start it. It wails and cranks away, coughs, and promptly stalls out.

Adam sighs and stares back at the red GEN light. "Ugh!" he exclaims. He shakes his head, swears softly then stomps on the gas four or five times, trying to coax it to turn over for him. It coughs and stubbornly, reluctantly stumbles to life for him. Adam relaxes, reclining back fully in his driver's seat and heaves a huge sigh of relief.

I'm sure Dad is listening to hear him drive off.

"Don't rev the engine or squeal the tires. I don't want Dad rethinking you taking me out for driving lessons, OK?"

"Ya mean revving like this?" he says, giving his car two quick boots to the pedal while it backfires in protest.

"Jeez. Sorry I even mentioned it now."

Adam laughs and squeezes my thigh. Finally, we head off for dinner.

"Ana, can I make you a coffee now that you're up?"

"No, Richie. I've just put some grenadine into my glass for a Tequila Sunrise."

"That stuff doesn't mix well with the Valium and Elavil you've been taking."

"Ohh, Richie, don't lecture me again about mixing alcohol and drugs. Astrid called me today and gave me another long story about how Geraint is behind on the rent at the store and owes his suppliers and creditors more than thirty-seven-thousand dollars in rent and outstanding accounts. I just don't know what to say to her about the situation. I know I've said this a hundred times before. But what did she expect when she married him? We both knew it was a huge mistake at the time. She had a good future with the bank and she gave it all up for a man with barely a grade nine education and limited prospects on the job front. Now look at where they're at. What are they going to do?"

"Ana, there's something I haven't told you. We've been discussing putting this place up on the market and moving into that new apartment building on Church Street going up where the old Notre Dame Nuns' convent is standing now. With Aaron heading off to College and Blackjack now getting older, you and I agreed to sell the house and use some of that money to finance his education and have some fun in our remaining years with the balance."

"Yes, yes, yes. Tell me something I don't already know."

"I'm getting to it, Ariane. It seems that Geraint has a friend who is on the St. Francis Xavier Church Committee. Someone who has access to the list of potential tenants expressing interest in putting a reserve in on those seniors apartments once the building is completed and ready for occupancy in 1980 or '81. As well, he somehow found out that we've talked to Paul Saunderson from Royal Lepage Real Estate. And he called me last week and asked to come and speak with me at the Hospital."

"Go on."

"Well, honey, he had the nerve to ask me if I'd consider selling the house to him because they were going to have the Bailiff come to lock him out of the store for outstanding rent and the percentage profit-sharing he has to pay them on a quarterly basis. And get this! He asked me to hold the mortgage for him on the sale of this place so he could set up shop here and carry on with his painting contracting business by selling paint and wallpaper out of the main floor while they lived upstairs!"

"God. It's worse than I thought."

"I almost kicked him out of my office, I was so angry. Imagine the gall of him... expecting me at my age and with less than a year to retirement to hold his mortgage and bail him out."

"Why didn't you mention this to me before now?"

"Ana, honey, I know you've been depressed with having to come to terms with the fact that Aaron will be leaving home soon and is almost an adult with his education plans locked down and a life stretching out ahead of him. We both love him—maybe at times too much, You're trying to deal with that. And, Ana, I just didn't want you to have to be hit with this at the same time."

"We share everything, Richie. We always have. The good and the bad."

"Then I think it's high time we deal with a few more blunt things that should have been said between us a long time ago, since we're getting into this now."

"We've both known about Aaron for a long time. I think you've known since he was three years old. I'm a faithful Roman Catholic and try to follow the Church teachings. But both you and I know about his sexuality. And I'll say this to you right now, I love our boy and God made him the way he is—not you nor I. Whatever Pope Paul VI and that damned Monsignor Cranston at St. Francis Xavier have to say from the pulpit about the damnations of Hell awaiting so-called perverts and sexual deviants—well, I don't accept that crap for one damned single minute! I well remember that old fart, Cranston pontificating to me when Astrid wanted to marry Geraint in the Catholic Church years ago. Telling me that if she were on birth control pills or pregnant and if Geraint refused to agree to raise their children as Catholic and have them baptized, he would refuse to marry them at St. Francis Xavier. He's lucky I didn't punch him in the face at the time... questioning my only daughter's virginity and having the nerve to say that to my face. I told him right then and there that Astrid was my child and a virgin and

75

how dare he make such a comment to me. Me! An upstanding member of his parish for over twenty years back then, and a faithful and dedicated long-time member of the choir as well. When I think of all the money I poured into his collection plate over the years—at times when we could ill-afford it, too—well, for him to say something like that to me. My faith in the Catholic Church was sorely tested back then. And I refuse to believe that our boy Aaron is an aberration and abomination... an affront in the eyes of God and will burn forever in Hell."

"Uhm, Richie, you should know that Astrid had more to say to me during our little chat this morning. I think I'd better help you here to fill in a couple of missing blanks from what Geraint and Astrid haven't said to you."

"Go on."

"Astrid told me that Geraint and his friend Carlo saw Aaron leaving work one night recently with what they labelled, *a known homosexual...* whatever that means. It may have been that man, Cliff Horton who you sing with in the church choir. I'm not sure about him, but I know he and Aaron get together every now and then for lunch, and he stops in at the paint store to say hello to Aaron whenever he's up there. I like Cliff. Or actually come to think of it, it might have been that young man he's been hanging around with who works in the womens' clothing department of Zeller's, Robert Galanos. You remember him, don't you? When Aaron first started working for Geraint, he and that nice young boy, Robert started to have lunch together up at the shopping centre, and he's been over here to the house a couple of times. Then Astrid proceeded to tell me that Geraint and Carlo were both testing Aaron to find out if he was really a homosexual by standing around him and rubbing their crotches and grabbing and scratching themselves to see if he would stare at them!"

"What?!"

"I'm not done quite yet."

"You mean to tell me there's *more*?!"

"Unfortunately yes. Astrid said to me that if we sent Aaron off to College and paid for all of his tuition and expenses, he wouldn't make it through the first-semester… that he would be wasting our money and we would be encouraging and supporting a deviant lifestyle because she and Geraint knew he was a homosexual."

"I can't hear any more of this! Disgusting! Horrible! A sister turning against her brother this way. This is wrong and goes against everything we taught that girl. That is before she married that damned poor excuse for a Welshman! Aaron can't know about any of this!"

"I agree, Richie. We'll handle Astrid and Geraint together and of course, support Aaron here. But you need to know, I promised Astrid last week that Aaron would continue to work for Geraint right up to when he has to start school. That was of course before she called me today. I told Aaron this and he is expecting to go up to the store tomorrow afternoon to help Geraint. How can we let him go now, knowing that Geraint and that uncouth, obnoxious fat friend of his, Carlo from the Radio Shack have been tormenting him and being so crude and ignorant? It just makes me physically sick to think that a brother-in-law would even think about trying to entice a family member into propositioning someone they know over money."

Richard pauses for a long pensive moment and then says, "Aaron is going to have to learn how to face ignorant and cruel people and stand up for himself sooner or later. Let's let him work there for the next month and I'll keep an eye on him. And if Geraint says or does anything more to bait him in any way, he'll be answering to me. I have a sneaking suspicion that Geraint is a coward beneath that bullying, smug Welsh façade. If he makes one more stupid move before Aaron heads off in September, I'll cut him off completely to help Astrid regain some element of control in their marriage and tell him exactly what I think of him. I've been looking for an excuse to give Geraint a piece of my mind for a long, long time. Trust me, Ana. If it weren't for those two little grandchildren he somehow managed to produce outside of immaculate conception, I swear that Geraint would be out on the street for all the crap he's handed Astrid and this family from the time they got married."

"OK, but on another subject, what are we going to do about this *Adam Blanchard* business?"

"For the moment, absolutely nothing. I'm not going to get into a long discussion with you about this tonight. I'm tired now, honey. This will be a conversation we save for another time and place. I have a lot of thoughts on the matter. And I want to hear yours as well. I think you and I should go out for dinner, just the two of us, this weekend or next and get everything we're thinking out in the open between us. But for the moment, Aaron is happy and focused and Adam is a good and decent young man. We both know that. Adam has had a tough life. But he is a good boy. We could be having to cope with much worse."

"That sounds like a good idea. I like that."

"Ana, uhh, uhm, I have a thought here. His mother, Delphine is a smart and intuitive woman. Maybe you and she could go out and have lunch together sometime. I'd like to hear what she has to say about Adam and what seems to be developing here between our two boys. But for now, let's just try to continue to keep him focused on September as best we can, shall we, honey? And who knows? Things may well sort themselves out, either before or soon after he leaves home here. After all, Ottawa and Brockville are miles apart in more ways than one."

"I knew there was a good reason I married you. Years ago at the time, I thought it was just purely physical, and being that it was 1946 and right after the end of the war. That, and of course my getting pregnant with Astrid and having to marry you for the sake of my reputation. But there are many layers to you and I've come to love them all over the years."

Richard grins and responds, "I just liked your legs and tush. The rest came later, honey."

"Sure as hell glad he didn't wanna go out to take a really good look at my old car," Adam says to me as he slouches down in his seat, spreads his legs and heads down Pearl Street to the restaurant. "Am having conflicting thoughts here about whether I'm more hungry or horny at the moment—what about you, baby?"

"Yes and yes."

Adam chuckles and then says, "Hmmm, then I think we're gonna take a little detour and head down to Blockhouse Island. Have ya ever watched the submarine races down there just after dark?"

"Uhh, uhm, if they're submarines, then wouldn't they be *under* the water?"

"You're startin' to catch on there, butt-boy."

Once we get there, he pulls his old car into a parking spot facing west into the fading sunset on the St. Lawrence River and kills the engine. Then he looks carefully around at any other cars and adjusts his driver's seat as far as it can go, pulls me over to him, spreads his long legs out and starts kissing me, while taking my hand to rub his big, furry pube-basket until I can start to feel a stain start to seep through the denim.

"Up periscope!" Adam laughs, then gives me one of his dirty-minded, suggestive grins as his big cock comes to life.

"Just had to do that. If I'd hadta' sit across from ya with a big fuckin hard-on in the restaurant, we both woulda gotten kicked out for sure. Now let's head on over to El Paso's and chew on somethin' else besides each other."

El Paso's Restaurant is just across from where the new Post Office was built in the late-sixties. A block away is the Public Library and St. Francis Xavier Church is just around the corner. Dad and I used to go to El Paso's every Sunday right after Church to have orange juice and cinnamon toast—that's a special memory for me. Down the street from El Paso's is Manoll's Fish-and-Chips, where they still add sea-salt and malt-vinegar to each order and wrap them in old editions of the *Brockville Recorder and Times* newspaper. It's still the best place in town for fresh-cut fries.

"Heya Louie! Looks like a quiet night for ya here this evening. Have you got a table for two for a medium combination pizza and a nice bottle of your special red house-wine?"

"I assume your young friend there has some ID on him for the wine, Adam?"

"Yes, Louie. Do you need to see it?" I say.

"Nah, kid. Just so long as you have it and Adam says you're over eighteen, then it's all OK with me."

"Yep, he's legal, Louie. It's all good. You know his mom and dad, Mr. and Mrs. Christie from the Psychiatric Hospital."

"Oh yes. That's all fine then. Take a table and I'll be back with your wine in a couple of minutes."

"Aaron, at the window or in the back? What do you prefer?"

"How about in the back. I'd really like to talk and get to know you better, if that's OK with you."

"Tonight's all about you. Whatever ya like, Cookie-Boy." Adam leads the way to a table and Louie brings over the wine and a couple of glasses.

"So, what great mysteries do ya wanna know about me there?"

"Well, uhm, When did you first realize you liked boys rather than girls?"

"Jeezus! You go right for the knockout punch, dontcha. Why not just start out by askin' me where I went to school and what my birthday is?" he says laughingly.

"OK. So when is your birthday?"

"October 19th. Same time. Same day. Same month. Every year. Funny how that works out, eh?!"

"What year?"

"1951."

"Where did you go to school?"

"Uhm, in Brockville… hello?" he says and then laughs. "Aaron, I'm not so great with twenty questions. So why dontcha just sit back and relax and I'll tell ya a little bit about me while you drink some more of that wine there. Will that work for ya?"

"Sounds good to me."

Several minutes later, Louie shows up with the pizza, a couple of chipped and cracked restaurant china plates, mismatched cutlery and paper napkins, and proceeds to cut up the slices and serve them to us while demonstrating his masterful flair of proud restauranteur showmanship.

"Thanks Louie, that's perfect," says Adam.

"Now uhm, where were we? Oh yeah—like I told ya already, it's just my mom and me here in town. She lives over on Broadway Crescent. And that's where I grew up and went to school. First to Commonwealth on Pearl Street and then to Brockville Collegiate across from Victoria Park. Mom has an older sister out around Nanaimo on Vancouver Island. She lives in a commune out there with a bunch of people and does yoga and makes stained glass shit and is a vegan. Mom hasn't seen her in years. Mom told me she thinks she might be a nudist, too. But they never, ever talk about that. They do still talk on the phone every once in a while though. That's about all we have in the way of family."

He pauses for a second and then decides to continue. "I'm know I'm getting kinda intense here, since we just met and all. But, ya know, I don't mind tellin' ya it was real tough for my mom and me when my dad disappeared. I don't remember that much about him anymore. Just that he and Mom yelled a lot at each other. And that she cried whenever he stormed outta the house on her. Just that and he really wasn't at home that much at all either. Most of the rest I've managed to block outta my memory. He disappeared in late 1967—late summer—just before my birthday. And she got a divorce from him in 1972 when she found out where he was and was able to serve him with papers from her lawyer. I guess I was around twenty or twenty-one or so back then. The last time either of us heard anything about him, he was supposed to be still out somewhere in Alberta. And that's about all we ever wanted to know."

Then he turns his attention onto me. "Uhm, Cookie-Boy, am I allowed to ask *you* questions here, too? Or is this gonna be the *Adam Blanchard Monologue?*"

"Of course you can ask me questions. What do you want to know?" I take a slice of pizza and smile at him between bites.

"Well, for a start, when did you first realize you liked boys rather than girls?"

"Ohh! That's an easy one to answer. The very first time I saw you in Tonner's."

"Real smooth there, Cookie-Boy. And the right answer, too!" he says and laughs. "But seriously, babe, how are ya feelin' about leavin' Brockville and headin' up to Ottawa to start College in September?"

"I *was* being serious with my first answer about boys and girls!"

"Yeahhh, right."

"Well, as for Algonquin and the Interior Design programme, I have to admit it's been a big decision to go back to school. And I'm really scared to fail because I don't think there's any turning back once I move up to Ottawa."

"You do realize how lucky ya are for your parents to be givin' you this opportunity, dontcha? Mom got me through high school and then one year of pharmacy assistant training before money started to run short.

I had to drop outta training at the end of 1970. And it was old Mrs. Tonner who stepped in to hire me at Tonner's. I've been there with her ever since. That was back in '72… five years ago."

"Have you ever wanted to go back to finish your training?"

"Ya know, I keep on hopin' for something to happen. There's gotta be somethin' more ahead for me than where I am just now. Gotta admit though, meetin' you has made me think things might just be turnin' around and there's more to life for me than just a dead-end job and a shitbox old car that costs more to keep on the road than what it's worth. Let's finish the wine here and pizza. Louie is looking kinda sleepy over in the corner there and I think I maybe might wanna take ya on back to my place for a while. Wouldya like to see my little place above Mr. and Mrs. Nicholson's garage?"

"Sure. Let's go soon. Let me finish my wine though first. Whenever you're ready there."

"Aaron! You're drunk!"

"Am not!"

"Aaron, baby! You practically fell up the stairs gettin' into my apartment in those platform shoes of yours. And now you're laid-out on my bed, spread-eagle! Like how in the fuck am I gonna explain this to your mom and dad?!"

"Uhm, nope, didn't fall up the stairs, uhh, just fell out of my shoes. Mmmm… nice and comfy big bed. Smells sexy, just like you. Mind if I get under the covers?"

"Jeezus fuck! You sure are a cheap drunk. Am makin' you some strong coffee right now. Get your butt outta my bed before I come in there and pull ya out of there right now!"

"Nope! You're going to have to come in and get me!"

"Fuckin' Christ! Your dad's never gonna forgive me for getting ya drunk!"

"Is the room supposed to be spinning around like this?"

"Fuck! Dontcha dare get sick in my bed! I'm not cleanin' it up! This really isn't funny!"

"I'm going to sleep now. 'Nite Adam."

Adam stands over me with his hands on his hips, then runs his hand through his hair in total and complete frustration and exasperation.

Think Adam! Think!

"Whoever this is on the phone, it's eleven-thirty at night! You'd better be dying, or you soon will be if this is a wrong number!"

"Uhh, Mr. Christie, sir, it's Adam Blanchard calling."

"Adam? What's wrong? Where is Aaron? Why haven't you brought him home yet? I have to drop Ariane off at the Hospital here in ten minutes to start her shift. Did your car break down again? Are you two stuck somewhere? Did you have an accident? Is Aaron OK? Are you OK? Adam! Talk to me. Adam? Where is Aaron?"

"Well sir, it's like this. Uhm, uhh, Aaron doesn't drink much does he?"

"What the Hell kind of question is that to be asking me at this hour of the night? Where are you calling from? What exactly is going on?"

"Well, Mr. Christie. You know he had a beer before we headed out to El Paso's."

"Yes, and ?!"

"Well, sir, we had a bottle of wine with pizza. And then he wanted to see my place here above Mr. and Mrs. Nicholson's garage."

"Yes, yes Adam. Skip the saga. Cut to the chase. Where are you both now? Are you both safe? Are you at your place now? Is he all right?"

"Uhh, well, Mr. Christie, sir. He kinda fell up the stairs here in those disco platform shoes of his and then started to deny he'd had too much wine and beer to drink this evening. Then he climbed into my bed and told me to wake him up in the morning."

Richard is laughing on the other end of the phone line. He says, "Boy oh boy! I wished I could have seen that! The kid's as big a lush as his mother!"

"I'm really sorry, sir that I let this happen. I think I can carry him back down the stairs here and load him into the back of my car and bring him home. I feel real bad about this, Mr. Christie. I hope you're not angry at me for lettin' him get drunk."

"Adam! I'm actually finding this whole story hilarious. He's the most creative, stubborn, exasperating and frustrating child any parent could ever imagine at times! How about we let him sleep it off there and then he can make his way home himself in the morning? It'll teach him hopefully to be more careful with his liquor in the future. Just dump him on your sofa and throw a blanket over him and go to bed. Don't give this a second thought. I remember doing much worse myself when I was his age. He's growing up and will have to learn how to deal with the ramifications of his behaviour and actions when he moves to Ottawa. Let this be a lesson for him he hopefully won't soon forget. Can you cope with him for one night there?"

"Yes, sir. That's not a problem at all, sir.

"Adam! I told you to stop calling me sir! Now just make sure he doesn't wind up shoeless or worse, half-naked out on the street there and we'll forget this ever happened. And one thing more… not a *word* to his mother about this. You got that, Adam?"

"Yes, Mr. Christie, I do. And thanks. I'm really sorry about this."

"Ahh, forget about it. This isn't your fault. We all have to do these things to in order to learn from them. I'll bet you got drunk at his age as well. I'll be laughing to myself about this tomorrow when I see how badly hung-over he is. Maybe I'll make him mow the lawn first thing when he comes in the door. You can take care of him until he stumbles home here tomorrow morning. Later, Adam. Sleep *tight*. Aaron certainly will!"

Once off the phone with my dad, Adam walks into his bedroom to find me lying sprawled cross-wise across the bed with my head under a pillow. "Fuck," he murmurs to himself. He starts to think—*My dong's gettin' all hard here just thinkin' about hoppin' in there with ya. But that's just not gonna happen tonight. Not with you passed-out. I won't take advantage of ya that way.*

87

Time to get those clothes offa ya, though.

First, the disco shoes off my quilt.

One, two, the shoes come off and he tosses them onto the floor.

Next, that tight fittin' shirt.

It lands on the floor on top of the shoes.

Socks next.

They land in a heap beside the shirt and shoes.

And now those sexy, tight white jeans. Like, how in the fuck can ya even bend over in 'em? Jeez!

Adam leans over the bed to undo my belt and starts to unzip my jeans.

"Jeezus fuck! He's wearing my goddamn Superman underwear!" Adam exclaims out loud and starts to laugh.

Twenty seconds of a World Olympic Record Moment later and Adam is completely naked in bed beside me, hard as a rock with his big cock shoved up tight against my butt-crack and his arm tightly wrapped protectively around me.

Sleep tight, butt-boy. Not exactly sure how much sleep I'm gonna get here. But I don't give a damn about that at the moment. Cuddling with you is gonna be just what I'm lookin' for tonight. Sleep can wait for you, Adam Blanchard.

He nestles as closely as possible to me, smiles and eventually falls into a warm, sleepy haze.

The Peacock Inn Restaurant is down a couple of blocks from our house and then to the right on King Street, just across from the Prentice ESSO gas station.

King Yee bought the property in the early sixties and proceeded to tear down the massive, dark-red brick, Romanesque Revival style Victorian mansion that had stood there for almost a century to build the peculiar building now housing his restaurant and living quarters above.

His new building is faced with thick-trowelled white stucco with half-circle, rounded arches, and long, low stucco flower planters in the front with bright red and burnt-orange geraniums and yellow impatiens overflowing from them.

Brockville was suffering the fate of many small cities in the seventies—a dying downtown core with shopping malls in the north end and teardowns of irreplaceable, historic structures… all in the name of so-called progress and economy.

I have to admit though that the interior of the Peacock Inn Restaurant is rather special for Brockville. Greeting you at the front door when you come in is a huge, fierce and angry-looking cloisonné peacock statue that resembles no such bird ever found in nature. Red shiny vinyl-upholstered booths and chairs, black lacquered tables, black lacquered hanging lanterns with red silk tassels hanging down from them and a big, long mural along the back wall of male peacocks in full plumage complete the theme.

It was all very exotic and foreign for small-town Ontario in the sixties and seventies and had become a favorite dining spot for many people in town, my parents included.

Richard and Ariane are seated at one of the booths toward the back. White wine, garlic spare ribs and vegetable-fried rice are set out before them as they start to launch into a serious conversation that had been long in coming.

"I'm just so worried about him, Richie. He's only nineteen. And all that trouble we had with him skipping school because of the boys taunting him in gym class. Do you really think he is ready to start College in a strange city?"

"Ana, sooner or later he will have to learn to stand up for himself. He's not a little boy anymore. We won't always be there to protect him."

"I know. It's just that I remember when he was seven years old and playing with that damned John Yaegar down the street—that awful John taking his marbles and toy soldiers and throwing them down the sewer grate when Aaron's back was turned. Aaron is a very trusting and naïve boy. I just worry about him getting taken advantage of or getting himself into trouble in Ottawa when he is away from me, errr, rather, us."

"Ohh, Ana! For God's sake, woman! You've never liked the Yaegars ever since Dorothy broke down crying in our living room sitting on the floor and told you her husband Don was cheating on her. And then this obsession of yours about their youngest one, Wendy, where you were so afraid she'd try to get pregnant and force Aaron into a marriage because you were convinced that was what Dorothy told her girls to do to trap a husband. Like that was ever going to happen in hindsight now."

"Honestly, Richie! You can really go off on tangents, you know, at times!"

"My point, Ariane, is that we must try to step back now and let him develop into who he will learn to become. We've done a good job teaching him to have common respect for others and understand right from wrong. Both you and I have worked long enough at the Psychiatric Hospital to see the damage done in the name of religion and what someone else thinks and deems is right for boys who just happen to turn out being different. Am I happy that he is gay? Well, no… I'm not, honey. I have the same fears for his future as do you. It can be a lonely life and a violent and unhappy one, with alcohol and drug dependency or worse. We both know that and have seen it happen time and again with the patients at the Psych' who have no family—or anyone for that matter to be there for them. But I think we have to accept and support and love him and just be there for the times, and there will be times that he needs us."

"Have you ever said these things to Aaron?"

"Well… no I haven't. I pray for him and ask God to keep watch over him."

"Your very liberal for a man for your generation."

"I saw a lot of unhappiness and sadness at the Hospital before I met you. And you've seen it, too. The way the damned Psychiatrists, Psychologists and the rest of the so-called professional staff tried to cure homosexuals with shock treatments and aversion therapy. Well, honey, I used to think to myself that they were the ones needing treatment and not the poor young men they were supposedly trying to fix. I've seen a lot of misery, both with the patients and the many orderlies I manage on staff. We are all human beings with our own hopes, dreams and desires. No one has any right to judge anyone else as far as I'm concerned. After all, no one is perfect. And when I think about it now, wouldn't it be one big boring world if we all were?"

"I know. I know. I'm glad we came out to talk about this. And oh yes, I did give Delphine a call and we are going to have lunch together at The Relax Restaurant later on in the week. I don't think she has many friends. Let's have her over here when Adam gets back to us with a date for dinner. Is that all right with you?"

"That's a good idea."

"Heya, Aaron! Are ya lookin' for more KY to buy there?" whispers Adam as he stands behind me in the store, chuckling.

"Uhh, no, Adam. I was just wondering if you wanted to go to the Capital Theatre with me tonight or tomorrow. *Saturday Night Fever* with John Travolta is playing and I really want to go and see it."

"You like to dance?"

"Yeah, I do. I've got a lot of disco, Motown and soul records and I watch *Soul Train* on the Rochester TV station… that is when we can get it tuned in on the cable on Saturdays at home."

"I kinda like Aretha Franklin, Lou Rawls, Stevie Wonder and some stuff from Chaka Khan," he replies.

"Are you off this evening then? Can we go? I'm asking *you* out this time."

"OK, sure thing. But how about tomorrow though? I'm off then. But dontcha be expectin' me to put out for ya without dinner first! Just kidding! I'll pick ya up around eight."

"Oh yes! I almost forgot. This is for you."

"Hmmm, somethin' in a plain brown paper bag. Is it that new *Joy of Gay Sex* book you've been readin' and tellin' me about? Ya know, you coulda at least wrapped it for me," he says and laughs.

"Never mind! Just don't open it here. Maybe go into the back when you open it. There's a note inside to go along with it, too. Read it first."

"Ya got me all curious now. Now, was there anything else I can help you with? Maybe like actually buyin' something? Or do I hafta boot ya outta here for loitering before old lady Tonner sees me wasting my time over here with you?"

"OK, ok. I'm going now. No big boner for me today I see."

"Saving those now for when I get to be alone and naked with you, or when I'm all alone and just thinkin' about you," Adam whispers.

I laugh and say, "See you tomorrow at eight then."

I head out the door with Mrs. Tonner giving me the evil eye and feeling Adam's eyes boring a hole into my back as I leave the drug store.

"Now what in the fuck did he put in this goddamn bag for me, I wonder?" Adam mumbles to himself as he heads over to Mrs. Tonner behind the cash. "Uhh, Mrs. Tonner, I hafta go out to get somethin' outta my car right now. Do ya mind if I go on break right now, ma'am?"

"No, that's fine." And then she says, "Wasn't that Mrs. Christie's boy just in here now talking to you?"

"Uhm, yes ma'am. He's goin' off to school in Ottawa in September and was asking me some things about when I was in College."

"I see. Well don't be too long and go on along now."

"Ya nosy old bat." mumbles Adam under his breath as he heads out the back door of the store toward his car.

I swear to God every time I hop in my wheels now, all I can think of is his hot, little boy-butt sittin' in my driver's seat. Now what in the fuckin' hell did he put in this bag? Adam stretches his long legs out in his front-seat and dumps the bag in his lap. The bag is tightly closed with a solid row of staples so he has to work all of the staples free to get into the bag.

Fuck this shit, Blanchard! Just rip it open.

Inside the bag is a sealed small yellow envelope. And on the front there is a printed message that says *open me first*. As well, there's a small, flat box that is perfectly wrapped in royal blue paper with a bright red bow on it.

"What a creative little bugger," Adam says out loud to himself and then thinks, *better read the note first, I suppose*. He opens the envelope and takes out the note—beautifully printed in Aaron's careful script lettering, it reads:

"Dear Adam,

... no, this is not a tube of KY...

I just wanted you to know that I am returning something of yours that I borrowed. I wore them all last week and jerked off in them every night thinking of you and your big thick dong. I've laundered them and hopefully they are clean enough for you to start to wear now because I don't want you showing your fuzzy man-ass and big, sexy pube-basket to anyone else but me from now on in the store.

And yes! You are The Man of Steel.

Yours very truly,
Aaron Cookie Christie"

Jeez! He can get me all fuckin' hard and horny now when he's not even around me! Adam thinks and then laughs as he stares down at the tent his cock is making in his pants. *Sure as hell can't go back into the store now to face Mrs. Tonner 'til I rub one out here. Now where is that goddamn cum towel under my seat? "Awww, what the hell. If he can use these to cum in, then maybe I'll jack-off with 'em, too and make him wear them tomorrow night at the movies, he says aloud. Two can play at this game!"*

"Well Geraint, Dad just hung up the phone on me," says Astrid as she puts down the receiver and starts to cry. He told me they can't help us anymore and that he knows what you've been doing to Aaron at the store. Also, that I should be ashamed of what we've tried to do, about him being homosexual and his going back to school."

"That little brother of yours is messing up my plans. If they don't help us, I'm going to have to declare bankruptcy and we'll have to move out west and start all over. You have to convince them to help us! They'll never get to see their grandchildren if we have to go. Maybe tell him that, the next time you talk to him!"

"I don't think he wants to talk with either you or me again for a long, long time. I really think we're going to have to put the house up for sale here and sell it. Whatever money is left over after, we can take to head

out to Alberta and make a fresh start. You still have your painting contracting business and your equipment. I can always get a job as a teller
again in one of the banks out there, in either Calgary or Edmonton. The
children are still young enough to adapt and make new friends and fit
into new schools. They say Alberta is the place to go to start over. I don't
want to lose Mom and Dad forever over this. I've never known Dad to
be so angry at me the way he is right now! He told me I was both a bad
daughter and an even worse sister!"

Astrid completely breaks down in tears then and looks pleadingly
at Geraint saying, "We have to do this! We just have to! There's no
other way!"

"Well, he's not gonna get his pay from me for his work at the store. I
dare your father to try and make me pay the little queer."

"Dad said to tell you that not only are you to pay him every cent you
owe him, but that if you didn't, he'd call the manager of the shopping
centre himself tomorrow to have the Bailiff come put the locks on the
store before you have a chance to take any of the unpaid stock and supplies out after-hours like you wanted to try to sell them off."

"Shit, Astrid! Your dad can be a real fucking, moral Catholic cunt
at times. OK then. He's backed me into a corner. I'll pay the little fairy
what I owe him. But I'm not going to hand it to him personally. Your
damned father can come and get the hundred bucks from you because
after that, I never want to see him or that little cock-sucking brother of
yours again."

It's the next day and Dad hands me an envelope. "Here, Aaron.
Geraint gave me this pay packet of money for you and said to say thanks
for helping him up at the store, but that he wouldn't be needing you
after all until September. He and Astrid put some extra cash in there
to help you with the first-semester for spending-money when you need
some, by the way."

I open the envelope and there are four crisp one-hundred dollar bills in it.

"Thanks, Dad. But this is waaay more than what Geraint owes me. And he hasn't been all that nice to me at the store since I got accepted at Algonquin. Still though, I guess I better call him to say thanks for it all the same."

"Uhm, no. That's not necessary, son. I had a long talk with him when he gave this to me. He and Astrid are extremely busy right now. They have decided to move out to Alberta right after you start school. They are focused now with meeting a real estate agent to sell their house. And Geraint is going to close up the store, remove the fixtures and close out the lease. I'll tell Geraint you said thanks for the money. You just focus on yourself now for the next few weeks. There's going to be a lot for you to take care of in that time."

"OK. But you always taught me to thank people when they do nice things. Don't you think I should at least call Astrid to say thank you?"

"She has a lot on her plate right now. Leave that for your mother and me to take care of. She'll know you are grateful for the extra money."

It's later that evening and Adam and I are walking out of the Capital Theatre and heading over to his car. I look at him and say, "So, did you like the movie, Adam?"

"Well, Cookie, I think the best part of it was havin' your hand rubbin' back and forth against my inner thigh during the whole movie. That and the red licorice and popcorn! And uhm, I'm sure as hell glad I brought my jacket along to cover up the hard-on you were makin' in my crotch!"

"Nooo, seriously. What did you think of it?"

"Well, the movie made me feel kinda sad. Travolta plays this guy drivin' around in a friend's car as old as mine who gets caught up tryin' to better himself to get out of the life he thinks is all his future has for him. I can kinda relate to that in a way. But fancy dance moves and white suits and tryin' to be popular and cool isn't how I think the way to be happy really is. I liked the music though, I hafta admit."

"What did you think about it?"

"Well, outside of you stealing all the licorice, I guess it was OK. It was pretty neat in the opening scenes when it showed him working in a hardware store and carrying gallon cans of paint around. That sort of reminded me a little bit of me working for Geraint in the paint store at the shopping centre. I think Travolta has a sexier man-ass than you do though, Adam."

Just then he grabs me and pulls me into a playful headlock and starts to laugh saying, "No fuckin' way, baby!"

Well, if you say so, handsome. And ohh, yeah, I kinda liked rubbing the inside of your thigh during the movie, too!"

Adam gives me a dirty laugh and says, "OK then. Let's hop in my car—that is once my dong simmers down here in a minute or so—we'll go somewhere quiet. Whaddya say? Not Blockhouse Island tonight though. Too many goddamn fuckin' straight people parked down there at this time a night. I have a special place I know of I wanna show ya, OK?"

"Sure thing. Let's go."

We walk over to his car in the parking lot beside the theatre and Adam says, "It's been runnin' kinda rough again since old Gerry fixed it up for me. Let's hope it starts up here 'cause I just don't need the frustration and fuckin' grief of havin' to cope with it crappin' out or breakin' down on me this evening. It gave me a real hard time when I was headin' over to pick ya up earlier. It damn well better not do that to me again!"

Luckily, it only hesitates briefly and then starts up for him. "Slide right over right tight beside me. I can drive just fine with one arm around you and one hand on the wheel. You can play with my dong and stick your tongue in my ear."

"Can I turn on the radio?"

"Yep, ya can. First turn the radio on. And then you can turn me on," he says with a suggestive wink, a sexy nose twitch and a laugh. Marilyn McCoo and Billy Davis Jr. are singing, "You Don't Have to Be a Star, Baby" as I snuggle next to Adam and as he drives slowly, heading east on Water Street.

"We're gonna park just before Centeen Park at the base of Park Street where the old Ault Creamery milk plant used to be and look out over the water," Adam says as we turn right to head down into the small parking lot there. "Cookie, didya know that Great Lakes steamships used to dock here to unload coal a long time ago? The moon is really nice tonight and it's dark and private and quiet. And I'm gonna give you some lessons on how to suck a man's cock."

"I thought I already knew how to do that?!"

"Well I figured I'd suck on yours for a change and maybe you'd pick up a few pointers from me. Ya know, there's all kinds of ways to teach and learn in this life."

"What did you do, Aaron?!"

"What?!"

"Uhm, baby, your pubic hair smells like *Eau Sauvage!* Jeezus fuck! What in the hell gave you the idea to douse yourself down there with my brand of cologne?!"

I start to get upset and shyly say, "Well, umm, uhh, it reminds me of you because it's what you always wear. And I can smell it down there whenever I put it on. It just really makes me think of you."

He sits up and puts his hand on my shoulder. I can tell he is stifling a laugh, which really embarrasses me. Then he pulls me in, gives me a big hug and starts to nibble on my ear lobe.

"I'm real flattered, but I really don't wanna smell my cologne down there when I'm goin' down on ya. I'm real good at this sorta thing. But so far I've never been able to suck my own cock. Besides, I'd rather suck yours there!"

He starts to shake with laughter and I'm almost in tears at this point.

"Aww, it's OK, baby. Dontcha cry or anything. Hold on. I got an idea. Reach into my glove compartment and pull out that tube of KY I stashed away in there."

I open up the glove compartment and his cum-stained Superman briefs and KY fall out onto the floor of the car. "Gimme those briefs and KY and I'll clean ya up a bit to get rid of the cologne-smell and getcha all juiced up at the same time."

He proceeds to squirt KY onto my penis and starts to massage it up and down with slow rhythmic, deliberate moves—back-and-forth—up-and-down—his thumb and forefinger twisting my cock head firmly until I begin to groan and squirm from his touch. Then he leans into me and whispers, "We'll do the blow-job lessons another time. In the meantime I'm gonna give ya a hand-job after I wipe ya down with my underwear to get rid of the damn smell of that cologne." Then he shifts over tight beside me so I can feel his beefy, muscular thigh rubbing next to my hip and says softly while barely able to hold back laughing, "And uhh, uhm, Aaron, just for future reference, I don't think Christian Dior meant for his cologne to be used down there, babe."

Ten minutes of his hands stroking my dick with him wrapped around me in his front-seat and I'm ready to shoot a cum load all over him and his old car. "Adam! I'm gonna cum!"

"Yeahhh, baby! I can tell! Gimme a sec' to get my mouth down there though 'cause we're not gonna need a cum towel tonight! You're gonna feed me!"

I explode deep in his mouth. He moans and grunts and sticks two of his fingers up my ass to increase the sensation.

"I think ya came there, Aaron. Whaddya think?"

"I think maybe yes… I did," I whisper hoarsely.

He laughs that wicked laugh again, pulls the zipper up on my jeans and then sits back in his driver's seat with his hand on the steering wheel. He gives me one long, appraising look.

"We always seem to be gropin' and doin' somethin' physical and sexual to each other. Not that I'm complainin' or anything. But let's just sit back now and look at the moon tonight and talk a little. Are you OK with that?"

"Talk about what?"

"Well, like, when exactly are you gonna be leavin' to start school for one thing?"

"Classes start on September 12th and I have to be moved in to a place and ready for classes for eight-thirty that morning."

"C'mon over here and put your arm around me. I wanna feel ya tight beside me right now. Ya know, I don't want this to end when ya move away. We're only just startin' to get to know each other, besides what we've got in our pants. How do ya feel about that?"

"Well I don't want this to end either," I say while burying my face into the nape of his neck and playing with his left nipple. "You said something about chemistry before. I don't know if that's what this is or not. All I know is that I want to be with you. And if I have to give you up because I have to move away and not see you anymore, well, I just don't know if I can do that."

"Ohh, Aaron, dontcha start to cry on me now. We'll figure somethin' out here. I gotta feeling we're gonna go right on with what we got started here 'cause I don't wanna be without you either." He holds me even tighter and nudges my ear. "Uhm, I checked my schedule from work and I'm off next weekend. Your mom can make dinner then, if she still wants to—maybe next Sunday. I wanna find out from your mom and dad what's got to happen with you between now and when you hafta move. I'm gonna step in and help with that, if they'll let me, just to stay in the picture. I wanna see what's in your bedroom that's gotta get moved and then you and me are gonna do that together to getcha all settled in. How does that sound to you?"

I stop sniffling and say to him, "OK. That sounds really good. And as for dinner, I'll tell Mom. I know she really wants to have you over."

"Now let's just be quiet for a while and look out over that water with the moon shinin' on it. It's really peaceful and beautiful tonight isn't it?"

A half-hour passes without a single word needing to be said. And then Adam moves to stretch and says, "Uhh, before I get more distracted than I am right now, I left a little somethin' of me earlier in my Man of Steel briefs for ya—a little thank you present. It'll be a real part of me rubbin' next to ya when you wear 'em tomorrow. Like, I'll really be in your pants. And knowing that'll keep me all juiced and boned-up for when I see ya next time. Now just kiss me for a while and then I'll take ya home."

The Relax Restaurant is another one of those Brockville institutions that has been around for like, forever. My mom and Adam's mom are seated together at a booth at the front overlooking the counter where the swivelling stools are. "This is very nice, Ariane," Adam's mom says as she looks over the menu at the Relax Restaurant. "I don't get out much except to shop for groceries and such. I'm so glad you called. I can't remember the last time I was here for lunch. It's been ages."

"Oh, please... call me Ana. I have to admit, with the midnight shifts I'm on, I don't get out much socially these days myself."

"And you call me Del—everyone does."

Just then Marie the waitress comes to the table with a couple of menus. They both scan the menus and order while Marie writes everything down on her little pad.

So, Ana, Adam tells me Aaron is heading off to College in a few weeks. I'll bet you miss him already. I remember how I felt when Adam left home. It was hard for me being alone. I didn't know what to do with myself without him messing up the house and needing my care. They grow up so fast, you know. How are you feeling about him leaving?"

"I don't think I've accepted it yet, Del to be truthful with you. I have to admit the house is going to be so quiet and I guess I'll just have to get used to the idea that he isn't my little boy anymore."

"He'll always be your little boy. Just as Adam will always be mine."

"Did Adam tell you he was giving Aaron driving lessons, Del?"

"Not in that old car I gave him, surely not! Is that even safe, I wonder?"

"Well, yes," Ana says, and takes a sip of the iced tea from the glass that Marie the waitress just placed on their table. "They've been spending an awful lot of time together. And well, uhh, Richard and I are just so pleased that Adam has taken Aaron under his wing. You know, Del, there are times I've regretted not having more children. I know he would have liked to have had a brother. I think it would have helped him in so many ways." Ariane's voice trails off and she looks away from Delphine, lost in private thought.

"You know, Ana, it was hard for Adam in his early-teens with just me for him. Sometimes I felt the same way about children. But the way things were with Jason, well, I'm just so glad we didn't when we were first married. You know when Jason left us, Adam had a very difficult time. He saw and heard too much when he was growing up. I don't need to tell you this, but I asked one of the Psychologists at the Hospital to spend some time with him during that time. He needed reassurance and safety and someone else besides me to talk to. He had a lot of anger and resentment inside him and was very protective of me. He was just a young teenager back then. It took a long time for him to heal and get past what his father had done to us. And I think Adam thought it was his fault because he was born somehow. I'd do anything to take those memories away from him, especially when he was little. I think he's managed to block a lot of them out, thankfully. I'm really glad he's offered to help out with your Aaron."

"So are we, Del. I have a feeling they are both looking for some direction in their lives. I hope I'm not being too presumptuous by saying that to you."

"No, you're not, not at all. I completely understand what you mean. I don't think either one of our boys fits the mould of a *happily-ever-after* life in Brockville." Delphine takes a bite of her toasted minced ham-and-pickle sandwich. Then she decides to confide a bit deeper. "Adam has been a loner and coasting for a while now. I worry about his future. Perhaps seeing Aaron moving ahead with his education and life may be a good thing for Adam. I worry about him. He wasn't a happy boy in high school. He got into many fights protecting me and trying to prove to his classmates he was as good as they were. I think being without a father during those years affected him deeply. Dr. Ledermann at the Hospital said to me back then that he thought Adam shut down emotionally after Jason abandoned us. Adam doesn't open up much with strangers and doesn't have many friends you know. I'm very pleased he wants to spend some time with Aaron."

"I'm glad we are having this lunch, Del. You've made me feel a little better about Aaron leaving for school. And from one mother to another, I know you've done a good job raising Adam. Sometimes, it just takes some children a little longer than others to find themselves. We worry so much about them, don't we?"

"Sometimes too much, Ana."

"Hmmm… funny you should say that. Richard said the exact same thing to me recently."

"Let's do this again soon," Del says, crumpling her paper napkin on her plate. It's been good to be able to talk with another mother. Let's you and I encourage their friendship. We women understand far more about what it is to have *friends* than men ever will. We'll always be their mothers. And they'll always be our little boys."

Ariane smiles and nods at Delphine. "I think we understand how difficult it can be to grow up in a small town when you're, uhm, uhh, well… when you're *different*. Maybe we'll just leave it at that. I think we both know our boys very well. No need to say any more. I'd like that, too. Thanks, Del."

It's the following Sunday and Aaron's mom is in the kitchen seasoning pork chops before putting them into the oven to bake. "Aaron, when did you say Adam was going to be here again?"

"He said around four-thirty or so. He needed to help his mom out with some things around her house."

"I wished she'd been able to come for dinner along with Adam."

"Maybe next time. And oh yes, I meant to mention to you, Adam was hoping to see my room. He offered to help with moving my stuff up to Ottawa when I start school. He wants to talk to you and Dad about that. I'd like him to, if that's OK with you both."

"You and he have become quite close friends in a short period, haven't you?"

If she only knew just how close...

"Uhm, yeah. I like him, Mom. He's a really nice guy."

"Well, you tell Adam to feel completely at home when he gets here. He was so kind and polite when he came over the other day and offered to help cut down some of the wild rhubarb in the back garden for me. In fact, I have a surprise for him. I've baked two rhubarb pies. One just for him and another for him to take home to Delphine."

"That was nice of you."

"I'm just happy he has taken you under his wing. You know, darling, friendships are rare and special things when we find them and not something to take lightly... or for granted. I hope you both will continue to be friends after you move to Ottawa. And Adam can come over here on his own any time he likes to spend time with your father and me. You tell him that, too."

Mom and Dad's house at 69 Bethune Street had been built around 1860 and was typical for several of the older houses in Brockville, loosely-based on Italianate style, Tuscan architecture with a shallow hipped-roof, heavily bracketed eaves, pale grey-coloured clapboard siding with white trim, two shuttered windows on the second floor and one down on the first beside an ornate, carved-wood fretwork front porch and finally, double front doors with a stained-glass transom above. If you were to use the big, brass door-knocker to announce yourself, chances are you'd likely be graciously invited into Mom and Dad's warm and welcoming home.

Mom had worked hard over the years to furnish the inside with slipcovered bright red, coral pink, hydrangea blue and lush green floral chintz overstuffed sofas and wing chairs, and some precious, treasured and much-loved family antiques and heirlooms her parents had left to her when they died.

My bedroom upstairs is on the side of the house where there is a two story, three-sided bay window above the dining room overlooking the driveway. I was given complete freedom to pick the wallpaper and paint for my room and what I chose surprised even Mom at the time.

My favorite colour is red. The wallpaper in my room replicates a classic colonial stencil-pattern with really small white hearts and dots on a strong, vibrant red background. It isn't nearly as girly and prissy as it sounds. The antique pine table desk that Rob Galanos helped me to find when we were out together looking in junk stores one day along with the big, tall pine armoire Mom was able to score for me at a local auction sale are the main pieces of furniture in the room, save for the bed that has an antique fireplace mantel serving as a headboard and shelf from the old Bank of Montreal on Courthouse Square when it was torn down in the early-sixties. There are pine shutters on the inside of the bay windows that match the lustrous, pine hardwood floors throughout the second floor of the house. Mom put a red Bokhara rug beside the bed to finish everything off.

It wasn't exactly a typical teenager's room from the seventies. But then again, I'm not exactly a typical teenager either.

Adam drives up just before four thirty and pulls into our driveway, right behind Dad's car. Dad has always been a Chrysler man. And the 1973 metallic turquoise, two door Newport Royal with the crazy, white paisley-embossed pattern vinyl roof he bought a few years ago is huge—a veritable land yacht.

Thank God we've got a big driveway, I think as Adam pulls into the driveway and hops out of his rusting, old Ambassador SST. He's just standing there with his mouth agape, staring at Dad's battleship destroyer of a car.

"Heya, Cookie! Jeezus, do ya think your dad bought a big enough fuckin' car? That thing must a real goddamn bitch and a half to hafta back up and parallel park."

"Can you understand now how I backed into Mrs. Larocque's garbage cans when he took me out to practice driving it?"

Adam laughs and replies, "Yep, I kinda can see that now."

"C'mon in. Dad's reading the weekend edition of the *Ottawa Citizen* he picked up from Ritchie's Cigar Store last night and Mom's in the kitchen. She said to say to feel right at home here and we'd have dinner around five or so."

"Where's Blackjack, Aaron? I brought him a nice bone from the butcher's shop."

"Dad will be really happy you did that. You know, he really is dad's dog more than mine."

"I wanna see your room first before I say hi to your folks."

"OK. Follow me up the back stairs and I'll give you a tour."

"Jeez, baby. I was expectin' to see shag rugs and a mirrored disco-ball and incense burners and macramé plant hangers with plastic plants and

Donna Summer posters plastered all over your room. This is not what I thought your bedroom would look like at all."

"Mom is pretty particular about what I can and can't put up on the walls. I like the room though. I picked out the wallpaper and some of the other things. And this being an old house with plaster walls and all, well… I just really like my room."

"Adam, Open up the armoire doors."

He opens the doors to find two posters taped to the back of each door. One is of Harrison Ford from *Star Wars* and the other one is of Diana Ross from *Mahogany*.

"Yep. That's more like what I thought," he murmurs.

"Look behind my clothes."

He shoves my shirts and jeans over on the hanging rod inside and looks at the back of the armoire only to find a giant poster of Superman with the caption *The Man of Steel* boldly emblazoned across the bottom and starts to laugh.

"And I'm wearing your Superman underwear right now. Uhm, Adam, do you see that hanger in there with those glen-check plaid pants? They're yours! I stole them from your car a few weeks back when I saw you up at the 401 Inn, along with that old brown tweed tie. I jerk off with them all the time." With this, I reach down to fondle his prominent bulge and ass-crack."

"So *that's* where those good pants and tie of mine went to! Jeezus! I was really pissed off about losin' 'em and kept looking for 'em back at my place for days and like, just couldn't fuckin' figure that one out at all!" The look of embarrassed shock and panic on his face is hilarious as I keep rubbing his crotch and pinching his left nipple.

"Jeezus fuckin' Christ! Dontcha be doin' this to me in your parent's house! What the hell are ya doin'? Stop grabbin' me! Get up off the floor and get your head outta my crotch! Nooo, honey, c'mon, just leave my dong alone! Settle down, Cookie! C'mon—nooo! Stop that! Leave my zipper alone! Jeezus! Get your hand outta there! Aaron, awww, Jeezus fuck, c'mon now! Stop teasin' me! Not here in your parents' house! Are ya fuckin' crazy?! What a little cock-tease you are!"

"Hmmm, no underwear, eh? Good! Now, Man of Steel, just let me rub it some more and then I'll put your cock back in your jeans so I can smell you on my fingers when we're having dinner."

"You're makin' me *abso'fuckin'lutely* crazy here! Knock it off!" C'mon now, it's all I can do right now not to throw ya down on your bed and do ya right here. And just so ya know, too, that tie's comin' back with me 'cause it was my dad's and I really missed it, ya kinky little shit! Now, behave yourself! Let's just simmer down here and go down to have dinner with your folks. That is, uhh, once my dong calms down here in a minute or two! Christ! I think I need a shower now."

Halfway through dinner, I cast an eye over at Adam and distract him with an amused, teasing expression on my face. My eyes twinkle and I give him a playful smirk once he catches onto the fact that I'm watching him. As we continue to eat dinner, he glances back at me every thirty seconds or so. I hold a couple of fingers up to my nose, pretending to sniff them whenever he does. Each time I do, he blushes deep scarlet red and quickly stares back down at the table, trying to concentrate on the breaded pork chops and garlic-mashed potatoes on the plate in front of him. God, I just love to make him blush like that! After a few minutes and in a futile and vain attempt to distract himself—me too, no doubt— he clears his throat and says, "Uhm, uhh, so, when are ya startin' school again there, Aaron?" He's clearly flustered, embarrassed, and uncomfortable shifting a bit in his chair. He spreads his cloth napkin out fully, trying to cover his jeans as we all continue to sit at the dining room table finishing up the meal.

I give him an innocent smile and say, "I need to be up there for September 12th to start my first-semester. But I have to find a place in Ottawa close to the Campus. And I have a final interview with Iona Ouspenskaya, who is Head of English Applied Arts/Interior Design on August 22nd."

Dad jumps in at that point. "I was looking through the ads in the *Saturday Citizen* for bachelor apartments and rooms to rent and there is a place at 37 Argyle Avenue, two blocks away from the St. Pat's Campus. It's just up from the Rideau Canal and close to Elgin Street and downtown. You'll be able to bike and skate along the Canal, and the school is just over the Pretoria Bridge and only ten minutes away. I won't be able to take you up though until Friday at the earliest. Hopefully, it will still be available and not rented out by then."

"Mr. Christie, errr, uhm, I can take Aaron up to look at the place, if you like," Adam says.

"I'm sorry, but not in that unreliable, old car of yours. I don't want him to miss out on this place to another student looking to rent so close to the school."

"It's OK Mr. Christie. Old lady, errr, uhm, that is Mrs. Tonner at the store told me I could borrow her car any time I needed it. I don't think she'd mind at all me takin' time to help you folks and Aaron out here."

"That would certainly be a big help to me if you could. I'd really appreciate that."

"Consider it done."

"Thanks very much, Adam. I would suggest no later than Tuesday though to try to get this done so we don't miss this opportunity. I'll call the Rental Agent to set up a time. You'll take care of him? Promise me that you will, Adam," my dad says while giving him a long, earnest and reflective look.

"Yes I will Mr. Christie. He'll be just fine with me. I promise ya that."

3   August / September

Adam pulls up in front of our house promptly right at nine and I'm out on the front porch waiting for him. He confidently boots Mrs. Tonner's car down the 401 until we get to Prescott and Johnstown and then heads north up to Ottawa.

An hour and a bit later we're driving by the Experimental Farm on Prince of Wales Drive and about to head onto Carling Avenue and Bronson. We're on our way over to 37 Argyle Avenue where Dad made an appointment with the Rental Agent to look at this bachelor apartment we've come to look at. At last, we pull up in front of the apartment building on Argyle and park on the opposite side of the street, facing the building. It's a red brick house similar in size and architectural style to most of the other houses on the street. At one time it must have been either a duplex or a very large single family home—three stories tall with covered wooden balconies above the front entrance. It's tight to the sidewalk and the street with no grass in front, save for some straggly weeds growing out of the concrete. There is a central door on the front façade... it's obviously a walk-up building with lots of stairs. Hopefully, the apartment we have to look at is either on the first or second floor. The prospect of carrying my really cool, turquoise Sekine ten-speed bike—the one I had saved up for and bought all by myself with my own money—as well as hauling laundry and groceries up multiple flights of stairs is not exactly thrilling. The lady who is to show us the apartment is waiting for us out on the covered front porch by the front door with the beveled-glass window in it.

"Hello. Which one of you is Aaron Christie?" she asks.

I reach out to shake her hand and say, "Hello, I'm Aaron. And this is my friend, Adam Blanchard from Brockville. Thanks for meeting us to have a look at the apartment."

"I'm Marisol, the Leasing Agent for the landlord. Your father explained to me on the phone when he called that you'll be starting classes at Algonquin close by in the fall. You'll probably find this place a little on the small side. It's really just one big living room with a kitchen alcove, an entry hall and a bathroom. The rent is two-hundred-and-five dollars a month, with a first and last month deposit and post-dated cheques required for the first year. Also, we don't normally rent to students, so we'll be needing a refundable security deposit of two-hundred-and-fifty dollars for any damages that may be incurred for the time you live here. Is that going to be a problem?"

"No. That sounds OK to me."

"Well then, let's go in and have a look and you can let me know what you think. I've had one person already looking at the place, so if you're interested you'll have to let me know before you leave."

"OK. May we see the place then, please?"

"Yes of course. Follow me."

"As you can see, it's on the first floor to the right, just as you come in the door—Unit #2. The place has new locks on the door and has just been freshly painted. The landlord bought the building a few years back. And with the exception of this place on the first floor, it's fully rented out. There are nine apartments total in the building. There are no laundry facilities on-site. But there is a laundromat three blocks down on Elgin Street beside Al's Steak House. The hardwood floors have just been refinished. This used to be the formal parlour or living room back when this was still a duplex. The fireplace is decorative and not functional. You have a big picture window facing out onto Argyle Avenue and the apartment building across the way. And as you can see, the place is heated with a hot water radiator just under the window over there. The bathroom has *really pretty, brand-new, peachy-coloured floral wallpaper* that I picked out and put up for the landlord. It has an original sink and claw-foot bathtub that came from another room when the place was converted into multiple apartments. You've got the IGA store for groceries, just over on Isabella Street. And you're close to the Voyageur Colonial bus station up four blocks on Catherine, just past the YMCA and Bank Street. Heat and hydro are included in the rent. Phone and cable are extra.

I had to suppress a grimace when she proudly stated it was she who had selected that *really awful* girly wallpaper…

Do you have any questions for me?" Marisol asks when she's done the tour.

"No, thanks, Marisol. Too bad the fireplace is painted over. I bet there is some really beautiful oak underneath all that paint."

"It has at least five coats of paint on it and would have needed far too much time and effort to strip it down to the original wood and re-stain it again."

"It's just so beautiful though."

"Tell you what. If you want to put the effort into refinishing it while you're here, then I don't think the landlord would have a problem with that at all," she says and slowly starts to warm up to me.

I keep looking at that fireplace, imagining those scrolled side pieces, fancy twisted, spiral wood columns and moldings, along with that original, old, cloudy, oxidized beveled-glass over-mantel mirror stripped down and refinished with a rich, golden stain to match the hardwood flooring. "Well, the kitchen is really small and there is only that tiny little alcove for clothes by the front door and those hanging hooks between it and the kitchen—I really like the place though—the location is perfect. It has some real character. If I were to take it, would you accept a deposit now by cheque and then when would I be able to have keys to move into the place?"

"Once the cheque clears and you give me the security deposit and post-dated cheques then I can hand you over the keys."

"OK. Well, Adam, I don't think I'm going to find anything cheaper, closer or better this close to the start of the semester. What do you think about the place?"

"It looks OK to me. That bathtub is really big," he says and gives me a sly little smile. The kitchen is smaller even than my place back in Brock Vegas. But you'll have the cafeteria at school. And there's lots of restaurants and fast food places along Elgin Street and down Sparks Street Mall. It's your decision, Aaron."

"May I give you a cheque now then, Marisol? My mom gave me a blank cheque before we left this morning. I can fill out the amount for first and last months and the security deposit and I'll give you post-dated cheques when I come up on the 22nd. I really like the place."

"Sounds good to me," she replies.

"I have to be up in Ottawa on August 22nd to meet with the Department Head and get myself oriented to find my way around the College. Can I pick up keys for the place at the same time? I think I'll want to move in around or just after Labour Day so I'll be ready for school to start."

"What are you going to be studying in school, Aaron?" she asks me.

"Interior Design."

"Well then! I'll certainly know who to come to whenever the landlord wants to do something around here. Just remember though that you can't paint or do anything that's going to alter the place, unless you ask permission first or you'll lose your security deposit."

Once everything is signed, Adam and I stand on the front porch surveying Argyle Avenue. He says to me, "Hey! This is great! Look over to the left. You're just a block up from the Canal. That'll be good for skating when the ice freezes over.

"Thanks for coming along with me," I say to him. "But what do you really think about the place now that I've rented it?"

"Well Cookie-Butt, that kitchen is smaller than a closet. And as for closets—well—there are none. And the ceilings in the place are at least twelve feet high. If you aren't plannin' on doin' more than makin' coffee and havin' toast in that kitchen—there is like, no counter in there at all. And if that hot water radiator in the main room heats the place so ya don't freeze to death in the winter, then it should be OK. Uhm, baby, I saw ya lookin' at and thinkin' about that fireplace. Don't do the landlord's work for him. It looks just fine painted the way it is now. You'll have more important things to do with your time outta school than takin' on somethin' like that—hmmm, yeahh—like havin' nice, long, hot bubble baths in that old-fashioned tub with me," he says with a dirty-sounding, suggestive chuckle. "Now, let's hop in the car and head over to the Campus 'cause I wanna see how far it is from here and just exactly where you're gonna be goin' for classes. After that, we're gonna come back here and take a walk down Elgin Street up to the Sparks Street Mall and Parliament Hill. Then you can buy me dinner 'cause I'm such a nice and sweet guy for bringin' ya up here today."

The St. Pat's Campus of Algonquin College faces directly onto the Rideau Canal along a roadway that is called the Queen Elizabeth Driveway. It used to be the railroad tracks coming along that side of the Canal in to Union Station, right across from the Chateau Laurier Hotel. That is, until the National Capital Commission and the City of Ottawa ripped up the tracks and beautified the entire length of the Canal to promote tourism back in the mid-sixties. It's quite touristy and beautiful now.

St. Pat's was purchased by Algonquin College a few years back and is an H-shaped, four-story, brown brick, vaguely Tudor-Revival period building that resembles many high schools built around the same period of time. I think they actually call it *Collegiate Gothic* style. It reminds me of Brockville Collegiate where I went to high school. *I sure hope the time I spend here is going to be better than when I was back at BCI...*

"I'll have to be up here again in late August to meet the Department Head and show her my portfolio. At least now I know how to get here from Argyle Avenue."

"That was the general idea. Looks like the place is locked up tight for the summer though, so I guess we won't be doin' any walkin' around inside. Too bad. I wanted to see what it looked like beforehand with ya."

"Maybe when I come up to meet Iona *whatshername* on the twenty-second."

"Depends on when I hafta work. We'll see. I'd like to though."

We head back to the car and hop in. Adam heads north on the Queen Elizabeth Driveway and turns left over the Pretoria Avenue lift bridge that spans the Canal. Then he follows the road to the right where it becomes Elgin Street. "Might as well park exactly where we were before on Argyle and take a walk up Elgin Street toward Parliament Hill. Ya know it's been like, a year or so since I was last up here in Ottawa. I know a bit about this area. I think you're gonna really like it here once you get yourself all moved in and settled."

We start to walk down Elgin Street and Adam says, "If you look over to the left, there is the Museum of Nature."

"It looks just like an *English castle.*"

A few blocks further along and Adam says, "Over there on the right is a laundromat and Al's Steak House is right beside it. Al's is famous and has been there for decades. Up ahead, you'll find a pharmacy. And dontcha go in there checkin' anyone out either!"

"You're more than enough for me."

"Ya got that one right there," he says and laughs while giving me a nudge with his shoulder as we walk along.

A few blocks more and he says, "Here's the Elgin Street Theatre. And look! They're playin' *Star Wars!* Wanna go see it after we eat somethin'?! I've really been wantin' to see it. I promise not to eat all the red licorice on you this time. In fact, I'll even buy it! Can we? Can we, huh? Uhm, uhh, can we, huh, puhleeze?"

"When do you have to have Mrs. Tonner's car back to her?"

"Not until tomorrow morning when I hafta start work. We've got the rest of the day just to fool around together and do stuff."

"OK, let's find somewhere to eat and we can catch an early show then. Hopefully, there won't be a huge, long line-up like there was when it showed in Brockville."

We head all the way down Elgin Street until we reach the Lord Elgin Hotel. Right behind it is a Ponderosa Steak House. At least it's something familiar and I'm guessing most of the government workers who work downtown probably eat lunch and dinner there. "How about we stop in here? Is this good enough for you?"

"Sure thing. I like my meat tender and rare. Just like you!"

Meanwhile I'm thinking, *Oh Jeez. Like, how corny is that?*

After eating, we stop at the corner of Elgin and Laurier Streets and Adam starts to tell me about the Lord Elgin Hotel. "Ya know, they have a gay bar down in the basement of this hotel and it's been there since the end of World War Two. It's called Pick's Place and is sorta like a classy kinda beer hall. Local boys call it the LE. There's also another place where we can go and dance sometime, just on the other side of where the old train station is on the other side of the Canal. It's called the Coral Reef Club. The guys up here call it *the oral grief club*!"

"How do you know about these places?"

"You gotta remember, I'm seven years older than you and have more experience with these things. Every once in a while before I met you and whenever I got lonely and really horny, I'd come up to Ottawa to check out these places. I wantcha to know about them. But I wantcha to promise to wait and I'll show ya them though, OK? I don't wantcha goin' into those places alone without me until you get to know the city better."

"OK. Sure."

"Now, let's see if we can get into the movie."

"Stop hitting me with that dumb piece of licorice! I'm trying to follow the movie," I whisper to Adam.

"It's my light-sabre and I'm attacking you, Luke Skywalker."

"Well thank God your dick isn't as limp as your light-sabre. Honest to God. Like, just how old are you anyway?" Adam laughs out loud and five people around us start to give him dirty looks.

"Wanna feel how hard my light-sabre is right about now?"

"Uhh, with your big cock, you're more like a Wookie down there, Chewbacca than Darth Vader. So let's say you just keep it in your pants until after the movie?"

"A Wookie and a Cookie!" Adam is killing himself laughing. Three bi-focaled geeks and one little old lady shush him. We both slouch down in our seats and giggle as quietly as we can for the next twenty-five minutes.

The ending credits start to roll on the big screen and Adam says to me as we are leaving the theatre, "So, do ya wanna feel my light-sabre and rub my Wookie fur when we get back to the car there, Luke Skywalker?"

I start to laugh and say to him, "Honestly, you're like a little boy sometimes."

"Only when I'm with you. And just what's so wrong with that anyway?"

"Nothing at all, Chewbacca. Nothing at all."

We head back down Elgin Street, and go past Pepper's Restaurant on the right just before the Museum of Nature. We're almost back to Argyle Avenue now.

"OK, Aaron, let's hop in the car and start to head back to Brock Vegas. I wanna go a different way home though—maybe along the Rideau River Road through Kemptville and Merrickville to North Augusta, and back on in to Brockville after that—we can stop in Merrickville for a Coke or somethin' there if ya like. Is that OK with you?"

"You're driving and I assume you know where you're going."

"Yeah. I know these back roads pretty well. We'll get home not too late after dark. Let's just take our time and enjoy the ride."

"OK, Chewbacca. My life is in your hands."

"It's not alive and in my hands until I take it outta your pants there. And it better not be cummin' to life for anyone else but me!" he says and laughs. Then Adam cranks up the radio and Bony M's "Daddy Kool" starts fill the inside of old lady Tonner's car with a driving disco beat.

The rest of the ride back is pretty uneventful, although the sexual tension between us is palpable as he steers Mrs. Tonner's car along the back country roads. "We're just headin' into Merrickville now. Didya want anything here before we hit North Augusta, Cookie?"

"Nah, I'm OK. I'm kind of tired though. And it's starting to get dark. Can I just put my head down in your lap and let you get us home please?"

"Just as long as my *light-sabre* doesn't keep ya awake down there Cookie-Boy," he says and grins.

About four miles south of Merrickville, Mrs. Tonner's car starts to cut out and then die and Adam has to wrestle it over to the side of the road. "What the fuck!" he exclaims.

"Jeez, Adam. What the hell is it with you and cars anyway?"

He gives me an irritated look, then looks at the gas gauge and realizes we've run out of gas.

"Jeezus Christ! We're outta gas! I can't hardly fuckin' believe this! Guess I shoulda filled up back in Merrickville."

"Just great." I say and give him a withering look.

"Dontcha be givin' me a hard time or I'm gonna throw you back into the back-seat and fuck your tight ass off. I still owe ya big time for stealin' my good work clothes outta my car that time and usin' 'em to jerk off with! Don't care if this is Mrs. Tonner's car. In fact, get ready for battle 'cause this Wookie's gonna take his *light-sabre* and turn ya over to *The Dark Side* like, right now!"

There's an old pillow in the back-seat I think I recognise from Adam's old Ambassador. Adam grabs me out of the car and pushes me into the back while he unzips his pants and hops in right behind me with his big cock fully aroused. "Suck my dong! It wants your tongue teasin' it! C'mon, Cookie, honey, get down there and suck me off like, now!"

So here we are with me going down on him in the back-seat of old Mrs. Tonner's car, inhaling and taking in the manly smell of his Adam Blanchard pube-forest while paying worship to his stiff cock under the veiled, cloaked darkness of early evening, with us stalled-out in the middle of nowhere.

This is all just too coincidental.

Ten minutes of him forcefully ramming his pulsating shaft deep into me and plowing my ass—grunting and working my dick at the same time and then he suddenly yells out, "Oh fuck! I'm cumming! Ohh, man! Ohh, fuck! Ohh, fuck! Ohh, fuckin' Jeezus fuck'! Am gonna cum inside you! Like, right now!"

"I don't think old lady Tonner ever did anything like this in her car," he quietly murmurs after his meteoric cum session and starts to really laugh.

"Oh God! Yuck! Ughh, what a gross thought!"

More laughter from him and then on a sudden impulse, he grabs me and pulls me out of the back of the car and drags me around to the passenger-side where he squats down and starts to give me a blow-job. "Too boned-up here to give ya tips on how to do this right. So you just lean back and let my lips and tongue to the talkin' while you lean back and enjoy the lesson."

He keeps holding tight onto the base of my cock to keep it rock hard while licking my sweet spot. I keep praying in the back of my mind that no one comes along and sees what we're doing, even though we're partially hidden by the car on the side of the road.

"Oh shit! Oh shit!' Adam, I'm going to cum real soon!"

"Just shoot your spunk into my mouth. I need ya to fill me up here."

"Too bad you didn't think of that with Mrs. Tonner's car back in Merrickville."

"Shhh! No funny talk outta you now. Gimme all ya got there."

I shoot a load of my creamy juice into his mouth. He swallows it and then gets up, wipes my cum off his mouth and takes his finger to trace the outline of my mouth with it. Finally, he passionately kisses me, enveloping me in a pervasive, hot, steamy embrace.

"Guess I'd better go and get the gas can I put in the trunk before we left Brockville this morning and fill up Mrs. Tonner's car so we can make it back the last few miles into North Augusta and then on in to Brockville," he says to me and grins.

"You mean to tell me you actually planned this?" I say to him in total disbelief, my mouth agape.

"Mmm hmmm, sure did. Figured we'd christen old lady Tonner's car and end this trip with somethin' memorable to mark it by. I like the look on your face when I shock ya. I kinda get-off on it. But then again, I get-off on just about everything about you."

"I get-off on just about everything with you, too. Now put your big, thick light-sabre away and let's go home."

Adam starts to howl and growl at me and laughs as he opens the trunk. He hauls out a full five gallon gas can. He slowly pours it into the gas tank while looking back at me, continuing to grin and chuckle away.

"Thanks for taking me up to Ottawa today," I say once we're driving again and about to pull into Brockville. "You've made me feel a little less anxious about moving there. It helps to know that you know a bit about the area where I'm going to be living and that you like it. I'm going to have a key made for you to come up any time you want. With the Voyageur Colonial stop so close, you can take the bus up on weekends and any time you're off. I'd like that a lot if you would."

"Will you stay with me tonight at my place please? I just don't wanna be alone this evening," says Adam, with a sad and tired look on his face.

"Mom and Dad are expecting me back to let them know how the apartment trip worked out in Ottawa. Umm, I guess I could call them from your place and give them some excuse for not coming home this evening. I wouldn't mind seeing your place without passing out in it like I did the last time."

Adam laughs and pulls me over tight against him as we turn off the 401 and head down North Augusta Road, then right onto Pearl Street.

"Your dad was pretty decent about that whole goddamn mess. Meant to ask you, by the way, did he really make you hafta mow the lawn that morning when ya went home with a hangover?"

"Yeah, he did. And then he told me I didn't have to go and work for my brother-in-law up at the store until September and gave me the money he owed me for working part-time up there over the past month. It was weird though. Geraint wasn't very nice to me when he found out I was going to go back to school. And then Dad said not to call him or my sister to thank them for the extra money they gave me over and above what he owed me."

"Whaddya mean he wasn't nice to ya?"

"Well, Geraint actually first started acting strange around me when he met Rob Galanos from Zeller's. Rob and I are friends. He and Cliff Hilton were the only gay guys I ever really knew in Brockville—until I met you, of course. Rob came into the paint store one day and we got to talking. He's a nice guy, Adam. He and I started having lunch at Howard Johnson's together. And sometimes he'd come and pick me up and we'd go to either the 401 Inn or the Skyline Hotel or even the Flying Dutchman Motel out at Long Beach with Cala and Wendy to have a beer and dance and talk."

"Should I be jealous of him there?" says Adam, his arm gripping me a bit tighter.

"Oh, God! Ohh, nooo. I don't like him that way at all. It's just that I never really had many friends in high school besides Cala Cuthbertson and Wendy Yaegar. And Rob was a lot like me in some ways... and we just started to talk. I got beat up a lot in high school, Adam. I don't like to think about those times now. The boys, once they thought I was gay, always bullied me. And it was weird. Most of them wanted me to suck their cocks afterward... and it really kind of messed me up. And the girls were even worse. I'd walk down the hall at BCI to my locker and a bunch of girls would be standing around and the first thing you knew,

I'd hear the words *fairy* and *queer*. Whenever I hear the word *queer* even now, it sends a chill down my spine and I just want to run away."

"Aww, same kinda things happened to me, too. I went to BCI and graduated a bit before you started there. It's a real snotty school with a whole lotta rotten, snobby kids goin' there. I remember my time there, too. Kids can be real cruel when they're growin' up. There was talk about my dad and mom. I got picked on 'cause I didn't have two parents and all. The girls all wanted me to date 'em—just wasn't interested though. I realized after I graduated, those girls were real mean bitches when they figured out you weren't really interested and didn't wanna date 'em. Most of what was said about me in school came from them. I had to toughen up a lot and had lots of fights with the boys and eventually they all learned not to mess with me. It was lonely for me though. I still have bad memories. Guess I always will. I kinda learned though not to let what others think or say about me ever get to me. Mom always said to me, 'Adam, what others think or have to say about you is none of your business.' It sure as fuckin' hell took me a long time to figure that one out, let me tell ya. You know, you're always gonna have people who don't like ya. You gotta understand though, you can't let 'em affect how you feel about yourself. Do ya understand what I'm tryin' to tell ya here?"

"I'm really sorry you got picked on in high school. I'm just glad we met and know each other now."

"Me too, babe. Me too."

We pull up in front of Mr. and Mrs. Nicholson's house on Pearl Street West and Adam parks Mrs. Tonner's big Plymouth in the driveway in front of the garage. "Sooo, butt-boy, think ya can manage the stairs up to my place without fallin' off your platform shoes this time?" Adam says with a laugh as he follows me up the stairs and grabs and fondles my butt.

"Uhh, I think so, uhm, yes," I say with an embarrassed look back to him as I reach the front door to his place on the landing at the top of the stairs. Adam deliberately leans over closely past me to unlock the door so I can really feel him behind me. He blows in my ear and puts his hand on the small of my back, with his middle finger poking down the back of my jeans to guide me into his apartment. This time I get to really see how he lives. And I have to admit, I'm fascinated with having the opportunity to really see what he's like when I'm not around him.

The kitchen is the first place you come into when you enter the apartment. It's immaculate with dish towels folded just like the linen displays in Walker's Department Store on King Street and a sign above the small window at the sink that says, *Kiss the Cook.*

I see a humongous colour TV set with a stereo phonograph record player and AM/FM radio, and what looks to be a liquor cabinet, all housed in one hulking, dark wood console credenza in his tiny living room. He has a couple of tall, dark wood bookcases reaching up to the ceiling, sagging, straining and groaning with the weight of hundreds of LP record albums on them and surprisingly, many hard-cover books as well. Looking over his books, I see quite a few on history and some as well on science fiction, birds/ornithology and outer space. He has a thick brown shag area rug on the floor with lots of big, plump, orange and blue oversize pillows on both the rug and a couple of blue, overstuffed upholstered armchairs where I'm guessing he must stretch out to watch TV and to read and listen to music when he's all by himself.

The bathroom has what looks to be very old, tiny little black-and-white hexagon-shaped tiles on the floor that remind me of what some of the stores in Brockville have outside their covered entrances just before you step inside to shop. Some of them even have the street number laid-out in small, black tiles with a border around them just before the front doors like that. I've always liked that kind of tile. I think they call it glazed porcelain mosaic.

He has a modern type of lilac-coloured, enamel steel bathtub with a big showerhead and spray. His shower curtain has cute little Superman comic strip characters all over it! And there is a white vanity cabinet with a matching lilac basin where his trademark Christian Dior Eau Sauvage cologne, shaving cream, soap, toothpaste, blow drier, brushes, razor and face cloths are neatly arranged on top. It all feels very personal and intimate for me to be looking at his stuff like this. I'm thinking, *he must really be comfortable with you to let you see all his personal things.*

His bedroom is a calm and restful inner haven. It feels like a cozy, intimate, extremely masculine retreat. The room has a dormer and window that look out over the next-door-neighbor's driveway and side yard—knee-walls climb up to waist height and then follow the angled roof lines of the garage, sloping up to a vaulted-ceiling in the middle of the space. I'm guessing that Adam must have painted the room when he moved in because it's a deep, rich colour of ocean marine-blue and is the only room in the apartment that isn't ivory-beige. His bedroom has a big, queen-size bed in it with an ornate brass and shiny-white enamel painted headboard and footrail. I sort of remember when I passed out on it and have some vague memory of him undressing me and sleeping with his arm wrapped protectively around me the night I got drunk on him. He has a stunning quilt on top of the bed in colours of deep blue and bright orange that looks handmade.

"Mom made that quilt for me. She's pretty good with her hands. She took a long time to find those exact fabrics and colours. They're my favorite colours there."

"It's beautiful, Adam. She's talented."

"My hands are pretty talented, too, ya know," he says and comes up close behind me starting to massage the back of my neck. You better call your folks to let 'em know you're gonna be stayin' over here with me tonight. I don't want 'em callin' the police and thinkin' we got into an accident or somethin' like that. The phone's on the wall in the kitchen.

You give 'em a call and I'll open a bottle of wine. That is, if ya promise not to drink the whole damn bottle on me like you did the last time."

"What time is it now?"

"Uhm, just after eight."

"I'll call them closer to ten and tell them we just got back then. Mom will be up and getting ready to go to work and Dad will be busy with her and having to walk Blackjack before bedtime."

"Your call there."

He goes over to the big TV stereo console, lifts up the top and the record player and liquor shelf rise up from inside the cabinet. "Ya know, this was the first piece of new furniture I got for this place from the Seaway Trader's down on Water Street when I moved in here. The liquor tray shelf has a gold-veined, *Elvis Graceland* kinda mirror on the bottom of the tray that raises up and down when you lift up the top lid of the stereo. It's kinda weird and freaky. But the colour TV is super big. And the record player and built-in speakers are really good. Wanna hear some music? What wouldya like to hear?"

"Whatever you like. I'm kind of curious to see what you've got in your collection."

"OK. Leave it to me then." He looks through his LPs and pulls out Chaka Khan, carefully puts it on the stem of the record player and flicks the switch. The arm and needle move over and "Sweet Thang" starts to play softly in the background.

"Here ya go. One glass of wine only for you and that's gonna be it for this evening. Let's cuddle on the floor on the pillows in front of the TV and you'll call your parents in a little while then."

"God, this is nice. You always feel so warm and manly next to me when you put your arm around me like that. And you always smell so good. It just feels so good."

Adam leans in to kiss me. His lips nuzzle my ear and then make their way down to my neck. I swear every time he gets close to me all I can sense is his virile masculine smell, and it's all I can do not to jump on top of him and rip his clothes off.

"Uhm, Adam, I meant to ask you. What's this thing you have about calling your big cock different names all the time?" He looks shocked and is speechless for about five seconds and then starts to really laugh.

"You mean my *crotch-rocket, stick-shift, big-dong there?*"

"Yeah. Like, what's with the *dong* thing? It seems to be the one you say most often."

"Well, baby, I don't know. I just *do,* that's all. "

"Well, you can stick your *big, monster King Kong dong* into me anytime you like."

Adam's mouth opens wide and after another few more long seconds of speechless surprise, he spills some of his wine onto the shag rug and starts to laugh uncontrollably while squeezing me in a head lock.

"Jeezus Christ! You're a funny guy, ya know. No more dong talk though for now. You'll just get me all hot and horny here and I'd like to just lie here beside you on the carpet and cushions and listen to some music and feel you close beside me. Is that OK with you?"

"Can we do it without our clothes on?"

"Maybe later, after you call your mom and dad. And remember, I just hafta get up to go to work early in the morning. So we're actually gonna sleep tonight and I'll drop ya off at home before I head on in to Tonner's."

"Where did you leave your car when you borrowed Mrs. Tonner's?"

"Out behind the store where I always park it when I'm workin'. Why do ya ask?"

"No reason really. I just thought of it now. I guess maybe just because it was the first place you ever kissed me."

"Less thinkin' and more kissin' there," he says as he leans in and starts to take his tongue to trace the outline of my lips. I can taste the wine on his tongue—*sweet and rich*—so nice.

Chaka Khan continues to play softly in the background.

"I think ya better call your mom and dad now so they won't be worried. The phone's on the wall in the kitchen by the front door. I wanna get that outta the way and then we can relax a little after today and get a good night's sleep. Hangin' around you makes me really kinda tired at times."

"Hi, Dad. We just got back from Ottawa and Adam still has Mrs. Tonner's car. He has to drop it back off to her first thing tomorrow morning. And I'm over at his place now. Can I tell you all about Ottawa in the morning when he drops me off at home?"

"So, you're staying over at Adam's place tonight then?"

"Uhh, yes. If that's OK with you, that is."

"You're almost twenty now and don't need my permission to stay overnight at a friend's house. Just as long as you call to let us know where you are so we won't worry. I'll talk to you in the morning over breakfast before I have to head in to the Hospital. I assume you rented the apartment then. Just please don't get drunk again on Adam over there. The poor lad was beside himself when he called me the last time."

"Ohh, Dad! Yes, I got the apartment. I'll see you in the morning."

"Good night, son. We'll have coffee and cinnamon toast in the morning."

"There, happy now Adam?"

"Yep, sure am. They don't need to be worryin' about ya. Now come on back here and lie down. Let's just listen to some more music and finish our wine and then head off to bed. My King Kong dong's' not gonna molest ya though, not tonight. Gonna be a busy day for me tomorrow. And I just wanna see if we can make it through one night together without jumpin' each other's bones and having ya play with and sit on King Kong!"

"OK. Just being close to you and feeling your sexy body-heat and smelling you and touching you all over will be good enough for me," I say as I bend over and start to rub my face in his armpit and then bite his shoulder."

Ahh, Jeezus fuck! Am gettin' all hard here again with that kinda talk from you." I reach down into his jeans and slowly start to rub my hand against his pleasure trail while reaching down to hold onto King Kong."

"Well maybe you can just jerk me off and then we'll hop into bed and sleep. And I do mean sleep this time." he whispers softly while holding onto the back of my neck and nuzzling my cheek.

"OK. That sounds like a good idea to me."

August 22nd arrives and I'm waiting at the Voyageur Colonial bus stop on Perth Street in Brockville for the morning bus to take me up to Ottawa for my orientation interview with Iona Ouspenskaya. Adam has to work today, and my dad as well. So I'm on my own to make this trip to finalize all my courses and pay final tuition for commencement of classes on September 12th. The bus is twenty minutes late and I'm starting to worry because my appointment is scheduled for right after lunch.

Finally, the bus pulls up in front of the station and I hear on the loud speaker, "Voyageur Colonial bus #43 with stops in Maitland, Prescott, Spencerville, Kemptville, North Gower and Ottawa is now ready for boarding. Have your tickets and baggage ready for loading, please. And *Thank You* for travelling Voyageur this morning!"

Just great, a milk run. Shit! This will take at least two-and-a-half hours to make it up to the Campus at this rate!

There is a twenty minute layover in Prescott that further adds to the time delay. *Nothing I can do about that now,* I think and sigh. Fortunately, the stops are quick enroute with very few people boarding or getting off. So the bus arrives at the Catherine Street station just before noon.

I know I'm close to my new apartment and the College Campus. So before leaving the station, I call Marisol, the Rental Agent to pick up the key to the place on Argyle Avenue after my interview. After that it's time to start to walk over to Algonquin to meet Iona. *Glad that Adam made sure I knew my way around when he brought me up here. I really wish he could have come with me today,* I'm thinking as I head out through the sliding doors of the bus station.

With the free time I have before my interview, I take the time to walk through the Design Wing of the Campus to check out the classrooms, labs, resource rooms, student lounges and the library.

There are six classrooms with folding full-height divider partitions to close them off when needed. I can see some three-dimensional models and sample boards, renderings and drafting plans and details sitting on the tables and mounted on the walls, from previous students I assume. There are long rows of tables placed length-wise throughout each classroom with drafting surfaces on top of them and stools that look like *Chinese-torture-devices* in front of each spot. There are huge southwest-facing windows along the exterior walls that flood each room with natural daylight.

I was told that typically in the first-semester there are between twenty to twenty-five students accepted for the English Applied Arts Interior Design programme. There is an English programme and a French programme that are completely separate with different rooms and Professors and instructors. I was also told that the drop-out rate is high in the first and second-semesters. Usually, by second year, the class size shrinks down to around fifteen students. And by third year and graduation, there are only six to eight students left to move on and enter the work force.

Most of these students wind up working for the Federal Government doing office-planning and design for government office buildings in the National Capital Region. A select few are lucky enough to land jobs in Toronto, or even outside of Canada and get to really experience the whole diverse spectrum of Interior Design with challenging and rewarding careers.

"*Vell*, so, you are Aaron Richard Christie," says Iona Ouspenskaya when she appears outside her office where I've been waiting in the hallway for my orientation interview. "All right, then. Come in and show me your portfolio."

137

I'm nervous and can't help but stare at her as I follow her in and sit down before her glass-topped desk. She has what looks to be a synthetic, platinum-blonde wig on. Talk about big hair! It looks bizarre on her as I estimate she must be at least sixty years old. *That damned, stupid wig would likely spontaneously combust if she ever came into close contact with an open flame.*

She is wearing a huge, blood-red velvet bowtie that I later learned was given the moniker *Iona's Lips* by students already in the programme. She has a tight, ill-fitting, grey, double-breasted pantsuit on that makes her boobs look like they're ready to burst out of it at any moment. And to top everything off, she's wearing these oversized, pastel blue, thick Coke-bottle lens, plastic-framed glasses with rhinestones embedded into them that effectively block any direct eye contact and that completely distract me. She looks like a weird, freaky cross between Carol Channing and Phyllis Diller.

I also later learned that she was supposedly able to speak five languages—apparently, none of them particularly *vell...*

I unzip my portfolio case and start to show her some of my work. She is completely uninterested in what I have for her to look at and then blurts out, "Just how old are you?"

"Uhh, I'll be twenty this December."

"No one coming from high school directly into this programme ever makes it through to the end. There are thirty-five hours of class time and at least the same number of hours required to complete the assignments every week. Most students quit during the first-semester. *Vhat* makes you think you can do it?" She stares at me balefully.

"Uhm, well, I always wanted to be an Architect. And when I started working for my brother-in-law back in Brockville in his paint and wallpaper store, I found I liked advising people and they seemed to like what I recommended to them. I studied the course-outline for this programme. And an Instructor I knew from a sales course I was taking at St. Lawrence College back in Brockville told me I had talent and recommended I apply for enrollment. Here is the letter of introduction she did up for me, by the way."

"Who *vas* this Instructor?" she asks imperiously.

"Cordelia Albescu. She teaches professional salesmanship courses part-time at St. Lawrence College."

"Albescu, that's Romanian, like me!"

The rest of the interview passes with Iona telling me her entire life story. Born in Russia and having moved to Romania when she was a small child with her parents, she used to be an Aeronautical Engineer who worked on drafting and design of weapons and armaments during World War Two, and after the Communist takeover of her country, immigrated to Canada with her son and eventually wound up as the Department Head of Interior Design at Algonquin College.

The interview told me everything I never needed to know about her and nothing about the programme I was about to enter. By the end of it I was sitting there and asking myself, *just what the hell have you gotten yourself into here?*

At the end of her diatribe, she finally stops talking about herself and looks me straight in the eye and says, "You are a very meek and quiet young man. You know you *vill* really have to get your *vire* up if you *vant* to survive in this programme, hmmmm... izzzn't it." When she said the word *vire*, she pointed directly at my crotch and my mouth fell open in complete shock and embarrassment. It was obvious she was trying to say *wire* with that ridiculous Eva Gabor accent of hers and was referring to my cock! *Like, wow! Did she really just say that?!*

I couldn't wait to get out of her office fast enough after that outrageous remark from her.

"Classes start promptly at eight-thirty on September 12th," she says and if you are late or miss more than three consecutive classes in any one semester, you *vill* get a failing grade for that course, and *vill* have to repeat it the next year. You *vill* have eight full and part-time courses to get through before the first-semester finishes at the beginning of December: Interior Design One, History of Design, Colour Theory, Design Basics, Building Construction, and basic Drafting. You *vill* have me for Interior Design One. Evan Copland *vill* teach you Building Construction. Elzbeth Mountebank *vill* teach you Colour Theory and Design Basics. Lynda Naagy-Birdsong *vill* teach you History of Design and Furniture, Massimo Visconti-Ciccone *vill* teach you Graphic Presentation and Interior Rendering, and Gaelen Goderich *vill* teach you Basic Drafting."

I walk out of her office in a complete daze and really wish I'd had either Adam or Dad with me to make some sense of what had just happened in her office.

Then it's time to head over to Argyle Avenue.

I'm standing on the front porch of the apartment building where I will be moving into with the Leasing Agent to pick up my key and I say to her, "Thanks for meeting me to drop off the key, Marisol. I just finished over at Algonquin and it looks like I'm going to have a pretty full itinerary and course-load for my first-semester."

"You look like you could need a boost of confidence from someone. I'm sure you'll do just fine, once you get settled and into the routine of classes and studies. Good luck, Aaron. If I can answer any questions you may have with respect to the apartment or any problems with it, here is my card and telephone number. Don't hesitate to call me any time. And I mean it. Good luck again to you."

There is a hardware store about five blocks down on Elgin Street. *Guess I'd better get keys made for Mom and Dad, and Adam while I'm here.* After I do that and start walking back down Elgin Street, I look at my watch and realize it is just past four- o'clock. Time for something to eat and then to catch the bus back to Brockville for five-thirty.

I then play it safe and head over to the Voyageur Colonial bus stop where I know they have a cafeteria-style restaurant. My mind is still reeling from that bizarre interview which really was just a diatribe on the life and history of Iona Ouspenskaya.

Jeez! I sure hope the rest of the Profs aren't as weird and wacked out as she is.

Luckily, the bus leaves right on schedule from the Catherine Street station and I can now just sit back and stare out the window and try to forget that stupid *wire* reference and those negative cracks and assumptions about my age from that crazy lady, Ouspenskaya.

To my surprise, Adam is waiting for me in the waiting room of the bus stop when the bus gets back to Brockville, just before eight.

"What are you doing here?! I thought you had to work late this evening."

"Figured you'd like to see my smilin' face waitin' for ya when you hopped off the bus. Are ya not happy to see me?"

"God! Yes! Am I ever."

"Well, c'mon then. I'll take ya for an ice cream cone at Smith's Dairy after ya drop your stuff off at your mom and dad's."

We hop into Adam's old SST and he starts to ask me questions while we slowly head over to Bethune Street.

"So, talk to me, Aaron. How did things go at Algonquin?"

"It was just so weird. That Ouspenskaya woman is really strange. How she ever got to be an Interior Designer is something I can't even begin to figure out. She's got this really stupid way of saying *hmmmm... izzzn't it,* after everything she says. She could be telling someone she has to go to the bathroom and she'd wind up ending her sentence with the words, *hmmmm... izzzn't it.*"

Adam starts to laugh and says to me, "Is that the *only* thing you remember from your interview with her?"

"Nope. I'm not done. She spent most of the interview talking about herself and couldn't have cared less about my portfolio. All she seemed to care about was the cheque for the College tuition. And she kept telling me that students as young as me never made it to the end of the programme. Then she made this stupid comment about me being meek and having to get my *vire* up in order to make it. She was trying to say *wire* with that stupid Eva Gabor accent of hers, I think! Jeez! And get this. Adam... she was pointing to my cock when she said that!"

Now he's killing himself laughing. "Well, your *wire's* never had a problem *cummin'* up for me," he says. "I wouldn't be too upset about what she said though. Sounds like she was tryin' to psych' ya up to expect a lotta work. And she maybe might even have a point about how young ya are. You're gonna do just fine, *hmmmm... izzzn't it,*" he says and bursts out laughing. "Now dump your shit off and tell your parents you'll be back in an hour or so."

"If you say so, *hmmmm... izzzn't it?*" I reply and laugh at him.

Adam then says to me, "Uhh, Aaron. say *hmmmm* for me one more time, will ya, please?"

Hmmmmouahhh. He bends forward and plants a huge, sloppy, wet kiss on my lips and then I hop out of his old car with my portfolio case in hand.

"Hi, Dad. Adam met me at the bus station and gave me a ride home. I'm just going to drop off my portfolio here for now to go and have an ice cream with him. Are you going to be here when I get back?"

"Yes, son. I have to take your mother in to work for midnight so I'll want to hear all about Algonquin and how you got along when you come back."

Adam drives over to Blockhouse Island and parks after we get our ice cream. When getting out of his car, he says, "Let's walk to the end of the breakwater where the light beacon is. It's a real nice night and we can sit and watch the lights on the other side of the river in upstate New York. Ya know, every once in a while, I like to come down here by myself to face west, waitin' for ships to clear the Brockville Narrows and Skeleton Island out there as they head east down the river toward the locks at Iroquois and Long Sault. It's really somethin' when one of the big Great Lakes freighters goes by in the main channel all lit up like a great big crystal chandelier or a Christmas tree. Ya know, I still remember that big freighter, the Edmund Fitzgerald, before she sank a couple of years ago in Lake Superior. That was real sad. All those lives lost. And she went down so fast, too."

"I remember that."

"C'mon. I wanna go sit out on the concrete base where the beacon light is. We can finish our ice cream and watch for ships and think about how lucky we are to have all of this here for us to appreciate. Brockville is really beautiful if ya just open your eyes and really look at it, ya know."

We have to pass by the World War Two Sabre jet that's mounted up on a concrete podium in memory of the fallen soldiers and veterans of World War Two on our way to the beacon.

"That Ouspenskaya woman told me she was born in Russia and then moved to Romania with her parents when she was four. She was an Aeronautical Engineer in Romania during the war, and that she had to come to Canada when the Allied Forces declared peace."

"Hmmm, Romania you say? She was probably a Nazi sympathiser durin' the war and worked for either Hitler or Mussolini, most likely. Lotsa those people wound up in Canada in the forties and fifties. Then again you never know, she coulda' just been tryin' to escape the Communists at the time."

"You really know a fair bit of history, don't you?"

"Just one of the interests I have there, Cookie—besides you."

"Here, Adam. I had a key made for you for my place on Argyle. You can put it on your Superman key ring thingy."

"Uhm, uhh, thanks." Then he stares at the key with a sad look on his face while rubbing his newly grown-in beard and moustache that I nagged him into growing just for me. "Guess this is really startin' to happen now. So when are ya thinkin' of movin' your stuff up to Ottawa?"

"Dad said he could move me up right after Labour Day. He has a trailer hitch on the car. And there won't be much to take up outside of most of my clothes, books and records. Mom said I could take the big armoire in my room. I'll have to get a new bed and I'll need to buy a drafting board and stool, and then I should be pretty well all set up."

"You don't want, or won't be needing me helpin' ya then when ya move?" says Adam with a disappointed look on his face.

"Well of course I do! I already told Dad you wanted to help and he said, "Thank God he offered, because I was going to ask him myself to help, otherwise." I take a couple of licks of ice cream that have melted onto my hand at that point and say, " I think he'd adopt you if he could. I told you he was a nice man."

Adam smiles finally, grabs my hand to lick the rest of my ice cream from it and says quietly to me, "Ya know, you're a lucky guy. I hope you know that."

After he drops me off, I head in the front door and Dad is in the living room waiting to talk with me. "So how did you make out with Iona at Algonquin? Did she look at your portfolio and did she have many questions for you?"

"Uhh, well, she seemed to want to tell me more about herself and didn't care so much about what I wanted to show her. She kept coming back to asking me how old I was and telling me most students my age never lasted to graduate until the end of the programme. She kind of scared me a bit."

"Sounds like she was trying to intimidate you in to either not enrolling or to standing up to her. What did you say to her?"

"Well, I didn't want to say too much back to her, honestly. I figured since I was already accepted into the programme, she could say whatever she liked. I'm going into this because I want to. And after listening to her, I thought that if she could make a career out of this, then I should be able to as well."

"Well, the final cheque for enrollment sure went through fast enough. She must have ran to the bank to cash it. You'll come to understand that what people think and say about you shouldn't matter a damn once you've set your mind to something. Your mother and I have faith in you and know you are going to do well, once you get into the pace and routine of the programme."

"Oh, Dad, uhh, before I forget, I had keys made up for you and Mom for my place on Argyle. And Adam was asking me about when to move my stuff up there just now. He'll need to know in case he has to take time off to help us. I was thinking maybe the Tuesday right after Labour Day, September 6th. Will you be able to take the time off that day? I really want you to see where I'm going to be living. Does Mom want to come, too?"

"I don't think your mother will come. You know she's going to miss you and seeing where you're going to be living might not help with that at the moment. I'm sure we can always take a drive up sometime later on to have a look at your place together once she gets used to the fact that you're not going to be living at home anymore. You know Aaron, we're both going to miss you very much."

"Labour Day's coming up real fast, Aaron. Can we do somethin'? Like, just us two together before I hafta move ya up to Ottawa?"

"Sure. What would you like to do?"

"Well, it's been a real fast summer and I haven't been out campin' at all or even outta town, except for taking ya up to Ottawa. I'm not complainin' though. Hows about I pull out the old tent from mom's garage and me and you can maybe spend the weekend together out at Brown's Bay? We can swim and cook outside and have camp fires in the evenings and get nice and cozy together in a sleeping bag in a tent under the stars. Whaddya think?

"You like to camp?! Jeez, there's still a lot I don't know about you. Sure! That sounds like fun, actually."

"Oh, and your driving test with the Department of Motor Vehicles is in a few days, right?"

"Yeah, it is."

"OK then. Well then, I'm gonna take ya 'out for a couple of driving lessons in the next couple of days. My damn car's been actin' up real bad again—you're gonna hafta use your dad's car for the test. But, I think as long as we stick close to town and don't get too aggressive with it, then the damn sonofabitch shouldn't give us too much of a hard time."

It's Friday, September 2nd and the start of the Labour Day weekend— my last free one in Brockville before commencement of classes in Ottawa. Adam has packed his mom's old, army-green, tourist-style, canvas tent into the trunk of his car, along with a big, double-sized sleeping bag. He's also borrowed a cooler from my mom and dad and packed it full of food and disposable boxes of cheap Italian rosé wine to last us through the three days we'll be camping together up at Brown's Bay.

Brown's Bay is about twenty miles west of Brockville on the old number two highway. The St. Lawrence River there is wide open and the main shipping channel along the river at this point is closer to the American side than the Canadian one. The Thousand Islands don't really start until about ten miles further west, where they stretch out between Rockport and where the St. Lawrence River meets Lake Ontario, up by Kingston.

Dad always took the Yaegar kids, John and Wendy along with me up to Brown's Bay every weekend when we were all in grade school together at St. Francis Xavier. I have good childhood memories of Brown's Bay.

"Looks like we've got everything packed up and ready to head out. Remember, there's no electrical to plug in your blow drier and ya won't be needin' a steamer trunk for twenty-five changes of clothes either."

"Very funny. I can rough it just as well as you can!"

"We'll see. I kinda doubt it though."

"This looks like a pretty decent spot to set up the tent. It's out in the open on pretty flat, bare ground, away from all those spruce trees and far back into the campground. Shouldn't be gettin' too much noise and disturbance from any other folks back here and there's a fire pit just beside us, so I can use some logs I brought and make a camp-fire for us to sit around after dark. Whaddya think? Is this good for ya here, Aaron?"

"I like that we don't have people on either side of us. Let's pull everything out of the trunk and set up camp."

Three hours later and Adam has a little folding hibachi grille set up and is cooking up hamburgers for us.

"Mmmm, they smell good. I'm hungry!"

"They'll be ready in a couple of minutes here. We'll save the steaks and baked potatoes I got for tomorrow and maybe head on in to Rockport to have dinner at the restaurant there right on the river on Sunday. I want everything to be perfect for ya before you hafta head up to Ottawa next week. Jeezus! I'm gonna miss you not being in town."

"I don't want to think about that. I just want to be with you right now, OK?"

"OK, baby. OK."

After dinner, Adam goes to find some kindling and then pulls a couple of fire-logs he took from his mom's garage out of the back of his trunk while I dump the charcoal into the fire-pit from the hibachi and start to clean up the grille and melamine dishes from dinner.

"This is so nice and peaceful. I'm really happy you suggested we do this." I smile over at him and then lean back, resting against a fallen tree trunk staring into the fire that he managed to build with the sparse kindling he had to work with around the camp-site.

"*Trick* was talkin' about some rain overnight on the radio this mornin', but it looks pretty clear to me," Adam says, as he moves over to lie back close beside me. "Here's a glass of wine for ya. Gotta love that burnin' wood smell from a camp-fire, eh? Let's just finish our wine and douse the fire and then crawl into that nice big sleeping bag I hauled along for us, OK?"

"Mmm, I like that plan. Can we get naked under the covers? "

"Keep talkin' that way and I'll generate enough heat to keep ya on fire all night long."

It's three o'clock in the morning. Flashes of lightening and loud rumbling crashes of thunder wake us both up. The old tent is starting to leak badly because of the torrential downpour from the thunderstorm raging over the river so close to the camp-ground. We both wake up to discover the open bare ground we set the tent up on has become a virtual river with both the canvas floor of the tent and the bottom of the sleeping bag practically soaked right through. The front flap on the tent is whipping back and forth and every twenty seconds or so a wind-gust sends a driving spray of cold rain onto us as we lay beside each other in the sleeping bag.

"Jeezus fuck! Quick, baby! Grab the pillows and I'll roll up the sleeping bag! We'll hafta leave the tent and cooler and stuff until it stops rainin' and hike it over to the car where it's gonna be a whole helluva lot drier inside than what this goddamn shit is right now. I'm really sorry about this," says Adam as he jumps up buck-naked and starts to gather up whatever is still semi-dry and runs over toward his car.

Once inside the car, Adam reaches down and adjusts both front-seats so that they recline back fully into what constitutes a bed of sorts. "Hey! I never knew you could do that with your car," I say to him as he grabs the pillow in the back and pulls me over tight next to him to snuggle.

"My old SST *still* has it's uses, baby," he murmurs as he wraps his leg over mine and shoves his half-hard dick up against my ass. "Let's get comfy and try to forget about the damn fuckin' rain outside, OK?

"Sure thing! You didn't exactly plan the weather. It's all good though. You've had to sleep in your car overnight. I guess spending one night in it with you isn't going to kill me either."

Adam and I spend the rest of that night entwined together in his car as the gale-force, wind-gusts from the storm relentlessly buffet and rock his old Ambassador back and forth. The driving rain keeps teeming down, obscuring whatever is happening outside the car and luckily for us, the action happening inside between Adam and me until first daylight. The last thing I remember before falling into a deep sleep was Adam slowly shoving his fully-aroused penis up my ass and whispering to me, "Honey, I'm gonna keep my dong warm by leavin' it in ya 'til we both fall asleep. OK, Cookie?"

"Works for me," I say. I fall asleep feeling his heartbeat and hot cock deep inside me.

Five o'clock on Saturday morning and the rain is still coming down in sheets. "Aww, fuck Aaron! Look at the goddamn tent!" Adam is leaning up on one elbow and staring over to where we had set it up. "It's like, totally collapsed!"

The tent poles must have given way overnight and the poor tent is spread out flat and soaking wet on the ground with only the cooler and whatever other stuff we couldn't grab and throw into the car last night poking through the front flap.

"What a fuckin' disaster this whole idea turned out to be!" he exclaims. "And I wanted it to be perfect for ya, too! Lemme throw on some clothes here from the back and we'll head on in to Rockport and have some breakfast there. Then we'll come back and grab the tent and cooler and head back in to Brockville. We can spend the rest of the weekend at my place. I'm so sorry about this, Cookie. I really am!"

After he retrieves a pair of baggy, soggy old jogging shorts and an old, mildewed, ripped and stained, wife-beater undershirt he uses to clean the inside of his car to throw on, he reaches down to grab the lever to adjust and raise up his front-seat back and then gets himself settled, leaning in while reaching for his key to try to start his car.

"Jeezus fuck! Ugh! C'mon, c'mon, c'mon, ya sonofabitch!" The rain keeps coming down in buckets and his old SST is not cooperating with him at all. It just keeps cranking away and refuses to start. "Ya fuckin' shitbox! Argh! C'mon, baby! C'mon, fuckin' start for me!"

I manage to adjust my seat back on my side while saying to him, "I don't think it's going to start!"

"Shhh! Argh! It's just gotta! C'mon! C'mon, c'mon, c'mon, fuckin' c'mon, man, ya goddamn fuckin' bastard! Ugh! Argh! Turn over for me, ya fuckin' cock suckin' piece-a-shit!"

He keeps brutally pumping his gas pedal and turning his ignition key. And then all of a sudden, his starter starts to squeal and make horrible noises like metal screeching and scraping against metal. There is a smell of something electrical burning inside his car and then blue and white smoke starts to rise and seep out from the front hood-vent where his windshield wipers are. His starter finally gives up completely and starts to squeal, then just click as he keeps turning his key and curses and swears. Then he slams his fist down hard onto his steering wheel.

"Jeezus fuck! Just fuckin' wonderful!" he yells. "Fuckin' stuck in this fuckin' goddamn rain with a dead shitbox of a fuckin' crappy car and fuckin' stranded here now! Argh, just fuckin' marvellous!"

"Well, uhm, if I have to be stranded, I'd rather it was with you than anyone else."

"Aww, honey! I'm sooo sorry! I just wanted this last holiday weekend before ya go to be perfect."

Then I can see tears starting to well up in his eyes as he stares out the windshield and shakes his head at the swirling, acrid-smelling smoke rolling out from the front of his car, hissing and vaporizing with the constant driving sheets of rain.

"It is perfect because I'm spending it with you." It's all I can think of to say to him. Then I wrap my arms around him to try to make him feel better.

"Well, now we're gonna hafta get fuckin' soaked and covered in mud here up to our ankles walkin' over to the pay phone at the front gate! I'll hafta give Mom a call and hopefully, she can come and get us and drive us on back home. I'll figure out what to do with my goddamn fuckin' car and the tent and crap later on."

Then he just sits there for a few long seconds, turns to me eventually and says, "Uhm, uhh, Aaron? Do you know what metaphors and symbolism mean?"

"Uhh, no, not really. I know what a symbol is. But honestly, I don't know what symbolism actually is though?"

"Well, it's kinda like a take on or idea for somethin' else. You know, like this old car of mine is sorta like a symbol. It's like everything else in my life right now. Holdin' me back and reminding me of my dad and how he let Mom and me down and how I'm not goin' anywhere right now. I just wanna cry. You're gonna be gone soon and here I am about to be all alone again. I don't wanna be alone. I just don't anymore!" Tears start to roll down his face and I know I have to say something to him to make this better for him, somehow.

"You're not alone. You have me! I don't know what I can say to make you feel better right now. But school and distance aren't going to break us up. That much I do know."

He pulls me into a tight embrace and buries his head on my shoulder, "I'm gonna miss you so much! I really am!"

"It's going to be fine. I just know it is."

"Jeez, Aaron! Sure am glad this armoire of yours comes apart. Gettin' it down the stairs would have been a real bitch if we'd hadta carry it down in one piece," says Adam as he starts to sweat, straining to carry the side pieces of it down the front stairs. It's moving day, and he has come over as he promised to help me move and make the transition.

Dad is down at the foot of the stairs and shouts up to us both,

"Careful, boys! Don't mark the wall or damage the chair-railing when you bring the desk and the rest of everything down to load into the trailer. That striped wallpaper is discontinued and we can't get any more of it."

"I think we'll be OK and I promise we won't hit the stair-bannister railing or the chair-rail or the wall when we get the rest of the stuff. Are there any more pieces of furniture to go after we bring the desk and stereo components down… then that last desk chair in his room?"

"There's a small pine washstand in the basement, along with an extra portable TV. I think that's it for the furniture. Then there are just the boxes of records and books and after that, just clothing. We can head out once everything is packed into the Rent-All trailer and maybe stop for breakfast in Johnstown at the Husky gas station and restaurant there before heading up to Ottawa."

"Dad? Can I take that rug Mom put in my room, too? It's my favorite colour and I think of Mom every time I look at it."

"I think she'd like to know that. And yes, take the rug. I'll tell her you said that, son."

"I wish she were here right now."

"She's having a hard time with you moving out and leaving. She's never been good with goodbyes."

"But this isn't really goodbye." I say. "I'll be back on weekends and holidays."

"It *is* a kind of goodbye to her. For me too, come to think of it. You're almost all grown up now, and moving into your own apartment in a strange city. Give her some time and she'll be fine, son."

Finally, the rental trailer is all loaded up and we're ready to head out. "Adam, you sit up front and ride shotgun with me—Aaron, you're in the back this time," Richard says as we sit in the driveway ready to go. "Looks like a good day for weather, and hopefully this should all go well."

With that, Dad backs the car and trailer slowly out of the driveway onto Bethune Street and manages to knock over two of Miss Janice Delahaye's aluminium garbage cans in the process. They start to noisily roll down the hill toward King Street. Adam quickly jumps out of Dad's car to run after them and bring them back, placing them back in front of her driveway. Then he hops back in, slamming the car door shut and starts to fasten up his seat-belt. Dad stares back at me in the back-seat and says sternly, "Not one word out of you there!"

Meanwhile, Adam is grinning in the front and I'm biting my tongue, trying not to laugh out loud.

Dad heads down the 401 to Prescott. "We'll stop in Johnstown to gas up at the Husky gas bar and Jon's Restaurant there to have something to eat," he says. "And I'm paying for breakfast and lunch, Adam to say thank you for helping us out. You know, you've been a really great support to us throughout this whole transition. Aaron's mother and I are grateful to you, son for pitching in and helping us all out here. She wants you to come over in the next couple of weeks to have dinner with us—just us three, after Aaron is gone."

"Happy to do whatever I can. We'll get him all set up and off to a good start here.

Once we make it up to Ottawa, Dad parks the car in front of the apartment building on Argyle and looks over to where I'm going to be living. "Well… we made it in one piece. Now let's test my key out here and have a look inside. Then we can start to slowly unpack."

He climbs the steps of the old front porch of my new home and once past the bevelled glass door and inside the entry hallway, turns to my front door and unlocks it. The door swings open to reveal the next few years of my life. "Hmmm, better, yes… much better than I thought it was going to be, boys," he declares, after scanning the space. "There is room for a good-size bed in here and that old pine desk of yours can go right over there beside the fireplace. You have some built-in book shelves in the wall there for your records, stereo equipment, and books. The armoire will fit just fine beside the door into the bathroom. And you'll still have room for a drafting board and stool in front of that big bright window at the front. The TV can go on top of the washstand and you'll be able to see it from the bed where the cable outlet is over there. Very good indeed."

"And I want that rug to go right in front of the fireplace. Thanks again for letting me have that."

"Let's just get everything placed for now and you can set up the armoire and get everything fixed the way you want it when you come up just before September 12th to start classes. Would that be OK, son?"

"Yes, Dad. I know this has been a long trip. Maybe Adam can help me with that stuff later on."

Adam responds with, "Sure thing. No problem with that. I'd like to actually."

The ride back to Brockville promises to be quiet and fairly uneventful. "Adam, you're driving back. I have to admit, I'm not as young as I used to be and this day has been rather tiring. Are you good with that, son?"

"Yes, Mr. Christie. More than happy to drive back."

I chime in from the back-seat at that point and say to Adam,

"Just make sure you fill up with gas before we leave Ottawa." He looks back at me in the rear-view mirror, rolls his eyes, smirks and shakes his head. Dad is oblivious to the exchange.

An hour and a bit later and Adam pulls off the 401 saying, "Mr. Christie, if you don't mind, I'll swing around over to my place. You can drop me off there and then you can take over to drive home to your place. Is that OK with you?"

"Yes, son. Good idea."

I pipe up from the back-seat, "Adam, can I go to the bathroom at your place? I really like, have to go."

"Yeah, no problem, sure thing."

He tosses his keys back to me and says, "I hafta get a load of laundry outta Mr. and Mrs. Nicholson's basement—go on in. You know where the bathroom is."

Dad smiles at Adam while waiting for me and says, "Thanks again for everything, Adam. Now remember, you come on over anytime you like to see us. And I was serious when I said we'll get together for dinner once Aaron is up in Ottawa. I know Ana would really like that. And so would I."

"Yes, Mr. Christie. And thanks a lot for the meals and everything. I'll see ya real soon.

I return from his bathroom and get back into the car, this time on the passenger-side up front, my father driving.

"Here's your keys back, Adam. I'll call you tomorrow at the store." I lean out from the passenger-side window of the car to hand him back his keys. Then Dad starts to drive away and we start on out for home.

Adam climbs up the stairs with his laundry basket, opens his door and steps into his kitchen.

"Fuck! I feel so alone and I miss that damn kinky, sexy little fucker already," he says out loud to an empty room. Then he looks up above the sink at his *Kiss the Cook* sign.

"What the fuck!" he exclaims in complete surprise.

I've taken a piece of white bristol board and added the letters I and E to his sign so it now reads, *Kiss the Cookie*.

And right below it is a note that simply says:

I love you, Adam.

4 September / October

"Hiya, Astrid."

"Aaron! Christ almighty! What the hell do you want? Why are you calling here?"

"Dad told me you and Geraint and the kids are going to move out west?"

"That's right, we are. Are you pleased now? What's it to you?"

"Uhh, well, I just wanted to call to say thanks for the extra money for school. I really appreciate it, Astrid."

"What the hell are you talking about? Geraint and I paid you what he owed you from the store. He didn't have much choice in the matter. I suppose this is sarcasm and gloating now because you're getting all that money from Mom and Dad for Algonquin and we're having to move because the store is going under."

"What are you talking about, Astrid?" I say in total surprise.

"Oh please, spare me. Don't give me that innocent little, baby-brother crap! I don't need any spoiled-brat shit from you. Thanks to you, Dad won't help us to get out from under what Geraint owes his creditors. And it's all your fault! It's always about you, isn't it? And now you have the nerve to call me! I know damned well you're going to waste every damned cent of that money they're handing over to you and will probably bitch it all away the first-semester. You're not going to make it, Aaron, you hear me? You're going to fail! I give you three months in that programme and you'll wind up dropping out. You and your damned homosexual friends are going to party with Mom and Dad's money and you'll probably wind up getting hepatitis or syphilis or gonorrhea from screwing all your pick-ups, or having them screw you up the ass. Geraint says you're a real little *man-whore!* Makes me sick to even think about it! Thank God Geraint and I are getting our children away from you. He says they don't need to be exposed to a perverted, sick, potential child molester like you!"

I am completely taken aback and tears start to well up in my eyes, "Astrid! Why would you say something like that? I thought you'd be happy for me that I'm going back to school! Why are you being this way?"

"Look, Aaron, I don't have time to deal with you and your creepy lifestyle and your stupid, gay ideas about becoming *a rich and famous interior decorator.* I don't want to hear anything out of your filthy mouth. You should know by the way, that I told Mom just what we thought about you and your *choice* to be a practising homosexual. Geraint told me he wants nothing to do with you! I'm sorry you're my brother. Now don't you call here again!"

She slams down the phone and I'm left listening to the dial tone in complete shock. I'm shaking and just can't hold back the tears.

Mom is in the kitchen and as I rush past her to head up the back stairs she stops what she is doing at the sink and asks, "What's wrong? What's happened?"

"I can't talk right now. I just need to go to my room and be alone."

"Was that you on the phone just now? Who was that you were talking to?"

"Astrid. Please, Mom! I just need to be alone right now," I say, tears coming down my face.

"Richie! I think you need to leave the office and come home right away. Aaron called Astrid and he's up in his room now crying. Please, Richard, come home now!"

"Damn! I told him not to call her! I'll be there as soon as I can get away here."

"May I come in?" Dad says as he opens my bedroom door and sees me lying face-down on my bed. He sits on the corner and hands me a handkerchief.

Funny the things I always think of when it comes to my dad. He never goes anywhere without a clean white handkerchief in his pocket. "What are you doing home from work?"

"Your mother called and told me you called your sister?"

"I just wanted thank her for the money she gave me and ask why they decided to move and then maybe wish her good luck and tell her I'll miss her."

"What did she say to you, son?"

"Dad! She said she didn't want her kids around me because I was a probably a child molester and sick and that I'm going to fail in school and probably get venereal disease. She said I was sick and perverted and that she and Geraint didn't want anything to do with me because I chose to be the way I am!"

Just then Mom comes into the room and stands at the foot of my bed behind Dad. "Richard, we should have talked to him. He shouldn't have had to hear this from Astrid."

"Not *now*, Ana. You go downstairs and get out that bottle of champagne we were going to open the night before Aaron was to take the bus up to Ottawa for school. I want to have a quiet talk with my son. It's time, honey. We'll be down when I'm done here.

Then he turns his attention back to me.

"Sit up, son," he begins, in a gentle voice. "There are a few things I want to say to you. You know that your mother and I love you very much. You do know that, don't you, son? That word is not easy for me to say."

"Yes, I know."

"I recognise that now I've never been very good with talking to you about sex and intimate, personal feelings in the past. You must have realized that when your mother told me to talk to you about those nocturnal wet dreams. I still remember the first time I tried to sit down with you when you were eleven to give you the talk about the birds and the bees, and you just looked back at me and said, "Sure, what do you want to know, Dad?

"After that, well… I never knew how to talk to you or what else I could do to explain sex except to give you that little pamphlet and tell you to keep yourself zipped-up and not to let it out until you fell in love and got married. I was hoping your high school gym teacher, Mr. Saladino would give you all the information you would need about sex.

That was until I found out he was having sex himself with his assistant football coach, Mr. Berenson.

"You know that we come from a long line of staunch Roman Catholics who grew up in Victorian England and never spoke freely about such things. When my parents died in England after World War One and my two older sisters and I were sent off to Canada from Liverpool to go work on farms and in kitchens for sponsoring Catholic families... well, son, those times were very, very different from today. But you need to understand that I come from that era. And it is still hard for me to express my feelings and talk about those things I now realize I should have said to both you and Astrid when you were growing up."

"Again, I do love you, son, very much—never forget that. I always have and I always will. When you made the choice to stop attending church with me at the age of fifteen, I prayed for you and still do. My faith is everything to me, Aaron and keeps me going. I believe in God and I hope that you still do, as well." He pauses at tis point and takes a long breath. "It isn't easy for me to talk to you this way," he says at last.

"I know, Dad. I appreciate that."

"You know the church teachings and what the Bible says about Sodom and Gomorrah. Monsignor Cranston from St. Francis has certainly had more than enough to say about that every damned Sunday from the pulpit during his interminable, long-winded sermons. You know the Ten Commandments and served as an altar boy for him for four years when you were in grade school. And you no doubt heard all kinds of talk and personal opinions and judgements about right and wrong from the Notre Dame nuns and Catholic lay teachers at Saint Francis Xavier back then as well.

"Well, Aaron, here is what I think is right. First off, and I've never said much about this to anyone else before, your mother included—you remember the story I told you about how I worked for the first sixteen years of my life after coming to Canada at the farm for the Jordan family in Carleton Place? As an orphaned young boy I saw all kinds of secret things that went on there. I had to grow up very quickly, son. As for what went on around me, it didn't really make much difference to me personally. And in hindsight, it wasn't any of my business as long as no one was being abused or hurt by what was happening. Live and let live. It took years, but I was eventually able to save up enough money and gain enough freedom and independence to move to Brockville on my own for the first time in my life to start training and working as an Orderly at the Psychiatric Hospital.

"I've seen a lot of good and bad in my life, son. The Hospital and the patients and staff there have shown me a lot, as well. And what I've come to learn over the years is that most of the good comes from kindness and wanting to help others in this life, and most of the bad comes from unhappiness and feeling the need to judge or harm others. Don't hate your sister right now, Aaron. She is having a hard time and is unhappy and needs to do whatever she must to save herself and her children. Deep down, she still loves you. Envy and greed are sins. Being who you are is not. The Last time I read the Ten Commandments, I don't remember God saying to Moses, 'Make an eleventh commandment forbidding any kind of love or physical intimacy outside of marriage—or between anyone but a man and woman. I bet you are shocked by what I am saying to you here. You know, son, outside of the Ten Commandments, most of what is in the Bible in both the Old and New Testaments was written by the Apostles or prophets and holy men interpreting what they thought God was intending for His flock. And what in the world twelve long-haired, middle-aged, unmarried men were doing following Jesus around all the time—well, that's one Apostle for Jesus for each month of the calendar year! We could even make a calendar of that, now that I'm thinking about it. Centrefolds of Peter for April, Paul for July, John for June Luke for October and Judas for December! I could go on and make a blasphemous joke about that, but I don't think you're in much of a mood to appreciate the humour so we'll just leave it alone for now. Do you understand what I am trying to say to you?"

My mouth drops wide open when Dad says this to me and I give him a sideways glance and start to blush. He laughs at me and says, "Didn't think your dad would ever come out with anything like that now, did you? I'm much more *hip* than you think!" then he leans over and gives me a shoulder nudge.

"But, Dad! What she said to me! It hurt so bad! I'd never hurt her children!"

"I know that, Aaron. Come here, son." Dad moves closer and puts his arm around me. "Your mother and I know that you didn't choose to be who you are. We do make choices in life, of course, but each of us is born into this world with a conscience and a soul. This, to me makes us all the same. It is God who determines what makes us different and I don't believe for one single second He would choose to make anyone less of a human being or less special or worthy of love than anyone else. It falls to each of us to take what He has given us—those traits and qualities that make us unique and special, and make the most of them, without hurting ourselves or others by doing so. Son, you are going to find in your life that there will be many, many people who think they are either God, or acting on His behalf, and who will judge you. You need to be true to yourself and take whatever special gifts He has given you to make your life and the lives of those you touch the best that you can, the way you know He would want you to."

"Thanks, Dad. I really do love you and Mom."

"We know that. You prove that every day just by being who you are. Now, I want you to take the gifts and talents that God gave you and move confidently ahead now with your life and continue to make us both proud. We have faith in you and know you are going to do marvellous things when you start school and graduate and go out into the world. And, by the way, the world is a much bigger and more fascinating place than small-town, Brockville, Ontario."

With that, he just sits beside me for a few seconds more with his arm around my shoulder before quietly adding, "And, Aaron, I want you to know the same holds true for Adam, as well."

"You really like him, don't you, Dad?"

"I do, yes. But I think he needs a little push and some mentoring right now to get him back on the road I see in front of him. You be sure and tell him he is welcome in our house any time. Now let's go downstairs and check to make sure your mother hasn't drank all that champagne. And from what Adam told me about you and your tolerance level for liquor, I'll keep an eye on your consumption, too."

He ruffles my hair and we both stand. Then he tells me that our father-son talk is just between the two of us and I tell him yes, of course.

"Are things better now?" Mom asks as Dad and I come down the back stairs into the kitchen.

"They will be, Ana."

"You know that we love you very much, Aaron, you do know that, don't you? We'll always be here for you, darling."

"Yes, Mom, I do."

"Please try to forgive Astrid for whatever she said to you in anger and jealousy on the phone. It may take a long time for healing and forgiveness, but brothers and sisters in the end are always there for each other when it comes to what's important in life. I truly believe that and hope that you will in time as well."

Two glasses of champagne, coupled with copious tears from Mom and too much emotional blather and blubbering about how she is going to miss me so much when I'm gone follow that little speech. At last, I turn to Dad and say, "Is it OK if I go over to see Adam?"

"I've already told you that you don't need my permission to spend time with him. If you need to go see him to talk, you go on ahead and do just that."

"His car really broke down badly again on him when he took me up to Brown's Bay for Labour Day and he was so upset about it. I haven't really talked to him that much since his mom had to come to get us— except for when he came up to Ottawa to help with moving—we really didn't talk much to each other then though. He hasn't called me in the past couple of days either. I just want to make sure he's OK and ask if he'll maybe take the bus up with me to Ottawa to finish with my unpacking and stay overnight before the Tuesday when I start classes."

Adam's apartment is three blocks north up Bethune Street from our house and then a fifteen-minute walk down Pearl Street. I walk along, thinking about everything Dad said to me and feel a little better with each passing block. *I'm really glad he included Adam in what he was trying to tell me. I'll tell Adam what Dad said about coming over to the house on his own when I move up to Ottawa—I think he'd really appreciate that.*

Crossing Perth Street toward Mr. and Mrs. Nicholson's house on Pearl Street West, I can see Adam's rusting-out, metallic silver-grey SST sticking its prominent, raised-up rear end out almost onto the sidewalk and overtaking the driveway. *Well, it was good at least he was able to get it towed back and parked here. I'll surprise him and knock on the door.*

I head up the exterior stairs on the side of Mr. and Mrs. Nicholson's garage and do just that. The place is in total darkness. After several minutes, I realize he's not there.

I just don't want to go back home right now. I don't want to be alone by myself in my room. I'm tired and I want to talk to Adam, right now. The only thing I can think to do is climb into his car and wait for him to come back from wherever he is. *He won't mind. Oh, good. He's left his jacket in his car. I can use it for a pillow, like he's told me he's had to do sometimes and smell him and feel warm and safe and pretend he's tight beside me.*

A half-hour later and I'm asleep in his car with his sports jacket over me, breathing in his comforting, all-enveloping, sexy Adam Blanchard man-scent.

At twelve-forty-five in the morning I wake up to hear the two long, loud horn blasts from the VIA Rail overnight passenger train passing the Perth Street railway crossing en route from Brockville station toward Toronto from Montreal. I'm holding a tear-dampened sleeve of Adam's jacket up to my face with my thumb and forefinger, rubbing the rough texture of the fabric. It takes me a minute to figure out where I am and what led to my being there, and then I realize Adam is quietly sprawled-out beside me in his driver's seat with my head in his lap and his right arm draped over the seatback. He's stroking my hair with his left hand and gazing down at me. How he ever managed to lift me up and slide in without waking me is a complete mystery.

"Cookie, I came home after midnight and looked in my car to get my jacket before headin' up to my place and found ya asleep in it. What's wrong? You have an argument with your mom and dad or somethin'? Or did ya just miss smellin' and feelin' up my sweaty old jacket sleeve and armpit there?"

"Oh, Adam! I missed you! Something really, really bad happened with Astrid and me today. And then Dad and Mom talked to me. I just needed to see you and you weren't at your apartment. And I, well, I just needed to see and talk and be with you! And you weren't here."

"Well, I was over with my mom earlier. I've been watchin' ya cry in your sleep and mumble stuff down there for the last half-hour. C'mere. Sit up and shift over closer to me. Hows about I getcha upstairs and then you can tell me all about it?"

"I'm too tired to talk now. Can I please just come up and stay the night with you and we'll talk in the morning?"

"Do your mom and dad know where ya are right now?"

"Yes. I told them I was coming over here to see you."

"OK, babe. Let's getcha upstairs then." Once inside, I hug him as tightly as I can and say, "Will you just hold onto me in bed tonight, please?"

"Sure thing. Lemme undress ya and help ya get ready for bed. Lift up your arms and I'll pull that sweater offa ya there. C'mon, climb into my bed. You'll feel a whole lot better after a good night's sleep under the covers, next to me."

Adam's mother, Delphine is one strikingly beautiful woman. It's obvious who Adam got his looks from when you meet her. I sort of remember that actress, Ava Gardner from a couple of movies. One was called *Night of The Iguana* with Richard Burton. And then there was that *Bluebird* movie 1 saw her in last year, along with Elizabeth Taylor and Jane Fonda. Picture Ava Gardner in those movies and you'll have the image of one sultry, sensuous, voluptuous, and earthy woman in her mid-forties. Those words serve to describe Delphine perfectly.

"Thanks again for comin' to get Aaron and me from Brown's Bay last Saturday, Mom," Adam tells her. They are sitting at the kitchen table in her house—though Adam would always think of it as his too, given all the years he grew up inside it. "It cost me another seventy-five goddamn bucks to have Gerry tow that damn piece-a-shit car back to Prentice Esso and then to my place. He checked it all over. It needs a new electric fuel pump, starter switch, ignition solenoid, and carburetor adjustment. And he said there's a slow leak in the gas tank and the tires are practically bald in the back. It's gonna cost me more than eight-hundred and seventy-five bucks to fix it! I guess I'm gonna hafta just get rid of it. I can't afford to keep pumpin' money into that old piece a crap car. I don't know what I'm gonna do now though. Gerry told me there was some guy in Merrickville who was lookin' for a parts car to fix up his old Ambassador to take out to car shows. He said he'd give the guy a call to see if he'd come and tow it away and maybe give me a few bucks to take it off my hands. Gerry said he'd even tow the car away for free to help me out. I think that's what I'm gonna hafta do. But after that, uhm, I'll just hafta walk, I guess."

"Adam, do you remember when you were young and we would sit around this table and have hot chocolate and talk?" says Delphine.

"Uhm, uhh, yeah, I do, Mom."

"You haven't come to really sit down and talk with me in a long time. It's good to know you feel you can still can, even though you're a grown man now. How do you feel about Aaron leaving Brockville and going back to school in Ottawa?"

"Uhm, Mom, well, I'm really gonna miss the damn little pain in the ass. I know he's a lot younger than me, but I got to know him pretty well in a really short time. And I just feel so bad now about losin' both my wheels and him at the same time. That Ambassador always reminded me of Dad, and not havin' it now is like having to go through him leavin' us all over again. And now havin' Aaron headin' off to school, well, I just feel really sad and alone. It's like everyone and everything is moving forward and I'm stuck here in Brock Vegas, not goin' anywhere."

"Adam, I had lunch last week with Aaron's mother."

"I didn't know that, Mom!"

"Ariane called and suggested we get together to talk a bit about our boys. You know she's depressed right now because she's afraid to let him go. I remember feeling the much same way with you when you moved away and started pharmacy training in Kingston. It's hard to let go."

"What else did she have to say?"

"Just that she and Mr. Christie were pleased that you and Aaron were friends and that she felt Brockville was not the place for either of you to be stuck in for the rest of your lives. And I happen to agree with her. She knows that about Aaron, but all the same it's hard for her to let him go. Adam, I want you to bring Aaron over so I can get to really meet him before he leaves for school. I know I've been busy and preoccupied with my life and work these past few months. And you may already suspect this, but I've been seeing Sebastien Forestier from the Hospital over the past while. He works there as an Orderly. I've wanted to keep that quiet though because we both work at the Hospital and people in this town gossip and seem to know everyone else's business. *Bast* is usually over here when you come to the house now, so it's time you know what's what. And, Adam, it's just so good to have someone in my life again after so many years of being alone. That's what I want for you, too, darling."

"Thanks, Mom. I kinda, sorta already knew that about you and Mr. Forestier.

After a long pause, Adam says, "Uhh, Mom, you do know I'm gay, dontcha?"

Delphine pauses and gives her son a long look before saying, "Darling, I've known that since you were eleven. I know we've never sat down and talked about it. And you've never come to me and said anything until now. I want you to be happy, Adam. I don't understand why you are the way you are, but it isn't for me to judge or tell you who to be or how to live your life. Acceptance is different from understanding. I love you, darling, and I'll always be here for you to talk to and to support you in whatever you do and in whatever way you must be to live your life and be happy. I want you to know that."

"I love Aaron, Mom."

"He's very young. What is he, nineteen, twenty? He has his whole life ahead of him and is barely an adult. I don't want you to get hurt, darling. With him moving up to Ottawa, things are going to change drastically in his life—and quickly as well. That being said, his mother and I want you both to continue to see each other. Ariane told me she's pleased Aaron has someone like you to be a mentor to him and hopefully watch over him when he's in school. It's not going to be easy for either of you. Distance and time can change people. And yes, Ana knows about you and Aaron, too."

"What did she tell ya!?"

"Not much. We didn't have to say all that much to each other. Mothers know their sons and she has the same fears and concerns for him as I have for you. She likes you, though… very much, and she's hoping you'll keep him motivated and focused on his schoolwork and be there for him to keep him out of trouble."

"Not sure how I'm gonna be able to do that, now that I don't have my wheels and he's gonna be so far away."

"You'll have weekends when he will either come home or isn't busy with his schoolwork. It's not going to be easy, but if you really care about him, you'll just have to be patient and hope that things all work out. And I'll lend you the car here when I'm not using it to go up and see him whenever you need to. I can't do much more than that except tell you again that I love you and that you are both welcome here any time. And, again, I want you to bring him over soon to meet me and Bast."

"Thanks, Mom. I feel a little better now, talkin' to you."

"You know you can always come and talk to me. I hope you realize that now."

Later that night, Delphine turns to Sebastien in bed and says, "Well, Adam finally told me he is gay. Bast, he doesn't know about, well, you know, about when Jason disappeared and all the talk at the Hospital. All I could think to say to him was to look for the same happiness I've been able to find with you over these past months."

"That's good," Sebastien says, and then lapses into French. *"Voilà, c'est bon.* He knows you love him. And that's all he ever needs to know. *Voilà, c'est tout.* You know, Del, I'll never understand what makes us fall in love with the people we do. *Jamais!* All I know is that love can come at unexpected times with the people we least expect and in surprising ways. *Vraiement, ma belle. C'est la vie."*

"Heya, baby."

"Adam! Hi. Did you hear anything back yet from the gas station about your car?"

"Uhm, yeahhh. It's done, finito, toast, history. I'm gonna hafta get rid of it. Can't afford to keep repairin' it anymore. It's just gettin' to be too damn expensive."

"Aww, Adam, I'm sorry."

"Me too, baby. We won't be cruisin' around any more now in it before ya head off to school."

"I'll miss the front-seat blow-jobs!"

"Well, baby. It's not goin' anywhere for now and neither am I. Whaddya say we have one last play-time in it before it gets hauled away?"

I'm on the way!

It's the last weekend before school starts for me in September and Adam and I are taking the bus up to Ottawa in order to get my new apartment set up before commencement of classes on the 12th.

Adam shows up at the bus station with a huge backpack filled with some tools, a rolled-up sleeping bag, and a change of clothes to hop the bus with me up to Ottawa. He's wearing tight jeans, a royal blue tee-shirt with a Superman logo on the front, and a pair of bright red Converse running shoes. *Thank God he left the cape at home*, I think and quietly chuckle.

"Did ya pick up the tickets for us yet, babe?"

"Yeah, I did. I'm glad you were able to get the time off to come up with me before I have to start school on Monday."

"I'll fix somethin' up for us to eat in that postage-stamp kitchen of yours when we finish with settin' up your armoire and after you buy a mattress and drafting board from Wallack's. It's gonna be fun going with ya to Colonial Furniture to test out mattresses together!"

"Uhm, by testing, I hope you mean just lying down on them to gauge their firmness and nothing else."

"Well, maybe just a little bit of bouncin' up and down to make sure the one you pick is gonna be strong enough to handle the action and abuse I plan to give it with you and me. But just so as I don't embarrass ya in front of the sales clerk, I'll try to keep most of my clothes on when I do. OK, Cookie-Boy?"

Oh, God!

"Jeez, Aaron! I had no idea a drafting board and supplies were gonna cost ya that much," says Adam as he checks the price stickers on the ones I've been comparing. "And that drafting thing, what did ya call it again, a *Paradraft* or a *Mayline?* Jeezus fuck! That thing alone is like, two-hundred-and-fifty goddamn bucks!"

"The tuition is cheap compared with what the materials and supplies are going to cost," I tell him. "I knew that coming into the programme. At least the drafting board and Paradraft and a stool and most of the other stuff I'm going to need are going to be one-time purchases. And since I was able to qualify for a Student Grant from the Ontario Government, most of that money will offset the more expensive items I'm going to have to get to do assignments from home and not have to live in the classroom twenty-four-seven, the way some of the other students will have to."

"If you say so." At that point, he grabs me by the shoulder, starting to drag me out of Wallacks while chuckling and saying excitedly, "Now, let's head on over to Colonial Furniture to check out those mattresses!"

Colonial Furniture is on Bank Street, down about two blocks from Wallack's Art and Drafting Supplies and Equipment. "May I help you, gentlemen?" says the female clerk as we walk into the store. Adam takes over completely saying, "Yeah, well, maybe. I'm looking for a good, strong, durable mattress and box-spring set that's gonna get subjected to a lot of *heavy-duty, big-time action.* Somethin' on the extra-firm, *hard-as-a-rock* side and not so expensive and *rinky-dink* that I'm gonna be afraid to really use and abuse it and wear it out, if ya catch my meaning." The moment he comes out with *rinky-dink* he hooks his thumb into his belt buckle while his hand cups his prominent man-basket.

The clerk colours up a bit and tells Adam that the mattresses are on the second floor. "If you need any help, my name is *rinky*, errr, rather, Marianna. I'd be more than happy to help you." Then she unconsciously looks down at Adam's delectable man-bulge with, no doubt, wild sexual images and fantasies running through her feverish little brain.

"*Rinky-dink*, Adam?" I say while giving him a questioning look as we walk away.

"Figured it'd make her look down at my big, furry crotch there and get her all juicy. Works every time!" he says and laughs as we head up the stairs and stare across a football-field sized room filled with mattresses and cheap plastic-laminate and tacky wood-veneer bedroom furniture suites.

"Once ya pick what we're gonna sleep on together, I'll give her one of my killer smiles and a look and I'll betcha we'll wind up gettin' a discount from her and maybe even free-delivery later on today, so we won't hafta sleep on the floor tonight!"

Four-hundred dollars later, and we've got a promise from star-struck Marianna that, yes, the mattress and box-spring set will, of course, most certainly be on a Colonial Furniture truck out for delivery later that afternoon. Adam and I head back to my apartment on Argyle.

The armoire goes back together fairly quickly, thanks to the tools Adam had thought to bring up with him. And then Adam secures a curtain rod into the top of the ornate wooden frame around the window. Watching Adam standing on top of the steam-heat radiator in front of the window with his long legs spread, a power drill in his hand, and his hard, shapely, sexy man-ass with those two cute, shapely butt-cheeks facing me while he installs the curtain rod is like XXX-rated pornography!

The mattress arrives just after four and we have drapes on the window and almost everything put away by dinnertime.

"I'm just gonna head on over to Boushey's Food Market around the corner on Elgin to see what I can scare up for us to eat," he says when he hops down. "It won't be fancy since you don't have much of a kitchen or stuff to work with, but I promise I'll make somethin' that won't give us food-poisoning, OK?"

"OK. I've just got a few more things to unpack and I'll help you when you get back."

I'm just finishing with unpacking the last box when Adam returns from Boushey's. He watches me take a framed-picture to place it up on the mantel ledge and has a look of astonishment on his face. "When the hell did ya ever get a chance to take a picture of me?" he says as he stares at the small, red-framed, black-and-white photograph of him in his old jacket and trousers I've just placed on the fireplace mantel.

"Uhm, uhh, well, I snuck my old camera into the store one day a few months ago before I'd actually met you and took it when you were busy with a customer. I know that sounds creepy, and I have to admit I felt like some kind of pervert stalker after I took it, but I just really wanted to have your picture to look at when I was alone in my room and needed something to remind me of you to jerk-off to."

"Jeez! You always manage to surprise me. Do ya want me to auto-graph that one? Hmmm, actually, I'll getcha a much better one than that the next time I come up, OK? Do ya want a life-size, full-length nude shot or will a close up of King Kong be good enough for ya?"

Then he drags me over to the new, as-yet-unmade bed, grabs me by the shoulders and lowers me onto my new mattress, still partially-wrapped in plastic, and then climbs on top of me. He says very quietly and seriously, "Uhm, I think dinner's gonna hafta wait for a bit 'cause I've got other plans for you and me at the moment."

Two hours later, we're facing each other half-naked, sitting cross-legged on the rug in front of the fireplace while dining on the chicken breasts and pre-cooked Cuppa Noodles he prepared on my ancient stove. Candles are casting a soft glow all around us in the room. I can't think of a more romantic way to have dinner.

After washing the dishes in the old porcelain sink and putting them away on the open shelves above, Adam undresses all the way, heads to the bed, pulls the freshly-made covers back, and climbs in. He pats the spot beside him and gestures for me to join him.

"These red satin sheets are really kinda slithery and cold-feelin'. Gonna hafta getcha some new ones. And, uhh, remember, I hafta be at the bus station for seven in the morning to catch the bus back to Brockville. And you'll be needin' to get yourself all pretty and cleaned up for your first class for eight-thirty. I'll have some instant coffee ready for ya when I wake you up. You're gonna be just fine on your own tomorrow. I wantcha to give me a call when Bell comes to install your phone later this week. I'm gonna hafta work this coming weekend, but we can talk on the phone and you can tell me all about your first week. And I'll be able to come up the following weekend to spend it all with ya, OK, Cookie-Butt?"

"Mmm, thanks for everything," I whisper as I pull the covers up and find a comfortable spot with my face nestled into his armpit, my arm across his hairy chest, my leg bent at the knee and rubbing against his warm, furry man-basket in our brand new bed. Sleep comes slowly though, as I have so many thoughts rolling through my head about my first day at school.

It's eight-thirteen in the morning... I walk into the school—my first day at Algonquin.

Right away, I discover to my dismay that the cafeteria on Campus is comprised of seven rusted-out vending machines and some mismatched plastic laminate tables and orange and yellow sixties-era plastic chairs in varying states of disrepair. There are cracked plastic ashtrays over-flowing with stale-smelling, lipstick-smeared, filtered cigarette butts on most of the tables. And judging from the look of the shrink-wrapped sandwiches in the vending machines, even the rats and mice would turn their noses up at them. I mean, really... *whoever imagined that the ham in a ham sandwich could be grey?!* Fifty cents for a paper cup of coffee that looks and tastes like coloured-water and then I head off to the first-year classroom in the south part of the main building to meet my fellow classmates and sign attendance for orientation.

"*Vell...* good morning, *hmmmm... izzzn't it?*" says the Head of Interior Design after we've settled into our seats in front of her.

"For those of you who haven't met me yet, my name is Iona, Iona Ouspenskaya. Most of you *von't* need to remember it though because you *von't* be here at the end of this semester." And with that as an introduction to our year, Iona has set the tone. She spends the next ten minutes repeating her diatribe about the high attrition-rate and how many drop-outs she expects by the end of November, and everyone seems to be trying to surreptitiously check everyone else out to make their own judgements about who will survive and who won't in the programme. *Not exactly a great way to start the first day*, I think as I scan the room and do a quick count of how many other students are in it with me.

I count twenty-one other students, aged nineteen to forty-five or so. There are two other guys and the rest are women.

"I *vant* you all to tell us your name and *vhy* you *vant* to be an Interior Designer, hmmmm... izzzn't it?" Iona says at last, having thoroughly depressed every person in the room. There are only five other students who even remotely look to me like they know what they've gotten themselves into and who have piqued my curiosity. The two other guys, of course, since we three are the visible minority males in the class, and then three women, all in their early to mid-twenties. Each says their name and gives a brief overview of why they decided to enroll in the programme. I scribble each name down so I'll be able to remember them: Alleyn Arendsdorff—Jakobe *Jako* Erikschöenn—Lynne Bergeron—Lorita Schaible—Melora Holt

Alleyn Arendsdorff is the first to speak.

He's the son of a recently-retired Canadian Ambassador who served out his last posting in some Soviet Bloc region I can barely pronounce, let alone spell. He works as a window display and merchandising assistant for the Hudson's Bay Company on Rideau Street but has decided to take a six-month unpaid leave-of-absence to decide if he wants to pursue a more challenging career in some form of creative design. I have to admit, he's sexy and sophisticated. Long, curling, almost black hair with a Tom Selleck moustache and an *Ohh-isn't-it-all-just-sooo-dreadfully-boring* way of speaking that would either intrigue or repel anyone who heard him. He's wearing a white silk shirt, unbuttoned halfway down to his navel and has a well-tended dusting of dark, not-too-thick chest hair, clearly visible and just waiting for someone to run their fingers through it. His shoulders look like they could support a steel girder. His pants look like they are molded right onto his thighs and I don't dare look down at his bulge, although I have to admit the thought is running through my mind.

OK, Aaron, get your thoughts off his moustache and chest hair and pay attention to what he's saying. And then I look at his eyes, which are just as dark as mine—almost black, in fact, and suddenly realize he's making eye-contact more with me than anyone else in the classroom. I'm sure

I'm blushing, so I look down and try to focus on what he's telling Iona and the class about himself. My ears really perk up though when he casually mentions that his parents live just east of Maitland on an old stone estate I remember well and now go past on the bus up to Ottawa on its route from Brockville. His parents' stone manor house with the curved stone stairs leading up to the royal blue, carved wood door and the adjacent carriage house is about ten miles or so east of my parents' house in Brockville on the other side of Maitland, just before the private school that used to be a Catholic Seminary there. And the other interesting bits of information I manage to catch are that he only lives about three blocks from me on Elgin Street in a pre-war, heritage-designated, three-storey, walk-up building with big, bright, diamond-pane, leaded-glass windows, and that he has an Afghan hound named, Marlene Dietrich.

The next one to speak is Lorita Schaible.

I will admit my opportunities to get to know or even meet anyone Jewish in small-town, English Catholic and Protestant Brockville have been few and far between, but I'm guessing both Alleyn and Lorita are Jewish. And when Lorita starts to talk about herself and why she enrolled in the programme, every stereotype assumption I was ever told by every stupid person who never, ever actually knew anyone Jewish back in Brockville, comes back to haunt me. Lorita talks with fast, nervous insecurity and pauses after every sentence to, I'm guessing, seek affirmation before continuing with her rambling story of how her mother wanted her to do something creative and make her proud because she could have been a famous designer herself, if she'd only had the chance.

God! Like, just who is her mother, anyway? Joan Rivers on diet pills? Wow. Talk about manic!

I can't help but smile at that thought. I could see Iona's eyes start to glaze over after three minutes of this drivel and then she cut Lorita short and said, "If I'd *vanted* to hear *vhat* your Mama had to say, I *vould* have enrolled her in the programme! You're done now, hmmmm... izzzn't it?!" Lorita gives an audible gasp and then shrinks on her drafting stool, seeming to disappear into a mass of fuzzy, black hair, teal angora, and white, bejewelled jeans.

Melora Holt is next.

Melora was studying to obtain her master's degree in Political Science at the University of Ottawa and had been planning for a career in the Federal Government, she tells us, but she's always had an interest in Interior Design and decided to take a break to pursue Applied Arts for one semester. Iona is quiet as Melora speaks, paying respectful attention to what she's saying. I get the distinct impression that Melora wouldn't take any crap from Iona, and decided right then and there at that moment that I liked Melora very much. *If she'd had a wire, Iona wouldn't be pointing at it and telling her she was meek,* I think as Melora continues with her poised, confident, and polished self-introduction.

Then Lynne Bergeron starts to talk about herself.

Lynne's father is an interior decorating consultant in Ottawa and has a showroom and store in the east-end of the city that sells high-end upholstered furniture and offers custom furniture fabric reupholstery services. Lynne's history is a bit similar to mine in that she works for her father in his store and, from that experience, decided she wanted to investigate the Interior Design programme at Algonquin with the objective of becoming a bonafide professional Interior Designer to help her father expand his business. Lynne is focused and I can tell just by listening to her she has discipline and clear expectations and goals for the programme. On top of this, Lynne is absolutely beautiful. Her intense blue eyes, clothes, makeup, and general demeanour suggest she shops in the most exclusive and expensive fashion boutiques in Montreal.

Jakobe *(Jako)* Erikschöenn is the last to speak.

He chose a seat as far back as he could in the classroom and leans back on his drafting stool with his legs spread as open as far as he possibly can, pretending he doesn't notice that Iona keeps staring at his prominent crotch-bulge every three minutes. Needless to say, Jakobe is gorgeous. Tall, with dirty blonde hair, and obviously straight, Jakobe is the kind of guy whose looks have surely made up for any intellectual or creative shortcomings in his life up to now. I think about those people who seem to be able to cruise through life without ever actually having to work hard at anything to achieve success as I listen to him speak. *Iona might have moist panties looking at him right now, but I'm wondering how he's going to make it through this programme if he thinks he can finagle and flirt his way through every assignment.* Then I have a bitchy, jealous thought and think, *I just bet Iona never pointed to his cock and told him he needed to get his wire up—although she probably would have wanted him to in another time and place.*

Once all the introductions are done and we've been handed out a smudged, barely-legible, photocopy map of the Campus and assigned lockers, drafting boards, and seat-spots in the first-year English student classroom, Iona finally begins to run out of steam and tells us to turn our stools in the other direction. At that, the folding wall between the two classrooms opens up and we are now facing Elzbeth Mountebank, who is about to start with our first class in Design Basics and Colour Theory.

Usually, I eventually came to learn, these classes consisted of hour-long lectures and practical instruction, and then three to four hours devoted to one-on-one critique *(crit)* sessions between the Professor and the student on whatever the assignment is for that week. Students always fight to get the best crit times, and if you have to wait until the end of a class, you'd usually get stuck with a brain-dead instructor who regurgitates boring, unoriginal and uninspired design concepts and recommendations that would likely wind up getting you a 'D', or worse, an 'F' for your finished work. I could see that this was going to be a brutal and competitive environment. My *wire* was starting to pay attention.

Later I was to discover the fabled life story of Elzbeth Mountebank *(Ela)*. Her chief claim to fame was that of being a nubile, young Carnaby

Street girl in a micro mini-skirt and white patent leather *go-go* boots, dancing her way through London in the sixties to Herman's Hermits and The Rolling Stones. She had a clipped, posh British accent and, apparently, some kind of obscure fine-arts education that helped her land this teaching gig for her in the design programme. I'm sure that in her mind, she is still as skinny as Twiggy and just as fashionable, wearing her plastic op-art jewelry and traffic-stopping, bold, graphic, Piet Mondrian-inspired, Dior-knock-off dresses. But to me, she just looks like some tired, forty-something Emma Peel/Diana Rigg clone from The Avengers in complete and total denial.

By the end of the first day, I have two assignments dumped on me with the clear instruction from both Iona and Elzbeth to use *their* name when buying materials from Wallack's Art and Drafting Supplies. No doubt they each either get a kick-back, or the Interior Design programme benefits financially somehow.

Narcissistic lessons in Interior Design—always look for a discount—never give anything away for free—always demand acknowledgement and praise when giving a recommendation. I was certainly beginning to learn.

My trip to Wallack's to pick up what I needed for Iona and Elzbeth's assignments was first on the agenda. One-hundred-and-forty dollars later and I head back to my apartment to start to get to work.

Iona's assignment deals with abstract two-dimensional planes. No… not the ones that fly—more like what she told us in class about points, lines, planes and volumes, which are the primary elements of design. I had an idea about circles increasing and decreasing in size made from what she told us had to be thick white Bainbridge board. The idea was to use the two-dimensional planes to create a three-dimensional sculpture that could be viewed from all sides and that flowed smoothly from each viewing angle.

Cutting the Bainbridge board with a geometric compass and an X-Acto knife becomes an exercise in masochism after the twentieth circle. For every perfectly-cut circle, four wind up being either ruined or dirty and have to be thrown out. Iona's last comment to us when we left the class was that craftsmanship and perfection were as important as the concept we were trying to convey. I work throughout the evening and, at four in the morning have all the circles cut into different sizes and am ready to have a crit later on that week with her.

Elzbeth's first assignment is to have us pick up paint-chip colour samples at different paint stores. We are to look for harmonious colours and then do up twelve 1/2"-x-4" bands on a piece of Bainbridge board, using no less than three distinct colours per strip. The final effect was to look like semaphore signals—or flags—or military medal ribbons. The idea is to achieve pleasing colour combinations using both similar and contrasting colours in varying degrees of size and width within the confines of the bands. Once again, craftsmanship and perfection are important for the final submission.

I had to visit four different paint shops to get whatever paint-chip samples I could lay my hands on. This takes almost as long as doing the actual assignment! It isn't until much, much later that I clue in to what some of the other students have done—namely, buy what's called an Architect's colour-fan paint-deck that shows virtually all the perfectly gradated colours I would need in order to complete this assignment. I really wish I had scammed a couple of those paint decks from my brother-in-law's store back in Brockville when I'd had the opportunity.

In the end, I simply run out of time to complete Elzbeth's assignment and wind up using fluorescent colours and some really intense, saturated, bright ones like safety-orange, and school-bus-yellow which really did not work well together at all. As a result I receive an 'F' for my very first assignment with her and an official note on College letterhead informing me that, as men were more likely to be colour-blind than women, and in view of the assignment I had just handed in, I should go to the College medical-clinic as soon as possible to be tested for suspected colour-blindness!

As an aside, I was later to learn that Elzbeth was a very bitter and unhappy woman because her long-time partner had left her for a young man several years before.

Iona's *crit* sessions with me go somewhat better. We play around with the circles in class together and I explain what my thinking is. She is agreeable and receptive to what I am trying to do. Her one comment is to remember that, whatever I do, time and effort are important factors.

"You may have *zee* best idea in the world, but if it takes more time to achieve than *vhat* your client is *villing* to pay for, then you must edit and not do something for nothing, hmmmm... izzzn't it?" This was her parting morsel of wisdom to me before all the students' models were to be completed and presented in class the next week.

There were other memorable moments I took from my classes that first week.

Gaelen Goderich was a fleshy, stiff, pompous, somewhat conde-scending and supercilious, proper British gentleman who used to work with Evan Copland in Toronto before coming to Algonquin to teach. He always seems to wear ill-fitting, grey flannel double-pleated and cuffed pants and generally speaking, looks as starched and stiff as his oxford-cloth dress shirts. In his first class, I remember him saying to us straight up to think of him as either a client—*or God*—taking great delight telling everyone that no one who was left-handed, like me, would ever receive a grade higher than a 'C' in his class, as they could not draw without smudging their work when working from left to right. Then he handed out an assignment for architectural lettering on a huge A1 size sheet of white velum that I knew would take hours and hours to complete.

My first impression of Lynda Naagy-Birdsong was that she was as flighty as her name. Again, we got the entire life-story of everything we never needed to know about her. Honey-blonde, carefully-coiffed and on the far side of forty, Lynda was yet another one with some kind of undefined fine-arts training and background. She took great pains to explain to us that, yes, while she was married to some high-level, Federal Government Deputy Minister and didn't need to work, she was teaching as a time-filler and hobby because she felt her talent just couldn't go to waste and just simply needed to be shared with us, her students.

Massimo Visconti-Ciccone was a short, paunchy, fifty-something Italian stallion of heroic proportion, originally from Venice with degrees in European History and Fine Art Restoration. Passionate about art and design, he loves to walk around with an artist's sable brush tucked behind his ear that he uses to gesticulate theatrically whenever he wants to emphasize a concept or make a point during his lectures on graphic design, interior-rendering, and graphic presentation. He's a fascinating, sophisticated, and altogether intriguing character. The gossip is that he is secretly Iona's long-time lover with a thick, fat, Italian-sausage monster dick and that this is how he became part of the programme's faculty.

The only one of all the Professors and instructors who seems to be normal, to me anyway, is Evan Copland. He's in his mid-forties, has an Ernest Hemingway beard, a deep baritone voice, and a patient, engaging manner. Out of all the first-week classes and assignments, his was the most valuable as he *actually has* an architectural and design background and education and worked for Cadillac Fairview, a major Toronto real estate developer doing hotel and condominium planning and design for the Harbourfront buildings on Lake Ontario before he and his colleague, Gaelen joined the Interior Design English Applied Arts programme.

God! What the hell have I got myself into with these bizarre, freaky people?! I wish I had my phone installed now because I really need to talk to Adam and Dad.

"Thanks for the easy-to-remember phone number," I tell the clerk at the Bell Telephone service kiosk in the Billing's Bridge Mall. "My older sister is mentally-retarded and can only remember simple number sequences, so I think 233-0330 with only three numbers for her to remember will work out just fine." *Thank God Adam gave me that spiel about having a mentally-challenged family member to score a good phone number. God, I wish he were here with me right now.* "Yes, The installer can come Thursday afternoon to hook up my Contempra wall phone." I say, and then I leave the kiosk.

It's a few days later when I pick up the phone to call Adam.

"Heya, baby! You got your phone installed, I'm guessin'?"

"Hi, Adam, uhm, yes, and my number here is the same area code as you, 613, then 233-0330. Thanks for the advice about getting an easy-to-remember phone number. It worked out perfectly."

"Told ya I'm not just a pretty face, ya know."

"Well, actually, yes you are. But I prefer your big cock and sexy, fuzzy man-tush and I wish they were up here right now with me. I miss you, Wookie!"

"Aww! I miss you, too, honey—big time!"

Twenty minutes of conversation starts to wind up with Adam telling me he's jerking himself off on the other end of the phone. I say goodbye with a promise to meet him the following weekend at the Catherine Street bus stop, right after nine.

A new week and more assignments... Iona's class starts first thing Monday morning, and I walk into class to find that Alleyn Arendsdorff is occupying the drafting stool right beside me, having bribed Yolanda Vargas, an exchange student from Guatemala to exchange places with him.

"Hi, Aaron! Figured we guys should stick together in this class. Hope you don't mind me sitting beside you?"

"Uhm, no, I guess that's OK."

"You and I live close to each other. And I know where your house is in Brockville. It's a quaint little place your parents have there. Uhh, maybe we could go to the Coral Reef Club or Sac's in Hull or the Lord Elgin sometime. That is, when we don't have any assignments to do."

"I promised my boyfriend, Adam I'd let him take me to those places."

"Well, maybe some time when he isn't around then."

"Shh, Alleyn. We'd better pay attention. Iona's coming in now."

"*Vell*, good morning class, hmmmm... izzzn't it. Let's see *vhat* you've all been able to do *vith* your first abstract planes assignment."

She has a long, wooden pointer in her hand and is wearing that ridiculous dark, blood-red velvet bow tie.

Alleyn leans over and whispers in my ear, "Well, at least she has her *lips* on straight today."

She walks up and down the long tables where each student has placed their Bainbridge board assignments, and smashes some of them and knocks them off the table with her rod.

"Carap, gaaarrrbage, sheeeet! If I'd *vanted* something that looks like it *vas* copied out of the Elements of Design textbook, I *vould* have said that! Nooo! *Carap!* You've missed *zee* point! *Vhat za* hell is that supposed to be?"

One by one, projects that would have taken at least ten hours to complete land on the floor and break apart. She gets to Lorita Schaible's project and stops for a moment. "Nope! *Vhat* is it? *Gaaarrrbage!*" It lands on the floor and falls apart into small pieces. "It actually looks better that *vay*, hmmmm... izzzn't it?" she exclaims as Lorita gets up and rushes out of the room in tears.

"Let's see if *ve* can pick up the pieces and make something good out of this piece of *carap.*"

Fifteen minutes later and Iona has manipulated the pieces of Lorita's project to create an aesthetically beautiful work that flows from all angles and appears to meet all of the assignment's prerequisites. With this, it all becomes clear to everyone what the project was to demonstrate as Iona loses herself in the process of creating while explaining her thought process. It is simply brilliant to be able to watch and listen to her.

"Now, *vhen Principessa Schaible* gets off the phone crying to her Mama, *vill* someone tell her to glue *zeese* pieces back together exactly the way I've arranged them and I *vill* give her a 'D' for the assignment? Hmmm... yes, izzzn't it?"

When Iona got to my model, she does exactly the same with the notable exception of knocking it off the table with her pointer.

Twenty-five minutes later, after she's performed a complete and total autopsy on my model and left it in pieces, she says, "Now, Aaron, put it back together again the way I left it and I *vill* give you a 'D', like *la Contessa Schaible.*

I just look at her and don't know where I find the balls, but I say, "In your first class, didn't you tell us *not* to do something for nothing?"

She stares at me for a couple of long, uncomfortable moments, smiles, and says, "*Vell, vhat* is it you *vant, il mio giovane,* little Aaron Richard Christie?"

I replied, "A grade 'B'."

I got both a 'B' and respect from her from that moment on.

Vell... izzzn't zat just great!

There is something very seedy and dirty about the Ottawa Voyageur Colonial bus station after nine in the evening. The fluorescent lights give everyone's skim a sickly grey pallor. The smell of diesel fumes is nauseating, and the shrill, rasping loudspeaker announcing arrivals and departures is grating.

Finally, the bus from Brockville carrying Adam arrives—not a moment too soon for me, too, as I'm really not comfortable at all with the old men there cruising me and the endless stream of disenfranchised people coming and going.

"Heya, Aaron!" he exclaims as he spots me in the waiting area and heads over to give me a big bear hug. "I've missed ya! I wanted to give ya a chance to get yourself all settled in classes so I didn't call. But now this weekend is just you and me. I missed ya so much."

"I didn't go to the grocery store yet," I tell him. "I'm sorry, but there isn't anything in the fridge and I haven't had any time to get a bottle of wine or anything. I'm really sorry."

"Aww, dontcha give it a second thought. You and I can head over to the IGA on Isabella tomorrow morning and I'll get ya all set up for food for the next couple of weeks and we can have a nice romantic dinner, just the two of us. How does that sound?"

"It sounds like I want you up here all the time. God, I missed you too so much."

He laughs and gives me one of his dazzling smiles and, suddenly, all the challenges and disappointments and hard work of the past week at school seem to fade into an endorphin-charged fog.

He's wearing a well-worn, weathered, tight-fitting, black leather bomber jacket and those same pair of man-ass-accentuating dark jeans he wore when he came over to meet my mom and dad. A black crew-neck sweater and his trademark red Converse running shoes complete the image. That familiar scent of Eau Sauvage, mingling with his own unique *Adam Blanchard man-scent* envelope me as he hugs me one more time before we leave the station to walk the four blocks over to Argyle.

Just outside the front entrance of the bus stop there is a dark alcove. He drags me into it, drops his knapsack, and roughly pulls me into him for a passionate deep, demanding kiss.

At the same time, he is grinding his half-hard, Chewbacca light-sabre into me and whispering, "Just hadta do that 'cause I don't think I coulda walked all the way to your place with the big boner I got when I first saw ya waitin' for me when I got off the bus! Hell, I missed ya, butt-boy! By the way, I bought ya some new sheets for that nice new bed of yours. No more slithering around like horny snakes on those red satin things ya got. The only snake in your bed is gonna be the big one between my legs tonight! And we're gonna be nice and toasty this evening with what I got for ya. Consider them a housewarming-gift there."

"As long as there is some red in them, I'll like them."

"You'll be seeing all the colours of the rainbow when I'm done with ya in bed later. Now, let's hike it over to your place."

The minute we get in the door, I say, "Adam? Tonight maybe could we try Chapter Eleven?"

"Whaddya mean? Ya wanna go bankrupt?!" he replies and then starts to laugh.

"Nooo! I want to have you lying down on the bed on your back so I'm able to straddle you. I read that if I do that, it'll be easier for you to rub against my prostate gland. The only time I jerked-off this past week and a half was right after when I called you to give you my phone number. I need to have you inside me tonight. Squeeze your Cookie hard enough and his Oreo cream-filled centre will spill out all over you."

"Sounds messy and juicy to me there. But before we get too distracted, your mom sent me up with a care-package of her homemade peanut butter cookies and I'm thinkin' I wanna chew on one of those before I take a bite outta you. Besides, I have a plan for this evening. So, patience, little one and we'll get around to takin' care of your tight little butt-hole later.

"Uhm, uhh, Adam, I also want to rim you tonight. You've never let me do that to you and all I've been able to think about the past couple of days is your hot, sexy man-ass. I really want to make you feel as good as you did to me when we went to the Lyn Pit. Can I do that, please? Can I? Can I, puhleeze? Huh? Can I?"

"We'll take a long, hot bubble bath together in that big, old-fashioned tub of yours before we hit the sack later on. And after that you can stick that tongue of yours wherever the hell you want—in me, on me... whatever, wherever."

After that, Adam reminds me he promised to take me to the Lord Elgin and Coral Reef Club the last time he was up. He suggests we show up over there to dance and maybe have a beer or something before we rip each other's clothes off and have hot and sweaty sex. I tell him one of the guys in my class, Alleyn Arendsdorff had mentioned that he and I should go to the Lord Elgin some day after class one day, and that I'd told him I'd promised my boyfriend I would only go with him.

"Good boy. I just wanna make sure you don't get yourself into any trouble in these places. You're very young and the guys have a nickname for guys your age. You're a *twink*. Not a Twinkie, as in my special little cookie, but a twink. Lotsa guys go after really young guys your age. And yes, I'm bein' overprotective and probably jealous and possessive here. But I just don't wantcha gettin' yourself into any situations where you're gonna get taken advantage of by someone who's just interested in you 'cause you're young and innocent and all."

"Well, Adam, I promised you I'd let you take me. So whenever you want to go, that's OK with me."

"OK then. Maybe we'll just go to the *oral grief* Club tonight and dance for a little bit. You don't need to be stared at by all the old guys in the Lord Elgin. And, Aaron, the men's washroom there, just so ya know... well, there's no goddamn way I'm lettin' ya go in there without a safety net around ya. Anytime you go to the Lord Elgin from now on, you go into the stalls and steer clear of the urinals. There's lotsa perverted, horny creeps in there who'd love to get a peek at your cute little *Cookie Monster* down there. And that particular pleasure is reserved just for me. Besides, there's security guys who check that washroom out every half-hour or so and call the police to come and hassle the guys who spend too much time in there. You need to know these things. Can't have my little twink gettin' himself into any trouble 'cause he doesn't have a clue about this stuff. Do ya understand?"

"Yes. And I don't want anyone looking at my cock either, no worries there. My dad took me to the men's washroom in Kingston a long time ago at City Park, around Barrie Street and King because I had to go like, really badly. There was a hole someone had made in the partition between the stalls and Dad told me to put my jacket over it when I went to pee. I think I must have been around eight or nine. Dad stood outside the stall while I pee'd and kept talking to me until I came out. I remember that to this day. There was someone else in the stall right beside me and I'm pretty sure they were trying to look at me. Dad could see their shoes. I still get bashful now, so I'm extra careful when have to go. Otherwise I just can't. About the only time I'm not shy is when I'm with you."

"Hmmm, good to know, baby. Good to know."

The Coral Reef Club is in a basement beneath a multi-level parking lot close to the historic court house and the Department of National Defense on Nicholas Street. You'd never find the place unless you knew where it was. The door down to the club looks like an anonymous emergency-exit door beside the pay-ticket-meter and barrier toll-gate to drive into the parking lot. The only clue that there's anything down there is a small, square, fire-rated, Georgian-wire glass window in the door and a tiny, hand-stencilled, amateurish sign just inside that reads *The Coral Reef Club* in pink and turquoise clunky-looking letters. The minute Adam opens the door and starts to head down the stairs, all I can hear is KC and The Sunshine Band blaring out "Get Down Tonight." There is a ticket wicket with a window and a pass-through at the bottom of the stairs where some older guy with a porn-stache, looking extremely bored, is sitting.

"Coat-check and entry fee. Ya got some ID there, I hope?" he asks me.

I pull out my wallet and show him my brand-new driver's licence that Adam was able to help me get—just in time before his old car completely conked-out on him back in Brock Vegas.

The guy takes the dollar cover-charge and my jacket and hands me a round plastic token with a number on it to claim my jacket when I leave.

"I wantcha to stick close by me 'til we figure out how crowded and nuts this place is tonight. Ya got that? Here, grab onto my hand, 'cause I'm not lettin' ya loose on your own 'til we get ourselves a drink and find a place to sit down, OK?"

"Uhm, yes. I'm kind of nervous anyway so I'm going to stick close to you. Besides, from what I can see so far, this place is kind of creepy. The music is good, but the rest sort of looks like the cafeteria at the College with all those long tables arranged in rows and those plastic chairs."

"What'll ya have to drink? I'll go to the bar while you sit here."

The place is packed tight with people. Mostly thin and super good-looking men in their twenties and thirties—just like Adam. I don't think I've ever seen so many bell-bottom jeans and platform shoes in one place. And it seems like every guy has a David Cassidy shag haircut, too. I have to admit though that I prefer Adam's shorter hair, along with his fully-grown-in beard and moustache—*so much more masculine somehow*. Polyester double-knit shirts, suede-fringed vests and leather beaded-chokers, or neckerchief scarves seem to be the trendy fashion for a lot of the guys dancing on the tiny little dance floor that looks like a scaled-down version of the one John Travolta danced on in *Saturday Night Fever*.

There are at least twenty guys at the bar with their stuffed, bulging pube-baskets thrust out, pretending not to check each other out. Every so often someone leans over to someone else and asks for a light for their cigarette. Usually five minutes later, they pair up on the dance floor where they shake their booties to whatever disco music the DJ is spinning from his sound booth above. To the right of the sound-booth and the dance floor is a little stage. I was to discover later that there are weekly performances by local drag queens there every Wednesday night. Also, that Thursday nights are for women only, when all the lesbians get together to drink, smoke, dance, and probably talk about their motorcycles, pottery-kilns, and the cheapest places in town for a mullet haircut and where to rent a U-Haul trailer.

The bar has pink flamingos painted on the wall behind where the glass shelves hold all the liquor bottles. Pink flamingos are the main theme throughout the place… the plastic garden-variety ones people put in their yards seem to pop out everywhere. I even see a few pink feather boas drooping down from the columns in the room. Instead of doors into the restrooms, there are long, shiny strands of thick, silver tinsel.

The mirrored disco-ball above the dance floor is the biggest one I've ever seen.

"Here ya go, Cookie. Cheers! So, whaddya think of the place?"

"It's kind of tacky, actually. I can feel all the older guys in here staring at me. I'm really glad I'm with you right now."

"You'd be shocked if you knew who many of them are. You've got married men and teachers and politicians and even priests and ministers who come in here to try to pick someone up for sex. You're right, it is all kinda, sorta tacky and sleazy."

Just then, I happen to look over beside the bar only to find my high school gym teacher, Mr. Saladino in an acid-green leisure suit, unzipped halfway to his navel exposing all of his sweaty chest hair with five or six tacky gold chains and medallions hiding in it. He's chatting up some anemic, skinny blonde guy with terminal acne and a weak chin who I think I recognize from College.

"Oh my God, there's my gym teacher from Brockville over there! He's married and has four children. What the hell is he doing in a place like this?"

"I've seen him in here before. And I've known about him for a long time. Wouldya like me to call him over to say hi?"

"Hell, no! He was just awful to me in sex education class in grade ten. He kept saying that homosexuality was unnatural and that guys who had sex with other guys usually wound up getting hepatitis and venereal disease. And now look at him, posing there with that big erection poking at the other guy in his lumpy polyester pants, and that look on his face! He looks just like a horny, Jolly Green Giant!"

Adam is speechless for a moment and then starts to laugh.

"You just kill me," he says. "But dontcha be goin' and judgin' other people. If he's not tryin' to pick ya up, then I got no problem with him bein' here and neither should you. Now let's dance, 'cause I like this song, and it's a slow one."

Stevie Wonder sings "And I'll Be Lovin' You Always" from the big speakers at the back of the dance floor. Adam grabs me and pulls me into him and starts to move in gentle rhythm with the music.

"You're a really good dancer," I tell him.

"It all comes down to who ya got in your arms when ya dance," Adam whispers into my ear and gives me a little kiss. We move together and forget about everyone else in the place.

The next song is "How Deep is Your Love," by The Bee Gees. And then the DJ cranks Donna Summer's "I Feel Love" up to eardrum-splitting volume. The dance floor begins to overflow with haughty guys muscling each other out of the way to gain a square inch to strut their stuff.

"C'mon, baby, let's sit this one out. Too many fuckin' attitude queens on the floor now. Like, fuck this goddamn shit."

"Adam, I'm kind of hungry. There's an Italian restaurant on Rideau Street, across from the Bay. It's just around the corner and on the way back home to my place. We could split a pizza and maybe have a beer or something. I'm paying, too, since I asked you. It'll be kind of like my little date inside of your big date. And, no, I'm not trying to sound sexy or suggestive when I say that. Of course, that is, unless you want me to be, and that would be OK, too. Would you like to do that?"

A stunned look of surprise from Adam and a dirty laugh, and then he bends down and blows into my ear. "Cookie-Boy," he whispers, "I've had enough of this phoney tinsel-palace for one night and I can't think of a nicer thing to do with you than sharin' somethin' to eat. C'mon, let's go."

The front windows in The Bay are set up for Canadian Thanksgiving and Halloween. I tell Adam about how my classmate, Alleyn Arendsdorff used to do the window and store displays for The Bay, and that he still goes in part-time. I tell him Alleyn works with someone named *Mother* who weighs three-hundred pounds and walks around with a silver-handled, ebony cane and fans himself while his assistants do all the work. And that his parents live in an old stone estate just east of Maitland with a carriage house and stone pillars at the front gate, and that he lives just around the corner from me, too, on Elgin Street.

"Those store windows are pretty cool," Adam says. "Those mannequins with the *pumpkin-heads* and the *lipstick-painted lips* are pretty freaky. That reminds me, Mom wants you to come over to have Thanksgiving dinner with her and Bast and me when ya come down to Brock Vegas that weekend. I think she's gonna surprise me with a cake from Tait's Bakery for my birthday."

"That would be great. And you'll come over to Mom and Dad's for dinner that weekend, too, I hope?"

"Sure thing, Cookie. Your mom's already invited me."

When we finally make it back to my place Adam opens his knapsack and pulls out a bag, casually tossing it over to me. "Here ya go, just like I promised," he says and smiles. "A little housewarming present for ya."

Inside the bag is a set of gorgeous Egyptian cotton sheets and matching pillowcases. They're primarily dark hunter green in colour, but also have alternating thick red and orange and thin baby-blue stripes on them. I know they're unique and expensive. The plastic they are shrink-wrapped in has the name Ralph Lauren and a cute little logo of a polo player with a mallet and sitting on a horse emblazoned on it. It must have taken him quite a while to find those sheets in those colours, especially the red and orange together like that.

"Figured I'd getcha' somethin' that has both our favourite colours in 'em. Do ya like them?"

"I love them, Adam! And, and, I love you, too."

"Aww, honey, right back atcha. Anything for you."

"Let me put them on the bed to see how good they look. "

"You do that and I'll go brush my teeth and clean myself up a bit. Then we can test them out, break them in, wrinkle them up, whatever ya have in mind for me once we turn out the lights, OK?"

"I'll be quick."

He walks over to where my books are stashed away beside the fireplace, pulls out the newly-published and released 1977 first edition of *The Joy of Gay Sex* hardcover by Edmund White I bought, and opens it to a random page.

"It says right here on page 231 you should never be too quick when it comes to sharin' your bed with your man," he announces.

"I'll have to remember that when you're naked in it with me."

Once in bed together I turn to him and say, "I've been staring at your sexy man-ass all night long. Uhm, can I rim you? I really want to lick you down there to see if I can make you squirm the way you do with me. Then I want to suck King Kong until you're just about ready to cum. And then you can fuck me and fill me up so I'll be walking around tomorrow with you deep inside me."

An animal grunt and a Wookie-worthy growl and he grabs me and thrusts his tongue down my throat.

"Jeezus fuck! Do whatever the hell ya want to me. My body is all yours tonight," he groans as his hands seek, fondle and grope every inch of my body.

Two-and-a-half hours later, with the sheets half on and half off the bed, we finally fall asleep, coiled, snake-like, around each other.

5 October / November

In the weeks to follow, the assignments continue to be piled onto to us and one by one, we start to lose more and more people by the curbside. As Adam's birthday and Canadian Thanksgiving approach, the first-semester English class dwindles from twenty-one students down to fifteen. A partial refund of tuition fees is available to those students who change their mind about the programme within the first month after commencement. Some decide to cut their losses and drop out rather than continue to endure the brutal pace and demands of the programme.

I'll be honest, there were more than a few times when I became completely discouraged and wanted to just hop the bus and go home. But I remembered that last horrible phone call and the awful conversation I had with my sister Astrid before she and Geraint moved away. And in some twisted way, she really did me a favor when she told me I wouldn't last through the first-semester. I was damned-well going to prove her wrong. And so I persevered and tried to keep focus on why I was there and what my end goals were.

The sacred five, whom I thought would be the ones to make it through the first-semester—Alleyn—Lorita—Melora—Lynne—Jakobe—each offer up their own surprises. As we enter the first week of October, Lynne drops out, followed closely by Lorita.

I must admit, Lorita was not a surprise to me.

Lynne however, well, that totally shocked me. I was to learn later that her father had been diagnosed with lung cancer. And, as he was divorced and as Lynne was his only child, she was stepping in to provide health-care and support to him. I was truly sorry to see her leave the programme. She had talent. I hope she returns to the programme sometime in the future, should her father's cancer hopefully go into remission. I know though had it been one of my parents, I would have done the exact same thing without a moment's hesitation.

Jako continues to chat up every gullible female in the class. And it always seems to me that his projects and presentations assimilate design concepts that are suspiciously borrowed from those fellow classmates who fell under his spell.

Alleyn always seems to manage to complete his assignments and continued to maintain his 'C+' average. He remains just under the radar and avoids the dreaded wooden rod that Iona continues to brandish like some crazy, near-sighted empress. As the weeks roll on, I have to admit his sarcasm and biting, sometimes cruel wit and observations make me glad he is sitting beside me, even though he makes me feel less than him somehow when he compares my parents and background with his at times.

As for Melora, well, I was determined I would be her partner for the group assignments we were told would be coming up in the second and third terms. She was my hero.

My marks seemed to be all over the place this first-semester. I try to focus on the important courses that are prerequisites for progressing to the next stage. For example, Interior Design One is a precursor to Interior Design Two and such, until the final year, when a major thesis-project on hotel and restaurant-planning will complete the full programme. We have some *fluff* courses that are added to the curriculum to meet requirements for professional accreditation and provide opportunities for creative expression. They touch on Industrial and Graphic Design, Professional Photography, History of Art and Furniture, and

English of all things! And while they do little more than create additional stress with their workload, I have to admit I find some of them to be fun and a welcome respite from drafting and building construction and assembling abstract models that reflect design theory and principles.

Lynda Naagy-Birdsong's major assignment for my first-semester is really stumping me. Even so, I find her lectures on History of Design and Architecture, as well as her ones on History of Furniture Design to be interesting and useful. Giving Lynda credit, she sure knows how to hold a student's attention and is knowledgeable on the subject matter she speaks about in her classes. But the one major project we were given by her to be handed in for sixty-percent of our grade for the first-semester is one I just cannot seem to get my head around. It's to be either a presentation booklet or series of display boards reflecting architectural history from our own personal, creative perspective and is to demonstrate our knowledge of certain periods of architecture. As well, it's to be a visually-appealing, professional-looking presentation, integrating best practices of graphic design on whatever relevant subject matter we choose to cover.

"Hi, Mom! I'm glad you called! How are things back in Brock Vegas?"

We're both laughing at the sarcastic term to describe the city and then she says, "Hello, darling. Everything is good here. Blackjack misses you. And he's been *moping* around the house for the past month. You *are* coming home for Thanksgiving on October 10th, I'm assuming?"

"Yes of course. I'm coming home for the whole weekend. I could use the break. And I'm looking forward to Thanksgiving Dinner with you and Dad. Your strawberry pie is something I wouldn't miss. Oh, and thanks for asking Adam, too. I know he really appreciated the invitation."

"That was one of the reasons I called you. Please give Adam a call and get him to ask his mother to come as well. She'd probably welcome a break from having to do up her own dinner for Thanksgiving and let someone else entertain her for a change."

"OK, Mom, I will. And I'll ask him to get back to you."

"We miss you, Aaron."

"Me, too, Mom."

I hang up with Mom and then dial Adam's number to speak with him. "Hey, Adam!"

"Heya, Cookie-Boy! I miss ya! I'm glad you called. What's up, besides what you're most likely grabbin' onto there and shakin' right now with your right hand?"

"Well, Chewbacca, we haven't talked all week and I miss you, too. I just got off the phone with Mom. She called me and told me to ask you about having your mom come to join us all for Thanksgiving dinner. Would you ask her and maybe give my mom a call to let her know if she can come, too? She said it might give her a nice break from having to cook herself."

"Ok, sure thing. But she might be havin' her own dinner with Bast though. And remember, she wants you to come for dinner, too—maybe on the Friday when you're down that weekend. I sure hope you're gonna be hungry that night."

Well, the food up here is the pits. So any home-cooked meals would be appreciated. You know I think I've actually lost weight."

"Nooo, baby! You're only a hundred-and-thirty pounds soaking wet now—ya just can't afford to lose weight. I don't wantcha gettin' sick up there."

"Yeah, I know."

"Uhm, uhh, Aaron, I'd better warn ya about your mom before you come down that weekend. I went over to help her get her garden ready for winter and she, uhm, well, she, uhh, kinda looks a little bit different since you started school."

"What do you mean?"

"Well, she's dyed her hair bright flamin' red and was wearin' a one-piece, zipped-up, bell-bottom jumpsuit when I was over there last time, and platform shoes, just like what you have. She sorta looks like she's tryin' to look like that Shirley MacLaine actress outta the movie that's playin' right now at the Capital Theatre, *The Turning Point*. And she asked me to teach her how to do *The Hustle* 'cause she wants to go out sometime to the disco out at Long Beach!"

"What?! Tell me you're kidding! And what's the big idea comparing my mother to her!"

"Nope. I'm bein' dead serious. I asked your dad about it and he just kinda shrugged his shoulders and said somethin' about her goin' through menopause. Then he laughed and said she'd been goin' through it for the last twenty-five years of their marriage! It's actually kinda funny what he said."

"Oh my God! Thanks for warning me."

Then he changes the subject and says, "So, how are the assignments and courses going? I know you've been busy. It's been real hard for me not to pick up the phone to talk with ya, but I really wantcha to concentrate on your assignments and studies there."

"Adam, I'd rather you call me… even if only to talk for a couple of minutes than sit around here and wonder why you haven't. Let's make a deal to call each other every couple of days, OK?"

"Uhh, OK, babe. Now, uhm, do ya want me to pick you up on October 9th and bring ya on back to Brockville for the weekend? Mom isn't usin' the car that night. And she thought that maybe you and I could come over for dinner once we got back with her and Bast. She promised no turkey though 'cause we'll be havin' that with your mom and dad. Wouldya like that?"

"That would be great, yes! How are you there? "

"Like I said, I miss you. I've gone over to see your folks a few times and had a couple of suppers with 'em, too. Your mom's garden is lookin' real good. I've been helpin' my mom, too—a bit. And other than that, just work as usual at the store. Not much really happenin' back here in good old Brock Vegas."

"I wish I could say the same. I've got this one assignment I have to do for sixty-percent of my mark for History of Architecture and I have no idea what I am going to do yet. It's beginning to really bother me, to tell you the truth."

"Well, let's you and I just forget about work and classes and assignments that weekend and walk around town here and enjoy the fall weather, and each other. Does that sound like a plan to you?"

"Sounds like a perfect plan, since you're a part of it."

"Aaron, I miss you so much."

Friday, October 9th arrives and Adam pulls up in his mom's Volvo sedan to pick me up. "Heya, baby!" he says as he closes the front door of my apartment and moves in to grab me in a tight embrace. "What the fuck are all these pillowcases stuffed with? Have ya not done a laundry since I was last up?"

"Uhm, no. I just haven't had the time to go and sit in the laundromat and wait for everything to wash and dry. I know Mom won't mind if I do it down there. God! I missed you so much!"

"Judging from how hard my dick's gettin' at the moment, I'm guessin' it musta missed you, too!"

I reach down to grope Adam's big basket and realize he's as hard as a rock and not wearing any underwear, given the wet spot that's starting to seep through the warm crotch of his jeans.

"I'm going to do you right now, Adam. I've missed how you taste and smell and I just have to like, right now."

"Well, my dong was half hard drivin' all the way up here. So if ya wanna taste of my light-sabre, then get down there and do me now before we hop into my mom's car to head back to Brockville. I'm not gonna have ya suck me off in Mom's car 'cause that would be just too weird."

"That kind of spoils my plans to play with your light-sabre on the way back. We'll have to negotiate that on the way home, Chewbacca!"

"Well, Cookie, to quote you, all things are negotiable."

"You've been readin' more chapters in that *Joy of Gay Sex* book, given how you're goin' down on me there," he says, his voice husky with craving and sensuality.

I can smell his provocative man-scent and my hand is massaging his pleasure trail. He has to lean against the wall to steady himself. And all I can hear are his soft moans of pleasure as I take his entire cock in my mouth while my finger plays with his anus.

"Jeezus fuck! I'm gonna cum like anytime now! Keep strokin' my balls! I gotta get rid of some of my ball-juice and I'm gonna shoot deep inside your mouth, like, right fuckin' now!" He is forcibly thrusting back and forth into my mouth and he yells out, "Aww, fuck! What a perfect way to start a Thanksgiving weekend with ya. Jeezus, I've missed ya so much, Cookie."

After one huge, explosive cum session, I look up into his big eyes and say, "I've missed you, too, so much, Wookie." And then I start to zip him up—massaging his muscular inner thighs while slowly rubbing my nose back and forth across his spent-cock inside his jeans—inhaling deeply—shoving my nose deeply into his heady, pheromone-scented crotch.

After a few minutes of pleasurable sighs and grunts, Adam bends down and starts to pull me up from the floor to face him and reluctantly reminds me he's promised his mom we'd be back no later than seven-thirty for dinner with her and Bast. So we pack up all my crap and get on the road right away. But not before I give him an early birthday present. I tell him I want him to open it now.

"Better not be a pair of your cum-stained bikini briefs there. I'm not gonna wash 'em for ya! Seriously though, honey, ya really didn't hafta go and do that."

"I know I didn't..."

Adam gives me a stunned look of surprise and we both laugh.

"You didn't think I was going to forget now, did you? I didn't have time to wrap it, so the plastic bag will have to do."

Adam opens up the bag and pulls out an Algonquin College sweat-shirt—dark evergreen with the College-crest logo and white lettering. He admires it for a few long seconds then says, "Aww, this was really thoughtful of ya. Thanks so much."

"It should fit you and I hope you like it."

"I'll wear it to bed to remind me of you every night," he says.

He's oddly quiet while checking the size and washing labels on the sweatshirt and I know he is thinking something. "Is it OK? Is it the right size? Do you like the colour? Would you have wanted something else?"

"Well, Algonquin is where you're going to school up here. And to be honest, I'd rather I was wearin' *you* to bed every night. But it's a really sweet present and I'll wear it when you're not around and when I miss ya… which is like, almost all the time now."

He reaches out and pulls me into him and my hand somehow makes its way into his shirt. I rub his chest hair until he sighs and says, "No more of that for now or we'll never get outta here and down to Brockville in time for dinner. Thanks again for the present. I *do* love you, ya know."

"You better. That sweatshirt cost me thirty-five bucks!"

He laughs and says, "I'm worth it, butt-boy!"

We pull up into the driveway of Adam's mom's house on Broadway Crescent. It's a raised-ranch style, split-level house with a low-pitched, gable-roof and a two-car garage on the basement level that's right on the curve of the crescent at the top of a little hill. The front garden and hedges look carefully-clipped and manicured. The house has a big, curved five-pane bow window beside the double front doors and frosted-glass sidelights. It's very different from my mom and dad's house. I'm guessing it was built in the early to mid sixties.

"Mom and Dad bought the house when it was first built and this is where I grew up," Adam says as he hops out of the car and comes around to my side. "Now, you just be yourself and don't think you need to impress anyone to get 'em to like ya. We're gonna have a nice dinner. And after that I'll take you on over to your parents' place, OK, baby?"

I have to admit, I'm a bit nervous with meeting and really talking to his mom for the first time, but Adam's words help to alleviate some of my nervousness and trepidation. Just then, his mother comes out the front door and heads toward us. Sebastien follows.

"Hi, boys!" she exclaims, a welcoming smile on her face. "Glad you made it back before dinner. You certainly made good time on the road. Adam, you know Bast already. Aaron, this is a good friend of mine, Sebastien Forestier from the Hospital. He works for your father as an Orderly there."

"Very nice to meet you, Mr. Forestier."

"*Salut, ça va, allo, Aaron et bienvenue chez Del!* Welcome! Call me Bast. *Tout le monde, mais* everyone else does. We want to hear all about how your first few weeks of school have gone for you. Del, that bottle of wine I brought over. *C'est vraiment un celebration içi cette soirée.* Let's open it." Adam and I follow them back into the house and hang our coats up in the front hall entry closet.

The first thing I see when I walk into the dark, wood-panelled living room is a humungous 'L' shaped sectional sofa in an avocado-green and burnt-orange, wild-looking, abstract floral-print fabric with clear plastic slipcovers over it, along with avocado-green, sculptured-pile, wall-to-wall polyester carpet on the floor. On the wall above the biggest monumental combination stereo television liquor cabinet console I've ever seen, a beautiful, quilted piece hangs from a maple rod that I'm guessing Adam's mom must have made.

"That hanging quilt is really quite beautiful, Mrs. Blanchard."

"It's Del, dear—call me Del. And my last name is Bogaert now since the divorce from Adam's father. My family was originally from Belgium.

Thank you for complimenting my quilt hanging. Now, how have the first few weeks at Algonquin been for you? I'll bet they've been exciting!"

"Oh, I'm sorry, Mrs. Blanchard, errr, Bogaert, uhh, Del. They've just gone by so fast. I haven't had the time to sit back and really think about them. I have a feeling Christmas is going to come and I'll still be trying to finish my assignments."

"When does your first-semester end, Aaron?"

"The last day for actual classes is Friday, December 2nd. And all my assignments have to be complete and handed in for the following Friday, December 9th."

"How are the other students in your programme making out?"

"Well, it's funny you should ask that. We've had, like, six or seven drop out already. At the rate things are going, I can see a few more dropping out before the end of this first-semester. There's a lot of class-time and assignments to get through. I think some of them had no idea what they were getting themselves into before they enrolled in the programme. It's good though, because it gives the rest of us more time with the profs and instructors. It's been pretty good so far, all things considered."

"Have you had much chance to get out to experience life outside of the College?"

"Not yet, no. I'm finding just trying to keep up with my classes and course load to be pretty demanding. And I really haven't had much time to do much else, to tell you the truth."

"I can vouch for that, Mom, given the five stuffed-full pillowcases of laundry he brought home with him," laughs Adam in the background. "I'll need to remember to get that stuff outta the trunk when I take ya on home to Bethune Street."

"Ohh, yes! Thanks for letting Adam pick me up with your car, ma'am. That really helped me out a lot."

"You're more than welcome. Now I'm curious, what has been the biggest surprise to you now that you're settled into your new apartment in a new city?"

"I guess not having someone around telling me what to do all the time. I have all this freedom now to come and go whenever I like. Does that make sense to you?"

"It's called growing up and becoming an adult. I'm sure you'll do very well, once you get a chance to catch a breath and experience life outside the Campus—Brockville, too, for that matter," Delphine says, casting a glance at Adam. "Have you managed to make friends with any of your classmates yet?"

"Not really friends, no. But Connie Caserta and Melora Holt in my class have been pretty nice—and Alleyn Arendsdorff, who sits right beside me. His parents live just east of Maitland. And, well, he is probably the one person I've had a chance to sort of get to know in the first few weeks. He's OK, but I don't know if he's going to stick with the programme after this first-semester. He's taking a leave-of-absence from his job to see if he wants to go through the full programme. It's pretty competitive. So I don't want to get too friendly with anyone until I know they're going to stick with it."

"Well, here's to you, Aaron," Sebastien says, reverting back into French again. *"Si bon de vous rencontrer.* Let us all celebrate your first few weeks in College and hope you continue to grow with your studies. *Cheers! Santé! La meilleure chance à toi*—good luck to you, little one."

We hoist our glasses and then Delphine heads into her *harvest-gold* kitchen to serve up dinner.

Before Adam takes me home later that evening, he heads down to where we parked before, just west of Centeen Park. "I wanna talk to you about a few things before I take ya on home, OK with you, Cookie?"

"Uhm, uhh, OK." I look over at him inquisitively as he pulls into the parking lot and parks his mom's car to face out over the water.

"It's times like this I miss my old Ambassador, baby. I'd like to snuggle in that big front-seat and be close to ya right now. These bucket seats and gear shift console are the *fuckin' shits*. Uhm, I've been givin' some thought to when I was last up in Ottawa with ya right before school when we went to the Coral Reef Club and I think we need to talk."

"About what? Did I do something wrong? You sound very serious."

"Aww, no, Aaron, nothin' really to worry about. But I've been thinkin' about the age difference between you and me, especially with my birthday comin' up and I'm thinkin' that if what we have here is goin' to last, then I'm gonna hafta give ya some space to grow a bit on your own and experience the same things I did at your age. I don't wantcha later on to feel like you missed out on anything 'cause ya spent all this time with someone who's almost eight years older than you. Do you understand what I'm saying to ya here?"

"No, not really. Are you saying you don't want to see me anymore?"

"Oh, hell, no! No way! That's the *last* thing I want. But you're still so young and I don't wanna be someone who controls you. You're a smart young man and both you and me need to have freedom to grow and do whatever it is we want in life. That doesn't mean we hafta be apart though. I think what I'm tryin' to say is that, for this relationship to last, we hafta come at it from the perspective of mutual respect and as equals. That's gonna be real tough, given the age difference between us. I wantcha to know though that I see you as an equal partner here. You're doin' just great with your education, and that's makin' me think about where I am with my life and what I wanna do. I haven't figured that one out just yet... but I know I'm gonna wanna hafta make some decisions for me real soon. And I wanna make sure you're an important part of that—but not at the expense of you havin' to sacrifice anything for me. There has to be respect and trust and support between us. And by that, I mean not just me watchin' over you to stop ya from making some of the same mistakes I've made in my own life. I don't think that's gonna happen anyway. You're a lot more mature than I was at your age. And I think you're damn smart, too. I love you, Aaron. But you know that already."

I sit there beside him absorbing his words for a bit before responding. Then I say, "I need you to be there for when I make mistakes though. I love you, too, and I don't think of you as a *daddy*, err, uhh…that is, I think they call them that anyway—or a big-brother or a father-figure or anything like that. It's just that you happen to be a *little* bit older than me—I like older guys because they usually are more mature than the ones my own age. And, like you, they're usually a whole lot sexier, too. Especially you! I get flutters in my stomach that shoot right down to my cock every time I'm close to you. And I don't ever see that stopping. All you ever need to do is look at me a certain way and boom, my cock swells-up and gets hard and all I want is to be with you."

At that, Adam gives me one of his indecent, dirty laughs and says, "And I find cute, horny, kinky, little buggers like you just as sexy. I'm no pervert *cradle-robber* though. There's just somethin' unique and really special about you."

"OK then, Adam. So what you've just said to me, what does this mean for us now?"

"Well, uhh, I've thought a lot about this. For one thing, ya don't need me to be takin' you to places like the Lord Elgin, and the *oral grief,* and bars like that. Of course, I'll always go with ya whenever I'm up in Ottawa and when ya want me to go with you. But you're gonna get lotsa interest from guys and I'm just gonna hafta get used to that and not be jealous or overprotective. I don't want you to be goin' into any bath houses like the Club Baths at 1069 Wellington, though. The police raided that place last May and the *Ottawa Citizen* threatened to publish the names of all the men who were either in there at the time or who were registered members in the log-book for the place. Twenty-seven men got rounded up and hauled into the cop shop that night. The whole gay-scene up there in Ottawa just hasn't been the same since then, I've been told. Lotsa guys and women are scared for their jobs and safety right now. And the Ottawa police and RCMP are still out to get anyone they think is gay 'cause they all just fuckin' hate us. Promise me you won't be goin' into any places like that 'cause I don't wanna hafta worry about you gettin' arrested, or beaten up, or gettin' crabs, or VD, or anything like that."

"Uhm, OK, Adam."

"And I think you need to have a few friends close to your own age you can spend time with while I'm back here workin' for now. I'm thinking about my job and apartment back in Brockville, and I've almost come to a decision about what I wanna do in the next few months. But I'm not ready to talk to you a lot about that just now. Mrs. Tonner was talkin' to someone from the Shopper's Drug Mart Group and they maybe wanna buy her out as part of their expansion program by openin' up a franchise on King Street downtown. She's somethin' like eighty now and not gettin' any younger. She won't always be around. And that's really made me think. For now, all I know is that I want and need you and want us to be together like, all the time. But I don't want to come between you and your schoolwork. And I don't want to smother you either. Unless, of course, it's with my *sweaty old jacket and dress pants* that getcha all hot, horny and juicy for me!"

He laughs a bit, then turns serious again and asks, " Uhm, honey, do ya understand what I'm tryin' to say to you here?"

"I do now. Yes. And I miss you, like, all the time now, too and want you to be with me. I've heard stories from Alleyn Arendsdorff about the clubs and going out every night and smoking-up during class breaks and doing *poppers*, whatever they are, and getting drunk and… and, well, I'm just not interested in those things."

"I wantcha to feel like you can make those choices on your own, baby," Adam says. "I'll always be there to support ya, you can count me for that. But I don't wanna be havin' to babysit you or tell ya what to do all the time either. Some days I feel like I'm barely able to make my own way in this life. So you just might hafta help me, too."

"Sounds like a good plan and basis for a relationship to me."

"Me, too, baby. Me, too."

"I still get to suck your King Kong dong whenever I want. And you get to fuck me whenever you want though, eh, Adam?"

"That's not negotiable! And judging from how hard ya started to make me just now by changing the subject and bringin' up sex, I'm gonna let you go down on me. What goes on in Mom's Volvo stays inside Mom's Volvo though, deal?"

"Shhh! I can't suck your big dude-piston and talk at the same time."

Twenty minutes later and Adam quietly says to me, "I'm pickin' ya up tomorrow morning and we're gonna take a long walk downtown together. Your dad promised me some back bacon and eggs and coffee first thing, so I'll be joining ya both for breakfast. And Blackjack is real happy when I take him for walks now. He doesn't get enough exercise. And your parent's backyard isn't big enough for him to run around and play in. I've gotten to really like him. He's a good dog and I know he misses you a lot. Also, I was thinkin' about your architectural assignment for that *bird-brain* lady and you and me are gonna walk around Courthouse Square 'cause I think I might just be able to give you an idea or two while we walk around. Sometimes an answer can be staring ya right in the face. But it might take someone else and their eyes to

218

push you into seein' it. I'll see ya tomorrow. And be prepared to spend some time walkin' around with me and enjoying the fall weather and the leaves, and each other."

"Good God, Aaron! Lucky for us we've got a king-size washer and drier down in the basement," Mom says after I've hauled my pillow-cases of laundry into the front vestibule hall. "I'll get into this tomorrow morning while you and Adam go downtown. He said something to me about helping you with one of your assignments when he was over here earlier in the week. Don't get used to me doing your laundry for you though. I'm only going to do this for you this one time, you hear me?"

"Uhh, yes, Mom. Thanks."

"We're so glad you are home now for Thanksgiving with us," Dad says and reaches out to give me a hug. "I've missed you, son."

"Oh no! Richard, look at Blackjack! He's pee'd on the rug in front of the sink! He's so excited to see Aaron."

Blackjack's tail is going a hundred miles an hour. He's running around in circles, chasing his tail with his tongue hanging out, barking every thirty seconds.

"I've missed you too, Blackjack."

"Mom, uhh, your copper-coloured hair and that jumpsuit and big, wide Bianca Jagger headband! Uhm, Adam said something about you wanting to learn how to do *The Hustle* and go out to the Flying Dutchman sometime to their disco. Uhh, well, what made you decide to do that with the big wide hair band and your hair?"

Dad is sitting there with a bemused look on his face, just waiting for Mom to respond.

"I just felt like it was time for me to make a few changes, given that change is happening with you and Astrid and life in general. Why? Don't you like it?"

"The jumpsuit looks pretty cool. I'll just need to have some time to get used to the hair. It's brighter, too—all the *grey* is gone out of it."

Dad chokes and quickly jumps in at that point and says, "There never *was* any grey in it, Aaron! For a young man who is supposed to be so good with colour, I'm surprised you would even think that. Your mother still looks like she's in her thirties—with the butt to prove it, too, in that outfit."

Mom turns fifteen shades of purple and says to Dad, "Let's not discuss my butt in front of Aaron, Richard."

To which he replies, "OK honey. We'll take that conversation upstairs when we go to bed then."

"Oh Jeez, Dad! When is the next bus back to Ottawa?!"

"Have you heard anything from Astrid now that they are out in Calgary?" I ask them both.

Dad answers by saying, "They were able to make it out there safely and arrived about a week or so ago. They have rented a house for a year in the northeast end. And apparently, someone that Geraint had hired to work for him back when he had his commercial painting firm in Brockville here offered him a job. Your sister is looking to find a job with one of the bank branches out there. They're going to be just fine. Don't you worry about them."

"I still think about what she said to me. I hope they're going to be OK."

"We know son, we know."

"Did you talk to Adam about having Del come over to join us for Thanksgiving dinner?" Mom asks.

"She's having a dinner for her and Bast for Thanksgiving."

"Who is *Bast*?"

"Oh no! I don't think I was supposed to say anything about that. Uhh, oh well, Bast is someone she's been sort of dating for a while now. It's a big secret though. Dad, you know him. He works under you at the Hospital, Sebastien Forestier. He's an Orderly there. Do you know him?"

"Oh yes, Sebastien, I know him very well. Hmmm, I wonder if he might be uncomfortable coming over to have dinner at his boss's house. I'll bet that is why Del has been turning us down for dinner over here. Also, the staff at the Hospital like to gossip and create all kinds of unnecessary speculation and drama at times. Both you and I know all about that Ana, don't we?"

"Indeed we do, Richard," she replies.

"Tell you what Aaron. You *didn't* tell us this. Leave this with your mother and me to handle with Delphine and *Bast*—is that how you say it?"

"Yes. He was really nice to me at dinner earlier. He seems like a pretty good guy."

"He is. He's a very quiet and shy man when on duty. He keeps to himself most of the time. Leave this to me. I'll make sure he and Del feel they are welcome over here anytime."

"Thanks Dad. I know Adam would really appreciate that, too."

Later that night when they are in bed together, Richard turns to Ariane and says, "So how about that?! Delphine and Sebastien… shacking up. I never would have thought the two of them would get together in a million years."

"Oh, I don't know, Richie. Del has been alone and on her own for many years now. And she said to me she found it lonely and really tough when Adam moved out on his own. I'm happy she's found someone. Now, instead of you jumping in here and putting your big foot in your mouth with Sebastien, would you please just leave this for me to speak about privately with Del? I want her and Sebastien both to know that we would like to have them over here. And I don't want the fact that he works under you to be a source of discomfort."

"OK, Ana. Now, on another topic, honey—since when have you ever thought my feet were *big?* Is there anything else you'd care to comment on with respect to size on me now that we're in bed together?"

"Oh shut up, Richie and just kiss me you damned silly old fool! The door is locked, I hope, isn't it?"

"Double-bolted from the inside. Blackjack can sleep down in the kitchen tonight!" he laughs and responds while cuddling up close.

It's just after breakfast and the next morning—Adam and I have just covered the four blocks from Bethune Street to Courthouse Square.

"OK Aaron, here's my pitch to ya about that History of Architecture assignment you've been worryin' about. Hear me out on this. And if ya like it I won't charge you a consulting fee for my services!"

"You can take it out in trade if I like it." I say and then laugh.

"OK, here goes. We're standin' in the middle of Courthouse Square right now. Start with the Courthouse and go clockwise. Count the number of historic buildings going right down to King Street and back up until you get to the Courthouse again... and remember to include the ones that got torn down in the past couple of years like, where the old Comstock Block building was."

"Uhm, OK. Not sure where you're going with this. But I'll play along." So, I start to count and name the buildings off in my head—the Old Courthouse, the Wall Street Methodist Church, the new Bank of Montreal where the old one used to be, the First Baptist Church, the land where the old Comstock building used to be, the Toronto Dominion Bank at the corner of King and Courthouse, the Cossitt Block, The old Post Office, the Brockville Club, the George Street Episcopal Church, Courthouse Terrace and the First Presbyterian Church.

"OK, I got twelve. Do I get a prize now or something for it?"

"Not just yet. Now uhm, how many hours are there on the face of a clock?"

I'm starting to get a little impatient with him but still playing along. "Twelve. Where are you going with this?"

"Patience, Butt-Boy, patience. Now architecturally, how many different types and styles of buildings would you say there are here? And over how long a time period would you say they've been built?"

A lightbulb is beginning to go off with me. "Adam... uhm, uhh, are you suggesting I maybe take these buildings and describe them and relate them back to their time-periods and then maybe compare them to the hours and hands of a clock that tracks progress and time? Is that what you are trying to tell me?"

"You got it! You wouldn't have to go too deeply into describing 'em—just their architectural style and then take photographs—black-and-white ones of all of 'em. Then you could put 'em all into a booklet or somethin' like that. Whaddya ya think of that idea?"

"I think you just gave me my first 'A' for the semester! God I love you! Thank you so much, Chewbacca."

"I even help ya with the photographs. It'll be fun. And, Aaron, remember—sometimes, the best ideas come from the most surprising inspirations and unlikely sources. Never forget your hometown and where you're from. Brockville is a historic city and its architecture is really important and worth recognizing, preservin' and respecting.

"Hullo, Del, how are you? We haven't talked since our lunch together."

"Hi there, Ana. Happy Thanksgiving weekend to you," says Delphine into the phone.

"Thanks, Del. I just wanted to call to say thanks for letting Adam drive Aaron home from Ottawa. I don't think the five overstuffed bags of laundry he brought with him would have fit into the overhead-bin on the bus!"

Del laughs and says, "Welcome, Ana to the world of a College-student mom. I can still remember when Adam did that to me years ago when he was up in Kingston."

"Listen, Del, I'll get right to the point here and hope you won't be embarrassed or offended. Aaron let it slip quite accidentally that you and Sebastien Forestier are seeing each other. I'm absolutely thrilled for you. But I have to ask, are either of you nervous about coming over here because he works for Richard and we all work together at the Hospital? Please be honest with me."

After five or so seconds of dead silence on the other end, Delphine says, "Ana, I really don't want anyone to know about Bast and me. But, yes, he is apprehensive about having the staff at the Hospital know about us right now. It's still early in our relationship and you know as well as I do how nosy those folks are. Neither he nor I need to be talked about."

"I understand completely. And that's why I'm calling. This is confidential information, but I'll let you in on the fact that Richard intends to retire sometime next year. He will be sixty-three then, so please reassure Sebastien not to worry about reporting to him and coming over here. And please, Del... bear in mind that Richard's planned-retirement is not something we want to have circulated at the Hospital for the moment, any more than you and, is it *Bast*?"

"Yes, he likes to be called *Bast*. He's the *best* at being *Bast*, as he reminds me all the time."

Ariane, giggles just then at Del's mildly exasperated respnse.

"Good! Now that we've confided in each other, I hope that settles that. And as for you and Bast, I have to say I'm thrilled that you've met someone and are not alone. It's none of my business, I know, but I remember our lunch together and am feeling a little lost and lonely myself here now with Aaron away at school. I'm just so pleased that you have someone for you there now."

Thanks, Ana. I do appreciate that."

"Now, about Thanksgiving dinner. I have a suggestion and a proposal. I know you are doing up dinner there for you and Bast—Aaron let that one slip as well—how about coming over to have dessert with us later on in the evening? Do you think Bast might be comfortable with that?"

"I'll have to ask him. Can I get back to you?"

"Absolutely. We'd love to have you both come over, truly. Call me back when he lets you know. And, Del, I swear that no one will hear about you and him from Richard or me. That is your business. But I do want you to know that we are both happy for you. You deserve happiness, you really do!"

"Thanks for that, Ana. I'll let you know later on today."

"Are ya hungry, Cookie? Wouldya like to maybe pick up some fish-and-chips over at Manoll's and maybe head on down to Hardy Park to watch the ships on the river before the main channel freezes over in a few weeks' time? Then maybe we can go back to my place for a while. Whaddya think?"

"It's going to be one of the last nice days to do that before the cold weather sets in. Sounds good to me."

Once we make it down to Hardy Park and after we're seated at a picnic bench with everything unwrapped, Adam pulls one of the fish apart with his fingers, then looks over and says, "You sure do like your ketchup there, dontcha, Cookie-Boy?!"

"It's good with the beer batter-coated haddock. And, I forgot how good these fresh-cut french-fries are."

"So now that it's just you and me, tell me more about how you've been doing like, really. We haven't had much chance to be alone and talk since I drove ya back. Ya know, I remember my time away at College. It was kinda lonely for me at first. Have ya really not gone out much at all or done anything outside of your classes with your classmates?"

"Well, like I said last night, I just don't want to get too close or friendly with anyone right now. Connie Caserta's been really nice to me though. She's married to some really important man who's with some big international bank in Ottawa. It's been a riot driving over to Wallack's to pick up supplies and stuff with her in her big, silver, twelve cylinder Jaguar XJ sedan! She's really something... just sooo sophisticated, funny—super, incredibly talented, too. Then there's this one guy named Jakobe in my class. The women call him *Jako* though. He's straight and always chats everyone up. Then before you know it, his assignments look like someone else's when it comes time to hand them in. I don't trust him."

Adam chuckles and asks me, "Did you say his name was *Jack-off* or *Jerk-off*?!" and then he starts to laugh.

"Oh piss off, Adam. Jeez!" You really are like a ten year old at times!"

"OK, OK, OK. So, what about the rest of your classmates?" he asks.

"Uhm, uhh, well, there's Alleyn Arendsdorff." He seems OK. But his parents are really rich and part of the Diplomatic Corps and he makes me feel like I'm some kind of pathetic charity case sometimes when he talks to me. I may be wrong though—I just don't know."

"You're just as good as anyone else. Dontcha ever let anyone make ya feel bad because of what they have and what you don't. Take it from me. I aughta know. And money isn't the measure of what makes ya good— or happy for that matter."

"Thanks Adam."

"You're welcome! Now… are there any other projects or great mysteries of life you want me to help ya with right now? Or can we go back to my place and maybe practice Chapter Fourteen of your *Joy of Gay Sex* book there?"

"Hey! No fair! You've been reading ahead and are ahead of me now. I don't know what Chapter Fourteen covers."

"Everything Chapters One to Thirteen doesn't. Now let's hike it back to my place like, right now!"

"I'll race you there!"

"Sometimes it's all about the journey and not just gettin' to your destination," he says as he gathers up the newspaper fish-and-chips wrappings and tosses them into a garbage can.

The gulls swoop down to fight each other to snatch up the last few fries on the ground.

"You *have* lost some weight! I can see your hip bones stickin' out more than normal. How much did you say you weighed now?" asks Adam as I climb fully naked onto his bed.

"I think I've lost maybe between five and seven pounds."

"Well, that's just not gonna happen anymore. I can't have ya wastin' away to just skin and bones. You have to keep your strength up. Winters up in Ottawa are damp and cold. And I don't wantcha comin' down with the flu or bronchitis or anything like that."

"Since you're the drugstore wizard, I expect you to keep me healthy."

"I'm bein' dead serious here. I know I said you hafta grow up and learn at your own speed. But I do worry about you and don't wantcha gettin' sick on me—you got that?"

"Yes sir, I do!"

"Good. Now, let's see just how tight your little butt-hole is there. I think it needs my tongue teasin' it and gettin' it ready for a full-scale *Star Wars Imperial Star Fleet attack! My light-sabre* might need some chargin' up from you though to get it ready for battle. Think ya can manage that for me, honey? Chapter Fourteen is all about *Sixty-Nine*. Do ya know what that's all about?

"Nope, no idea," I lie.

He has his clothes off in record-time, climbs over me on his comfy, big brass bed and says, "All right. Now roll over onto your right side and get ready to take me in your mouth while I lean on my right side the other way and do the same to you. I'm gonna play with your butt and suck the livin' crap outta your little Cookie Monster down there. And you're gonna do the exact same thing to me. Then, when you really like what I'm doin' to ya down there, I wantcha to imitate it and do the exact same thing to me. That way I'll know what gets ya off. Not that I don't already have a pretty damn good idea of that now already though."

Every time I go down on him now, all I can think of is his hairy pleasure trail and the base of his big, thick shaft. I like to squeeze it at the base, because he moans and groans when I do and his big cock seems to swell up even more. Pulling his foreskin up and down on his shaft really gets him off. I know that when I do this, his cock head gets super sensitive and his sighs of pleasure get louder. All I have to do is focus on what I'm doing to him down there.

The scent of his fully-aroused cock is something I swear I would recognise instantly in a darkened room. It's pungent, totally masculine, and virile. And I wish I were a pair of his Superman underwear briefs at times so I could be in his hot pube-basket and have his man-smell between his furry legs and in his crotch on me all day long.

"I love how you smell."

"Jeezus, Aaron! You're one kinky, perverted little fucker at times. I don't think you'd be sayin' that after gettin' a whiff of me after three or four days without a shower. But if that's what gets ya hot, I'm OK with it. Now, I wantcha to stick your finger up inside me. My butt needs some attention. We'll shower up together after this—maybe in four or five hours or so—after we've had five or six messy cum sessions together. And I just might fuck ya in the shower when we're in there together, too. Whaddya say, Cookie?"

"What I really want to eventually do is play with your hairy chest and nipples."

"Once I shoot my ball-juice all over ya then you can do whatever the fuck you want to me there. Is that OK with you?"

"I'm so boned-up now all I want to do is just keep sucking on King Kong and have you cum all over me."

"Well, you just keep on with what you're doin' down there to my light-sabre and I promise ya I'll explode all over ya like, anytime now!"

"Jeezus fuck! Where in the fuckin' hell did you ever learn how to squeeze my dong in that exact spot when I'm cummin' like that? It felt like I was gonna pass-out. And I've like, never, like, ever shot a load that hard before. Like, Jeezus, Aaron! Feel my heart in my chest. It's still racing here and my sphincter muscles in my ass just keep flexing. How in the fuckin' world did ya ever manage to accomplish that? I just gotta know so I can do that to you, too."

"Maybe I'll be giving you some lessons soon. Think you can afford my hourly-rates?"

"If you can make me do that, then I'll pay you whatever your weight is in fish-and-chips."

"Your face when you cum is payment enough for me."

"Come here and snuggle close to me. I wanna feel your heartbeat next to mine. Let's just stay this way for a while, OK?"

I'm so relaxed and half asleep. All I can do is nod and nestle inside his armpit and close my eyes.

It's Thanksgiving dinner at the Christie household and feels like a surreal, bizarre, twisted scene out of either *The Walton's* or *The Brady Bunch*. Jeez, I hate those shows! I remember how the girls used to call me *John Girl* in high school. Those bitches!

Fuck...

We're just finishing up the last of the stuffing and turkey and Mom is starting to take the plates away from the table when the doorbell rings.

"Now I wonder just who that could be interrupting our Thanksgiving dinner?" Mom says to Dad with a little smirk on her face. Sebastien and Delphine walk into the dining room and Del says, "Happy Thanksgiving everyone! Hope there's some dessert and coffee left for us. We've brought a bottle of Grande Marnier over to mix with the coffee."

"Well, well! Anyone bringing liqueur with them is always welcome for Ariane's homemade-pie and coffee! Adam, Aaron, pull up a couple of chairs for Del and Bast. Happy Thanksgiving to you two!"

Just then Mom comes into the dining room carrying a *Charlotte-Rousse* birthday cake tied with an orange silk ribbon from Tait's Bakery on King Street with twenty-eight matching, orange-coloured, brightly twinkling and flickering candles on it.

"The pie will have to wait, Richard. Adam's birthday is this coming Wednesday! And given that Aaron will be back in Ottawa at school, Del and I decided that Adam was going to have *two* birthday cakes this year. Happy Birthday Adam! Now, make a wish. And I'll take the cake back into the kitchen and serve it up shortly."

Adam is silent as he looks at the cake, then over to his mom, then to me and then finally, at everyone else. "I don't know what to say. I think some of my wishes came true this year. And most of 'em are about the people around the table with me right now. I do have one more wish. But I'll keep it secret 'cause I really want it to come true. Thanks everyone." He blows out all the candles and smiles.

Mom hands Adam a card in a sealed-envelope. "Now Adam, this is a birthday card from Richard and me. Don't open it here though. You take it home with you and open it there later by yourself. And again, a very Happy Birthday to you."

The evening ends with everyone in front of the fireplace in the living room having coffee and Grande Marnier. Brock Vegas Blackjack is flaked-out completely, quivering and twitching and snoring in front of the fire. Every thirty seconds or so, he lets out a little yip and his tail thumps on the floor.

Dad gestures to Bast and signals him to come over to talk. "Now Bast, I know you report to me at the Hospital. But when you're over here, it's just you and me and Del and Ana. Do you understand that?"

"*Oui. Merci*—errr, rather, yes Richard. And thanks, *merçi la*—I do."

"Good! Then let's get really drunk and pretend it never happened on Tuesday when our shifts start again at the Hospital." Both men share a private laugh together while Delphine and Ariane give them both suspicious looks.

"Uhh, Aaron, can I see ya in the kitchen for a minute? I wanna take home a piece of that cake, if that's all right with you, Mrs. Christie."

"It's all yours, Adam. Take as much as you want." Then Mom turns to Delphine and says, "Del, I have some tequila in the pantry. Have you ever had a *Tequila Sunrise*? They're absolutely delicious! Let me make you one when we finish with the liqueur."

"Sounds wonderful! Thanks, Ana."

"Aaron, baby, do ya wanna know what my wish was when I blew out my candles?"

"I think I might already know. It was for a new car." I answer him and then laugh.

"Nope. Not exactly. I think you know what I wished for. I love you, Cookie. I know I've said that like, ten times already today. It isn't easy for me to say that word either, ya know. Can I please see ya before tomorrow before ya hafta catch the bus back to Ottawa?"

"How about me staying over at your place with you tonight? Would you like that?"

"That would be the nicest birthday present I could ever receive. Let's make up some lame excuse no one will ever believe and leave 'em to finish off their coffee and liqueur by themselves. Does that sound like a plan to you?"

"A perfect plan."

Once back at his apartment, Adam reaches into his laundry hamper and hands me one of his shirts. "Uhm, when ya go back to Ottawa I wantcha to take this good white dress shirt of mine back with ya. I've been wearing it to bed and sleepin' in it on purpose for the last four or five days. It smells kinda salty and sweaty and uhh, uhm, I sprayed some of my cologne on it. You can wear it to bed and fall asleep thinkin' of me if ya want. I know how much you love how my jacket and old pants feel and smell. It's a real kinky, fetish kinda thing to do. But ya know, and I never told ya this until now, but you wearing and gettin' off on my clothes after I wear 'em really gets me hot and makes me feel really possessive and protective of you, almost like I need to douse ya with my man-smell to claim ownership, if that makes any sense to ya at all. It's like some basic kinda primitive animal instinct thing. I think the word is *primal* or somethin' like that, anyway. Ya know, I'd be walking around

233

with a permanent hard-on thinkin' about fuckin' ya all the time if you were to just wear one of my old white dress shirts from work and nothin' else around here with your hot little boy-butt and sexy legs teasin' me. When I see ya sleepin' with my old jacket or pit-stained shirt coverin' you, it kinda makes me feel like you hafta have me to be like, all over ya, inside and out to feel safe and protected and really belong to me. But, honey, I really need that jacket and those pants for work right now. And this is the next best thing I can think of for ya to have me wrapped around ya to feel good when you're tryin' to fall asleep. Willya promise me you'll wear it for me?"

"Well, Adam, your old clothes are a really masculine touchy, feely kind of thing for me. I like to rub my face back and forth on them to feel your big hard cock inside them. And I don't care if that's perverted or weird or not. I don't know if you can really understand that. But sure, you bet I will! Can I have your Superman briefs, too."

"Yep! Sure thing! Ya know, every time I put on those old pants and start to zip up the fly, I think about you. Then I get half-hard and all distracted and horny—like every fuckin' damn time, baby! Whatever gets ya' off works for me. Knowing it does too keeps me all boned-up and juicy for ya. Guess we're both kinda a little bit kinky that way. Who knew, eh?"

"Yeah, who knew?"

"Uhm, uhh, changing the subject here and while I'm thinkin' of it, too, I'm really gonna try to stop calling ya *babe* and *baby* all the time. I've been givin' that a lot of thought. You're growin' up and really, almost an adult now. So Cookie and honey are what I'm gonna try to remember to call ya from now on."

"When you come up to Ottawa next time to spend the weekend with me, would you maybe wear your old clothes? I really do get-off on the feel and smell of your hard cock inside your pants when I get to play with it. It really makes me horny and crazy when you go commando and your big dong is poking out at me and to quote you, *sayin' hello.*"

"Butt-boy, any old damn thing I can do to keep you interested in what's hangin' between my legs works for me. Now let's go to bed 'cause tomorrow is gonna be busy for us both. Nite, honey."

"Nite, Adam."

Several days later and I'm back in Ottawa sitting in Elzbeth's Colour Theory class...

"Oh come on Aaron! We've only got a few weeks left until we have to start our final assignments for the semester! One night out isn't going to make a big difference at this point and I really want to party this evening since it's Friday!" says Alleyn as we head out the front door after enduring yet one more interminably long and painful journey down Carnaby Street with Elzbeth Mountebank.

"God, she is such a nasty bitch, that woman! I handed in that first assignment I had to redo for her weeks ago and she *still* hasn't graded it. I swear her cunty face was as icy as her vagina probably is when I asked her about it."

"Now you're sounding just like me! That's really funny! Now let's dump our things over at my place and we can head out to the LE and then catch a cab over to Sac's on Rue Principale in Hull to drink and dance our asses off until they close after three in the morning."

"I don't suppose it would do any harm to go to the Lord Elgin. Adam will be up later on tonight though. So Sac's will have to wait for another time."

"He must be really something, this Adam of yours. Why don't you just leave him a note and he can join us at the LE when he gets off the bus from Brockville and gets to your place?"

"Uhh, I don't know about that. He's expecting me to meet him at the bus station."

"He'll understand. Now come on! I have to walk Dietrich, and then I'll lend you something of mine to wear with your jeans. We can make a Hollywood grand entrance together through the doors of Pick's Place and watch everyone pick their jaws up off the floor when we get there."

"Alleyn, he's worked all week long at Tonner's behind the pharmacy counter and will have been on the bus for more than two-and-a-half hours coming up here just to spend the weekend with me! I can't just leave him stranded by himself at the station. Would you like it if someone did that to you?"

"Well, you'll never catch me taking a bus anywhere. So I guess we'll never know."

"Alleyn. I'd like to go. But I'm not leaving Adam alone. And I think my own clothes are good enough."

Alleyn stares me up and down from head to toe and finally shrugs and says, "Well, don't say I didn't offer."

"Look, Alleyn. I'd love to see your dog and apartment. Dietrich sounds beautiful and actually, I've seen you walk her up and down Elgin Street. I don't know where you find the time to keep her so well-groomed. Afghan Hounds need at least a daily-brushing. We never have to worry about that with Blackjack at home. He constantly sheds and my dad takes care of that."

"Well, she is a purebred sighthound and my parents help me out with money for a dog-walker and professional groomer for her," he says. "Tell you what. Come on up and you can see my place and meet Dietrich. And I have a really nice red silk shirt I think you really should wear tonight. In fact, I'll even give it to you and you can leave that old one you have on now with me and I'll have it taken care of. How does that sound?"

"Wow! This place is fantastic. Are those real maple inlays and pegs in the oak hardwood floor? And that wood panelling in the front hallway and living room—is that what Lynda Naagy-Birdsong was describing as English Tudor-style, linen-fold panelling? It must be five and a half feet high around the entire perimeter of the room! And the fireplace surround, is that real pink *Breccia* marble?"

"Well of course it's real," Alleyn says, bristling. "But then I couldn't really expect you to know that. When my mother came back with Father from one of their postings abroad a few years ago, she found this place for me. And as for that nineteenth-century, mahogany Biedermeier fall-front secretaire desk and two matching bookcases there, well, she had those brought back from Germany through my Father's diplomatic channels. And I wound up with them because they were a matching suite and the bookcases were too tall for the library in their country house east of Maitland. Oh yes, and that late nineteenth-century, Irish Waterford crystal chandelier with the converted gas jets—another one of Mother's impulse purchases gone horribly wrong. It's all OK here though, I suppose."

"It's incredible. Ohh! I love that William Morris wallpaper in the front entry hall. I recognise the pattern. It's called *Ianthe*, isn't it? Those pale teal, navy blue and blood-red colours are just so beautiful together."

"Uhm, uhh, yes. I'm quite surprised you would actually know that. It's imported from Liberty of London. But my mother brought it back with her when she was there for a fitting for her annual spring and summer wardrobe at Norman Hartnell. He dresses the Royal Family, you know. I wouldn't have anything else but an original Art Nouveau,

William Morris pattern in there. I have a galley-kitchen through here. And I like to sit and look out the window over at the Museum of Nature with a cup of double expresso in the morning. That is of course, after I walk Dietrich and before I head in to class. The mosaic marble tile floor in here is the *same* tile used in the main gallery hall of the Museum. This building was built in the early-twenties. I think they must have used some of the leftover materials from when the Museum was built to finish the interiors of these apartments."

I'm speechless at the richness and elegance of Alleyn's place.

He continues to lead me through his place, describing it all the while.

"There is a separate room with a big diamond-pane, leaded-glass window just past the main salon, or the living room as you would probably call it. Actually, it's more like a double parlour with the columns separating the two spaces and I think that solid wood, sliding rod-pocket doors must have been installed there in those wall-cavities behind them at one point. They would have needed to be more than ten feet tall as the ceilings in this apartment are fourteen feet high. The columns with the fluting going half-way up them are of course, solid oak, as is the panelling, that crown molding, the doors, and casings. And my bedroom is in here."

There is only one piece of artwork in his bedroom. A tiny black-and-white abstract print with a huge white matte and a simple, thin burnished silver frame hanging on the wall.

"That print is beautiful."

"Oh that," he says. "Another one of my mother's mistakes."

Dietrich lounges on a white down duvet with a cream-coloured cashmere throw casually strewn on top of his brass bed as Alleyn leads me into his bedroom. At the head of the bed there are huge, fluffed-up, goose-down pillows that I swear have not one single strand of dog hair on them.

"Where do you actually do your assignments, Alleyn?"

"Oh those. Well, umm, uhh, *Mother* at the Bay lets me use his office there that has a drafting board and work table—sooo much easier for me that way."

"You don't have anywhere to sit down in your living room though. Just that beautiful fireplace and the desk and those bookcases."

"I like to live simply. And less is more. Especially when it's the best." He laughs and then continues with, "But seriously though, I just roll out my nineteenth-century, oriental Caucasian dragon-patterned carpet in the entry hall closet and take the pillows off my bed whenever I want to lounge in there. Mother had that rug shipped to me in a diplomatic pouch from Kirghizia which was Father's last posting abroad before he retired. Strange that they call it a *pouch* at the Ministry of Foreign Affairs. But those things, which can sometimes be as big as a shipping container are never subject to inspection or customs-duty when they come into Canada. I actually do *rather* like that rug. At least my mother didn't screw that up, for once."

Ten minutes later and Alleyn has Dietrich's Tiffany-blue, patent leather collar on her. "I have to take Dietrich out for her walk," he says. Go into my closet and find that red-coloured, raw silk shirt I promised you. It has a Chinese band collar on it. I think it's in a pile along with the other ones on the floor. They're all new and I just haven't had a chance to hang them up yet—*it's all just-sooo-dreadfully-boring*—oh yes, if you need to wash up you'll find fresh, white terrycloth towels in the bathroom. You may even want to use some of that cologne in there, too. It's called Grey Flannel by Geoffrey Beene and it's so much more sophisticated and subtle than that cheap Eau Sauvage crap you seem to like.

"Uhm, well, OK. Thanks."

I can't help but compare my little apartment on Argyle with this amazing place and feel a bit like a poor country hayseed to what Alleyn and his mother have managed to create here for him. And that comment he made about the Eau Sauvage—I just wonder what Adam would have to say about that.

"Yes! I just knew that shirt would look perfect on you," Alleyn says once he returns with Dietrich. "You know, the first time I saw you, you were wearing red. Leave that other old thing of yours here. Just throw it down on the floor in the corner at the foot of the bed and I'll have my housecleaner see to it."

"Uhh, Alleyn, Adam gets in around nine at the Voyageur Colonial station. Do you want to come with me to meet him there?"

"No. Not there. I don't do bus stations… sorry. I'll see you both downstairs in Pick's Place at the LE when you get there."

"OK. Your place is amazing and Dietrich is beautiful… and thanks for the shirt."

"No problem. Later then."

The bus gets in twenty-five minutes late from Brockville. And Adam is the first person off, looking dishevelled and tired.

"Heya, babe! That goddamn fuckin' bus this time. Let me tell ya. All I could smell was the stink of stale piss and disinfectant from the washroom at the back of the bus, and I swear it seemed like everyone back there was smokin' their brains out. And I had to sit in a crusty, stained seat I'm hopin' someone spilled what was just Pepsi or Coke on it. It's times like this I really miss not havin' my wheels. How's your week been, baby?"

"It's been not too bad, except for today. I just got my final assignment from Iona for the semester and it's a big one. And that damned Elzbeth Mountebank, is she ever a fucking bitch. She made this stupid comment during crit time in her class today and said that Connie Caserta, Melora Holt, Yolanda Vargas, Lauren Marcato and I had all failed her class because, according to her attendance records, we'd missed more than three of her classes for the semester. I didn't though! I was just late! The lift-bridge was up one day when I went to cross the Canal because it was letting a sailboat through and I was more than fifteen minutes late for her class. I couldn't do anything except wait for the bridge to go down again to let me cross the Canal. I hate her! The other two times, well, once I was late again because of that stupid Pretoria Bridge. And I woke up with a really bad headache another morning and just didn't want to spread anything I might have had to anyone else. Then Elzbeth comes over and says, "Oh, Aaron, I'll get to you and your crit when I am done with *Jako* here." Honest to God, she spent more than thirty minutes with Jakobe outrageously flirting with him, and then she says she's going to fail me and then is still planning to give me a crit! I fucking hate that God-damned bitch!" I said to her, "Why are you *even bothering* to come over to crit my work since you've just failed me for the semester?! And you know what she *actually* had the nerve to say to me?!" Well, Connie Caserta was listening to all of this and was really pissed off at her, and Elzbeth said, "Well... I didn't actually say I was *going* to fail you, just that I *could* if I wanted to." Adam, I hope her vagina freezes over and she never, ever gets to have sex again—not that anyone would ever want her!"

"Well, you stood up for yourself," Adam says, having taken it all in. "That's good. Maybe that's what she needed—for you to hand it right back to her—to know you weren't gonna let her bully or threaten ya. I have a feeling she might not be so tough on you next semester. If she is, then you just go and report her to the Student Union and let them deal with her. And, uhm, the way you're swearin' there, you're beginnin' to sound like me!"

"I will. Thanks. God, I missed you so much!"

"Aww, me, too, you!"

"Did you bring your work clothes with you in that garment bag?"

"Sure did! You can play with King Kong in my pants when we get back to your place and I'll smother ya with my jacket. Whaddya say to that, ya kinky little fucker?"

"I say let's get out of here and I'll play with King Kong when we get back to my place."

Once back at the apartment and after I've had my fun with King Kong, I roll over on the bed to face Adam. He's just lying there, totally naked—smiling contentedly—his hands clasped together behind his neck. I stretch to lean up to bury my nose in his armpit and say, "You really surprised me when you came out of the bathroom wearing only your pants before. Hmmm... surprise me more often like that, Sasq'." I keep rubbing his hairy chest and he grins, squeezes me tightly and exhales slowly.

A few more minutes of me fondling King Kong and then eventually I say softly to him, " Oh yes, before I forget, I got to see Alleyn Arendsdorff's place on Elgin today. It's spectacular! He gave me a shirt of his and wants us to meet him at the LE for a beer or whatever this evening. Do you want to do that or would you just rather stay at home here? I'll do whatever you like."

"Well, honey, since you mention him more than the others in your class, I think it's time I get a good look at him and meet. I'll be wantin' to get myself cleaned up a bit though to get rid of the stink of cigarette smoke on me from the bus and throw on somethin' sexy so you won't be ashamed of me. Wanna hop in the tub and scrub me up while I play with your little Cookie Monster down there?"

"Hmmm, I have some new soap called Grey Flannel that Alleyn just gave to me.

"Uhm, just get the water hot and I'll letcha' rub me and scrub me and we can head out after that. Not with that Grey Flannel stuff though. We have it in the men's cologne section back at Tonner's. It's waaay too strong on me. I felt like a skanky man-whore when I tried it. I just like my own cologne. Now get outta those clothes and let's play rub a dub, dub, two sexy guys in a tub!"

The Lord Elgin Hotel is a historic landmark in Ottawa. It was built in the early-forties during World War Two and with the exception of the Chateau Laurier Hotel on the other side of the War Cenotaph, is probably the most elegant place in the city to host wedding receptions and important social and cultural events. I remember what Adam said to me about the washrooms there, and how I have to watch myself when I go down into the basement at Pick's Place and in what they call The Library, just off the main lobby on the ground floor.

There is a side door at the corner of Laurier Boulevard and Elgin Street that avoids having to go in to the main lobby where the hotel staff give you cold, judgemental stares if you go in that way.

I was to learn later on that the owners of the hotel were not exactly thrilled with the reputation of Picks Place and The Library being prominent, gay male cruising spots. But ever since the end of World War Two, according to Adam, the hotel was about the only place in the city where men could meet to have a drink and check each other out with the brazen intent of having sex together.

It's probably one of the worst-kept secrets in the city.

"Did ya know, Cookie that Lord Elgin was an Earl back in England and was the governor general of what was then, the province of Canada between 1847 to 1854? This place has been a hangout for gay men ever since the end of the war. Lotsa soldiers comin' back from the war stayed here. And with the Department of National Defence just on the other side of the Canal, and especially when the Union Station still had all the trains comin' right into downtown, its reputation as a hang-out for boned-up, horny guys lookin' to hook up for sex started way back then."

"Was history one of your favorite subjects in school, Adam?"

"Yep, honey, it sure was. Knowing the past can help ya understand the present and help shape the future. This place was just about the only place for men to meet in those days. Back then in the fifties and sixties, the RCMP started to monitor it to uncover government workers they thought were a threat to the security of the country. And they were ruthless when they interviewed suspected gays and lesbians at their headquarters right across from where the Russian Embassy is in Sandy Hill along the Rideau River. Lotsa men and women had their careers destroyed by those fuckin' bastards. They developed something stupid called *The Fruit Machine* they thought was a sure-fire method for uncovering suspected gay men and women. They shoved people into somethin' sorta like a dentist chair when they did too. I was told it was kinda, sorta like a camera/lie-detector type of thing that registered changes in the size of a person's pupils in their eyes and their blood pressure when they were exposed to pictures of naked men for guys and naked women for girls—and then somethin' like electrical shocks and buzzers and loud noises to record their reactions. Really kinda stupid when ya stop to think about it—because of those bastards, some of those poor folks even committed suicide after they were grilled. We're lucky we didn't hafta live in those times. I know that RCMP undercover officers *still* go into Pick's Place though and sit with their newspapers and take pictures of the senior government men who go down there—it's illegal to photograph folks without their permission, but they don't give a damn and don't care—some things never change. Ya just gotta be discreet when you go in there. You never know where you might wind up workin' when ya graduate. And the last thing you need is to have an RCMP file on you if ya ever need to pass a security check for a job or somethin' like that."

"I'm glad you know these things. I always feel safe with you."

"I'll always take care of ya."

"Uhm, uhh, Aaron, before we head down into Pick's Place, let's poke our heads into The Library. It's pretty classy and not like the meat-market you're gonna find when we go down into the basement."

The Library is drop-dead-elegant with beautiful, dark hardwood panelling and has a long 'L'-shaped bar with a brass foot-rail and a heavily-veined, luscious green serpentine slab marble top. The lessons that Lynda has been giving us at the College are starting to make me more and more aware of these things. There are seven or eight older men sitting at the bar drinking scotch, or whatever. I can feel the frank appraisals and blatant stares and interest from them as we survey the space. There are landscape reproductions of *The Group of Seven* Canadian artists and some black-and-white portrait studies of important politicians and celebrities by the famous photographer, Yousuf Karsh in thick, ornate, gold-leaf frames with picture lights illuminating them all around the room. As well, there are embossed, deep-gold velvet, heavily-lined draperies with elegant, sculptured pelmets, jabots, held with elaborate silk-tasseled tiebacks framing the big windows looking out onto the National Arts Centre, Confederation Park and the First Baptist Church at the corner of Laurier and Elgin. The atmosphere is hushed, like what I imagine a posh men's club would be like. And there are cushy chairs in green-and-gold-striped, heavy tapestry fabric, tightly clustered around low, round coffee tables that I'm positive would bang the shins of anyone drunk when trying to get into and out of those over-scaled, Queen Anne mahogany, reproduction wing chairs.

"A little too *fancy* up here for my taste. The downstairs is more my style. But just remember what I told ya about the washrooms here. You'll pass by them on the way down to Pick's Place on the landing where the stairs turn. Don't let appearances up here fool ya into thinkin' this isn't more than just a place where men go to get drunk and pick up other men for sex. And never ever let yourself get caught doin' anything here that you wouldn't want your mom and dad to hear about, OK?"

"I understand. I don't want anyone but you anyway."

"Just remember what I'm telling ya, honey, please. And oh yeah, when we go downstairs and through the doors into Pick's Place, you're gonna get a shock 'cause it's real loud and noisy compared to here. And if you hear guys sayin' numbers out loud, they'll be staring at your hot, little boy-butt there and rating it on a scale of one to ten when they check ya out. And remember, your butt's mine and it's a *ten and a half!*"

"And yours is a *twelve* there."

"Damn fuckin' right it is!"

There are pay phones in the corridor adjacent to the doors into Pick's Place and a couple of guys are standing around them. Another one with a really bad haircut is pretending to talk on the telephone while checking everyone who is coming into and going out of the bar.

"Yep. There's an RCMP cunt right there. I recognise the look with that bad haircut and those shitty clothes," says Adam as he heads into the bar with me behind him.

The sounds of clinking glasses and clattering beer bottles mesh with the high-octane, frenzied volume of lots of men getting drunk and high-pitched laughter filtering out into the corridor as I follow him inside and start to look around.

The place looks like a typical beer hall, like the Manitonna Hotel back in Brock Vegas—just not as dirty or stale-beer-smelling or littered with crushed peanut shells on the floor. It has some class to it. There are banquette benches in antique-brass-studded, bowling-green-coloured leather around the perimeter of the room and captain's chairs facing the banquettes with their backs to the main doors. Between the thick wainscot wood-clad columns supporting the hotel above in the middle of the room are more large round tables and chairs. All around above the banquettes and wainscoting are gold-leaf, framed pictures. But these ones are illustrations of what I think must be Grenadier British soldiers in full-dress with bayonets and rifles, posing to show off their military uniforms to reinforce the hotel's history and image. The noise is distracting because it seems like everyone is talking at once and staring continuously at the doors into the bar to see who's coming and going and what they're wearing and how old they are and whether they warrant a butt-rating when they go to sit down.

Seven-and-a-half, I hear when I start to head over to where Alleyn is sitting along the wall with a couple of people I don't know. "No, no, no! That's only a *seven*, if I ever saw one," says one guy to his friend beside him as Adam and I brush past. Adam gives them both a dirty look and then puts his arm possessively on my shoulder and whispers, "Aaron, your butt's a ten to me and fuck those two nasty old queens. They're just jealous 'cause you're younger than they are. Now, let's join your classmate over there and you can introduce me."

By the time Adam and I make it up to Alleyn's table, I can see both Adam and Alleyn staring uneasily at each other. At last, Alleyn breaks the tense silence by saying, "Well, I see you finally made it out tonight. Nice red shirt you've got on there! I had to fight with a couple of mean bitches, but I managed to hold onto these two chairs for you. Unfortunately, you won't be able to face the doors to check out anyone coming in or leaving. That's the best I could do, since it is a Friday and the place is packed with sexy, yummy guys tonight." With that, Alleyn brazenly checks Adam out from head to toe, laughs derisively, shakes his head, and starts to talk with his friends on either side of him.

"Uhm, Alleyn, this is Adam who I've been telling you about all semester."

Alleyn's eyes open wide in surprised amusement and then he says, *"Adam*, is it? Hmmm, you're sure about that? You look more like a *Paul* to me." And then he laughs again. " Sooo, *Adam*, you're the guy who works as a sales clerk back in Brockville who wears *Eau Sauvage*. You're *older* than I thought you'd be."

Immediately, one the guys sitting beside Alleyn covers his mouth with his hand to stifle a snicker.

I can see Adam is embarrassed and is clearly uncomfortable. He's just glaring at Alleyn with a threatening expression on his face and is dead silent.

"Uhh, uhm, yeahhh, right. Nice meetin' ya too there, uhm, Alleyn," Adam says with a thinly-concealed grimace, his unblinking eyes boring into him.

"And *there's* that *Brock Vegas* accent I was telling you guys about when I go down to spend those interminably long, boring weekends with Mother and Father!"

"How is your mother, Alleyn? Is she still buying up all the antique stores in Europe and having everything shipped back for their house in the country?" says the guy on the other side of Alleyn.

"Nooo, Jeremey. Father has her on a strict budget now. And she can only buy what he approves of—for antiques and furniture, that is—for hers and my clothes, well, we can still spend as much as we like on those.

He likes it when we look properly groomed. He says it reflects well on him and in the circles he travels… well, you know… *appearances are just so important.*"

Once again, he gives Adam a head to toe appraisal, smirks, shakes his head and then says to me, "Aaron, we're just about to head over to Sac's in Hull. It's so much more chic and lots more fun than this stale old place. We only come here to get a head-start on drinking and usually just cab it over to Hull from here after eleven-thirty when they crank up the dance music and we can dance and party until three. Sure you don't want to come with us? Ohh, yes. And you too, of course, uhh, uhm, Adam, was it? Did I get the name right… this time?"

Adam stares back at him with a murderous expression on his face and is deadly silent.

"No thanks," I tell Alleyn. "Maybe some time again. This weekend is Adam's and mine. And I haven't seen him for a couple of weeks."

"Well, whatever. We'll see you around then. G'bye."

Alleyn and his friends get up to leave, generating a cloyingly sweet, toxic and overpowering cloud of overly-applied Geoffrey Beene as they grab their coats and head for the doors. Alleyn looks back to see how many guys are looking at him leaving and then gives Adam a sardonic look before turning and heading out.

"So, that's the guy you've been sittin' beside in class, eh?" says Adam as he frowns and watches the doors as they swing shut.

"Uhm, yeah, that's him. He's pretty good-looking, don't you think?"

Adam ignores my question and says, "Let's finish our drinks and decide what to do after that. OK, Cookie?"

"Uhm, sure, ok, Adam." Just then, one of the waiters walks past us and dramatically places a bottle of beer with a burning birthday candle in it on a table in front of an older guy sitting all by himself a few chairs away. "What's with the candle in the bottle?" I ask Adam as he bends around to grab his wallet out of his jacket.

"Uhh, uhm, well, it must be that guy's birthday. The waiters here do that when they know someone who's havin' a birthday. Kinda sad actually, when ya really think about it—stuck sittin' in a gay bar all by yourself on your birthday—kinda, hafta admit, it sorta makes ya stop and think. Some of these guys are really lonely—they've got like, no one—no family for support to be there for 'em and are just plain lookin' for some friends and not only just for sex. Sometimes, it's the friends we *choose* who turn out to become our real families in life. You and me are lucky that way, Aaron. Me, with my mom, and you, with your mom and dad. Let's say we wish him a happy birthday when we get up to leave, OK, Cookie-Butt?"

"You're really something at times, Sasq' man. You have a good heart and are a really nice guy." Adam puts his arm around my shoulder and gives me a little squeeze while blushing deeply.

Just then that same waiter passes us from that guy's table. Adam has a huge smile on his face, waves and then gestures to him, "Wow! Heya, John! Good to see ya, man! Could I get a Molson Canadian and a dark rum and Coke for my friend here, please?"

Adam! We haven't seen you in here in a long time! Not since the police raids on the Club Baths at 1069 Wellington last year. So this is your new friend, is he? Nice to meet you, young man."

"His name's Aaron. You'll take care of him when he comes in here, will ya please?"

"Of course! For you, anything!" So good to see you back in Ottawa. And with someone, too!" At that point, John heads over to the back of the bar to fetch a beer and dark rum and Coke for us.

"John and André over there have been here like, forever," Adam says. "John must be almost seventy now and he's been servin' up drinks here ever since the hotel first opened-up. He's straight and married with great-grandchildren. He's a really decent guy. He always keeps his eye on us and makes sure we stay outta trouble with the local cops and the RCMP. And André, well, he's one hot-lookin' man. I've met his lover and I'm thinkin' André must have been workin' here now for at least ten years. He's pretty tough and has seen lotsa things in this bar over that time and can bounce anyone outta here if they get rowdy or give anyone trouble or too much attitude. They're good guys to have in your pocket, if you know what I'm saying."

"Speaking about pockets, I was looking at the other guys in here and you know something? Your fuzzy, sexy man-butt is a definite fifteen, compared with most of what I see in here."

"Aww, Cookie! That's real sweet of you to say. I don't think your friend Alleyn would agree, but he sure as Hell won't be seein' mine naked anytime soon, so I don't give a fuck whether he does or not. Uhm, after this, wouldya like to maybe head on back to your place and stop to have somethin' to eat at that twenty-four hour delicatessen place before we go past the Museum of Nature? Maybe we could curl up together and watch television or somethin'. It's been a really long day for me and I'm kinda tired."

"Oh God, yes. For sure."

As we are leaving, Adam walks over to where John and André are standing, just as I'm heading out the double doors. I pause there to wait for him.

"Heya, guys!" says Adam to both André and John.

"Adam! *Salut! Bonjour, mon ami!* Good to see you, man! Is that you're new friend? Aaron, right? Was that his name, John?" says André, as he turns to John, and then back to face Adam.

"Yep! He sure is!"

He's a *hottie*—a real nice piece of *chicken* for sure. If I didn't have *mon chum right* now, I'd be jealous!"

"Aww, thanks André. He's pretty mature for his age though just so ya' know, and not just some dumb twink. Uhm, guys, wouldya maybe keep an eye out for him whenever he comes in here to make sure he stays outta trouble? He's just about to turn twenty soon. And I'd really appreciate it if you kinda were as good to him as you both were to me when I first started comin' in here. Wouldya do that for me please?"

John pipes up then and says to Adam, "He reminds me of one of my grandsons. Don't you worry, we'll take good care of him. Rest assured of that."

"I can always count on you two. He's real special to me and it means a lot to know someone has his back when he's up here in College."

"Esti! Mon Dieu! Never mind his back there! I heard a couple of guys over there in the corner who were giving his butt a *ten* when he went out the doors just now!" says André, then laughs at Adam's shocked and overprotective reaction.

"Well, that cute, little boy-butt's all mine André! So hands off there, *mon ami!*"

André chuckles and says, "You've got no competition from me, judging from the way he's looking back at you from the doors right now."

"Oops! Gotta go! Like, right now! G'nite guys!"

Once outside, Adam turns to me and says, "Are ya cold there, babe? Wouldya maybe like my bomber jacket around your shoulders 'til we get to the deli?"

"Gee, you know, I kinda miss you not calling me babe and baby anymore. Would you maybe do that for me more when we're together, just the two us, maybe like every now and then, like you just did now?"

"Anything that makes ya happy, baby, anything at all."

Once back at my apartment, Adam flops down on my bed and says, "That deli place was sure as hell fuckin' packed. I'm gonna make sure we go over to the IGA on Isabella 'cause you just can't be eatin' out all the time. You're gonna turn into one big cheeseburger if I don't start gettin' after ya about what you're eatin'. We're gonna go do that together first thing in the morning. I'll load ya up with everything I think you should have in your fridge there to keep ya healthy and you can push the grocery basket around behind me. You sure as hell have enough practice workin' my *big basket!* Now come on and let's get those clothes offa ya 'cause I wanna see if you've put on a couple of pounds at least before my dong takes over and finds its way up into your hot little boy-butt there. C'mon, let's snuggle and my stick-shift can practice some long-division and maybe some multiplication scales on ya before we fall asleep. OK, Cookie— eh, hmmm, babe?"

"Hmmm, I need a pet name for you. Wookie and Chewbacca just sound really kinda dumb and childish. Can I call you Sasquatch, or just Sasq' for short when it's just you and me together?"

"Works for me there. My moustache and beard that ya conned me into growin' and my hairy chest you're always tellin' me gets ya hot and horny, and King Kong are just fine with that. Now, baby, let's get naked and review what we learned about sixty-nine in Chapter Fourteen of your *Joy of Gay Sex* book once again. Whaddya say to that?"

"I'm thinking I'm needing lots of practice with that one, Sasq' -man until I get the hang of it."

"It's not supposed to be hangin' when ya do that! Here, let me review that chapter with ya right now."

"Can I rim your sexy, fuzzy man-ass?"

"Oh Jeezus fuck, Cookie! Just do whatever the fuckin' hell you want to me! I'll be smilin' in my sleep with my dong stuffed up inside ya 'til we fall asleep soon enough anyway.

A few days later and Adam is back in Brockville. The phone rings in his apartment.

"Hullo?"

"Hi, is this Adam Blanchard?"

"Uhm, yeah, who's this. Who's callin'?"

"Hi Adam! I'm Cala Cuthbertson, a friend of Aaron's."

"Well, hi there, Cala. I remember Aaron talkin' all about you. I think I went to high school with your older sister, Cora-Leanne. She was just starting at BCI. And I was in grade eleven or twelve back then."

"That's right, Adam. She remembers you and said to say hi when I called."

"How is Cora-Leanne? Is she still workin' up at Black and Decker? Is she married yet? I haven't seen her in like, forever. Is she doin' OK? What can I do for you Cala?"

"Well, uhm, yes. She's still working shifts up at Black and Decker on the power drill and electric toaster assembly lines there. And she's still at home with Dad and me. Mom died last year when she had her last bad stroke. And my other sister Corinne is up in Kingston working as a prison guard at the women's correctional facility. She lives with her friend, Tina-Louise. And no, Cora-Leanne's still single. She's just got herself a new puppy, a little miniature Poodle she's named Melissa Etheridge— uhm, uhh… I mean *Melissa* for short. I don't think she's gonna get married anytime soon, Adam. Corinne neither, for that matter."

"I was real sorry to hear about your mom, Cala. Aaron told me you were the one taking care of her there at home after she had her first bad stroke a few years ago. That musta been really tough for ya. Well, you be sure and say hi to Cora-Leanne from me and tell her to pop into Tonner's sometime real soon to get caught up. I remember her from BCI and she was always real nice to me when I was there with her. And Aaron tells me you were nice to him too before ya, well… before ya had to drop out."

"It's OK. You can say it. There aren't any secrets in this *Peyton Place* of a town. Yes, I got myself pregnant when I was fifteen. You know, Adam, Aaron was one of the few people who bothered to speak with and be friendly to me when word leaked out and I started to show. I decided to give the baby up for adoption and then got my high school through correspondence courses and work now at the Sub Shop on King Street West."

"Oh, is that you in there in the evenings? You're pretty! I come in there once in a while. I didn't know you were Cora-Leanne's younger sister or I sure woulda said hi to ya. Have you heard anything from Adam? Is there somethin' wrong? Did he call ya about something? What can I do for ya?"

"Well, uhh, you and Aaron have been seeing a lot of each other, I know. And he's sorta occupied now with you and with school and all. He and I used to go up to the Skyline and the 401 Inn with Rob Galanos and Wendy Yaegar a lot before he met you in the summer. Not that I'm jealous or anything like that, but he's just been so busy with you these past few months and then with him moving up to Ottawa and going back to school. Anyway, you know his birthday is coming up on December 17th when he's back in Brockville on Christmas Break. You *do* know that's his birthday, right, don't you, Adam?"

"I sure do. I was plannin' on taking him out to the Town Haus Restaurant for dinner that night. I need to fatten him up a bit with some Beef Stroganoff and Spätzle! Wouldya maybe like to join him and me for dinner, and maybe you could give Rob Galanos a call and ask him if he'd like to come along, too? I think Aaron would be real surprised and happy if you both could come to help him and me celebrate his birthday. He's been real busy with his studies at Algonquin. It'll be a good chance for you and Rob to connect and get to spend some time with him. Whaddya think?"

"I can see why Aaron likes you. I'd like that a lot. And I know Rob has been missing him up at the shopping centre. I just met a new guy named Charlie Rieder. I'd like to bring him along to get to meet you guys, if that's OK. Charlie and I are going move out west to Prince Rupert in BC in the spring, and I really want to introduce him to Aaron before we go. I'll give Rob a call and get back to you to let you know if he can come, too. Thanks, Adam. We both miss him so much. Brockville just isn't the same without him, you know."

"Hell, Cala! Ya don't need to tell me that! Let me know and I'll make the reservation. And if you're talkin' to Aaron, let me tell him about dinner with you and Rob. I know he'll be happy and excited to see you all over the Holidays. And I'd kinda like to get to know you, too. He's talked about you a lot to me and I know it hasn't been easy for ya. And he's had his own problems in this city growin' up… just like you and me."

Adam hangs up the phone in his kitchen and starts to think and reflect.

Now she's a nice person who knows what real life's all about 'cause she's hadta' live it and survive it. My kinda person for sure. Not like that cheap fuckin' cum-slut, man-whore, Alleyn Arendsdorff and his snotty and creepy crackhead friends up in Ottawa. We're both gonna needta' hafta make some time for her and Rob Galanos. Jeezus, I'm sure as hell glad she called me. Actually, I'll give Rob Galanos a call myself and invite him. What the hell! No time like the present to meet one of the other decent gay guys Aaron knew in Brockville, before I came into the picture and got into his sexy, tight fittin' jeans.

6   November / December

October comes and goes in fast motion after Canadian Thanksgiving with Mom and Dad, and with Adam's birthday. The two major November assignments that take us up to the beginning of December and then to the end of the first-term-semester are from Iona Ouspenskaya in Interior Design One and Evan Copland in Building Construction.

They are intimidating with respect to the amount of work they require. I'm beginning to totally freak out.

Evan's assignment is interesting. We are to take what he taught us in class regarding what many Architects and Interior Designers follow when trying to develop perfect proportions for their creative work and apply what's called the *Fibonacci Sequence* to a scale model built from balsawood.

The *Fibonacci Sequence* is essentially a series of proportionate numbers in which each number is the sum of the two preceding numbers. For example: 1, 1, 2, 3, 5, 8, 13, and so on. Scale and proportion are important elements in architecture and design, and Evan is absolutely determined for us to understand these principles as we advance in the programme.

I had an idea about building a stud-frame, little house model based on the ratio of three, five, and eight and had discussed my ideas with him during crit times. Having heard his suggestions and listening carefully to what he was hoping to see in the final model, I was now on my own to build the damned thing to a scale of one inch equal to one foot.

Iona's assignment is equally demanding. It involves not only construction of a scale model constructed with Bainbridge board—seems like this is Iona's favourite material—easier to knock off a table with her wooden rod—we also have to do what was described as a programming study and design concept narrative booklet for what we were to hand in for fifty percent of our grade for that first semester. The assignment is to design and build a scale model of a student home-workspace that we could theoretically work in as Interior Designers.

So now we're going from abstract-theory into what most of us understand real Interior Design to be about—namely, *the design of real space for real people.* The programming study mandates that we measure every piece of equipment and material we would employ in the real world as Interior Designers for our work such as custom storage and cabinetry/shelving/filing, drafting boards, furniture like our drafting stools, and whatever else we think we would need in order to create an efficient and practical environment in which to work.

All the abstract theory and concepts we've been taught up to that point in her class with respect to colour, line, shape, texture, space, form, harmony and balance are to be incorporated to signify our understanding of the course. This is a daunting assignment.

Jeezus fuck… to quote what Adam always says!

I'm home in the apartment, reading the latest copy of Architectural Digest I picked up earlier in the week from Mags and Fags cigarette/magazine shop on the Market when the phone rings.

"Hullo."

"Heya, butt-boy, it's Adam. Howzit goin' up there, baby?"

"Hiya, Adam!"

"Figured I'd better call to letcha know I'll be hoppin' the bus up on Friday and should be up there around nine. How are ya makin' out with those scale-models you're workin' on?"

"Ohh, God! If I have to measure one more piece of Bainbridge board or sheet of drafting paper, or pen, or pencil, or marker, or piece of balsawood, I'm going to kill myself! She's got us measuring our drafting boards and stools, too. Next thing you know she'll be asking us to measure our asses to make sure they fit in the stools in the model!"

"I can sure help ya with that one. I already know it's a perfect fit for my big King Kong dong—the one that I'm playin' with right now!" Adam chuckles suggestively on the other end of the phone line. "Now seriously, babe, is there anything I can help ya with when I'm there, besides measuring your cute, tight little ass?"

"Well, uhh, you do know how to type, don't you?"

"Sure as hell do! I was pretty good in business-and-commerce classes back in high school. Why? Do ya need me to type somethin' up for you there?"

"Oh, God, yes! I have to take all of the measurements and design-concept information and put it all into a programming booklet, along with the scale-model when I submit it. Would you maybe help me with that? I'd be so grateful if you would."

"So no partying this weekend then? We get straight down to work and no foolin' around?" he asks me.

"Well, maybe some party-time when you measure my butt and after we turn the lights out. Does that work for you, Sasq'?"

"Mmmm, sure does! Oh yeah, and those black-and-white pictures I took for ya for that booklet for *Lynda bird-brain,* they turned out pretty good here. Maybe I can help ya trim them up and put them into that assignment you have to hand in for her History of Architecture course for the end of November. Ya know, you're gonna have to put me on the payroll if this keeps up for next semester!"

"Stop calling her *bird-brain*! I almost called her that myself last week because of you. And as for payment, just put it on my account and take it out in trade, Sasq' man!"

"I like those terms and I'll take the job!" he says and then gives me one of his dirty and suggestive laughs.

"Oh, yes! Adam, while I'm thinking of it, I got some groceries and some wine from the LCBO and I'll have dinner ready for you when you get up here. My cooking's getting a little better now. At least the last time I didn't have my upstairs neighbor here coming down and banging on my door because they thought I'd started a fire on my stove! Jeez, that was embarrassing."

"Just dontcha gimme food poisoning with whatever ya decide to make there and we'll be fine, Cookie-Boy."

"Maybe I'd better just make us some bacon and eggs."

"Over-easy then. And nooo, I wasn't referring to you either."

It's one in the morning, a few hours later, Alleyn Arendsdorff and his friends are dancing frenetically to the throb of their own personal highs at Sac's in Hull, on the Quebec side of the river. The flashing strobe lights and pulsing beat of "Relight My Fire" by Dan Hartman cranks up, just as "Love Machine" by The Miracles ends.

The dance floor is packed with beautiful, sweaty bodies in constant movement. Machines are blowing liquid nitrogen smoke into the air and it's suddenly *Saturday Night Fever* every night of the week for Alleyn and his ever-present amber bottle of poppers. "Here Jeremey, sniff some *Rush* and let's keep dancing!" he yells to make himself heard above the loud, pounding, vibrating speakers surrounding the stainless steel dance floor.

The bottle of isobutyl nitrate gets passed around to four or five others. And then the light-headedness and heart-racing, body-quivering dance moves take over while everything else but the music and the beat is forgotten.

Right beside Alleyn and Jeremey is this outrageous, three-hundred pound queen in a pair of glittery disco, high platform-sole running shoes with Seven-Up soft drink logos on them. He's wearing a match-ing green silk kimono jacket, huge cats-eye, dark-lense sunglasses that look like something Grace Jones would wear and a pair of denim cut-off shorts held up with suspenders that have battery-powered, little blinking-lights on them flashing in rhythm to the music. The shorts are cut so high up to his crotch that unfortunately, very little is left to the imagination. In each hand are oriental fans which he uses to hit other dancers with if he thinks they're cute. And when he does, he screams and then yells he wants to fuck them right then and there on the dance floor. "You go, *gurrrl*, shake it, *Mother!*" shouts Alleyn to his creative display director and boss from the Hudson's Bay Company store on Rideau Street.

The interior of Sac's on rue Principale is like something out of New York City or possibly the hot gay bar scene in Toronto, Vancouver or Montreal. It's the closest thing to Studio 54 one would ever expect to find in staid, boring, ultra-conservative, Federal Government Ottawa. Two tall, gorgeous, *head-to-toe-leather-clad* doormen command the front door controlling the black velvet rope they only open for the best-looking and coolest-dressed. One is white and the other black— ebony and ivory. Both are the sexiest-looking males you could possibly have wet-dreams about.

Once inside, there are three bars surrounding the huge dance floor. The entire club is painted with high-gloss, black enamel paint and the floors are gleaming, highly-polished black linoleum, so the sense of space seems to disappear and go on forever inside. Recessed pot lights are set on low dimmers in the ceiling, and they look like stars twinkling in a shiny, black midnight sky. The tops of the bars are stainless steel like the dance floor. Some people sit at the bars on black leather and chrome stools while most of the horny gay guys cruising each other stand at high tables on a raised platform to overlook the dance floor and pose like frigid Grecian statues, hoping someone will come up to them and beg them to dance or go have sex with them in the washroom stalls or out behind the club.

The strobe lights are blinding. Commanding the entire bar is a DJ booth that looks like a NASA space capsule about to re-enter earth's atmosphere.

One of the local television sports celebrities and on rare occasions, the station's replacement weather-man, Dexter von Kellner is sitting at the first bar discreetly hidden away to the right, and just past the coat-check where one enters the big, main dance floor space. He's got his back to the entrance and is trying to be incognito. It isn't really working. He has two very young, bitchy-looking, skinny French Canadian twinks sitting on each side of him—bilingual bookends. His reputation as a *chicken hawk* for seducing twinks is legendary. A couple of years earlier, he was arrested and charged for drunk-driving on the highway 417 Queensway after one of his live, on-the-scene broadcasts. He now has a personal driver to take him over to Sac's when his eleven o'clock, nationally-syndicated nightly sportscasts finish each night. The driver is down the bar from him wearing a chauffeur's cap, black suit and shirt, looking very straight, extremely uncomfortable, seated all by himself while nursing a Diet Pepsi.

"Hey Dex!" says Alleyn, as he, Jeremey and *Mother* pass him by on their way back to the raised platform where the rest of his friends pose like constipated swans in tight leather pants and a rainbow array of very expensive designer name silk shirts with Chinese-style band collars.

"How are you this evening, Alleyn? Did you get that stuff I asked you to get for me?" Dex says to him.

"Oh yeah! Here it is, Dex. It came in a diplomatic pouch from an embassy friend of my mother's in Uzbekistan the other day wrapped in some drapery fabric. Nooo, not *you, Mother!* My other mother," he says as he turns and laughs at his boss from The Bay.

Two plastic bags of cocaine are surreptitiously handed off to Dex. And then Alleyn and his entourage move on.

"I'll be in tomorrow to help you work on my assignments from school," he says to *Mother.*

"I'll need more of what you just gave to Dex, then."

"No problem. I have more back at my place and will bring it for you tomorrow. Oh! Let's head back to the dance floor! I absolutely love this song!"

Ten minutes later and back once again from the dance floor, Alleyn returns to his friends posing up on the podium, *Mother* then asks him in a lisping, high-pitched tone of voice, "Sooo, when do we get to meet this classmate of yours you've been bragging to us you're planning on seducing? And just exactly when are you going to bring the little piece of twink candy over to Sac's to receive my approval and blessing?"

"When I figure out a way to get rid that damned, fucking Brockville jerk of his that I sucked-off when I was stoned out-of-my-mind last year."

It's Friday and the weekend finally arrives—Adam and I are back from the bus station, and starting to chill-out together in my apartment. He wraps his arm around my shoulder, having shed his bomber jacket and backpack earlier and says, "We make a good team, Aaron. I'll take these notes and measurements ya scribbled back home with me and type 'em up for ya, no problem!" He continues to look over all the pages spread out on my old pine desk beside the fireplace. "And tomorrow, we'll clean up some of this damn mess around here and spread out those pictures I brought and start to lay 'em out for that other assignment ya have to have ready in a week's time for the end of November for Lynda *bird-lady* there."

"I wish you'd stop calling her *bird-lady*! I have to admit though, she does sort of remind me of that Tippi Hedren actress out of Alfred Hitchcock's movie *The Birds*. And that really doesn't help the situation at all, you know!"

He chuckles and says, "OK, OK, OK, baby, no problem. By the way, how's that Alleyn guy doin' with his assignments? Is he gonna stick with the programme after this semester? Or do ya know yet?"

"I don't really know. He seems to get all his stuff in on-time. And for the most part he's getting fairly consistent marks from the profs. I don't know how he's managing it though, because he tells me he is still going in to The Bay after-hours to help with that *Mother* person there and he hasn't missed any classes either. He always seems wired-up somehow though. And I'm not talking about the same *wire* that Iona seems to get-off on talking about when it comes to me. Sometimes I wonder if he gets any sleep at all."

"Hmmm, has he asked you to go out partying with him and his friends lately?"

"Well, yes, almost every night. He's beginning to really piss me off to be honest about it. I suppose I'll just have to say yes one of these times to get him off my back, I guess.."

"Tell ya what. Hows about you and me head on over to Sac's tomorrow after we finish with your assignment stuff to check the place out? A friend of mine from Merrickville, Conor Rekford is one of the doormen there. We went to high school together. Him and me, well, we haven't talked in a long time. He used to work up at Black and Decker, and then decided to get the hell outta Brock Vegas for a year to maybe find out what gay life was all about. He got a job at Sac's and has been up here now for about six or seven months. His dad's been real sick and I kinda, sorta, wanna talk to him to find out how he's doin' now. Whaddya say? Is it a date then?"

"Well, if you really want to go, then sure, let's do it. But not until I get to suck on that big cock of yours and maybe show you something new of mine down there before we head out tomorrow!"

"Hmmm, I'm *real* intrigued now. Just whatcha hidin' down there from me?"

"You'll just have to wait and see, mister commando."

Adam is laughing while trying to pull my jeans down and says. "I love you, my sexy, little butt-boy!"

"Now, what did you manage to make for me for dinner? And where's that wine ya promised? I'm hungry and hadta skip dinner to make it over to the bus stop on time to catch the bus up here. And it better not be just bacon and eggs either!"

The dishes, glasses and cutlery are already spread out on the carpet in front of the fireplace. Five minutes later and orange and blue taper candles are lit and flickering. The colourful aqua, damask-pattern cloth napkins I scammed from my mom's linen-closet are in place as I head into my tiny kitchen and pull a McCain's frozen pepperoni pizza out of the oven.

"Thought you said you were gonna *make* and *cook* me somethin' for dinner," he says as I put the cardboard plate down and start to carve up slices.

"Well, I managed to turn the stove on and get the temperature right. So that's like cooking, hmmmm... izzzn't it?"

"C'mere, baby. I wanna measure your tight little butt right now to make sure ya haven't lost any more weight. Let me get my tool out and we'll see if my eight-inch-measuring-tape can tell if you're healthy or not."

"Never you mind. You can have your cookie for dessert later... if you behave yourself. Now, kiss me and then eat what I made for you."

"Oh yeah, speakin' of food there, when you're home on Christmas Break, am gonna take you someplace real special for your birthday. I have a big surprise waiting for ya—besides the one hidin' in my good pants—which by the way, kinda miss ya these days. They're real lonely all by themselves and told me they're gonna hafta go back *into the closet*. They keep sayin' to me they won't be *coming-out* again 'til you're back in town! Not to worry though. They're pretty *well-hung* in there."

"Very funny, very funny. Hah, hah, hah." Meanwhile, I think, *just how lame and corny can this guy be at times? Jeez...*

"Yeahhh! I kinda thought so, too," he says with a smug grin on his face as he bends over to bite my lip and gently kiss me.

"My old jacket said to say hi to ya as well. It misses ya almost as much as I do, butt-boy."

"It's just jealous of your shirt. It'll have to get used to the fact that I have more than just one love-interest now that I sleep with. I wear it every night. And it still has that sexy *Adam Blanchard scent,* too. You know, I don't think I'd make it through a whole night without it to help me get to sleep."

It's late Saturday morning. Adam shakes me awake with a hot cup of strong black coffee in his hand and says, "Let's crank-up the music in here and start to get into these black-and-white pictures. Where's your X-Acto knives and that expensive piece of linoleum cutting-board surface ya got ripped-off on from Wallack's?"

He heads over to my stereo and pulls out Diana Ross. Suddenly, "Love Hangover" starts to play and we make some room to start working on Lynda Naagy-Birdsong's History of Architecture assignment.

"These pictures are perfect! I'm glad you insisted we do them up on glossy print paper. The black-and-white contrast in them is incredible. You should be a professional photographer, Sasq' man!"

"Thanks. You told me what you wanted and how to frame them in each composition though. So you take credit here too—it's a group effort. But no one ever needs to know that. I just like helpin' ya."

Diana Ross continues to sing in the background.

Three-and-a-half hours and three more cups of instant black coffee later and all the pictures have been cropped and cut precisely and laid-out on twelve pages of expensive, white, matte-finish linen paper, ready for gluing and binding together. Between each page is a sheer white sheet of very thin, translucent rice paper that is like organza, intended to separate each page. The whole booklet will look extremely elegant once it's all done and ready to be handed in.

"Uhm, Adam, do you know what *Letraset* is?" I say to him as he carefully finishes up with gluing each photo down onto the linen pages the way we both decided they should be laid-out.

"Uhh, uhm, no, honey. What's that?"

"Well, it's kind of like a dry-transfer kind of typeface lettering you rub onto paper or Bainbridge board with a burnishing tool. Do you think you might want to help me by trying to do that with the lettering and numbers having to go on each page?"

"Sounds like fun. Let me try it and see what ya think.

"God, Adam! That looks amazing! Your spacing between the letters is really good. I'm glad you're here to help me. Are you still sure you want to go out later? I'm good if you just want to stay home with me here and snuggle and watch TV or something."

"Nope! We're goin', Aaron. I wanna see Conor and get caught up with him. His dad had a heart attack last year. And I wanna get another good look at that creepy Alleyn friend of yours."

"I don't really think of him as a friend."

"OK, good... errr, uhm, I mean, well, whatever, OK."

Later that evening and Adam says, "One great thing about this apartment is that ya never seem to run outta hot water for that big bathtub of yours." I'm gonna put some bubble-bath I brought up from Tonner's in it now and whaddya say we hop in there together before headin' on out to Sac's?"

"Yeah I'd like that. My back hurts from bending over to finish off all those pages for Lynda's booklet. It sure looks good though. Thanks again for all your help on it. If I get an 'A' on it, you can have a look ahead into Chapter Fifteen of the *Joy of Gay Sex* and I'll do anything from Chapters One to Fifteen you want me to do on you? Deal?"

"Fantastic deal there! He says and then laughs that indecent, dirty laugh I've come to love about him, along with everything else—not the least of which is that hard, fuzzy, shapely man-ass I catch sight of as he heads buck-naked into my bathroom and bends over the tub to pour in some bubble bath and test the temperature of the water.

"Jeezus fuck! Look at the fuckin' line-up tryin' to get into the place!" says Adam as we pull up in a Blue Line taxi right in front of Sac's at 117, Promenade du Portage in Hull.

There are at least seventy-five people in line waiting to pass inspection to gain entrance into the club. My classmate, Alleyn, along with his friends Jeremey and *Mother* are far back in the line-up looking very unimpressed that they have to wait in line along with everyone else.

Then suddenly, Adam spots his friend Conor at the front door.

"Hey! There's Conor, right by the front door there with that really tall, black guy beside him. I'll get us in here in no time. You just wait here and I'll be right back."

"Heya, Conor! How are ya, buddy! It's been waaay too long! How are your folks back down on the farm in Merrickville? Is your dad doin' better, I hope, since his heart attack? You never come into Tonner's to see me when you're back in town anymore. I've missed ya! Say, I really wanna talk to ya when you get a few free moments. Any chance you can get us past the line-up here? I've got my new boyfriend from Brockville here with me and I wanna show him the club. Hey! Aaron, c'mon over and meet Conor. Conor, this is my boyfriend, Aaron. Aaron Richard Christie. You might know his mom and dad from the Hospital. They're over on Bethune Street. He's all mine though, so dontcha get any smart ideas there, bud!"

Conor's mouth is agape when I head over toward and Adam to say hello. "You fuckin' lucky guy, Adam. How come I never got to meet cute guys like this when I was working at Black and Decker and living back in Merrickville?" he says, reaching out to give me a friendly hug. "I'd have never moved up here if I'd found someone as cute as you back there, let me tell ya!"

I promptly turn ten shades of red. Adam grabs me and laughs and gives me a big kiss on my cheek and says, "I think Conor kinda likes ya." And then he smiles back at Conor, who is beaming.

Then Conor says, "Jeezus, Adam, I'm really glad to see you with someone. It's about fuckin' time you met someone and settled down."

"I hear ya, Conor."

The black velvet rope gets opened up for us with a flourish, and people in the line-up groan and shoot us dirty looks. Conor introduces us to his black doorman counterpart, who's named Jean-Louis-Pierre-Francois and is from Montreal, originally from Port-au-Prince, Haiti. I swear they both must be more than six-and-a-half-feet tall, the two of them. And both are magnificent, with their tight leather pants, harnesses, military-flight leather-bomber-jackets, four-inch platform-heel, black leather, lace-up, mid-calf boots, and bare, chiselled, hairless, burnished torsos, exhibiting perfectly-toned six-packs.

"Thanks, Conor. Please, man, willya come and find me when you're on break. I wanna catch up on what's been happenin' with ya' and your folks, OK?"

"Sure thing, Adam. I will for sure."

"Ohh! And by the way there, Conor, I wouldn't be showin' up back in Brockville on King Street in that get-up unless you're wearin' a cock ring and holdin' handcuffs and a whip in your hand," he says as he gives his friend a big hug and lets out with a huge laugh.

"Oh! Fuck off! My nipples are turning to ice in this cold weather, ya bastard! You're just jealous because I'm so fucking hot and you're not!" Conor says while laughing at Adam.

"Want me to tweak 'em to see if they crack and break off? You say somethin' like that in front of Aaron and I'll fuckin' rip your tiny, shriveled up, little nut sack off! Remember, man—you and I hadta shower together when we were back in gym class at Brockville Collegiate. I know what you're packin' down there. You just better hope it's a *grower* man and keep it outta cold water!" Adam is killing himself, howling with laughter and dodges away quickly while Conor tries to grab onto his arm. They're both laughing their heads off while I'm standing alone and waiting for Adam to join me at the front door into the club.

"He's waiting for you and looks kinda lost there, Adam. Damn, he's cute! Now get inside there with him before *Dex you-know-who* gets a good look at him and decides to be Colonel Sanders looking for a *take-out-chicken-dinner* tonight! Enjoy yourselves!"

"Dark rum and Coke?" asks Adam as he steers me over to the bar on the left once we leave the coat-check and head into the club. "Try not to give too many guys a hard-on while I leave ya alone for a couple of minutes, OK?"

"Ohh, God, Adam! Just hurry back, OK?"

The music is cranked up to near ear-splitting decibel range and The Bee Jees, "You Should be Dancin'" is blasting out of the biggest speakers I have ever seen in my life surrounding the dance floor. The floor is vibrating. Dense cigarette-smoke blends in with the liquid nitrogen and I can hardly see anything because my eyes are stinging and honestly, I'm starting to get really tired from all the work Adam and I did earlier in the day on my projects.

"Let's dance!" shouts Adam as he dumps the drinks on the bar counter and grabs me and heads out onto the dance floor.

Five songs later with Gloria Gaynor, Michael Jackson, more Bee Jees, Diana Ross and Dan Hartman and I yell over to Adam, "Sasq'! I just have to go and sit down! I'm really tired!"

"OK, baby. I wanna go talk to Conor anyway. Are ya gonna be OK on your own? Do ya wanna come with me while I go look for Conor?"

"It's OK Adam, I'll be fine."

"Well, well, well... look who blew the doorman and got in before us, guys. It's Aaron from school!" says Alleyn as he sashays over to my end of the bar with Jeremey and *Mother*.

Mother appears beside him at this point and looks me up and down— then he grabs onto my arm. He hits me on the head with one of his stupid oriental fans and starts to shriek and screech while dragging me out onto the dance floor. "We're dancing! That's it, that's all!" he screams in my face.

"Disco Inferno" is blasting out of the speakers and we're getting weird sideways glances from everyone on the dance floor. I'm completely mortified, wishing I could sink down and melt into a liquid, sticky pool of dark rum and Coke on the floor. But, honestly, I really have no viable options other than to either make a scene or follow him onto the dance floor. Once out there together, he starts to grab onto my ass-cheeks while grinding his fat, gross body into mine in a disgusting and lurid display of what he must consider to be dancing.

"Shit! Adam! Where are you? Help!"

After about sixty seconds or so, Alleyn steps onto the dance floor and takes over from *Mother*, who is panting and fanning himself with those idiotic fans, yelling, "I'm hyperventilating here! Get me to a witch doctor! I'm having a "Love Machine" seizure!"

Alleyn laughs and says to me, "Just ignore him. He's just a big, old drama-queen." Then he pulls his bottle of poppers out and subtly puts them into the palm of my hand. "Here Aaron, try this. It's called *Liquid Gold*. Just sniff it and you'll get a rush and really get into the music. Trust me. It's OK."

"I'll take over from here," Adam says assertively as he shoulders Alleyn out of the way and starts to dance with me.

"He was dancing with me you big, clumsy Clydesdale," shouts Alleyn as Adam moves me over to the side and turns back to face him.

"You're right there, pretty boy. He *was*. But not now. Now, you take your goddamn bottle of *Rush* or *Liquid Gold* or whatever the fuck you gave to Aaron there and your freaky friends and move your fuckin' asses over to the other side of the bar or I'll have ya bounced outta here. You got that, or wouldya like me to act it out for ya in interpretive dance along with my friend, Conor at the front door?"

"Ohhh, fuck off, you rude, crude, pathetic, unsophisticated Brockville hick!"

"You forgot to add, bunghole… a hick with a smokin' hot, big, thick, man-size dick that's fuckin' Aaron—not you, ya fuckin' pathetic, phony asshole. Somethin' you're never gonna get to do with that shrivelled-up piece a stale, head-cheese stinkin' tube-steak between your sagging ass-cheeks and flabby legs. Now get outta my face, ya fuckin' mouthy queen!" Adam thrusts his angry face three inches away from Alleyn's shocked expression.

"Ohhh, puhleezzzze, spare me, Mary! I've already had your dick in the Club Baths, asshole, and it wasn't exactly memorable, *Paul!* That was the name you used on the club register log that night and what you told me your name was! You know, you're really nothing compared to me, you pathetic piece of low-class, Brockville trash... Paul, Adam, whatever the hell you want to call yourself!"

I'm standing there looking at them both with my mouth wide-open in shock and disbelief.

"Ohhh, fuck it all! This is all just *too-dreadfully-boring-and-common,"* Alleyn says after one more beat. "C'mon, guys. Let's go do some crack in the washroom and forget about this tacky, sleazy scene."

Adam grabs me by the shoulders and turns me to face him. "You stay right here! Don't you dare go anywhere until I go see Conor. I'll be right back."

He walks over to Conor, who is on break from manning the front door and says quietly, "Uhm, Conor, those guys who just went into the women's washroom back there. They're gonna either smoke-up or do crack. I know your boss here has had problems with the RCMP and the *Sureté du Québec gendarmes* before about illegal drugs in this place. I think ya better either bounce 'em outta here or call someone to come and bust 'em."

"Fuck! Adam. Thanks, man! There's been undercover RCMP officers in here a lot lately and they're just looking to shut this place down and arrest everyone. I'll kick those bastards out of here before they can roll a joint or do their first snort of crack up their noses. The owner here will be really grateful to you for letting me know this. I'm gonna let him know, too. I'll have them out the back door and on the street in no time. Hey! Jean-Louis! We got some freaks doing drugs in the ladies room! Let's bounce their asses outta here like, right now man!"

Adam turns back around then to find me and discovers that I've disappeared. Next thing he's at the coat-check and asking the guy there if I've picked up my coat and left the club.

"Uhm, yeah, you're talking about that skinny twink you came in with? He grabbed his coat just now and left. Shouldn't be too far away though, unless he was able to catch a cab out front."

"Aaron! Hey wait! Baby! C'mon, honey! Lemme explain!"

I'm halfway down rue Principale heading back to my apartment on the other side of the Interprovincial Bridge in Ottawa with Adam following as fast as he can, right behind me.

"Nooo! Leave me alone! Don't touch me! Let go of my arm! Nooo! How could you have sex with him? I don't want to talk to you! Don't follow me!"

Just then he manages to catch up to be in step with me and forces me to slow down by grabbing my arm in a tight vice-grip while starting to pull me toward him. "Well, Aaron, like it or not, you're *gonna* talk to me! That is, I'm gonna talk and you're gonna listen, without you yappin' for once!"

Several doors down from Sac's there is a restaurant that stays open long after the bars along rue Principale and Promenade du Portage close and where I was later to understand many people went to after three in the morning before heading home and falling into bed.

"C'mon! We're goin' in for coffee and maybe a burger or somethin' and you're gonna sit and behave yourself for once and be quiet while I tell ya exactly what happened with me and Alleyn last year! And no goddamn fuckin' around or attitude from you here either! C'mon, let's go.

"Well, OK, Adam, I'm listening. So talk." I'm sitting in this nasty, fluorescent flood-lit restaurant across from my boyfriend with my arms folded and a hurt look on my face.

"OK then. Uhm, uhh, do you remember when I told ya about the Club Baths gettin' raided about a year ago now? Well, uhm, uhh, I was there that night when the police busted the place and arrested everyone in there. Your classmate, Alleyn was in there at the same time and he was on his knees givin' me a blow-job when we both got caught and dragged outta there and put into a police van.

"Why were you in there?!"

"Ohh, come on Aaron! I told ya before, I used to come up here every now and then when I got horny! I didn't know ya back then. And that Alleyn was just some cheap trick who wanted my dong. I needed to get-off and he was more than willing. The sad thing is he was stoned and drunk and pretty damn fuckin' pathetic when it came down to sucking me off."

"I don't want to hear about that!"

"Fair enough. OK, OK. I get it. Well, both your *friend* Alleyn and I wound up spendin' the night in jail-cells down at the police station on Nicholas Street until that morning along with more than twenty other men. I thought I was gonna hafta appear in court before a judge and likely get fined and charged with public indecency! In the end, the police dropped the charges and let everyone go who got rounded up that night. Someone in my cell was talkin' about some really important, top-level security head guy from a government department who got caught up in the raid with his pants down in the Club along with the rest of us. I think that's why they most likely dropped the charges.

Either that, or they were just maybe tryin' to scare everybody, I think. It *was* all pretty scary, actually. That's why I haven't been back up here for a year or so now."

"Well, why would Alleyn say that back in Sac's? I don't understand that. Why would he want to stir up shit like that?"

"Ugh! Honey, c'mon, baby, he *wants* you! Ya just gotta smarten up there and start learnin' to figure these things out on your own! Now do ya understand what happened with him back then and that it has nothing to do with you and me and us now?"

"OK. Uhh, yeah, I suppose. Well, uhm, uhh, I guess so. It just totally creeps me out to know that he was playing with your cock. And having to sit with him in classes—well, that's going to be really weird from now on."

"Baby, the way he was mouthin' off back there in Sac's to me and you and with Conor and that Jean-Louis tossin' him and his friends outta the club, I don't think he's gonna give ya much trouble from here on in. And if he does, I'll take care of him. You can sure as hell count on that!"

"Well, I'm just glad you came to help me. I just didn't know what to do when that fat, obnoxious *Mother* guy dragged me onto the dance floor and then when Alleyn tried to take over from him.

"Remember what I told ya, Aaron. I'm always here for ya. Now let's go back to the club to say g'night to Conor proper-like and we'll catch a cab around the corner and head back to your place. Sorry this turned out so badly for ya. But I hafta say, I'm not one fuckin' bit sorry we ran into Alleyn and his goddamn freaky, fucked-up friends tonight."

"Heya, Conor! Thanks for lettin' us gate-crash tonight. Willya promise to come and say hi to me at Tonner's when you're back down in Brock Vegas?"

"Will do. And Aaron, really nice meeting you. You two make a real cute couple. Hope to see you both real soon now. G'night—*à plus tard, mes amis.*"

We're in the cab on the way back to Argyle and I'm thinking quietly to myself. Halfway there and then I turn to Adam and say, "You know something, Adam, I'm not really sure if you are going to get this, but I've been thinking just now about Alleyn and that first abstract-planes assignment Iona dumped on us at the beginning of the semester. You know, just like that first assignment, Alleyn seems to me to be like a flat, two-dimensional plane—nothing to him—he lives in his own little world in total denial of what his life is all about. The sad thing about it is that he'll probably never grow and develop into anything more than he is now, his own narrow, flat vision of who and what he thinks he is. Does that make any sense to you at all?"

"Mmm hmmm, you're learnin, baby'. And yes it does. But I think your brain's workin' overtime right now. Time to give it a rest and exercise another part of your hot, little bod' with me when we get home. Whaddya say to that?"

Meanwhile, the cab driver looks back in his rear view mirror, rolls his eyes and shrugs, thinking to himself, *esti, tabarnak... I don't get paid enough to listen to this merde at this hour of the morning.*

We're undressing and about to hop into bed when I say to Adam, "Turn your back for a second, while I take my jeans off."

"Why? It's not like you're bashful around me. And there isn't anything down there that I haven't had my lips, tongue, hands or mouth on... or my big dong shoved into, for that matter."

"Just turn around!"

"Uhm, uhh, OK, OK, babe… turnin' now."

"OK, you can turn back around."

I'm wearing a brand-new pair of Superman bikini briefs with the logo on my butt. Mine are different from Adam's because the Superman logo is on the front of his to show off his big bulge. I'm wiggling my ass and he is really laughing.

"My ass is truly yours now, Sasq' man. Now let's get naked and I'll suck your big, thick King Kong dong there, Man of Steel." He dives for me and we both fall onto the bed.

"Faster than a speeding bullet, it's Superman! Nope—it's Adam!"

Several days later, Adam is back in Brock Vegas, standing in front of an enormous, illuminated three-way mirror in Craig's Mens' and Womens' Wear Store on King Street, just down the block from Tonner's.

"Uhm, my inseam is a thirty-four and my waist is either a thirty-two or thirty-four, dependin' on how they fit. I take a forty-four long, usually, in jackets. But you can measure me up and then let's have a look at sports jackets and a nice pair of dress pants to go with 'em," says Adam as old Joseph, the geriatric sales clerk slowly shuffles off to find a tailor's cloth measuring tape.

"I got a date comin' up for someone's birthday real soon, Joseph and I wanna look real nice that night," he says to the clerk.

"How about this jacket here, Adam? It's Donegal tweed and not too thick and heavy that you can't wear it for three out of four seasons. It's on sale and very versatile and practical. The colours in the tweed would be good with your colouring and your new beard and moustache... and it should fit you well... especially in the shoulders and in the length."

Adam tries on the jacket, looks at himself in the three-way mirror and smiles. "Hmmm, I like the greys and blues in it. This orange and blue paisley lining is great—my favorite colours. And without any pocket-flaps or elbow-patches or any of that *pipe-smokin' professor* or *lord of the manor* crap, I'm thinkin' it looks pretty damn good on me. Uhh, the arms need to be lengthened a little bit though."

"Adjusting the arms and buttons on the cuffs won't be a problem. And I think it needs to be taken in a little at the lower back to emphasize your athletic torso. Our in-store seamstress can do that at no charge for you. I'll take care of that, no problem."

"Great. Now find me a nice pair of dark grey pants to go with it, wouldya please? No pleats in 'em or cuffs though. And I want 'em to fit me like a glove, if you catch my meaning."

"Ahh, yes. I think I know just what you're looking for."

Twenty minutes of tailor's-chalk adjustments, then pinning, tucking and hemming the pants to really show off his shapely, sexy man-ass—three-hundred dollars later and Adam heads back to Tonner's just down the street to finish his shift with a big sartorial smile on his face.

"I really don't know how to thank ya for the bonus, Mrs. Tonner. The new clothes will help a lot when I start to look for a new job. And that letter of recommendation you wrote to your friend at the Ministry of National Health and Welfare in Ottawa, well... I just wantcha to know that meant a lot to me."

"You know, Adam, I've always felt like an aunt to you. A nosy, crotchety and interfering old aunt at times, yes, I know. But not having had any children myself, I always considered you almost one of my own. The past five years you've been with me here have been a God send and a blessing. I didn't know what to do with the store when Mr. Tonner died. If you'd hadn't agreed to come and work here for me, I think I would have closed the store up back then. I'll be eighty-one this coming spring and it's time to finally step down and enjoy whatever is left of my life."

"Yes, ma'am. You know how much I'm grateful for the chance you gave me here. I'm real sad to see this place get taken over, but I understand. And the way the rest of Brockville is goin' these days, well, I suppose this was bound to happen, sooner or later."

"I'm glad you understand, Adam. I care a great deal about what happens to you. And I only wish I could do more to help you on your way now."

"Well, ma'am, laying me off will help me to collect unemployment insurance faster. And with the savings I've got and your letter and all, uhm, well, I think I'm gonna be just fine. Ya know Mrs. Tonner, things happen for a reason. And I think this is comin' at a good time for me. I haven't said anything to anyone about this yet, not even my mom. And I figured you'd wanna be the one to officially let customers know and all. Do ya have a firm date yet for when the Shopper's Drug Mart is gonna take over?"

"The end of February. We can close off the end of the calendar year here and hold a big sale for Christmas and early January—then do a final inventory of whatever is left after that. And Adam, you'll get another bonus from me then when I pay off the suppliers and after we clear out whatever stock we can sell between now and then. I'd be grateful if you could stay on with me until the middle of January. And of course, if you need time off for job interviews or whatever you're plans are before then, that won't be a problem at all."

Adam gives Mrs. Tonner a hug and says, "Ma'am, you know you've always been able to count on me. That's never gonna change, ya know."

She is holding back tears when she says, "Sit down for a moment with me behind the cash counter. You know, there are a few things I want to say to you here and now. First of all, I'm an old woman who's lived a long, long time and can say whatever the Hell I damn well please. People can either like it or lump it. I haven't got much time left to me and it seems to go faster with each passing year. I've seen a lot in this city—in my life too for that matter. I have watched Brockville grow from a small-town to what it is now. There are two types of people in this place, Adam. With all of the factories—Black and Decker—DuPont— Brockville Chemicals—Automatic Electric— Johnson's Shoe Factory —Phillips Cables—Stetson's Hat Factory—General Milk and Parke Davis Pharmaceuticals... you've got a lot of blue-collar workers making up most of the city now. And then you've got retired, rich old bitches like me who have been around forever. There's nothing in the middle. And I've always felt that this wasn't a place for you to live your life."

At this part, Mrs. Tonner heaves a big sigh and then hesitates to choose her words carefully before continuing.

"I remember your father, Adam. He just couldn't fit into the mold of factory shift-worker and happy husband, even though he grew up here. And when he left, I wasn't surprised. None of my business I know, but I felt you needed to hear that from someone who knew your father well back then. I know you've got your young friend who is in College up in Ottawa now. And I'm not going to judge or pry into your personal business. But there is something I want you to know about Mr. Tonner and me. I was ten years younger than him when we first were married more than sixty-years ago. It wasn't easy over the years. But we stuck together. And in the end, it was being together that made up for all the hardships and disappointments we had to endure over the decades. Age is just a number. Maturity and character are more important, Adam. If you care for someone, then be patient and love and trust them. It'll all work out in time. You live your life the way you want to and never be afraid to show others who you are inside. Do you understand what I'm trying to say to you?"

"Yes, I think I do. And thank you, ma'am."

Meanwhile, Mrs. Tonner with tears in her eyes says to Adam, "You're a good boy, Adam. I hope you'll come and see me after things wind down here."

"Count on it, Mrs. Tonner. I'll always be around for ya, ma'am."

It's Friday, December 2nd, the last day of formal classes with a week to go for hand-in of final assignments and also my last weekend alone with Adam in Ottawa before I head back to Brock Vegas for the Christmas Break. The bus is over an hour-and-a-half late because of the early seasonal blizzard that has descended upon the Capital. The Voyageur Colonial bus stop in Ottawa is steaming with humid heat while anxious passengers arrive and those who wait for them stare through fogged-up windows, heaving huge sighs of relief as each bus is announced on the loud-speaker and pulls into the station. Adam's bus finally pulls in, just after ten-thirty.

"Adam! The bus trip must have been horrible. It's been snowing heavily up here all day. I was starting to get really worried." I call out as Adam comes through the doors, looks around for me, and quickly sprints over to me to give me a big bear hug.

"The snow's gettin' real bad out there! We hadta' change buses in Prescott because the one we were on kept cuttin'-out and then crapped-out on the driver when we stopped there. A fuckin' full bus this close to Christmas and the driver hadta transfer all the suitcases and shit from that bus into another one they keep there for emergencies. We lost almost forty-five minutes in Prescott and then when we got to North Gower, the snow was so bad and roads so slippery we almost fuckin' goddamn skidded off into the ditch! I hafta really give credit to the bus driver though. He sure as hell managed to get us all here in one piece! I

285

really didn't think we were gonna make it here at all, to tell ya the truth. Jeezus! I'm sure as hell glad to see ya!"

"Well, you made it and am I ever glad you did! Let's get the hell out of here. I've got the heat cranked up in the apartment. And I got us some rum and wine. Hopefully, you can warm up when we get there."

He gives me another big hug while people rush by him to catch cabs or meet those waiting for them outside in warm, idling cars. Then he gives me one of his suggestive laughs and says teasingly to me, "Well, ya wanna know somethin'? At least the *front* of me is startin' to heat up now."

"Gimme your back pack. It's the least I can do to carry it back for you. You look exhausted."

"Nah. Not exhausted, just so fuckin' relieved to see ya and to make it up here in one piece. I'm thinkin' when we get back to your place, I'm gonna be feelin' a whole helluva lot better. Let's go."

"I've got a million things to tell you, Sasq' man. But for now, I just want you to take all your wet clothes off and get dry. Do you want me to run a hot bath for you to help you warm up? Would that help? I can dry you off afterward? I'd really like to do that, actually."

"I've got a better idea," he says, as he pulls me into a tight embrace and slowly starts to remove his coat, sweatshirt and tee-shirt. "I'm thinkin' you've got too many clothes on yourself there," as he yanks my coat off of me and tosses it over on the floor by the front door. "I wanna do ya like, right now! We can talk later and tomorrow. But right now I'm so fuckin' hot for you, my balls are gonna burst if I don't shoot my load inside ya."

His tongue thrusts deep inside my mouth with a demanding, passion-ate kiss, playing with my tongue and exploring every deep recess while his hands roughly fondle and grope every sensitive part of my body. I can feel his thick, hard cock thrusting against me with a determined and urgent rhythm as my hands paw and knead his strong shoulders and hairy chest, caressing and squeezing his hard, sensitized nipples. He moans with intense need and pleasure as I pull and start to lick and suck them with my tongue. I can feel my own cock responding. And all I can do is to keep exploring him boldly all over with my tongue. His armpits are starting to perspire with the heat and humidity in the apartment and the intensity of the moment. His pungent *Adam Blanchard male pheromone scent* is blocking everything else out of my senses as I drop down in front of him to tug and yank the zipper down on his jeans, shove my face into his fragrant, thick, furry pube-forest and grab onto his pulsating dick.

"Shit! I love your man-scent. I wish I could live down here all the time. You make me crazy! Your hot, sexy pube-package is all mine, Sasq' man!"

"Shhh, baby! Gimme a sec' to take my pants off or I'm gonna hafta fuck ya in 'em! My dong's got a mind of its own tonight and I'm not gonna argue with it, and neither are you. Not tonight. I just wanna cum in ya, on ya, and all over ya 'til it settles down, baby—suck on my achin', full balls and hide your head down there in my funky-crotch all night long!"

I do just what he says and bury my head down between his inner thighs and slowly start to work my lips and tongue up until I get to the base of his hot, tight scrotum. His dark pubic hair tickles my nose. All I can do is inhale deeply and take in his unique manly odor and masculine spice while thinking of nothing else but pleasing him and worshipping his hard, pulsating tool. He always groans with mindless, unrestrained surrender when I grab onto his ass and clutch and fondle it with both hands tightly groping each perfect globe-cheek simultaneously.

He shoves his cock down my throat as roughly and deeply as he can. I gag a bit at first, then pull back and whisper to him, "I want to swallow you up whole and then ride you on the bed until you cum deep inside me. I can't get enough of you tonight. It's like the first time for me with you!"

I can feel every inch of his hot, perspiring body on top of me and am obsessed thinking, *Aww, he's making me fucking crazy!*" Adam is groaning and says urgently to me, "Fuckin' hell, baby, am gonna toss ya on the bed and work my tongue all over your body 'til ya beg me to bury my dong deep inside ya. I wanna hear ya moan and beg for me tonight. It's been waaay too long. King Kong has missed ya. Now keep on goin' down there with those magic lips and tongue of yours on the tip of my cock!"

Somehow he manages to get both of us onto the bed. I feel him lifting me up gently while I bury my face into his armpit, biting his shoulder and softly moaning. Next thing I know he's down between my legs, urgently biting and sucking on my inner thighs and rolling my balls in his mouth while greedily squeezing, clutching and clawing my backside and butt-cheeks.

"Jeez! I can't get enough of your mouth and tongue. You're driving me nuts with your hot body and big cock tonight!" I cry out while thinking, *he's making me crazy! The more he does what he's doing to me, the more I want him inside of me.* "I want you to fuck me like, now, Adam! Like, really, really fuck me!" I think, *just like the first time when we came together at the Lyn Pit. And just like I hope it's going be with you every time, from now on.*

Animal-sounding snarls, grunts, groans and growls emanate from him, involuntarily surging from his throat as he clamours and scrambles to shift his position, roughly rolling me over and starting to forcibly finger my anus with single-minded determination. His hot breath on the back of my neck is like a two-hundred-degree heat lamp radiating and beating down on me.

"I'm thinkin' you're lubed-enough on your own down there for me to shove my dong inside ya without any KY or foreplay."

"Fuck the foreplay! I need your cock inside me, so badly! I want you to shove it in there fast and hard and fill me up like, right now!" I can feel every inch of King Kong spreading my ass cheeks, moving deeper and deeper into me while my sphincter muscles flex and squeeze him, driving him crazy with intense desire and need.

"Awww, baby, you feel so damn good. Fuck the snow and cold outside right now. My dong is tellin' me it's a hundred-and-ten degrees inside your tight, juicy little ass tonight!" His thrusts become more and more aggressive and urgent, his breathing more ragged. I can feel his hard, hairy chest expanding and contracting with rapid deep breaths.

"I don't care how raunchy this is. I just gotta have your hot, thick spunk inside me and really fucking soon, too." I sigh and whisper breathlessly to him.

"Ahhh! I'm cumming! Clench your fuckin' hot ass-cheeks around my dong down there and squeeze the livin' shit outta my crotch-rocket. I'm gonna shoot my load in ya, like, right now!"

At the same time I exclaim, "Ahhh! Shit, Adam! Me, too! Me, too! I'm gonna cum! Fuck me! Fuck me hard! Make me cum hard, now!"

Once I catch my breath, I roll of the bed to go and stand by the window staring at the snow outside. Adam rolls over as well, still on the bed and bends down to grab his tee shirt. He tosses it over to me. "Here, baby. Throw on my tee shirt so ya don't catch cold over by the window. Where's that wine you were talkin' about earlier? And have ya got anything in your kitchen that would feed a starvin' hungry hunk like me?"

"There's some Fig Newton's on top of the fridge. And I think there might be some unsalted crackers, cranberry-and-brie cheese, and peppercorn pâté somewhere in there, too. "

Adam pads into the kitchen and pours wine for us both. He looks in the fridge and grabs the pâté, Fig Newtons and crackers sitting on top of it and comes back, flopping back down on the bed after he hands me a glass of wine. "Ya, know, you're gettin' kinda *classy* on me with the pâté there, baby."

"Anything I can spread on a cracker works for me these days."

"Hmmm, you're givin' me an idea for the next time I bang ya!"

"You just like the words *spread* and *bang*, Sasq' man. I'm onto you."

"Onto, into, around, under, on-top-of, it's all good, butt-boy. Now, drink some of your wine. Let's snuggle and get caught up. You were sayin' you've got a million things to tell me before Armageddon happened around here just now. Jeezus! I can't hardly see the floor 'cause all the damn pillows and clothes and shit are all over the place. Now let's get comfortable and snack on these Fig Newtons and crackers so I can get my strength back to do ya all over again."

"Uhm, uhh, OK, Adam. But first I want you to have a look at my student workspace assignment for Iona hmmmm... izzzn't it?' Ouspenskaya. It's under the plastic garbage bag I'm using to keep the dust off it over on my desk there."

We walk over to my maquette and I dramatically pull off the bag. Adam looks at it for a long while before saying anything.

"Fuck me, man! This is fuckin' great! But lookin' at the scaled-down drafting stool there, I'd say it's too big for your cute, sexy, little Aaron Richard Christie boy-butt though. Ya really shoulda let me measure your ass the last time I was up."

I laugh then and reply, "Oh, piss off! I can just curl the edges of it up like this and then it will hug my butt just the way you do. Really now... take a good look at the model and let me know what you think."

He does, leaning into the project, circling it, peering into its corners. He smiles at the precision of my measuring on the table-top and work-surface heights. He notes my choice to put a narrow shelf between the lower and higher one to make them look like they line up... and the Paradraft I've made for my drafting board, complete with a couple of set squares. He notices all the bins I've made for drawings and Bainbridge boards, and that I even put pins with little white round heads on the drawers to make them look like knobs. And all of it measured to-scale and cut from white Bainbridge board. "I'm really impressed," he says. "And don't let me forget to give ya the programming and design study I typed up. It's in my backpack."

"Thanks Sasq'. I really appreciate that."

"Now, didya hand in that Lynda *bird-lady* assignment last week and has she got back to you with a grade on it yet? I'm real interested to see what she thinks of it."

"She was super impressed. I didn't know, but she has in-laws living down in Brockville. She knows the city well, and really liked what I handed in. I won't be getting my grades until next Friday though, but I'm pretty sure I'm going to do well with that one."

And that Professor Evan *whatshisname's* model on the *frikken-nachos theory*, or sequence, or whatever the fuck ya call it, where is it? Can I see it?"

"*Fibonacci*, Adam! Jeez! It's an algorithm. And Fibonacci was a thirteenth-century Italian, not Mexican!"

"Yeah—yeah—yeahhh, whatever. So, like, where is it?"

"I've had to leave it back in the classroom and work on it there. It was getting to be too fragile to carry back and forth. And well, uhh, I didn't want to wreck it by trying to get it over to the College."

"Uhm, you don't leave a lot of your work there alone when you're not there, do ya, baby?"

"Well, sometimes I do. There's usually someone there to keep an eye on stuff. In fact, some of the students have been bringing coffee-makers and sleeping bags into the classroom to spread out under the drafting tables to work on their stuff all night to get them done in time for submission. I know Melora Holt and Yolanda Vargas have been doing that this past week."

"Aaron, I don't wantcha to leave your work unattended. That fuckin' scene with that goddamn Alleyn and his strung-out, crack-smokin' friends when we went to Sac's really freaked me out. That guy is a goddamn psycho'. I'm not sayin' anyone would try to sabotage your work. But, ya never know. And I don't wantcha takin' any chances this close to the end of your first-semester. Just thinkin' here out loud. Uhm, honey, does the College have any night-watch Security Guards to patrol the halls and classrooms. And do they like, lock the outside doors late at night? Is there a guard-desk to let students and people in and out?"

"Yes they do. No one gets in unless they check in there and have a valid student photo ID card. And, trust me, I'm way ahead of you with Alleyn. In fact, he hasn't shown up for class all this past week. I'm glad he hasn't, too."

"Good to know."

"Now, can we suck and chew on each other's tongues for a while here? And can I rub your Sasquatch fur or do you want to talk some more?"

"Well, maybe five or ten more minutes of kissin' and gropin' 'cause I wanna taste that red wine on your lips and tongue. But after that then, I've got a few things to talk to you about, too. Does that work for ya?"

"Are ya all nice and comfy there with your head shoved up into my armpit?"

"Sure am. Now what did you want to talk to me about?"

"...well, once upon a time, there was this cute, sexy, young guy named, Cookie-butt, and he loved a hairy, hunky Sasquatch, called Sasq' man..."

"Sounds like one twisted, fractured kind of bedtime story to me there."

Adam chuckles and then says, "Seriously now, remember when I was tellin' ya I was startin' to think about my future and where we're goin' together in this relationship?"

"Uhm hmmm, yep, I do." I start to yawn, stretch and curl up closer to him as he continues talking quietly to me.

"Well, how wouldya like it if I moved up here and crashed with you here in your little apartment until we found a bigger place together closer to the end of your lease? Do ya think we could manage together in this mouse-cage for a few months together?"

"Ohh, Adam! Would you?! I'll do whatever I need to around here to make space for you! What made you think about doing this?"

"Well, I'd hadn't really for sure made up my mind 'til I was on that fuckin' *abominable snowman* bus ride up here tonight. Do ya remember me tellin' you about Mrs. Tonner talkin' to some folks about sellin' the store and about them maybe opening up a franchise back in town?"

I nod.

"Well, I've known about this for a week or so now. Mrs. Tonner is gonna be eighty-one in the spring. And she's tired and wants to move into a seniors' retirement-home back in Brockville."

Just an aside here: Mrs. Tonner and her late husband when he was still alive lived in an imposing, red-brick and ornamental stone, bay-fronted Queen Anne, mid-Victorian style mansion just behind Tonner's Drug Store at number 10 Fulford Avenue, right at the base of the steep hill. The house has a massive, stone-faced staircase leading up to an exterior court or piazza and the mahogany, double front-doors with etched-glass windows. It was three stories in height and boasted steeply-pitched roofs, multi-coloured slate shingles, rooftop finials on the end-gables and a slender, round corner turret with a conical, copper roof and a weathervane.

Adam continues with me by explaining, "She told me a while back that her big, old house just behind the store on Fulford Avenue was gettin' to be too much for her with the stairs and all. And she just wants to slow up now a bit and enjoy the rest of her years in peace. She's been really good to me about the whole thing. She actually gave me a nice big bonus and a letter of recommendation and spoke with a friend of hers up here in Ottawa at the Ministry of National Health and Welfare. Seems like they're interested to interview me for a job. I'm not gonna get too excited about it just yet though. And I don't wantcha to get your hopes up either. But, baby, Mrs. Tonner agreed to lay me off to collect unemployment insurance right away and I have some money saved up. She wants me to work the store with her through Christmas and January and then the Shopper's Drug Mart Group will take over in late February. So, wouldya like me to move in with ya here in the short term and then maybe start to look for a bigger place for us both at the end of your spring-semester in May? I think havin' you in this bed here with me every night would be the best Christmas present I could ever hope to get. I love you, Aaron and I know it's gonna be tight here in this tiny postage-stamp excuse for an apartment, but I want for us to give it a try. So, whaddya say, baby?"

"If you can put up with me and my cooking and mess around here, then let's do this."

"Uhh, I'll be doin' the cookin'! I wanna live to see the New Year. You just leave the place tidy and keep that tight, little ass ready at a moment's notice whenever I wanna get into your pants and we'll sign a formal binding contract to that effect and move on from there. Deal?"

"Deal!"

"Good. I know my old jacket and pants are gonna be real thrilled with havin' to share space with your sexy jeans in your armoire there. You can take 'em out and abuse them any time ya like, you perverted, kinky little fucker. How does that sound to ya?"

"Do I have to break the news to your shirt, Adam, or will you do that?"

"Awww, c'mere, honey. I think that old shirt can learn to share."

I smile, burrowing even more deeply into his armpit, yawning every thirty seconds. Sleep will come easily to me tonight for sure.

"Now, Aaron, I'm gonna talk to your mom and dad about this when we're back in Brockville together over your Christmas Break and ask my mom and Bast to store some of my furniture and stuff in her garage. We'll do just fine together, that is, if we can manage not to trip over each other on the way to the bathroom in the middle of the night."

"God, I love you!"

"Awww, Cookie, me too, you. Somethin' else, too, before I start to get hard here again and King Kong takes over the thinkin'. Your friend Cala Cuthbertson called me a couple of weeks ago and she and I had a real nice, good long talk on the phone. I know her older sister, Cora-Leanne from BCI. We're gonna have your birthday dinner with her and Rob Galanos from Zeller's on the seventeenth. Or, if your parents are doin' dinner for ya that night, either the night before—or just after. You haven't seen or talked to them since ya moved up here and I don't wantcha forgettin' about or takin' your old friends for granted. They miss you a lot and wanna see ya. Cala's got a new boyfriend named Charlie. He's an independent, long-haul truck driver and Cala told me they're plannin' on movin' out to BC in the spring. And Rob's met someone too named, Bryson Steyn, and they really wanna meet both you and me and maybe get together once in a while when we're either back in Brock Vegas, or when Rob and Bryson come up to Ottawa. They're good people, and trust me, friends like that are really worth holdin' onto."

"I know I haven't called Cala since September and I feel really badly about that, too. And Rob, well, he was just beginning to date Bryson when you and I first got together, and I just figured he was busy and not really thinking about me and all. You're right though. It's been way too long. And I miss the times we all got together and danced up at the Skyline and the 401 Inn. It seems like a lifetime ago now. But, they were there for me then, and I guess I'd better make time to be there for them now."

7

December / January

"Heya, butt-boy! I'll be up on December 9th to pick ya up and bring ya on back to Brock Vegas for Christmas break. Your dad said to use his car and to make sure the trunk was empty for the nineteen pillow cases and plastic garbage bags of laundry and shit your mom is expectin' you to bring back with ya."

"Very funny! *Hah, hah, haah.* I'm just killing myself laughing here, mister Sasquatch-man. Can't you hear me? Uhm, but why isn't Dad coming up though?"

"He has to practice with the choir for Midnight Christmas Mass at St. Francis Xavier that night. And he and your mom are busy with gettin' the house ready for Christmas. At least that's what he said to me."

"Ahh, OK."

"I think he's just tired these days and probably just doesn't wanna hafta drive all the way up there and back. I talked to him and your mom about movin' up there with you in the New Year, by the way."

"What did they say?!"

"Well, they're worried about the size of the place ya have there and don't wantcha gettin' upset or distracted with me bein' there all the time distractin' you from your studies—which I can understand."

"And?!"

"Well, we talked for a long time."

"Yes… and?!"

"Well, uhm, uhh, I hadta promise 'em I wouldn't get in your way and that I'd get myself settled with a job just as soon as I can. I think they were happy I was gonna pay half the rent and food and all. In the end they said it was your decision. So whaddya say? Can you put up with me movin' in with ya there?"

"Do you even have to ask me that question?!"

"Well, I figured I would, just so I could say I did!"

I can hear the music playing in the background at Adam's apartment. Chaka Khan is grooving with "Dance Wit Me".

"I'll be waiting for you back here after I pick up the last of my projects and get some of my marks for the semester in the afternoon then."

"I'll be there. And oh yeah, has the ice frozen over on the Canal yet for skating?" Adam asks.

"They're working on it now. They've been drilling holes in the ice and flooding the surface every night. I've been going down to watch the guys from the National Capital Commission doing it. The change-huts for lacing up skates are there now. And the concessions for hot chocolate and beavertails are almost done. I think everything will be ready for skating right after New Year's Day."

"Good to know. We're gonna enjoy that together—along with lots of other things we can do, with our clothes on for a change."

Going to have to get my laundry done this week for sure, I think as I hang up the phone and stare into the corner of my bathroom where most of my clothes and Adam's beautiful new bedsheets are piled in a huge heap.

Meanwhile, the music in my apartment continues to boom, with The Jackson Five singing "Enjoy Yourself."

Hmmm, oh well, I'll get around to doing the laundry later...

"Has anyone seen or heard from Alleyn this week at all? Melora? Yolanda? Connie? He wasn't here for last week's classes. And now I don't see any of his final assignments in the classroom for submission. Does anyone know what's going on with him?" I ask my classmates the next morning during the break from our first class of the day with Massimo.

"Oh, Aaron!" Melora says right away. "You haven't heard then! I thought you would have been one of the first to know. Alleyn got fired from The Bay last week for stealing clothing when he was there after-hours. He was caught red-handed on a closed-circuit TV camera and was stopped by Store Security. Apparently, he's been doing that for some time. I heard that from someone who knows his friend, Jeremey. Then, just after he got fired, he was over at the *chez Henri* one night and apparently OD'd on quaaludes with too much alcohol and poppers. He's lucky to be alive! Last Jeremey heard, he was back in Maitland with his mom and dad and won't be coming back for next semester and maybe not even back to Ottawa."

"Holy shit! I had no idea, Melora. Is he going to be OK, or does anyone know yet?"

"Well, I think his friend Jeremey said his parents were going to admit him into the Elmgrove Unit at the Brockville Psychiatric to help break his cocaine addiction after Hanukkah. Then they were going to look to try to sublet his apartment and have him move back home with them for a while until he got himself straightened out."

"A cocaine addiction! Oh my God! What about his dog, Dietrich?" I ask.

"I think Jeremey told my friend they were returning Dietrich to her breeder."

"Oh jeez! What a damned shame."

"I know. I had no idea about his cocaine habit, did you, Aaron?"

"Well, Melora, I always wondered how he managed to keep up with his projects and assignments, and it always seemed to me he never slept. I guess cocaine and poppers and whatever else he was on must have kept him going. This is really too bad. I feel sorry for his parents and that poor dog of his."

"Hi, Dad."

"Aaron! Well, hello, son. How did you make out with your grades and did you manage to hand in that last assignment for Mr. Copland's class you were so concerned with on time?"

"Uhm, uhh, yes, I did. I managed to get everything done and handed in. Evan Copland's project was the one really holding me back, but I got it finished. And whatever mark I get on it I'll be fine with, just as long as I pass. I got an 'A' on that History of Architecture project that Adam helped me with for Lynda Naagy-Birdsong. And I even got a 'B' in Drafting from Gaelen Goderich for the semester. Not bad for a *leftie*, eh?

"Good for you!"

"Thanks. And thanks, too for letting Adam come up to get me next Friday with the car. I really appreciate that and I hope you're OK there."

"Yes, son, I am perfectly fine. Monsignor Cranston made me the lead male vocalist for Midnight Mass this year and I have a couple of solos I must practice with Sister St. Evelyne-Bernadetto that evening. So I asked Adam to come up to pick you up, that's all."

"Oh, OK. Good. Uhm, but Dad, there's something else I wanted to talk to you about. It has to do with one of my classmates up here, Alleyn Arendsdorff. I think I mentioned to you and Mom that his parent's live just east of Maitland there."

"Yes, I remember you mentioning them to us. What about Alleyn?"

"Well, he's had to drop out of school because he was fired from his part-time job and almost died from a drug overdose last week. I don't know him all that well, except for sitting together in some of my classes. And Adam met him and told me to be careful around him."

"Well, good for Adam. Go on, son."

"Uhh, well I don't know for sure. But I heard his parents are going to admit him into the rehab clinic in the Elmgrove Unit there at the Psych' right after Christmas."

"Addiction for what? Do you know?"

"I heard it was for cocaine and something else called *quaaludes?* Like, what is that, Dad? I figured if anyone would know about this stuff, you would. I suppose I could ask Adam just as well. But I really wanted to talk to you about all of this."

"Well, son the medical name for quaaludes is *methaqualone.* And they are a powerful depressant like barbiturates or sleeping pills. They affect the central nervous system and, among other things, can reduce anxiety and create a false sense of happiness or euphoria. It's a wonder that young man is still alive, mixing them with cocaine! Did you know this boy very well?"

"No, Dad. I was over at his apartment once. And Adam and I ran into him a couple of times. But if you're wondering if I'm a friend of his, well, no, I'm not. Not at all."

"OK, son. Good. I'm sad to say though that his parents are going to have a long rehabilitation road ahead of them trying to help him break his addictions. Both cocaine and quaaludes are highly addictive. You say he's going to be admitted into Elmgrove?"

"That's what I heard. Yes."

"I'll speak with the doctors there and make sure he gets the best care and resources to help deal with his addictions."

"Thanks, Dad. I feel really badly for him."

"Now, Aaron, on another subject, seriously now… about Adam. I suspect you know he's told us about Shopper's Drug Mart taking over from Mrs. Tonner and him moving up to Ottawa. I want you to be completely honest with me now, as we are concerned. Are you going to be able to focus on your studies up there and not have them suffer? It's all well and good that you want to help him get a fresh start—your mother and I do as well—is this something you are absolutely sure you can cope with in that tiny, little bachelor apartment?"

"Well, Adam said it would only be until the end of the lease here. Then he said we could find a bigger place and he isn't too worried about getting another job. You know, he's actually been a really big help to me with some of my projects. I've thought about it a lot, too. And honestly, I think it will all be fine, I really do."

"Well, I told him the decision was yours in the final analysis. So, as long as you are completely sure there."

"I really am, Dad. It'll all be OK. Now what do you really want for Christmas?"

"Peace on earth and good will to man. And just maybe the ability to get through Midnight Mass without any *off-key* notes in my solos. Umm, you *will* be coming to Midnight Mass this year?"

"Can I come and sit up in the choir loft with you, like I used to?"

"I'd like that. Very much."

"Ohh, Dad, what colour is Mom's hair going to be *this time* when I get there?"

"Just never *you* mind, young man! And whatever it is, it's *beautiful*, you got that?"

"Yes, Dad..."

It's finally December 9th and I'm staring out the window at home patiently waiting for Adam to show up. Dad's Newport eventually pulls up and Adam hops out of it, ambling over to the front door of my apartment building. He bursts into the apartment and exclaims, "Heya, butt-boy! I made real good time comin' up today. Are ya hungry and wouldya maybe like to stop for lunch on the way back to Brockville? You're buyin' too!"

"Let me grab a couple of eight tracks to play in the car on the way back. I've got a couple of Christmas presents to go, too that are stacked over there, and my duffle bag and the bigger suitcase right beside it."

"You mean to tell me you don't have any laundry to take back with ya and that I cleaned your dad's trunk out for nothin'?!"

"Uhh, uhm, well... the pillowcases are in the bathroom."

"Jeezus fuck, Aaron! At this rate you're gonna need a permanent U-Haul van on-call to getcha' back and forth! I'll be havin' to make friends now with butch lesbians to get good rates on truck rentals!"

He hoists the first of seven full pillowcases and five green plastic garbage bags of laundry over his shoulder and starts to head out to dad's car which is idling away, double-parked out in front of the building.

"Just hold on for a minute there, Sasq'. I have to check on something first." I reach down to grab his furry pube-basket and start to shake it. "Hmmm, OK. Good. It's still there."

"Well, where the fuck did ya think it was gonna go, baby?! It'll be there for ya for the next three weeks when you're on break—and *in* ya for most of that time, too!"

"Just checking, that's all."

"Well, you can play with King Kong after we have lunch and are on the road. There's a place in Kemptville I wanna check out. We can eat there and then head back through Merrickville again. Is that OK with you?"

"I remember the last time with Mrs. Tonner's car. This time, no running out of gas and no back-seat sex in Dad's car."

"OK, OK! Oh well, there's lotsa stuff we can do in the front anyway!"

The fresh fallen snowscape is blindingly beautiful as we pull into Kemptville, Adam pulls up in front of the Rideau View Motel, just north of what constitutes the main street in the village. "Did ya know that Rob Galanos's sister, Gemma runs this place?" he says as he opens his door and starts to get out of Dad's car. "Let's get warm inside and find a table to sit down and have somethin' to eat. I hear the food in the dining room here is just fantastic!"

"I want to tell you what happened with Alleyn once we get inside. You won't believe what I heard from Melora and Elaine and Connie back at school."

"Yeah, well, we've got lotsa stuff to talk about. But let's get outta this freezing weather. My nuts are freezin' right now."

Once inside and having shed our winter coats and gear, I look deep into Adam's eyes, giving him a huge smile. It's been a long stretch and I've missed him. Our conversation continues.

"Just so ya know," Aaron says, "I went ahead and talked to Mom and Bast about storin' some of my stuff in her garage for a few months. She's got no problem with most of it. I think as long as I can fit a little dresser with some drawers in your place and carve out some room in that armoire of yours for my clothes, we should be OK for a few months. The rest we can figure out in the next couple of days when you come over and we start to figure out what comes, what goes, what gets stored and what stuff I'm gonna wanna donate or get rid of. I'm gettin' kinda excited here and once we get through Christmas, things should come together pretty quickly, I'm hoping."

"That huge, monstrous *elephant-in-the-room* console stereo thing of yours isn't going to fit up here into the apartment. You *do* know that, right?"

"It's OK. Bast wants to buy it from me, babe. We'll figure it all out though—I'm not too worried. Now, what were ya telling me about Alleyn Fuckface when we were gettin' outta the car just now?"

"Well, uhm, I'd hadn't seen him in class since we were all over at Sac's. And when I went in this morning to get one of my project assignments and most of my final grades for the semester, Melora was telling me he got fired and banned from coming into The Bay because he was caught stealing clothing and other things after-hours from the store. Then she told me he had to be taken by ambulance from the *chez Henri* one night to Emergency at the Ottawa General Hospital on Smyth Road for a drug overdose! He's back with his parents now in Maitland, as far as anyone knows. And they're probably going to have to admit him into the Elmgrove Unit at the Brockville Psych' to help him deal with his addictions to cocaine and quaaludes, according to his friend Jeremey. He won't be coming back to the programme in January."

"Wow! I sorta, kinda knew he was fucked up. But I sure as hell didn't think he was doin' fuckin' cocaine! Jeezus fuck! What a dumb asshole he is! The *'ludes* don't surprise me though. The way he was doin' poppers on the dance floor that night, I was scared he might try to slip ya a 'lude. I didn't wanna hafta deal with him tryin' to drug you to getcha back to his place and molest ya. I just had a feeling he would try to pull some weird, fuckin' kinda shit like that on you that night."

"I asked Dad about quaaludes and he told me they make you really relaxed."

"Well, butt-boy, I'd be sayin' a whole helluva lot more than relaxed. They make ya super-fuckin' horny and take away all your inhibitions. Some people call 'em *disco-biscuits*. People put 'em into people's drinks and then wind up gettin' 'em into bed for sex. And no, before ya even say or think it, that's never, ever gonna happen with me and you. Not that we need any drugs to help us get-off. That kinda shit is dangerous and just plain stupid."

"Has anyone ever done anything like that to you?"

"Yep... about three or four years ago now. That's how I know about 'em. And I felt helpless and couldn't do a damn thing about it either at the time. Shit like that's never ever gonna happen again, either to me or someone I care about. There's right and wrong, and there's the words yes and no. I know the pharmaceutical side-effects of those things. Especially when ya mix 'em with poppers and cocaine, of all things! Jeezus fuck, the stupid cunt coulda' died doin' all that crap together like that. I don't like him for the shit he tried to pull in Sac's that night with you and me. But I sure as hell wouldn't wanna see him dead from bein' so dumb with drugs. He's obviously not a real happy guy. But I'm sure as hell glad to know he's not gonna be in your programme anymore, that's for damn fuckin' sure!"

"Well, Dad and I talked a lot about Alleyn. And I told him you said to be careful around him. Dad said he would keep an eye on Alleyn if he goes into rehab and make sure the best doctors and professional assistance would be given to him and his parents.

"Yep, that's exactly what I'd be expectin' your dad to say, too. He's really somethin'. I keep tellin' ya how lucky you are to have a dad like that." Adam's voice trails off and he looks away, deep in thought. Then he shakes his head and returns back to reality and the half-eaten club sandwich, and fries-and-gravy sitting in front of him.

Now, I heard back from Cala and Rob and they really wanna do somethin' up special for your birthday. You gotta get yourself all prettied-up that night, 'cause I'm gonna get all showered and shaved and make ya proud to show me off." He says all this with a cute grin on his face and a twitch to his nostrils that just kills me every time he does it.

"So, I won't be able to lick the man sweat off your balls that night then?"

Adam gives me a wink and a suggestive, dirty laugh and says, "Well, maybe you can come over beforehand and hop in the shower with me after ya bury your face in my crotch and suck me off first. And then I can fuck ya silly in the shower and we can head on out after that. Whaddya think of that plan, ya kinky little twink?"

"My cock is liking that idea, big time. But I don't want to have to wait until the seventeenth to do that though. Can I play with you when we get out of here?"

"Thought you said no sex in your dad's car."

"I was lying when I said that!"

"Ahh, I see. Well, uhm, maybe after we've had a piece of pie and some hot, strong coffee. I'm missing my Cookie big time. But I want more than just one dessert right at the moment. Now settle down there while I play footsie with ya under the table."

Fifteen minutes later and Adam tries to hide his big, hard dick straining inside his bulging crotch with a crumpled-up paper napkin. He urgently calls over to Gemma behind the counter at the cash register, "Uhm, uhh, cheque please!"

Once in the car and after I've managed to undo Adam's belt and unzip his jeans to start to go down on him, suddenly I lift my head up to look at his smirking face and say, "Uhm, Adam? Did you happen to spray Eau Sauvage between your legs?"

He is shaking with laughter and replies, "I just wanted to make ya feel right at home down there!"

"Ohh! You bastard! You're not *ever* going to let me forget that are you?"

"Nope!"

"Well, you just wait! I'll get you back for that, Sasq'!"

"I was hopin' you were gonna say that! Anytime. Anywhere. The challenge is on!"

There is one time of the year that Brockville is at its most festive and picturesque. And that time is Christmas. The six-foot-tall, stuffed, brown bear with the Santa Claus hat and jacket and bells is placed out in front of Craig's Men's and Women's Wear Store every year. One of the Craig men shot the bear and had it stuffed many years ago now. And it has been rolled out to help children and harried shoppers celebrate the festive Holiday Season every Christmas since then. All the street-light standards along King Street are festooned with big candy cane and tinsel illuminated decorations. And the Nativity crèche in front of the World War One War Memorial on Courthouse Square is always in place, just before the Santa Claus parade to remind people of the true meaning of Christmas. The snow that falls in December is mostly crisp and pure and covers the city with an innocent and fresh white mantle of seasonal joy and happiness.

What the hell am I going to buy for Adam for Christmas?! I think as I head down King Street and go through a mental list of possibilities.

Having stopped in to Tonner's to say hello to Mrs. Tonner and wish her a very Happy Holiday, and after having checked Adam's hot, sexy, fuzzy man-ass-cheeks out while he was waiting on a customer behind the pharmacy counter, the search is now on to find that perfect gift for him for Christmas.

"Hiya, Joseph. I bet you've been really busy in Craig's with Christmas coming up in a few weeks time. I'm really just kind of looking right now. But, well… is there anything new that's come in that maybe I could have a look at for both Dad and a friend of mine?"

"Well, hello and Merry Christmas, Aaron. I guess you must be back in town now for the Holidays. I know your dad was in here recently looking for a new winter overcoat. You may want to consider a scarf and gloves, or even a new Fedora hat for him to go with the coat. He does like his hats. We've just received several new Fedoras in from Stetson's Hat Factory on Park Street. I can show them to you if you are interested."

"I really like the suggestion about the scarf and gloves. Maybe something like a silk and cashmere scarf and a pair of dress gloves. What colour was the coat that Dad bought?"

"Charcoal. Perhaps something in navy and red, along with black or charcoal leather gloves would work with that."

"Perfect! And as for my friend, I was thinking maybe one of those Peter Scott virgin wool crewneck pullover sweaters. You know the ones I'm talking about. I've bought a couple of them for myself."

"Yes, I remember. Did you have a particular colour in mind? And a size?"

"Uhm, uhh, well, *anything* but *orange*. Maybe something either in navy or royal blue. Something that he can wear with either blue jeans or something dressier. And a size extra-large, extra-long, please, because they shrink a little after dry-cleaning them."

Leave it to me. I'm sure we can find everything you're looking for."

"Hiya, Cala!" I say to my old friend, once I've settled onto a swivel-stool just beside her. She's come to meet me for coffee at the old lunch-counter in Woolworths and it's been months now since we last saw each other. I tell her Adam has told me about her new boyfriend, Charlie Rieder, and then ask for all the juicy details.

"You'll get to meet him soon enough. He and I met just after you left for school in September. He's a really big, beefy guy with a full beard and a pony-tail. And I don't want you giving him funny looks about his studded, black leather biker jacket or boots when you meet him. He comes across as really tough and mean. But he's a real sweetheart underneath all the hair and the clothes. And before you ask, yes, he knows you and Adam are gay. And he's perfectly cool with that, too."

"Adam says you're moving out west to BC with him in the spring?"

"Yep, I am. I love him. He's good to me and there isn't much keeping me here in Brockville anymore. Dad will be just fine with Cora-Leanne here. And just like you, I want to get out and see what else there is to life outside of Brock Vegas."

"So, how is Rob Galanos and that new boyfriend of his?"

"Ohh! His new friend, Bryson Steyn is sooo sexy. He's as skinny as you and has long, dark brown, wavy hair, a cute beard and moustache, a beautiful smile and is a really funny guy. With Rob's blond hair, they make a nice couple. Rob is still living in that apartment of his in Courthouse Terrace. He's been talking about moving up to Kingston though to study Restaurant and Hotel Hospitality Management at St. Lawrence College. Bryson lives up there now, so I guess they'll eventually move in together. He's really pretty happy. I think we're all doing great right now. How are things with you and Adam? I really like him a lot. He loves you, you know."

"I love him, too, Cala. He's going to move up to Ottawa to be with me early in the New Year. Dad really seems to really like him. And as for Mom, well—you know Mom. She's got him doing all kinds of dumb stuff for her around the house. And he's just been so good to them both."

"By the way, I saw your mom downtown with that crazy hair and headband a few days ago. Like, what in the world was she thinking, dying her hair that bright copper-red colour? It looks like her head is on fire! I barely recognized her."

"I stopped trying to figure Mom out a long time ago, Cala. Now if I could just find her a decent Christmas present."

"Go and have a look in Symington's Home Hardware. They have a brand new adult novelty and gag gift section down there in the basement where your old toy and hobby department is. I found a couple of really hilarious gifts there. Maybe you could get her something funny. And if that doesn't work, then go into Kami Hair Design and pick her up a gift certificate to fix that horrible hair colour of hers."

"You're just as mean and bitchy and funny as ever, Cala! That's why we're such good friends. God, I've missed you!"

Symington's Home Hardware has been a familiar and stalwart fixture on King Street in Brockville for generations. It has a huge main floor and a basement with a toy and hobby shop that is always packed with customers shopping for children's toys and gifts at this time of year.

Mr. Elasse the franchise owner supplies all the Christmas gift toys for the children of those who work in many of the factories in the city. They do a huge business with selecting gifts based on gender and age, then wrapping them and delivering them to each staff Christmas party for each company in December.

I know this because I had to wrap all those hundreds and hundreds of dumb, stupid gifts for the past two Christmases I worked there before I started to work for Geraint at his store franchise.

Mr. Elasse's fat, red-headed, near-sighted great nephew, Mat will go and play Santa Claus for an additional fee. It's about the only time of the year he actually works at something, other than being a spoiled, entitled brat and bully.

Down in the toy and hobby shop and in the model car kit section, I see a Revell scale-model plastic car kit for a 1967 AMC Ambassador SST coupe and start to think, *Hmmm, I wonder if Adam would ever put something like that together. He's always bragging about how good he is with his hands. Maybe I'll give them something else to do other than grope and feel me up all the time. On second thought, uhm, maybe not...*

Back out again on King Street, I head back east on my way home to Bethune. I know I still have to pick up something really nice for Mom. Since Tonner's is closing up and they have a big clearance sale on, I figure there's no reason I shouldn't go back in and ask Adam to help me. I really don't have any idea what to get her. There was absolutely nothing in Woolworth's and there's no way I was going to go into Lipson's Department Store with John Yaegar working in the stockroom and on the sales floor. *That homophobic bastard prick and his damned bullying cousin, Jimmy. Nope! Not gonna go there. No fucking way.*

"Back again, Mrs. Tonner. I need to get something nice for my mom for Christmas."

"Adam is in the back right now. You'll probably want him to help you. I'll let him know you're here."

"Heya, baby." he says quietly to me as he sneaks up behind me in the perfume and cosmetics section of the store. Are ya looking for some more Eau Sauvage to spray in my pants, or what can I help you with there?" He chuckles softly.

"Ohh, Jeez, Adam! Nooo! Stop teasing me about that. I have to get something for Mom for Christmas and I haven't got a clue what."

"Hmmm, I know she was lookin' at those silver-plated comb, brush and hand-mirror dresser sets up at the front of the store. Also, she wears that Dior perfume and is into dusting powders and stuff like that. I'll sell ya some of that Dior if ya promise me you won't tell her you douse yourself with Christian Dior between your legs, like ya do with my Eau Sauvage!"

"All right, mister comedian. You really should consider taking your act on the road. Now… are you actually going to help me here with something constructive? I could really use your help."

"Honestly, I think the Dior would be a good and safe choice. And then maybe you could stop into Evangeline's Dress Shop and pick her up a scarf, or somethin' like that. If you run outta ideas completely, you could always get her a crate of tequila for those Tequila Sunrises she seems to like. Jeezus, she's even got my mom drinkin' 'em now!"

"Gee, thanks, mister helpful. I'll know who not to ask for suggestions in the future."

"Aww, now, Cookie-Butt. Seriously, you might wanna go and get her some wool and a couple of patterns down at Kitty's Wool Box. She's promised to make me a fisherman rib-stitch knit sweater in the New Year and is startin' to get into knitting again. Maybe that might a good gift for her. Somethin' to keep her busy and occupied."

"Now that's not a bad idea! Maybe that and something personal just for her. Gimme some of that Dior and I'll go and see Kitty down at The Wool Box."

Jeez! What a guy to suggest I go and buy Mom some wool to make a sweater for him! I'll go in and exchange the sweater I got for him for a fisherman cable knit sweater at Craig's and then stop in at the LCBO to get his mom and Bast a really nice bottle of French vintage red wine and then get some wool for Mom to make something for herself! Jeez, what a guy!

His suggestion about scarves in Evangeline's Dress Shoppe, however, did make me think about that ridiculous Bianca Jagger headband Mom was wearing.

When I was just a little kid, Mom and Astrid used to drag me into Evangeline's all the time with them when they went shopping for dresses and such. I used to hide in the clothing racks and giggle whenever they couldn't find me. Then, when I was a little bit older and got bored while they aimlessly thumbed through all the stock on display that never seemed to change, I'd hide again in the clothing racks and jump out exclaiming "Pick me! Pick Me!" whenever strange ladies came close and started looking at the clothes hanging on them! After a couple of those exciting, exhilarating and wildly-entertaining episodes, Eveline and Angelica told my mom and Astrid to please leave me at home or get a babysitter because the customers were starting to complain! I still laugh about that to this day.

"Hi Angelica. Those scarves in the window there, they're really beautiful. And there's one with copper, grey, yellow and jade green in it. May I see it, please?"

"Hi, Aaron. Back home for Christmas, are you? I'm assuming it's for your mom for Christmas. Those scarves are from Italy and are similar to those done by the fashion designer, Emilio Pucci. A copper-coloured one in that wonderful Pucci-inspired print would work well with your mother's new uhm, uhh, hairstyle."

"Well, it's either that or an Elizabeth Taylor turban!"

Angelica chuckles and then says quietly to me, "Between you and me, Aaron, that scarf is big enough to serve as a kerchief once her hair starts to grow out. Just let me get it out of the window display and then you can decide."

Once purchased, I spot a beautiful Christmas card inside the bag showing downtown King Street, all lit-up at night with Christmas lights and a message that simply says, *Season's Greetings from Eveline and Angelica of Evangeline's Dress Shop.* This card and gesture, for me at least, is the true small-town heart and soul of Brockville. It will always remain home for me, in so very many ways.

Every year the Town Haus Restaurant is a Christmas kaleidoscope of colours, sights, sounds and scents. The Nutcracker soldiers standing guard at the front door into the restaurant have seen many Christmas's come and go over the decades. Inside is a veritable Bavarian fairyland of German-themed ornaments such as wooden, candle-powered carousels, exquisite painted-wood and delicate, antique silvered-glass tree ornaments, pine cone wreaths, and one marvellous tree beside the fireplace in the main dining room.

The aromas of delicious foods, mulled-wine, and tangerines spiked with cloves, gingerbread, pine boughs, holly and burning fire-logs enhance the entire festive atmosphere and experience.

I know I have to look nice for my birthday. Adam told me to be at his place for five because our reservations are for seven-thirty to meet Cala and Charlie, and Rob and Bryson.

I'm on the phone to confirm the time with Adam and ask if I can shower and change over at his place.

"You can change over here and we can head out then, no problem. Does that work for ya?"

"Do I get my birthday present before we go for dinner or after, Sasq' man?"

"Yes and yes."

"Like, what the hell, Adam?" I exclaim, while laughing at the sight of him stark naked and boldly posing for me just inside his front door. He's wearing a bright red fireman's helmet and has a piece of orange silk ribbon loosely tied around his penis and testicles. The ribbon looks suspiciously like the one from his birthday cake back in October.

"What's with the helmet, Sasq' man?"

He responds with, "I'm auditioning to be the next member of The Village People! Figured they needed a sexy hunk with a big hose to join 'em! And then he starts to roar with laughter.

I roll my eyes and say, Umm, uhh, OK… and the ribbon around King Kong…?"

"Well, since it's your birthday, I figured I'd get dressed in my birthday suit to greet ya. Happy birthday, baby!"

"Oh jeez! How lame and corny is that?" I say while continuing to roll my eyes and shake my head. "You *do* realize you've finally lost your mind… you *do* know that, don't you, Sasq'?"

"Never you mind! I'm wearin' our favourite colours, baby! Now just get your cute little mouth down there between my legs and give my balls a good tongue-lashing 'cause they've been really bad and raunchy boys lately and need a real firm hand… and maybe some tongue and lip action on 'em to keep them in line!"

"Happy fuckin' birthday." He groans softly as a big load of his thick spunk shoots out of his throbbing crotch-rocket and washes down my throat. "Now, let's hop in the shower together and soap, shampoo and lather each other up. Then we can get dressed to go meet Cala and Charlie and Rob and Bryson."

"Do you think ya might be done in the bathroom and ready to head out before your *next* birthday rolls around there?" says Adam, having long finished dressing in his new clothes in his bedroom.

"You want me to look nice, don't you?" I yell back at him as I pull up my pants and start to throw on my sweater.

"I can see now we're gonna need two bathrooms when we start to look for a new place in Ottawa."

317

"Nah, It just takes you less time because you're so perfect and handsome and tasty and sexy already." I laugh and say, "Just a couple of more minutes and I'll be done."

"Yeah—yeah—yeah, just speed it up in there, butt-boy. I'm not gettin' any younger out here, ya know."

"OK, Sasq'."

Once out of the bathroom and stepping into his bedroom, I stop dead in my tracks to take in the sight of him in his new clothes, leaning back on his bed and smiling provocatively back at me with a raised eyebrow while twitching his nose.

"Oh My God! You look incredible! Wow! Next time, give me some kind of clue before you decide to give me heart-failure. Wow! Can I jump on you and maybe we'll forget about dinner?"

"Nope. You're not gonna mess up these clothes, ya horny, little perv'. You can play with my old ones all ya' like. But these ones are gonna stay clean and pressed for job interviews in Ottawa. Now come on over here and you can sit in my lap for a few minutes and we can stink up the room with the Eau Sauvage I'm guessin' you sprayed in your bikini underwear. You can rub my Chewbacca chest hair and then we just gotta head out."

I'm thinking, *Yay! Happy birthday, Aaron!*

Different families observe and celebrate the Christmas Holidays in ways that are as unique and special as they are. At our house, Mom is always the one to dictate how the house would be decorated and what customs would be observed. Strict tradition with respect to fragrant, freshly-cut blue spruce Christmas trees and holly and ivy garlands and boughs of pine are always the rule. Mistletoe and multi-coloured, bubble-lights on the tree—more multi-coloured festive lights and a pine garland draped around the front door where a handmade pine wreath with a red silk ribbon bow greeting visitors is a long-standing family tradition. Decorations collected over the decades, some handed down from her parents are proudly displayed and carefully hung from the tree. The effect is timeless.

Contrasting this, Adam's mom is, without doubt, a contemporary seventies woman who likes to keep up with the latest modern trends and styles. She has a shiny, silver aluminum Christmas tree with a rotating wheel that casts glowing red, blue, green, and amber-coloured light onto huge gold and white globe decorations—a total contrast to what I've grown up with. The exterior of her home on Broadway Crescent is decorated with blue and green flashing Christmas lights that hang along the eaves and huge silver artificial floral sprays with blue and green ornaments at the double front doors. This is her special way to welcome guests into her home for the festive Holiday Season.

The common thread between both families is the kindness and warmth of the women who open their homes to all over the holidays and the love they have for their friends and family. I came to finally realize this year that it is this spirit of love and acceptance, and the desire to want to share happiness and goodwill that is very much part of the true meaning of Christmas.

"You really needed a tree in your apartment," I tell Adam and then place a tabletop Christmas tree I got from The Flower Shop on King Street on top of his stereo console cabinet. It's white and has red, gold, and silver decorations and green bows on it. It's kind of a mix between his mom's house and mine, I tell him. "I thought maybe we could combine the two families and traditions into one tree. I hope you like it. Merry Christmas!"

"Aww, that's real sweet. I like the sentiment and you're right. This place sorta kinda needed somethin' to make it look festive. There's just one thing ya forgot, though. I got some real mistletoe and hung it just outside the bedroom door." With that, he pulls me into the doorway of his bedroom and kisses me deeply under the mistletoe.

"*Now* it's Christmas. Merry Christmas!"

Then the question of how we will spend our first Christmas together comes up for discussion.

"Uhm, Adam, I'm going with Dad to Midnight Mass at St. Francis this year. I haven't done that with him in years. And I want to go and sit up in the choir loft with him while he sings in the choir and say hi to Cliff Horton at the same time. We usually come home after that and open our presents. What do you and your mom do? Do you usually open gifts on Christmas morning and then have dinner later on? I assume Bast will be there with you this year. I'd like you to be part of our traditions this year, and of course if your mom wants me to be there, I'd really like to be part of yours, too."

"Mom was asking me about that before I came up to pick ya up. She was thinkin' maybe instead of having to eat two turkey dinners this year, she'd do up a honey-glazed Christmas ham and maybe make a *tourtière* to keep Bast happy, with him being French Canadian and all for mid-day. Ya know, when I was still living at home growin' up, we always opened up our gifts on Christmas morning. It's only you damn Catholics who can't wait until Christmas morning to open up your gifts!"

"Don't say that in front of Dad or he'll have Blackjack pee in your Christmas stocking!"

"So, how do you want to celebrate with me here then, Cookie?"

"Well Sasq', how about we come back here after Christmas dinner with my parents and we can have our very own first Christmas together, just you and me?"

"Hmmm, guess I'll be goin' out to buy lots more mistletoe then and hang it all over. Now, do ya maybe think you could grab onto my dong again like you did when I picked ya up at your, errr, I guess I should be sayin' *our* place now to bring ya on back to Brock Vegas? You were so concerned it wasn't down there before. And right now, I can promise ya it's very much here and wants ya to know it too. It was tellin' me it wants to wish you a Merry Christmas!"

"And hopefully a Happy New Year, too..."

"Damn straight! Remember what I always say to ya... you can always count on me. And just so ya know, my King Kong dong doesn't discriminate. It observes all the major holidays, statutory, religious and otherwise."

"Ahh, yes, I remember it mentioning something to that effect at Thanksgiving. Your penis can be very chatty and communicative at times—a real talking head." Meanwhile I'm thinking. *Jeez, Aaron, you're beginning to sound as lame and corny as Adam!*

Then Adam comes out with, "It's only shy around strangers. Once it warms up to someone, it practically never stops yackin' and jackin'!"

Oh God... !

8 January / February

"These CCM Professional Series men's hockey skates are really gonna be good on the Rideau Canal when we go skating. They're like, the perfect present. Thanks, baby!"

"And these Faber Castell technical drafting pens are going to come in handy when I have to work on Gaelen's drafting assignments in the New Year, Adam. How did you manage to pick them up in Ottawa without me knowing?"

"I didn't. Wallack's has a branch store in Kingston on Princess Street and I got my mom to pick 'em up when she was up there shoppin' a few weeks ago."

"I keep breaking the really extra fine-point nibs on the ones I got back in September. Your timing here is perfect for the next semester! Thanks, Sasq'."

"The sweater is nice, too, Aaron. It kinda makes me laugh when I remember it's an *Aaron, fisherman, cable-knit sweater*! It's sorta like I'm wearin' *you* on my back."

"Merry Christmas, Adam!"

"Aww, Merry Christmas to you, too, honey!"

Later on that evening, the subject of New Year's Eve and spending it up in Ottawa with Rob and Bryson and Cala comes up again. I remember the idea being tossed around by Adam during my birthday dinner at The Town Haus."

"So, whaddya say, Aaron? Cala and Rob and Bryson are all wantin' to go and dance at Sac's and maybe those two clubs Conor Rekford was telling me about when he came in to say hi to me at the store last week when he was down visiting his parents for Christmas. Valentino's on 160, rue Montcalm and *Le Trou du Diable* on 200, rue Victoria in those big new government office complex buildings they're buildin' over in Hull there. We could even stop in at the *le chez Henri* on boulevard, Sâcre Coeur if ya like. That place is somethin' you should really see. It's legendary and has been around like, forever."

"Le Trou du Diable? Isn't that like, *the devil's hole* in French?"

Adam chuckles and replies, "Yep, my tight, little butt-boy! It sure is! But I kinda prefer yours though. It's more than hot and toasty enough for me in there."

Ten minutes of an Adam Blanchard *grope-fest* and then I try to distract him by saying, "I'm really excited about skating on the Canal with you. Are you a good skater, Sasq'?"

"Yeah, I am. How about you?"

"Well, kinda, sorta." Then I start to think about my time growing up in Brockville.

The first time I ever went skating, my dad took me. I think I was around seven back then. He was pretty good with holding me up until I got the hang of it. The ever-present handkerchief in his pocket dried my tears the first few times I fell on the ice.

Just then, I start to think, remembering the times I used to go skating with John and Wendy Yaegar every Saturday when we were little kids back at St. Francis Xavier.

I'm not the greatest skater in the world and am never going to be an NHL hockey player. But I have to admit, I really did look forward to and enjoy those Saturdays at the Memorial Centre on King Street West—going with the Yaegars and then stopping back into the toy store inside Symington's on our way home to look in the Matchbox car display case and the HO scale model-train layouts.

It was the *Spirograph* and *Gumby and Pokey* phase of my childhood.

I can still remember the music they played on the loudspeakers at the Memorial Centre as everyone went round and round the inside oval hockey rink for one or two hours, until they headed back in to unlace their skates and grab a hot chocolate and green relish and mustard-slathered hot dog wrapped in tin foil at the concession counter. Music like Herb Alpert and The Tijuana Brass with "Limbo Rock" and Henry Mancini tunes such as "Moon River", as well as that Mancini theme from the Jack Lemmon movie, *Good Neighbor Sam* played on a harsh, tinny-sounding, continuous repeat-cycle by ancient, static-filled loud-speakers. I can still remember the piano orchestral version of "Alley Cat" from the early-sixties by some obscure Danish Jazz group—it's one of those tunes that got burned into my brain back then, and will likely stay in there forever—along with all the other useless information I manage to retain in there on any given day of the week.

Then puberty and high school came and smacked us all on the upside of the head. Suddenly, that was that for my Saturday afternoons with John and Wendy. John and I stayed acquaintances for maybe another year or so until he turned thirteen and his hormones started to kick in. He and I went swimming every week at the Rotary Pool beside the Memorial Centre during that time. He was one year older than me and Wendy was one year younger, almost to the day, in fact. But when the other kids started calling me fairy and queer, he started to avoid me like the plague.

And it was only years later that Wendy and I became sort of friendly again. She got free drinks from me in the bar and I got a dance partner who didn't care that I was gay and who served to allay some of the unkind gossip, rude speculation and ignorant jokes about my sexuality when I was in the bar with a girl. The arrangement worked out perfectly for the both of us.

Their chubby, loud-mouthed, bullying first-cousin, Jimmy made my early and mid-teenage years miserable. He would snicker and lunge at me and make like he was going to punch me in the face whenever he and I passed each other on King Street, before I moved away to College. If I saw him first, I'd cross the street just to get away from him. I now wonder just what it was that was so awful in his life that he felt he had to bully and torment me so badly. Oh well, I guess we all carry our own *diables* around inside us.

I then stop my sentimental reminiscing and return to reality, saying to Adam, "There's a change-hut to lace up skates and leave our boots just down on Argyle from us on the Canal. The ice should be in really good condition once I start back to school in January."

"I think that's gonna be really romantic. You and me together, just the two of us and sharin' a beavertail and some hot chocolate together. And then we can head on back to our little place and warm each other up after skatin' the whole length of the Canal from the National Arts Centre right down to Dow's Lake and back. It'll be lotsa fun and the exercise will do us both good. It'll keep our butts in shape for sure!"

"You really are one single-minded Sasquatch at times. You *do* know that don't you?"

"You love it, butt-boy—your *trou du diable* is all mine and dontcha forget it either!"

"Uhh, I'm OK, Adam, if you want to spend New Year's Eve in Ottawa with Rob and Cala. Can you get your mom's car to take us up and then back the next day? I suppose we could all crash at our place that night after partying, if we had to."

"I'll ask her, honey. She'll be with Bast that night so I don't think that's gonna be a problem."

Chaka Khan and Rufus are singing "Once You Get Started" in the background.

"In the meantime I'm thinkin' Chaka Khan there is tellin' us she likes the way we do it and the way we move. Whaddya say we move it into the bedroom and continue this discussion in there?"

"Thought you'd never ask."

"I can hardly wait until we get to do this every night when you're with me up in Ottawa," I sigh and smile as he finds his way into my *trou du diable.*

It's December 31st—the last day of the best year of my life.

"Ugh! C'mon, Aaron! Jeez. You sure as hell take long enough to get yourself dressed at times! Cala and Bryson and Rob are waitin' for us to pick 'em up! It's fuckin' freezing out there! We just can't keep 'em waiting. I promised them we'd pick 'em up at Rob's place on Courthouse Terrace for seven-thirty and its way past that now! Now let's get movin'! We hafta be at Sac's to wish Conor a Happy New Year and then on to

Valentino's and the *Trou du Diable* before midnight. And I mean mid-night *this* fuckin' year, too!"

"OK—OK—OK! I'm just having trouble deciding what to wear."

"Oh, for fuck's sakes! You're gorgeous and sexy whatever ya put on or take off. Now let's get going! New Year's is gonna come and go and you'll still be starin' at yourself in that mirror, debatin' whether your jeans are tight enough—which, by the way, they are! Now, c'mon, let's move it!"

"Before we go though, Adam, can I have my New Year's Eve kiss now?" I say this while reaching down to grope King Kong.

"Aww, Jeezus fuck, you're gettin' me all hard again here. You can rub my pube-forest and I'll shove my tongue down your throat and grab your cute little ass-cheeks and then we can head out then. Will that make ya happy?"

"Happy New Year, Sasq'!"

"You too, baby."

It's still early when we all cross the Alexandria Bridge over to Hull and start to make our way to Sac's. It's a special night for the club and only VIPs and invited patrons have been issued silver-embossed invitations to celebrate the New Year's Eve festivities inside. Conor Rekford pulled some strings with his boss to get us tickets for the night. The owner of the club remembered Adam's tip about Alleyn, Jeremey, and *Mother* and the nasty drug incident in the washroom.

The tickets were his way of saying thanks to Adam for getting him out of a potential jam with the RCMP and Quebec *gendarmes*.

"I think we're just gonna park around the corner from Sac's and say hey to Conor at the front door. I just gotta see what his boss has him wearin' this time!" says Adam as he starts to chuckle. "I sure hope his nipples are covered up with this goddamn deep-freeze!"

"Conor! Heya, man! I see ya got a bit more clothes on ya this time, buddy. Happy New Year to you!" Adam gives his friend a big bear hug.

"I'm wearing thermal long-johns under these tight-fitting leather jeans, Adam! And if I didn't have this goddamn skull toque and padded, down-filled bomber jacket on, I'd be an ice sculpture right about now like the ones at Dow's Lake during Winterlude, man!"

"You remember Aaron, Conor, dontcha? And these are our friends, Cala and Rob and Bryson from Brockville."

"Sure do, Adam. Nice meeting ya guys. Hey, are ya legal yet there, Aaron? And Cala, I remember you! Your sister, Cora-Leanne worked on the assembly line with me when I was at Black and Decker. How are you? And how is Cora-Leanne?"

"Hiya, Conor! Cora-Leanne is doing just fine. And I remember you, too! But not with skin-tight, black leather pants and four-inch platform boots! Guess it woulda been kinda hard to work an assembly line in those back in Brockville. You look just like a porn star! God! Hell, why is it all the really hot and sexy guys seem to be gay?" she sighs and whispers as she leans over to Adam and shares a quiet laugh with him. "Don't you ever, ever tell Charlie I said that though."

"Conor, we just wanted to stop by to wish you an early Happy New Year before things get crazy. You mentioned that *Trou du Diable* place and then Valentino's. Figured we'd check those places out first and then head back here for around eleven or so to ring in the New Year with you."

"Forget about that *devil's hole* place, Adam. It really is a fuckin' hole, as in hole in the wall! I found out some organized-crime guys outta Montreal just rented some space for a few months until the office towers are finished and the government start to move their workers into them. Those Mafia guys are trying to gouge all the gay guys who go in there with overpriced drinks, and undercover drugs, and male prostitutes. And I hear they've been recording names and taking pictures of some of the government senior men who visit. God knows what the fuck they're doing with that information—I don't wanna know, either. I went in there myself and the place is a real dump. It looks like it's still a construction site. The walls aren't even painted yet—drywall tape and plaster still, with just some folding card-tables and chairs, and a real shitty DJ and sound system, too. I'd be staying away from there, if I were you."

"Holy shit! Thanks, Conor. I can always count on you to have my back. I appreciate that."

"And as for Valentino's, well... Adam, just be real careful when you're there, too. Something really strange is going on with the bars in Hull right now. The owner here has had to hire security guys to watch this place 24/7 'cause bars have been mysteriously burning down in Hull on a pretty regular basis. Seems like those guys in Montreal are trying to send a message to all the bar owners here about allowing access for selling drugs and prostitution. It's getting kinda scary, to tell you the truth. Just last week, someone drove by Valentino's and threw a bottle of gasoline with a burning rag in it at their front door when the place was packed! Just be careful, OK, Adam, please?"

"Jeezus fuck! I will for sure. Thanks, man! Uhh, we'll be back here before midnight. If you're off later just before the bar closes, maybe you might wanna join us at the *chez Henri* before we all go home and crash. Whaddya think?"

"I'm outta here at one-thirty and my new boyfriend Nicolas, errr, that is, *Nico* will be meeting me here just before midnight. I'll let you know when I talk to him, OK?"

"So, you're datin' someone now, too. That's fantastic, Conor! Guess that means you'll be stayin' up here for a while then. I'm movin' up here real soon now myself—full-time, to be with Aaron."

"We'll be hanging around then lots, that's great news!" Conor says as he smiles and gives Adam another big hug.

"Later, Conor!"

Valentino's looks like a clone of Sac's in that it's pitch-black inside to the point where you almost need a flashlight to make your way around the place. There is a long black bar and multi-level, carpeted, raised ply-wood-platforms/bleachers all along the walls where people could either lean or recline, like in some debauched scene from an ancient Roman noble's villa. It's much smaller and, in a way, more intimate than Sac's. The place reeks of stale cigarette smoke, spilt beer, and *Drakar Noir,* cologne-masked, rank body odor. The ever-present, mirrored disco-ball is over the dance floor and a tiny DJ booth is tucked into an obscure corner. The dance floor is smaller even than the ones in the *oral grief club* and Sac's.

As for the crowd, they're decidedly more Gatineau French than English. Above the music, all you can hear is raucous laughter and vulgar French epitaphs at the bar and on the dance floor.

"C'mon, Cala, let's dance!" Adam shouts. He grabs her and elbows his way onto the dance floor. "Don't Leave Me This Way" by Thelma Houston is cranked up and there's frenzied movement on the dance floor.

Once he's back from dancing and watching the scene with me, Adam keeps scratching himself and then finally grumbles, "Jeezus fuck, I sure as hell hope they clean the goddamn shag carpet on these platforms more than, like, once every ten years or so. I feel like I'm sittin' inside someone's hairy armpit or furry pube-basket here with you leanin' back into me and your sexy butt rubbin' against my dong."

"That wouldn't bother me! I'd have no problem being inside your armpit or sexy bulge down there anytime! So let's switch places and you can pretend you're leaning into me. I can shove my hands into your pockets and play with King Kong then. You know you're my big, hairy hand-warmer, don't you, Sasq' man?!"

Adam blushes and pulls me back into his bulging, half-hard man-basket. "You just wanna get me hard in public to make me blush—I figured that one out a long time ago."

"Well, actually, I like getting you hard to make everyone in the bar jealous of what I get to play with, and they don't!"

"Ya *do* know, Cookie, that's just plain teasin' everybody, including me, dontcha?"

"Well, Adam, just like you always like to say to me, if my ass is all yours, then your cock is all mine!"

"You kinky little fucker!" he says, and laughs.

"And that's why you love me, Sasq' man!"

"Yeahh, right. Uhm, just so ya know, I'll be hoppin' into the bathtub when we get home in case I get a rash or pick up bed-bugs or head-lice from this damned, stinkin', arm-pit-smellin' shag carpet! We're sure as hell headin' right back to Sac's just as soon as Rob and Bryson get off the dance floor. And what's inside my jeans can warm your hands up there if ya promise to behave. Does that work for ya?"

Once back inside Sac's, I have to laugh and say to Adam, "Aww, you look so cute wearing that Happy New Year tiara with the fluffy white marabou and silver stars!"

"You're really gonna regret it when we get home if ya keep on teasin' me! Conor made me wear it when we came in the door. In fact, he gave me one to put on you, too."

Just then, he hauls a matching one out of his back pocket and plunks it on top of my head.

"Now that's worth a picture! Smile, guys!" Rob and Bryson are both laughing. Rob pulls out a tiny little instamatic camera and snaps a shot of the both of us.

"Oh my God! Ugh! C'mon, Cala, we came here to dance." I drag her onto the dance floor to get away from Paparazzi Rob and his flashing camera.

A half-hour later, at two minutes to midnight, six fat drag queens holding wands and wearing purple and pink Halston fashion designer-style jersey caftans converge onto the dance floor and start to throw pink glitter dust into the air while swaying back and forth and singing "Auld Lang Syne" to a disco beat.

"Gotta admit, this is one pretty fucked-up way to ring in the New Year, eh?" whispers Adam as he starts to nibble and tease my ear lobe with his tongue.

"It's been the best year of my life, Adam. I love you. Happy New Year!"

"Happy New Year, Aaron. I love you, too."

After we leave Sac's, Adam muscles his way through the packed bar and grabs the last remaining dirty table for us inside the *chez Henri*, just before last-call.

"Too bad Conor couldn't join us."

"Well, honey, he was wantin' to spend the rest of the night with his new boyfriend. I can sure as hell understand that."

He puts his arm protectively around me and starts to survey the people in the packed bar. "Yep, this place hasn't changed one damn bit since the last time I was here. Ya got drag queens, transvestites, motorcycle dykes, and everything else in here—I wanted ya to see it all with me. This is no place for you to come into by yourself though. Drug-dealers, addicts, motorcycle gangs, and every other damn criminal and creep you can think of winds up in here for last-call on weekends. The place used to be a real respectable hotel decades ago. And if you look real hard, you'll still see some of the leftover reminders from that time. Like, just look at that big, hand-painted mural on the wall behind that beautiful, old brass and mahogany bar. It's like, fuckin' fantastic!"

The mural is huge and while badly-stained now after decades of neglect and coated with a thick, brownish-film of nicotine, it's still very imposing and actually quite gorgeous. I'm guessing it must be over forty feet long and at least ten feet high. It reminds me of a Pierre-Auguste Renoir painting, or maybe something from Henri de Toulouse-Lautrec. It's full of movement and depicts a ballroom scene from what I'm guessing would date back to the time when the hotel first opened at the turn of the century. Men in white waistcoats, black tail-coats, and tight-fitting trousers are waltzing with blushing women in swirling, late-nineteenth-century, pastel-coloured ball gowns with bustles, wearing jewels, birds, and feathers in their hair. The scene looks to me like something out of the Paris *demimonde* from the 1890s."

"That's a real special, piece of history there," Adam tells me just as the waiter comes to clean our table with a dirty cloth.

By the time they start to flick the lights on and off to let people know the bar is closing at last-call, Adam looks over at Cala, Bryson, and Rob and then turns to me and whispers, "Uhm, they all look like they're about to fall asleep. Let's get 'em out to the car and I think I'm gonna drive us all back to Brockville tonight. They can be comfortable and get to sleep in their own beds when we get home. And you can sleep with me. Whaddya say?"

"That's a good idea. Happy New Year! It's going to be a great new year."

It's just past official moving day for Adam and we're crammed into my tiny excuse for an apartment.

"Uhm, uhh, Aaron, like, why have ya got three of the exact same shirt in the same size and four pairs of identical Howick jeans in the same size and colour?" Adam says, trying to shove his clothes into my armoire. "This just isn't gonna work if ya can't give up some of your space for me. Ya know, most of my stuff went into storage in Mom's garage. But ya just gotta gimme some room for my clothes, and that little dresser... and what I moved up here with from Brockville."

"But, Adam, why did you pack every single solitary book you own and not leave some of them back at your mom's? They're taking up all the space in the front when I come in the door. And I can hardly get past them to reach for my coat and put on my boots to go outside."

It was just a week ago that Adam finished moving his stuff to the apartment, except for what he still needs to finish up working for Mrs. Tonner in January. The challenge is now to find space for everything he has, along with what I moved up with in September.

This is going to be a real problem.

"OK—OK. I guess we're just gonna hafta be patient with each other and do the best we can 'til we find somethin' bigger."

Adam sighs and then tries to shove nine shirts, six pairs of pants, five sweaters, plus his navy blue jacket and new grey tweed one into the armoire.

"I guess I *could* take a box of yours there when you're done with it and stick some of my extra shirts and stuff in it and shove it under the bed for now. Would that help?"

"Yep, it sure would. But like, I just hafta ask—like, why the fuck have ya got three identical shirts? Like, I just don't get that at all."

"Because they were pretty and I liked them… and I didn't want anyone else to have them."

"Ugh! Jeezus fuck! Like, fuck me over with a two by four!" he mutters under his breath.

"What did you say, Adam?"

"Uhm, nothin' honey. Nothin' at all."

Later that evening, we're out skating on the Rideau Canal when I have to stop for a minute to catch my breath and shout over at Adam, "It's like, frikkin' twenty degrees below zero out here on the Canal! You've made me skate all the way from the National Arts Centre to Dow's Lake! That's, like, more than three miles and we had to fight the wind against us all the way. We're going to stop at Patterson's Creek on the way back for a hot chocolate and a *beavertail*. And you're buying, too!"

"OK, butt-boy!" Adam skates back toward me and suddenly skids and brakes in theatrical and dramatic fashion, spraying ice and snow up at me from the frozen surface of the Canal. Then he gives me one of his provocative, dirty laughs and says, "A *beavertail*—gotta admit… pretty weird name for a piece of pie crust with brown sugar and crap on it, eh? Like, that's the closest we're ever gonna get to a beaver!"

"Oh, I don't know. It's flat and sort of looks like a beaver's tail the way they spread it out with a patterned rolling pin before deep-frying."

"Wasn't exactly referring to that kinda beaver there."

"Ohh, you're so dirty-minded at times, you know!"

"That's why ya love me. Now, c'mon and move those cute boy-buns! I'll race ya back to Patterson's Creek."

At the rest stops along the Canal, the National Capital Commission has set up little fires in oil drums so skaters can warm themselves. The smell of wood smoke along with the coloured-lights and music at the concession stands is pretty.

Winterlude starts at the end of January, filling the area with ice sculptures that volunteer groups do up for charity on Dow's Lake. It's a major spectacle, very unique to Ottawa and the National Capital Region."

"Sure is nice to be able to experience all this, eh, Cookie?" We're lucky to be livin' so close to the Canal. And these new skates you got me for Christmas, well, I can skate rings around ya!" At that, he skates backward, dodging, weaving, and spinning around to make his point, and generally-speaking, to piss me off.

"It's not a competition!"

"Nope, I'm guessin' not, given the way you skate there!"

"Ohh! You bastard! Just wait until I catch you, you big, hairy, hunky Sasquatch!"

And then the game of tag continues all the way down the Canal until we get in front of the Colonel By Campus and our tiny little apartment on Argyle.

"Hullo?"

"Well, well, *allo, bonjour, la*, Aaron. *Salut, mon petit*. How are classes coming along? It's Bast from Brockville. Is Adam there?"

"He's right here, Mr. Forestier. Hold on."

"Heya, Bast. What's wrong? Is there anything wrong? Is Mom OK there?"

"Salut, Adam. Ahh, mon Dieu! Non, non, Adam, not at all—pas du tout, mon jeune. Mais, I was driving along Water Street today and saw your old *voiture*, errr, car, that is. Do you remember the winter *carnaval içi* here in Brockville when they take an old car and put it out on the ice on the *rivière*, then sell raffle tickets to guess when it will break through the ice and sink to the bottom? *Bien. Câlice! Sacrifice!* Your old, grey SST *Ambassadeur* is out there now, right where the Brockville Rowing Club is!"

"Nooo! You're fuckin' kidding me, right? *Tell* me ya are!"

"Mais non! Mon Dieu! Pas du tout! Just like years before, they've got the sign up and are calling it *Old Meg* and there's a *placard*, uhh, sign with a *numéro* to call to buy tickets and make a *prédiction* of when it will go down in the spring! *Incroyable! Esti! Câlice!*"

"I sold it to that guy in Merrickville who was going to use it for parts! Why the fuck did he get rid of it, I wonder?"

"*Alors*, it looks like he stripped it right down, *absoluement, totalement!* There's no windshield or windows in it and the rear tail light lenses, door handles, and hubcaps are gone. *C'est juste*, it's just the rusted-out body *la* and it looks like most of the *interieur* is gone. They spray-painted the name *Old Meg* on the side of it *avec*, errr, with the *numéro de téléphone* to call for tickets! *Je crois*, uhm, uhh, I believe the more people who buy a ticket to make a *prédiction* when it will sink, the bigger the prize will be."

"Ahh, man—my poor fuckin' car! After all the years it served Mom and me! It sure as hell deserves a better goddamn finish than this! I'm really upset here, Bast!"

"Your mom thought you would be and that is why I call you now, *mon ami*, to let you know. *Je suis vraiement désolé, mon petit. I* am sorry.

"Tell Mom I'll call her in the next day or so, OK, Bast?"

"*Absolument*, absolutely."

"We'll talk later."

Adam slowly puts the receiver back onto the wall-phone and sighs heavily.

"So what did Bast want?"

"Jeezus fuck, baby! They took my old SST and it's out on the ice in front of the Brockville Rowing Club for the Brockville Winter Carnival! I'm kinda upset about it here. My poor old car deserves better than that! Bast wanted me to know, instead of me havin' to see it out there when I'm back down in Brock Vegas."

I'm tempted to make a smart-ass crack about it feeling right at home with the underwater submarine races and hot, periscope-sex in it off Blockhouse Island, but think better of it and let him continue.

"God, Aaron. My dad's poor old car! How fuckin' sad and pathetic is that?!

"Uhm, do you remember telling me how you thought it was a symbol for you when it broke down out at Brown's Bay?"

"Uhh, yeah, baby, I do. What's your point there?"

"Well, seems to me that it served everyone pretty well for all the years it was running. You know, Adam, if it hadn't been for that car, you and I might never have gotten the chance to meet each other. And now with you ending one life in Brockville and starting a brand new, fresh one up here with me, well, uhm, maybe this is a kind of a fitting closure and goodbye. You could look at it that way, I suppose."

"That's kinda romantic there, baby. A real nice sentiment. I think I kinda, sorta like that. There's a word for that. But I can't come up with it right now.

"I'm pretty sure you're thinking of the word, *lyrical.*"

He snaps his fingers and exclaims, "Yeahh! That's the word all right! That makes me feel a little better, actually. Thanks."

"I think you and I should buy lottery tickets to see when it will break through the ice in the spring. I'll get Mom or Dad to do that for us. Sometime around Easter this year, I'm guessing, because I think we're going to have an early spring."

"Hah! Did you get that outta the Fisherman's Almanac magazine ya bought from me at Tonner's that time when you were pretendin' to shop for stuff while checkin' me out?!"

I couldn't help but laugh over his remembering that episode with me in Tonner's at the cash-register and cashier's counter from last spring.

"Nooo! I read somewhere that men's hormones get stronger in the spring and you seem to be constantly horny and boned-up around me lately, so I figured *spring fever* must be just around the corner!"

"Get on over here! Kiss me, ya kinky, fuckin' little twink!"

9 February / March

The first month or two of living together brings with it a series of challenges that test the limits of compromise, patience, humour, and understanding for Adam and me—at times to the absolute max. He's been on his own for more than five years and I know there are times when I frustrate him with my habits and quirks. He tries so hard not to distract me with my schoolwork, and I have to admit, I'm happy when he comes over to the school to say hi to my classmates and check on what I'm doing. They all just absolutely love him, too.

"Jeez, baby, what's Gaelen gotcha workin' on now?"

"Hi, Adam! I'm just testing out some line weights on these mechanical pens you got me for Christmas. They're really a beautiful set of drafting instruments. He wants us to do an axonometric drawing in ink of our student workspace from last term. I think it's looking not too bad. What do you think?"

"Well, I think it looks like it could jump right off the page atcha. I'm thinkin' the thicker lines on the outside edges make it look like you could reach down and put your hands around it and pick it up."

"That's the idea. They give it dimension. And that's what Gaelen taught us in one of his last drafting classes."

"So, what else have they gotcha working on right now?"

"Well, Evan gave us kind of a fun assignment, actually. I'm going to team up with Yolanda Vargas to come up with something that Evan says is more like Industrial Design—a team project to stretch our creative limits and to make us think outside the box. We are to design a package or protective enclosure to hold an egg that has to withstand a drop from a second-floor window without breaking. Isn't that insane?"

"What the fuck does that have to do with Interior Design?"

"Nothing, actually. It's just something to make us learn how to work together—to think analytically and come up with a workable and cre-ative solution to a challenge. If the egg survives the fall, we pass. If it doesn't, we fail. It's as simple as that. I think the idea is kinda neat!"

"OK, OK, I get it," he laughs and then asks, "So, whatcha' got in mind for that one?"

"Not sure just yet. Yolanda said she had some ideas. But I haven't talked with her yet about them."

"Are you gonna be done here soon? I thought I'd walk with ya back home for dinner. I made some spicy chili up for us and picked up some cheese, sour cream and french bread at the IGA. Thought we could have some of that and then head out onto the Canal again to skate down to Dow's Lake to see the ice sculptures. The fresh air will be good for ya'. Whaddya say?"

"Give me five minutes to pack up and we can head out then."

We're walking down the hallway and past the lounge area where there are two lumpy, smelly, ancient brown sofas and a blueprint machine when Adam stops for a second and motions over to a door, asking me, "Uhm, what's behind that door there?"

"Oh, that one? That's where they keep some old fabric and wallpaper sample-books and the bottles of ammonia, velum and sepia paper and mylar rolls for the blueprint machine."

Just then he grabs onto my wrist roughly and starts to drag me over to the door.

"What are you doing?!"

He reaches down to grab the lever to see if the door is locked and discovers it isn't. The next thing I know, he's shoving me into the room, which is not much larger than a janitor's storage room. He pushes me tight up against a metal shelving rack and starts to undo my jeans and roughly yank them down.

I'm laughing at him and burst out with, "Jeez! We're in my school! What the hell are you doing?!"

He has this lunatic expression on his face while continuing to pull my pants down and squats down on the floor right in front of me.

"I knew it! I just knew it! Ya damn little shit! You stole the last clean pair of my goddamn underwear this morning and left me with nothin' in my drawer! Take 'em off! Take 'em off like, right now! Time for you to go commando for a change there!"

I'm laughing my head off and standing in front of him with my jeans down around my ankles while he starts to pull his underwear down on me and orders me to hand them over to him.

"You can free-ball for once! Now you get yourself outta those damn jeans so I can grab those *tightie-whities*!"

At last he has his briefs in his hands. He sniffs them, rolls his eyes at me, balls them up in his hand and then roughly shoves them into his ski-jacket pocket.

All of a sudden I can hear Connie and Lauren just outside the door waiting for their prints to come out of the blueprint machine.

"Shhh! Adam! I can hear people just outside the door!"

Adam has a frightened look on his face which makes me giggle even more.

"Shhh! Aaron! Stop laughin'. We're gonna get busted here for sure! Shhh! Quiet!"

Then he quickly straightens up and starts to clumsily pull my jeans up, fumbling with my zipper and belt. "Shhh, now!"

The only thing I could think of to do was reach down and grab onto King Kong and bury my face into his shoulder to muffle my laughter. Meanwhile, I'm shaking and trying to be as quiet as possible.

Adam swats my hand away from his crotch and starts to softly chuckle and grin himself. "You're doin' the goddamn laundry tonight at the laundromat after dinner!" he whispers as Connie expounds to Lauren at great length and in precise detail about the health benefits of free-range, grain-fed chickens and all the different classifications and grades of eggs just on the other side of the door.

Later that evening, we're out skating on the Canal at Dow's Lake when I shout over to Adam, "Give me your hand and let me spin you around!"

"Just dontcha dump me into a crack in the ice."

"Ohh! You mean like the last time you did that to me, Sasq'" I say and laugh while starting to skate away.

"Ottawa is beautiful this time of year when it isn't a hundred degrees below zero, isn't it ?" Adam says as we skate circles around the ice sculptures all along Dow's Lake.

"Sure is. These ice sculptures are amazing. The only time I ever saw anything even close to them before was in Kingston at Queen's University. But the ones there were nothing compared to these. The coloured-lights on these ones and the work and skill carving the ice is just incredible. And we can just skate up close and right around them. That one there with the *Star Wars* theme, there's just one thing missing though on that big Wookie sculpture. They should have used *you* for a model."

"Nah, that's reserved just for you," Adam says. "Speakin' of which, my nuts are startin' to shrivel up with the wind blowin' across Dow's Lake here. Whaddya say we head on home and you can blow some hot air on 'em to see if we can unfreeze them before the spring thaw? Sound like a plan to you ?

Once back home and while cleaning up the dishes together, Adam says to me, "I meant to tell you earlier, I got a call this morning from the Ministry of National Health and Welfare from that contact Mrs. Tonner knows. They want me to come in next week for an interview for a job they have comin' up at the end of March. That's the start of what they call the government fiscal new year when they get their operating budgets. The job they're thinkin' of for me deals with supervising clerical staff and processing prescription drug applications and approvals for senior citizens on pensions. And they want me to learn French to become bilingual if I qualify for the job. I'm kinda nervous about that."

"Gee, you could do me in both official languages. Your French kissing already gets me off."

"Very funny. But do ya think I could actually learn a second language? I haven't been in school in years and I hafta admit the idea scares me a little."

"Adam, you're already losing some of that Brock Vegas *woulda—coulda—shoulda* accent and I'll bet you didn't even notice it. You adapt well and aren't afraid of change. I mean, really, just think about this past month. You're smart. You're determined. And you're just too sexy and tasty for words." At which point, I bend down to cup his big bulge while leaning in to tongue and tease the nape of his neck. "You'll do just fine, I have no doubt of that. Just don't get too sophisticated for me because I love you just the way you are."

After the initial phase of adjustment and getting used to the concept of sharing space and living together, I must admit it really didn't take all that long to learn and accept each other's unique habits and foibles. He has his eccentricities, like having to fold towels a certain way and being right-handed, putting dishes away exactly the opposite to how I would. Little things like that can make living in a small apartment challenging. The fact that we are together and approach life with a sense of humor and patience, *most of the time* make habits like that seem very minor in the overall scheme of things. I think some of my favorite times with Adam now are when I head down to the LE to meet him after my classes, only to find him sitting there in Pick's Place reading the *Ottawa Citizen*, waiting patiently for me. Early in the evenings, he gets the chance to say hi to John and André and sometimes his friend, Conor pops in to catch up with him before his shift starts over at Sac's.

It's the morning of Adam's interview with the Ministry of National Health and Welfare. "You look so good, Adam," I tell him when he comes out of the bathroom wearing his new clothes. "Do you remember telling me once to relax and just be myself and everything would turn out OK?"

"Yeah, I do. And thanks. Hafta admit, I'm nervous. But I'll do my best and we'll see what happens."

The day of Adam's interview with a Mrs. Andrea Gauthier starts with me heading off to class for nine and him heading down Elgin Street to meet her at her office on the Sparks Street Mall.

His interview is for ten-thirty.

"Do come in, Mr. Blanchard. So nice to meet you. I've heard so many good things about you already from Mrs. Tonner. Did you know that I used to work for her and her husband years ago before I married and was still living back in Brockville?"

Adam self-consciously clears his throat and thinks, *now Blanchard… lose the damn Brock Vegas accent and try not to sound like a goddamn hick for a change.* Then he nervously smiles at Mrs. Gauthier saying, "No, ma'am. Mrs. Tonner never told me that."

"Her husband gave me my first job fresh out of high school and I'll always be grateful to both him and Mrs. Tonner for the start they gave me back then. Now, I want you to relax and my co-worker and I have just a few questions for you that hopefully shouldn't be too difficult to answer. There is one question in particular, however that will comprise most of the grading we are obligated to do for this position, given that it is a supervisory management role with staff reporting to you and you, in turn reporting to senior management. But we'll get down to the questions in a few minutes. Tell me, how are you enjoying Ottawa now that you have moved up here permanently?"

"Well, ma'am, to tell ya the truth I haven't had much chance to get out to really see the city just yet. I've been up here often enough before when I was back in Brockville. But outside of skating on the Canal and gettin' myself settled into an apartment on Argyle Avenue, it's been busy for me. I'm looking forward to getting to really know the city though. It's beautiful and I'm excited to be given the opportunity to grow and experience all it has to offer."

"Very good. May I call you Adam?"

"Yes, ma'am, please do."

"OK, Adam. We have four questions for you and have already gone over your resume and the letter of recommendation Mrs. Tonner wrote on your behalf. Just relax and take your time to answer these questions to the best of your ability. The first question is really more of a formality and needed for the official record. Are you willing to undergo Federal Government training at the government's expense in order to become officially bilingual in order to meet the requirements of the position we would be offering to you?"

"Yes ma'am, I am."

Mrs. Gauthier's co-worker poses the next question. "This is an important question, *Monsieur* Blanchard. It involves a scenario wherein you are about to enter a boardroom to discuss important finance issues with another government department. Your hand is on the door knob leading into a boardroom where you are to meet with them and where they are sitting waiting for you, along with one of your staff who reports to you. This employee was responsible to provide you with critical information for this meeting and as you are about to step into the room they confess to you that they haven't done the required work and as such you are now in the position of having to explain this to those waiting inside the room. What do you do?"

Adam shifts a bit in his seat and starts to think about how he is going to answer this question.

"That's a really great question," he says, at last. "Uhm, uhh, I think this comes down to accepting responsibility and accountability. First off, I'd be completely honest with the people I hafta meet. I'd apologise and tell 'em that I don't have all the information necessary to conduct the meeting. I'd then suggest a follow-up time and place to meet again as soon as possible, at their office, with the promise I'd have all required facts and information for them at that time. I'd take full responsibility myself as a supervisor for not bein' prepared and ask for their patience and understanding and hopefully then end the meeting."

"Is there any more you would like to add to that?"

Adam hesitates for a moment and then adds, "Uhm, yeah, errr, yes, there is. If I were a supervisor in this position, I'd hafta ask myself how I let this happen. Did I not meet enough with this employee beforehand to understand and know the progress they were makin' with their work? I'd sit down with this employee and ask them if I coulda helped 'em more after the meeting. Did they feel my request was too difficult? Did they need my help or more time to do what I asked 'em to do? Were they afraid to come to me to ask for help or tell me they didn't understand what I was askin' them to do? Like, in other words, what could I have done to prevent this from happening? I'd want to hear anything they have to say to me so I could help them in their job, and with mine, too, for that matter, to avoid anything like this from happening again."

"Anything more?"

"Yeah, errr, yes, that is. I'd make sure I have everything down in writing on the chance my boss would get a call about this and let 'em know right away what had happened. I wouldn't want 'em to be blindsided if someone from the other government department complained about the waste of time and effort."

"That's fine *Monsieur* Blanchard. Would you like to add any more to that, or are you satisfied with that answer?"

Adam has a frown on his face and ponders his response. Then he says, "Well, uhm, uhh, maybe just one more thing. After I'd done all the above, maybe I'd go and meet with another supervisor over coffee to ask how they woulda dealt with a situation like this and ask for any suggestions they could make to me that would help me make sure somethin' like this didn't happen again."

"Thank you very much, *Monsieur* Blanchard."

There are two more questions dealing with the *Mission Statement* for the Ministry and knowledge specific to the Section Adam would be expected to work in. Luckily for him, he was able to find some research material at the National Library and managed to ace each one of the last two rated questions.

Then the focus shifts back to Mrs. Gauthier, who is openly flirting and smiling at Adam as she asks, "Adam, are you willing to undergo a full security-screening process at Federal Government expense in order to meet the requirements of this position?"

Adam hesitates for a moment, looks slightly uncomfortable, and then replies, "Yes ma'am. Uhm, uhh, that's OK."

And then the final question—really not much of a question at all, "Adam, the position will be available on a permanent, full-time basis starting after March 31st which is the new Federal Government fiscal year. Would you be ready to start as of that date, should you be the successful candidate for the position?"

"Yes ma'am."

"Excellent! Well, that concludes the interview. We have a number of applicants still to see. However, we will get back to you within the next month as to our decision. Thank you so much for your time. Do you have any questions for us regarding the position?"

"Maybe a couple, uhm, yep, err, yes. Like, how many people would I be responsible for as a supervisor with this job?"

"At the moment there are three employees reporting to this supervisory position. Although the number may increase to four, or possibly five, if our budget is approved in the new fiscal year."

"Uhh, how big a budget would I be responsible for? And would I be workin' with the public or only with inside government staff?"

"A supervisor in this role would only be responsible for the staffing budget for their employees and any extra people, like special consultants on an as-need basis. And yes, there may be times when this supervisor may have to interface with the public, along with senior management... although that would depend upon the circumstances. Any more questions, Adam?"

"No, ma'am. Thank you for this opportunity. It's been a real pleasure to meet you both."

"We won't take long to get back to you, Adam," says Andrea as she gets up to walk with him out to the elevator.

Once Adam has left the office, Andrea and her co-worker Hilary sit down to discuss and review the interview questions and the notes and check-marks they jotted down regarding his answers. Eventually, Hilary says, "Well, I have to admit, that was the *best* answer we've received by far to-date regarding that scenario challenge. He seemed to go full-circle and think of it from all aspects and checked off every box on what we were looking for in an answer. And he was very good with the other questions, too."

"Ohh, come on, Hilary! He's perfect for the job! You know it and so do I! And wouldn't it be nice to have that *Ottawa Rough Riders tight-end,* that smiling face, those gorgeous hazel-brown eyes and that tall, lanky, hunky body hovering above us in the office every day?"

"Don't think I didn't notice! But that stays just between you and me and these four walls, OK?"

Both woman chuckle together as they leave the boardroom to head off for mid-morning coffee.

Later that afternoon, I cut one of my classes short to meet Adam at the LE for a beer and then out for a quick dinner at the Ponderosa restaurant behind the hotel.

"Heya, Cookie! You're here kinda early. Did ya skip a class for me?"

"Uhh, yeah, I did, kinda, sorta. I kept thinking about you all day and my class this afternoon was with Iona and it was only for a crit, so I left early—she didn't mind."

"OK, but dontcha be makin' a habit of that. My interview went just fine. They asked me one question I really hadta think about. The rest of them weren't even exactly questions—more like would I take language training and would I be ready to start work at the end of March and dumb stuff like that. That one question really made me think though. And I kinda owe you a thanks for helpin' me with it, too. Do you remember when you had to do that assignment for *Lynda bird-brain* and you did the assignment based on following the hands of a clock?"

"Uhm, yeah, I do."

"Well, that sorta helped me to answer the question. I remembered that damn stupid clock when they asked me what I would do. And I worked it out step-by-step and think I covered a full circle of what I'd do and who I'd speak to. I started with one and ended up at twelve—me in the middle of the clock. I think I did pretty well with my answer. They're gonna let me know in a few weeks' time. Until then, I guess we wait."

I'm smirking and, with sudden inspiration, come out with, "Well, I hope your arms and hands didn't get stuck when they reached six thirty!" Then I lean into him and quietly whisper, "I wished you good luck this morning. Can't hurt to say it again."

"Thanks, butt-boy. I appreciate that. Now, let's finish our beer and then we can head out to have somethin' to eat before headin' home. Are you OK with that?"

"*Home*—you really feel at home with me now?"

"Sure do," he replies with a grin as he reaches under the table to squeeze my thigh.

Several days later and I'm doing some research at home when the phone rings. It's my dad. "Hi, Dad. I'm glad you called. How are Mom and Blackjack doing?"

"Hello, Aaron. We're all just fine here. I know you've been busy and I didn't want to interfere with your studies. But it's been several weeks. I wanted to touch base with you to find out how you and Adam are managing and how you are making out with your assignments. Are you keeping up-to-date with everything? And how is Adam making out with the job-search?"

"Well, Dad, actually he had his interview with the Ministry of National Health and Welfare a few days ago, as a matter of fact. He told me he thinks he did pretty well, too. He'll know in a few weeks and I'll let you know once he hears back from them."

"And you're not getting behind with any of your classwork, I hope."

"Nope. Adam is making sure I stay up-to-date. He's really good that way. It's all good."

"Uhm, son, Bast told me at the Hospital about Adam's old car and *Old Meg* and all that Winter Carnival nonsense. I assume you know all about it there."

"Yes. In fact, would you and Mom mind calling that number and getting a couple of lottery tickets for Adam and me, please? He's actually pretty much OK with it all."

"Sure, son. Just let me know the time and date you each want me to give them and I'll take care of that, no problem."

"Thanks, Dad."

"Now… back to why I really called, Glad to hear you are managing to keep up with everything there, son. I did have another reason to call you other than to say hello and ask about Adam though. I promised I would let you know about that Alleyn Arendsdorff fellow you were with in school last semester. His father and mother finally contacted the Hospital to discuss admitting him into Elmgrove for rehab. I made it my business to meet with them personally when they came to the Hospital to look at the facility. His mother is very worried. Apparently he somehow managed to involve her and some of her friends in some illegal, drug-related smuggling business overseas and she was beside herself when she discovered what he was doing. He is one entitled, thoughtless and self-centred young man. His father is extremely angry with him for damaging his reputation within Foreign Affairs, and for using his mother and their diplomatic channels to have drugs brought into the country. It's one big, complicated legal and political mess for them all to sort out and I understand that the RCMP and the Ministry of Foreign Affairs are doing a full internal investigative review of it all. I'm so relieved you didn't get yourself mixed up in any of that."

"I never really felt comfortable around him. There was just something not quite right about the way he behaved and tried to make other people feel like they were beneath him. I guess now that I think about it, he was trying to cover up his own insecurities and fears. Uhm, you do know he's gay, don't you, Dad?"

"Yes, son, I do. As well, his mother told me that they are trying to sub-let his apartment up there. Alleyn mentioned to her that I'm your father, and she told me to say thank you for being a friend to him in school and letting me know they were going to put him into Elmgrove. She is shaken up badly over this whole unfortunate episode, and I fear she may need some counselling herself in order to get through it. She asked me if you and Adam might consider taking over Alleyn's apartment."

"Wow! I don't know what to say about that. I have to stay here until at least the end of the semester to finish with the lease on this place. And I'd have to talk to Adam about it, too."

"I explained to her about the lease on your apartment and she said that she would cover the cost of the outstanding rent on it until your lease expires if you would just take over and pay the rent on the place they rented for Alleyn."

"How much is it?"

"She said it was three-hundred and ninety-five dollars a month and that they wouldn't be wanting back any of the light-fixtures and carpets and such they put in there to fix the place up for him. Also, if you wanted any of the artwork or dishes or anything like that, you could have them.

They only want to keep the antique furniture and will probably auction all of it off up there."

"I'd really have to talk to Adam about this. When does she need to hear back about it?"

"No later than the beginning of March."

"OK. Oh, and by the way, Adam and I are coming down to celebrate your birthday in a couple of weeks. Can we take you and Mom out to celebrate?"

"Ohh, I think King Yee at the Peacock Inn can save us a table for four. You *did* say that you and Adam were paying. I *did* hear that correctly, didn't I?"

"Yes, Dad."

Once I get off the phone, it starts ringing yet again. Adam heads over to answer it. "Jesus! Grand Central Station here tonight!' He grumbles and picks up the receiver.

"Oh! Heya, Mom!"

"Adam! I was just wanting to give you a call, darling. How did your interview go today?"

"I think it went pretty good." Two women interviewed me and one of them used to work for Mr. and Mrs. Tonner in Brockville before she got married and moved to Ottawa. I didn't get her last name before she got married though. She seemed real nice and the other one, well, she was alright, too. They really didn't grill me too badly. There was one I had to really think about though. They seemed pretty satisfied with the resume you helped me with and that letter from Mrs. Tonner. I should hear back from them in a couple of weeks or so. They asked me if I'd be able to start right after the end of March, so I think that's a good sign. How're things with you and Bast down there?"

"We're driving down to Quebec City next week for Winter *Carnaval and Bonhomme!* Bast hasn't been down to see his cousins in a couple of years. And he wants me to meet them and experience the city with him. I'm actually excited he suggested we do this. It's going to be fun!"

"That's great, Mom!"

"So, I take it you and Aaron haven't killed each other yet in that little apartment. Really now, how are things, Adam? Is everything going well with the two of you there?"

"Yeah, it's all good. It was kinda touchy for the first week or so 'til I was able to get all my clothes and stuff put away and got used to sharin' a place with someone else. But we managed, and I think it's gonna all work out just fine."

I stare over at him, then roll my eyes and scowl when he comes out with the word *touchy*. He looks back at me, shrugs his shoulders and smiles that silly, stupid grin of his... all the while continuing to talk with his mom.

"I think it will, too, Adam. I'm very proud of you, you know. It took a lot of courage to do what you've done. Remember that I'm always here for you if you need anything or even just to talk. I miss you not coming over to the house now. But I love you and want what's best for you."

"I know that, Mom. Thanks"

Several days later and Adam is busy in the kitchen trying to brace up the sagging shelf where the dishes are stacked. He is interrupted by the phone ringing. It's Conor on the line. "Conor! Heya, man! Glad ya called, buddy. What's up?

"Hey, Adam. I forgot to mention to you last time we were at the LE about Valentine's Day coming up next week. I was thinking maybe we could take our boys out for dinner together down on The Market. They've got a place there called Daphne and Victor's that Nico here has been bugging me to take him to and we were thinking it would be a perfect time to meet everyone. We could pick you two up. What do you think?"

"Shit, Conor! Jeez, man. I forgot all about Valentine's Day! Sure as hell glad you called. I've been so busy gettin' settled myself and then with the job interview and tryin' to keep things calm and sane around here with Aaron and his school schedule and all. You know, that sounds like a really great idea. I'd like to get a good look at this Nicolas Marulli, *Nico* guy you've been tellin' me you're seein' and I know Aaron really likes you and wants to get to know ya better, too."

"OK, Adam, great! I'll call them today and make reservations. I'll swing around and pick you guys up with Nico and we can head out from your place then. I know it's on Argyle. What number on Argyle and can I park in front there?"

"Yep. Ya can for sure. Parking is no problem and its unit #2 on the first floor at 37 Argyle. If you see or talk to Aaron beforehand though, dontcha say anything to him. It'll be a surprise for him that way. OK?"

"You're sure about the surprise part there?"

"Yeah, Conor. He's been way too focused on some of his assignments at College this past couple of weeks. I think I might wanna shake things up just a bit for him. It's all good."

"Uhm, uhh, OK... if you say so. We'll pick you guys up then at seven . And I'll make reservations for seven-thirty."

"Actually, Conor, I have to be downtown and close to the LE that afternoon to get my driver's license changed with the new address up here now. I need to get a new health insurance card, too. I'll meet you guys in front of the LE and we can head on over to pick Aaron up after that. OK with you?"

"Sure thing, Adam. We'll pull in and pick you up at the main entrance, just off Elgin there."

February 7th, 1978…

I'm sitting with Yolanda in Evan's class and she leans over and starts to whisper to me, "Now that we've got that axonometric drafting assignment finally done for Gaelen and before we have to start coming up with ideas and a concept for that retail-store design assignment from Iona for our mid-term grade, we'd better start with this chicken-and-egg thing we have to do for Evan's class. I know you've been preoccupied with Adam moving up and getting settled in, so I went ahead and did some research and think I might have an idea here."

"God! Thanks. I owe you big-time. Uhm, I was thinking of something maybe like using elastic panty-hose and cotton-batting inside a really big box that could be dropped out the window. But I just don't know. Seems to me there must be better ways to think about this and come at it from another angle. What have you got?"

"Well… Evan told us there were absolutely no limitations to what we could do here. Only that we have to make sure the egg doesn't break or we fail the assignment. And since neither you nor I are going to jump out of a second floor window holding the egg while wearing a parachute, I think I might have something that could work."

"Go on. I'm listening."

"Well, the yolk and the shell are the most fragile parts of an egg. Are you with me on that one so far?"

"Uhm, yeah. Go on."

"Well, what if we were to inject some kind of chemical or something like that into the egg to make it's consistency more like jelly and then coat the outside of the shell with an industrial-enamel paint to make it super-rigid and hard? Everyone is concentrating on doing something to protect the egg without thinking about somehow actually changing the physiology of the egg itself."

"Hmmm, you're right. Evan said there were no restrictions or limitations here. But do you really think he'd let us do this to the egg? We could still do up some kind of enclosure to hold the egg and either use a little parachute or wings and a tail rudder so it could glide and sail like a paper airplane down to the ground."

"He said himself to come up with something out-of-the-box and to be as creative as possible. If we market the idea and present it well, he really can't say we didn't comply with the requirements of the assignment. I say we do this! What do you say?"

"Well, Yolanda, it sure beats having to go into a lingerie store to buy panty-hose. I'll say that much for it."

Just then Evan stops his lecture on building construction materials and stares back at the two of us.

"Just what are you two giggling about back there? Something you'd care to share with the rest of the class?"

"Oh, nothing Evan. Nothing at all..."

After Evan's class, it's my crit time with Iona for Interior Design and I'm next on the list to discuss my retail store design project with her.

"Vell, Aaron, *vhat* have you decided to do for a design for a retail-store in Fifth Avenue Court? *Vhat* are you going to amuse, astound, and amaze me *vith* today?"

"Well, Iona, I had this idea about maybe an exclusive small retail boutique that sells high-end designer bathroom accessories and towels and such. I've already started to develop a programming study for it and I have a name for it, too."

"Vell, vhat is this *vonderful* name you *vant* to use?"

"I was thinking about when people take long bubble-baths and use loofas, natural sea sponges, expensive Egyptian and Turkish cotton bath towels, and exclusive designer soaps and such. And I thought maybe the idea of *bubbles.* Actually, I want to name the place, *Bubbles Bath Boutique."*

She stares at me for several seconds and then breaks into hysterical laughter.

"Bubbles is a name for a stripper *vith* balloons in a Burlesque theatre! Or a clown *vith* a big red bowtie, silly glasses, and a curly *vig* in a circus!"

The second she mentions the clown bit, I look up at her synthetic blonde wig and then down at her trademark red velvet *Iona lips* bow tie and have to bite my tongue. Tense moments follow until I pull out the signage logo I've already developed for the store and hand it over to her.

"Here, Iona, I know it can be hard to get past stereotypes and preconceived ideas and notions. But take a look at this. I've come up with a unique and elegant, slim typeface lettering style and logo for all the letters in the word bubbles based on a round circular bubble shape. You'll notice the blue-green water droplets that are above the letter S at the end. Maybe, instead of adding the words bath boutique, I should just call it *bubbles*. Also, Iona, I was thinking of maybe including things like limited-edition, designer towel bars and soap dishes and imported tiles, and maybe even having the store offer an Interior Design service for anyone looking to have their bathroom professionally-renovated—also, a service and space where contractors could give lectures and seminars to customers wanting to do the work themselves. The store wouldn't just sell stuff. It could offer design consultation services, too."

"Vell, maybe. Better. Hmmmm... izzzn't it? This is taking a huge risk *vith* who you *vant* to come to shop in the store. *The* name could *vork* though. It has suggestive and intriguing double entendres that *vould* amuse sophisticated customers. Either that or they *vould* be scandalized and afraid to come in to shop... especially in Ottawa. *Vords* have connotations and different meanings. Remember that. I *vant* to see how you carefully develop this and how you *vill* present it. And I don't *vant* to see strippers climbing out of a tiny clown car *vith* balloons popping out of its sunroof in the front *vindow* of your store *vhen* you do. Promise me that, Aaron!"

As she is walking away I can hear her muttering to herself, "Clowns, strippers, bubbles, balloons, hmmmm... izzzn't it?!"

She starts to cackle hysterically once again.

Early February continues to drag on and the pressure and pace of the Design programme continues to build forcing more students to give up and drop out. I'm focused on the next several major projects to complete before winter break at the apartment in the late afternoon when the phone rings.

"Hullo?"

"Hi, is this Aaron?"

"Uhm, yes. Who's calling?"

"It's Alleyn, Aaron, Alleyn Arendsdorff."

Something like a gasp came out of my mouth at that point and all I could think of to say was, "I thought I recognized your voice. What do you want, Alleyn?"

"I just *had* to speak to you. I can't stop thinking about that night in Sac's with that loser idiot boyfriend of yours. He's no good for you. You could do so much better!"

"Alleyn, I'm not interested in anything you have to say about Adam. He's living up in Ottawa with me now and was just interviewed for a job at the Ministry of Health and Welfare. I'm really busy with projects right now and don't have time for this. Is that the only reason you called?"

"I *love* you, Aaron! I need to be with you!"

I'm completely taken aback and stumbling to say something back to him.

"Alleyn, I'm sorry, but, you have some serious issues. You need to get professional help. I know about your addictions. I hope you get yourself straightened out there before it's too late for you. I don't hate you, but I don't want to have anything to do with you, the way you are right now either. I hope your parents can help you. My dad works down there at the Psychiatric. I'll have him talk to your parents."

"Fuck that shit! They just wanted to dump me there rather than leave me with the maid and the groundskeeper in Maitland while they take off to Europe again! I'm getting out of Maitland just as soon as I can!" He starts to cry. "Nobody loves me."

"Well, Alleyn, that's your life and your decision. In the meantime, please don't call here again. You're not someone I want to have any involvement with. You really need to get yourself straightened-out. I feel sorry for you, actually."

"Feel sorry for me'?! Well, fuck *you*, you dumb, pathetic little twink! Feel sorry for *yourself* there, loser boy! You know something, Aaron, you'll never amount to anything! I'll just be waiting to see how far you make it in life before you fall down flat on your face and fail!"

That comment made me think of what my sister Astrid said to me months before.

"Don't call here again, Alleyn! I mean it. Get some professional help. You really need to stay down there with your mom and dad's staff in Maitland. Their maid and groundskeeper can take care of you, or you can get yourself admitted into Elmgrove—that's entirely your decision! And Alleyn, you just leave Adam and me the *hell* alone from now on!"

After I slam the phone receiver back into it's cradle on the wall, I look up to see the reflection of Adam in the mirror standing just inside the front door with his jacket half off, staring intently back at me.

"Was that that fuckin' shithead, Alleyn asshole on the phone with ya there?!"

"How long have you been standing there?" There was no way I could lie about it to him now. So, I just take one big breath and turn around and say, "Uhh, well, uhm, yeah, it was."

"What the *fuckin' hell* did he want? I thought he was in the Hospital down with his parents in Maitland. What the *fuck* is he doin' callin' you here? Was he threatening you just now? Sounded to me like you were tellin' him to leave us alone. What's goin' on?!"

"I don't know why he was calling! Let's just forget about it, OK?"

"No! It's *not* goddamn well OK! Now… what did he say to ya? I wanna know!"

"I don't want to talk about it—just leave me alone!" My mind is reeling from Alleyn's stupid declaration of love and all I can do is slowly walk back to my desk, collapse down into the chair and spread my arms out while shaking my head in utter disbelief.

Suddenly then the front door into the apartment slams violently while Adam storms out into the depressing February gloom.

"Hullo, Jeremey?"

"Alleyn? Is this really you?"

"Yes it is. I'll be back in Ottawa before you know it. I called because I was wondering if your uncle is still with the RCMP there."

"Uhm, yes he is. Why do you want to know?"

"Well, there's something I need you to do for me. You know you owe me big-time for all the times I set you up with local drug-dealer contacts up there—now I'm calling in the favour. If your uncle ever found out about all the drugs you do, I don't think he'd be too impressed.

Jeremey gasps and after a few seconds of hesitation says, "That's blackmail, Alleyn!"

"You sound surprised there. Now… just listen to what I need you to make happen and let me know when you've done it."

A short while later, I'm sitting in the LE and on the hunt to find Adam. "Hi, André. Was Adam in here earlier at all? "

"*Mais non, mon petit*, not tonight so far. It's early though, Aaron. Can I get you a beer or something?"

Yeah. Thanks. A dark rum and Coke, please."

The LE is really dead at this time in the evening, since it's only a few minutes before eight and nothing much ever happens in there before nine—most nights anyway. There are maybe ten to fifteen guys total in the bar and just my luck, one of them happens to be that Jeremey friend of Alleyn's, pretending not to notice me sitting by myself across the room from him along with some really tough, strange-looking guy I don't recognize.

"Thanks Andre. I'm just going to poke my head into the Library upstairs and hit the washroom. If Adam comes in, would you please let him know I'm here and maybe watch my coat and drink for me?"

"Sure thing there. *Pas problème la, mon petit, ça marche.*"

Just then John the waiter calls over to André. "André, there's a phone call for you in the back."

Once back from the washroom, I make it back to my table and look around to spot a few more guys now in the bar. I'm so damned depressed that Adam stormed out earlier. *Like where the hell did he go? I just don't want him knowing anything about Alleyn. He'd hurt him if he ever found out Alleyn told me he loved me!*

"Uhm, André, where did this second drink come from? I didn't order anything before I went up to the Library."

"Some guy who was with that Jeremey Kessler guy on the other side over there sent it to you," he says, gesturing over to where Jeremey had been sitting minutes before. "Hmmm, that's strange. They were both over there a couple of minutes ago. Must have left just now. *Bizarre...* "

"OK, thanks, André."

It's after nine-thirty now. I'm finishing that second rum and Coke and Adam still hasn't shown up. *Like, where the hell else could he have gone?* I begin to get really paranoid, thinking he might have gone to the Club Baths or something like that. *No, he wouldn't do that! No way.* I start to think, *hmmm, this rum tastes really strong and the colours in the bar seem a lot more vivid and sharper than what I remember.* I begin to hallucinate—all the soldiers in the framed prints on the walls, advancing and running toward me with their bayonets extended—just can't seem to stop obsessing on their rifles and how badly I'd like to shoot that damned Alleyn for sucking Adam off in the Club Baths, and continuing now to harass him and me. Suddenly, everything in the bar seems out of focus—feels like I'm trying to see underwater—*like, why am I so dizzy?* I'm tingling all over. *I don't feel well at all—I don't like this—this is like, sooo weird—I think I'm going to pass out...*

"Look at him, John! His pupils are dilated! *Maudit! esti! Tabarnak!* And he can hardly move his arms! *Câlice! Maudit!* Adam's going to kill us both if anything happens to him! Some guy sent a drink over to him earlier. *Esti! Putain!* I took it over to him, and a couple of minutes later he called me back over and asked me to take it over to Aaron when he was away from his table. *Fuck! Esti! Tabarnak! Sacrament!* I'm going to get him upstairs to the lobby and take him in to Emergency at the General! Cover for me here. I think that guy with Jeremey Kessler must have dropped something into his drink! Shit, man! *Merde! Câlice! Sacrifice!* I was supposed to be watching it for him, too! *Sacrament! Crisse! Esti!*"

Adam pokes his head into Pick's Place just after ten-thirty, having finally calmed down from the scene played out with Aaron in the apartment earlier. He was shocked not to find Aaron waiting for him in the apartment. He spots John in the corner juggling a tray full of beer bottles and dirty glasses and waves over to him.

"Uhm, John, have ya seen Aaron in here tonight?"

"Adam, André just drove him in to the Hospital! We thought he was drunk because he almost passed-out in here over an hour ago and André had to help him upstairs to the lobby. André thinks someone may have put something into his drink."

"Ohh! Jeezus! Thanks, John!"

André hijacks a wheelchair and manages to get Aaron out of his souped-up F150 pick-up. He wheels him into the Emergency Department where a young student doctor takes him immediately in to the Emergency Ward to check his vitals. Temperature, pulse, breathing rate and blood pressure are all quickly taken and the suspicion that he has been drugged is confirmed.

"Get him hooked up to an IV and on an oxygen machine, stat! He's overdosed on PCP and we have to keep him breathing or his respiratory system will shut down!" The doctor turns to André saying, "Are you the one who brought him in?"

Andre is hovering around the admissions station, anxiously waiting to find out what is going on behind the swinging doors into the Emergency Ward.

"Yeah, I did. *Oui, vraiment.* He was in the bar at the Lord Elgin and his eyes got really dilated and I brought him in here to have you guys take care of him. Is he going to be OK?"

"Are you a relative or is there someone we can speak with?"

At that moment Adam bursts into the waiting room, sees André and heads straight to the ER desk.

"Is he OK, André? I got here as fast as I could. What's happening?"

"They won't tell me anything because I'm not a relative."

"Thanks for gettin' him in here, man. I really appreciate that."

"No worries. *Pas de problème.* You can take over from me here now, right, *oui, ça marche?*"

"Yep, sure can. Thanks again, André."

"You can speak with me." Adam lies to the doctor, saying, "We're related. I'm his big brother. It's OK. I've got his health card here. Now, what's happening?"

"We've got him on a respirator right now to keep his lungs functioning. He's overdosed on PCP. Do you want to go in to see him? You can if you want to. Here, put on this mask and Hospital gown. He's barely conscious."

Adam stands there staring back at the doctor in disbelief as the smell of the place begins to permeate his senses.

Funny how all Hospitals reek of rubbing alcohol, antiseptic, Lysol, adrenaline and fear.

The Emergency at the General is hyperactive that night. There had been a bad accident on the 417 and nurses are running back and forth trying to keep up with all the hectic activity happening on the ward. As well, there are two armed and uniformed Ottawa Police swat team officers standing guard over a prisoner, shackled and handcuffed to his bed, yelling and threatening to kill everyone there if they don't let him go.

Aaron is in a small alcove, shielded behind a sickly, hospital-green coloured curtain. With the respirator and the IV tube hooked up, Adam just stares sadly at the pale, skinny figure in the bed and is barely able to hold back tears as the sound of the respirator keeps up with a constant dull, droning rhythm.

"Is he gonna be OK, doc?"

"We'll know more in the next couple of hours. Usually, a PCP episode lasts anywhere from between four to eight hours. He's lucky someone got him in here so quickly for an intervention. We won't know anything more for a while. But I think he may recover... as long as we can keep his lungs functioning, and we continue to avoid any complications."

"I'll sit with him, doc, if that's OK with you."

"Absolutely. You go right ahead." Just then, three more gurneys are quickly wheeled into the ward and the intercom blares out with, "Attention, attention—Code Orange—all staff to stand by and wait for further instruction. *Attention, attention—Coder en Orange—tout le personnel pour qu'il se tienne et attendre d'autres instructions.*"

"Sorry, sir, you'll have to excuse us now and stay out of the way."

Adam pulls a chair up close beside the bed and runs his hand through his unruly, dishevelled hair. After sitting down, he gently holds onto Aaron's cold hand as the minutes pass slowly by. "Honey, I know ya probably can't hear me right now. I'm really sorry I got so angry with ya before, but, baby, I just can't protect or help ya if you won't communicate with me. I love you, Aaron." Finally he falls into an exhausted and fretful sleep, bent over almost double in that sorry excuse for a visitor's waiting chair.

Three hours later—Adam is suddenly shaken awake when three nurses and an intern rush in to Aaron's cubicle to verify his vitals and adjust the settings and controls on his respirator.

"What's goin' on? What's happening?!"

"You've *got* to move out of here *now!* His blood pressure is dangerously low. We're monitoring his breathing and vitals from the nurses' station. His lungs are heavily-congested and his breathing is ragged and very laboured. You *must* move now to give us a chance to try to stabilize him. Go and sit in the chair outside there by the nurses' station. We'll let you know when you can come back inside." Then the green-coloured curtain gets yanked back, leaving Aaron alone with the intern and nurses, and Adam staring back at it feeling a sense of deep anxiety and despair.

For the next half-hour, Adam continues to sit there in a dazed stupor, obsessed with self-recriminatory thoughts. *What am I gonna say to his parents if they find out about this? What am I gonna do if he doesn't make it? I can't lose him! Fuck! This just can't be happenin'! Not now! No way!*

It's six o'clock in the morning, and the ward starts to wake up while the nurses finish up their shifts before the next staff-rotation change. One of them is removing the IV tube and breathing apparatus from Aaron.

"How is he, ma'am? Is he gonna be OK?" Adam says as he stretches and shakes his arms to get the blood flowing to bring the circulation back into them. Then he rubs his coarse, trimmed-beard and looks keenly over at her.

"The doctor took his vitals earlier and he seems to be slowly coming out of it now. He's a very lucky young man," she says.

"Am I gonna be able to take him home then when ya tell me he's ready to leave?"

"Yes. He'll need to sign a release-form at the desk beforehand, and then we can get a wheelchair and you both can leave after that."

"Thanks for everything, ma'am."

"Just doing our job here. Glad everything turned out so well for him."

The Blue Line taxi sprays dirty slush and melting snow and chunks of ice all along Smyth Road on our way back to Argyle from the Hospital. The view outside the filthy window is depressingly grey, drab and overcast, which seems to accurately mirror the mood and general atmosphere inside the cab as we head home.

"Your parents are *never* gonna find out what happened here last night, Aaron. You and I are gonna keep this secret just between the two of us. You got that?!"

"I still don't know what happened. One minute, I'm just sitting there, hoping you'd eventually show up in the bar, and the next thing I know, I'm in the Hospital!"

"Well, things turned out OK in the end. So let's just forget about it and move on."

"I remember seeing that Jeremey guy who was friends with Alleyn Arendsdorff before I went upstairs to check to see if you were in the Library. He and his friend weren't around though when I got back to my table. That's about all I can remember."

"That fuckin' name, *Arendsdorff!* Jeezus fuck! I don't wanna *ever* fuckin' hear that goddamn name again!"

Once home, it doesn't take long for me to shrug off my clothes and fall into bed. Adam just climbs in beside me, too exhausted to undress and says, "You're gonna stay in bed here today, baby. You can afford to miss one day of classes. Do ya want me to call someone at the College to let 'em know ya won't be in today?"

He gets no answer as I've already fallen into a deep comatose sleep.

The last thing on Adam's mind, however, is sleep. His brain continues to fixate and churn away on overdrive as he ruminates and obsesses about what has transpired over the past twenty four hours. *Why does he keep comin' back into our lives? Like, I just don't get that at all. And now this business with his goddamn friend, Jeremey. I just know that fuckin' crackhead Arendsdorff has something to do with what happened to Aaron. Like, what the fuck. What's goin' on?*

Twelve hours later and it's almost nine o'clock in the evening. I need to pee badly and have a splitting headache. I'm stiff and sore and have to stretch my arms. I toss back the sheets and quilt on the bed to get up. There's a note propped up on the desk that I can see from the bed.

"Aaron, baby,
Had to catch the bus down to Brockville.
I'm staying overnight with Mom.
Don't worry about me.
I'll see you tomorrow or the next day."
Sasq'

"Thanks for lettin' me sleep over tonight, Mom. There's somethin' I just gotta finish up here in Brockville and then I'll catch the bus back up to Ottawa, either tomorrow or the next day. Uhm, do ya think I could maybe drive ya in to work tomorrow morning and borrow your car? I'll pick ya up after your shift ends. Is that gonna be OK?"

"Oh, don't worry about that, darling. I'll just get Bast to drive me home after work. Just leave me some gas in it though, please. You keep the car for the day. That'll be fine."

The old number two highway, just east of Maitland is only two lanes wide with dangerous blind curves and is very hilly. It used to be the main highway between Montreal and Toronto, until they built the 401 back in the mid-sixties. The St. Lawrence River is wide-open at that point, and stretches between the Ogdensburg Bridge at Johnstown and Brockville. It's frozen solid at this time of year and the icebreaker out of Prescott will soon start to break up the ice in the main channel, just before the spring season commences once more for Great Lakes shipping traffic and the Canada Steamship Lines.

Adam slows down driving through Maitland and continues for about a mile or so until he spots the imposing fieldstone country manor with adjacent carriage house and barn buildings that constitute the Arendsdorff estate on the left side of the highway.

There's the place, alright. Yep. Aaron described it perfectly. That bright blue door and the ones on the carriage house would be pretty hard to miss.

Adam slowly drives past Alleyn's parents' house and makes a U-turn, just out of sight of the main stone pillars before pulling over to the shoulder of the road. It's a waiting game now.

Adam sits in his mom's car and fixates on stalking Alleyn as the minutes drag on.

After thirty minutes or so, a massive gold-coloured Lincoln town car appears at the end of the lane and turns right onto the highway leading in to Brockville with two distinguished-looking occupants—one, silver-haired and the other, platinum blonde—comfortably coddled, cosseted and cocooned inside.

Not long after that, a rusty old brown Datsun mini pick-up truck pulls out of the driveway and turns left to head east in to Prescott. It goes right past Adam, who slumps far down in his seat to shield himself from the man driving it and the woman sitting beside him. *Must be that caretaker guy and the maid headin' in to Prescott. Perfect. The fuckin' cunt's alone now.*

Adam hops out of the car and after hoofing it on foot up to the front driveway and gate to the property, he makes his way stealthily up the long, uneven flagstone path toward the curved stone stairs and the front door.

The light comes on inside and is visible through the fanlight above the door. The front door opens after a few seconds and Alleyn comes face to face with Adam. Alleyn has no time to react before Adam's tightly clenched right fist slams into his jaw.

"Ya fuckin' cunt! I know ya had somethin' to do with Aaron and the PCP! Don't know how ya fuckin' managed it. But you're gonna pay for it big time now, ya fuckin' goddamn piece-a-shit!"

Another blow smashes into Alleyn's face from an expertly-executed, lethal, left hook.

"Stop! Stop! I didn't do anything!"

"I'm gonna fuckin' kill you, ya sonofabitch!" A barrage of blows to Alleyn's jaw force him to hold his hands up in a feeble, pathetic defence against the furious attack that Adam continues to dole out.

They're both inside the entry vestibule. Alleyn is down on his knees flailing his arms wildly while hopelessly yelling for help and trying to deflect the flying fists that keep punching away at his bleeding nose, chin and forehead.

"You can't even fuckin' fight like a man, ya cock-sucking bastard. Jeezus fuck, I'll bet you *fart glitter!* Come on, *sparkle tits!* Stand up, ya goddamn psycho'! Stand up or I'll kick the livin' fuckin' shit outta ya right down there on the floor!"

There is blood all over the white marble vestibule floor and the delicate, hand-painted Chinese floral wallpaper just inside the front door. Alleyn is crying and holding onto his jaw.

"That bowl over there on the table, it looks expensive," he says to Alleyn and laughs. He steps over Alleyn, who is moaning and writhing in pain and grabs an extremely rare, translucent porcelain, mid-nineteenth century *Qing Dynasty* bowl with his gloved hands. He lifts the bowl up, casually tosses it up into the air, catches it, then smashes it with brute force down onto the marble floor where it shatters into hundreds of tiny shards.

As well, there is a deep-green, museum-quality, mid-nineteenth-century *Japanese Edo Period*, ceremonial kimono hanging from an ebony wood stretcher on the wall... further into the vestibule and just beyond the table. Adam violently yanks it down, breaking the hanging rod and ripping the rare, prized textile-piece in the process. He tosses it over onto Alleyn, who is holding onto his jaw, crying and moaning in intense pain.

"No fingerprints. No evidence. There, Geisha boy! Explain that one to your damn parents, ya fuckin' pathetic, fat-ass drama-queen!" he shouts as he stares down at Alleyn's bloodied, horrified facial expression and laughs. "Now, pretty boy... if ya wanna *stay* pretty from here on in, you're gonna leave me and Aaron the *fuck* alone!"

As he heads back down to his mom's car, he's smiling and silently thanking the groundskeeper/handyman for having plowed the driveway earlier in the day.

Bare pavement—no footprints—no evidence—fuckin' perfect, man...

February 14th, 1978…

"Happy Valentine's Day, Aaron!"

Adam yawns and stretches out to his full length beside me in our bed. Then he rolls over onto his side to pull me into a playful head-lock while thrusting his probing, teasing tongue into my mouth. "I got a surprise for you later and not the big one that's pokin' atcha right now under the sheets."

I've rolled over to face him. "Mmmm, Happy Valentine's Day," I say. "I have a surprise for you later, too, Sasq'. Now let's just stay this way for a little bit longer, OK?" I snuggle close and bury my face into his warm armpit.

"I'll be out when you get home from classes this afternoon. I hafta renew my health insurance card and driver's license downtown with the new address here. I'll be back here around seven or so though. And then we can do somethin' romantic for a late Valentine's Day dinner after that. Are ya OK with that, butt-boy?"

"Yup, that works out great for me. I'll be finishing up that egg assignment with Yolanda today and we have to present it this afternoon. I'm curious to see who passes and who fails this one. Everyone's been really secretive about what they're doing, so there's some suspense and drama and mystery happening at the school for once. Even Jakobe is being quiet and not trying to check out everyone else's work which is really shocking for him."

"OK, babe."

It's the end of the day and the final make-or-break test—literally—Evan's assigned egg project. The entire class is in the fire-escape stairs on the second floor of the College where the only window that opens wide enough to enable us to throw our egg projects out the window is located. Evan is there with a fancy clipboard, checking each assignment off as each pair of students throw their project out the window.

"OK. Yolanda and Aaron, you're next."

"Here goes," Yolanda says as she tosses the unlikely named and scarlet-painted *Red Peril*—my favourite colour—the delta-winged glider with the chemically-altered egg inside it out the window.

It's beautiful the way the air picks it up and it glides gently down to the ground. That is until one of the wings snaps off in mid-flight and it starts to nose-dive into a death spiral and eventually crash onto the paved parking lot where the rest of it breaks into several pieces.

Evan shouts down to the safety-helmeted spotter standing below, "Did the egg break or not?"

"The egg survived!"

Just then Jakobe comes bounding up the stairs with a live chicken that's wearing a collar and is on a leash. "Here you go, Evan. Nature's perfect protection for an egg. Meet *Leona Leg Horn*. We got her from a farmer down on the Market!"

The poor hen is traumatized at the sight of all of us staring and laughing at her and promptly craps all over the stair landing. Evan is killing himself laughing and then Jakobe asks, "So, do I throw her out the window to see if the egg inside her survives the fall?"

Everyone laughs until Melora Holt shouts out, "Nooo! Chickens can't fly! You'll kill her if you throw her out the window!"

Evan is bent over laughing at this point and he says, "OK, Inga and Jakobe, I'll give you credit for imagination. Let's consider this one a pass. Now, what are you going to do with the chicken?"

"Inga then says, "It's OK, Evan. I have to drive by a chicken farm on my way home to Manotick. I'll just dump her into the pen where he keeps all his other hens. It'll be days before he figures out he has one more than he thought he did. That poor farmer will never figure out how he suddenly wound up with an extra full-grown chicken. It'll likely be a question he carries to his grave.

As an anecdote here, the next day, Inga came back and told everyone, including Evan that the hen she left with the farmer was the only black one there. Apparently, all the farmer's other hens were white...

Adam is waiting in front of the LE as Conor and his boyfriend, Nicolas swing in to pick him up. "Thanks for pickin' me up Conor. It's just down a few blocks on Elgin Street and then ya turn left onto Argyle."

Then Adam leans forward to grab Nicolas's hand from the back-seat. "Nice to finally meet ya, Nicolas. Aaron's gonna be real surprised we're all goin' out for dinner. I didn't say anything to him 'cause I wanted it to be a surprise."

"Call me Nick, Adam. Nice to meet you, too."

"C'mon in for a minute to meet Aaron and see the little place we've got here for now, guys."

"OK Adam. I'll just park in front and you can lead the way in," says Conor.

"Heya, babe! I'm home. Happy Valentine's Day, honey! And look at the surprise I brought ya!"

"Adam! Sasq! *Happy Valenti—ohhh, shit!*" I exclaim.

Adam, Conor, and an open-mouthed Nick discover me stark naked, except for an obscenely short, white cotton apron with big, goofy-looking red hearts plastered all over it. It's a full-frontal that leaves almost nothing to the imagination… a view for which I was hoping Adam would be alone to discover! To top that off, I'm holding the *Kiss the Cookie* sign Adam brought up with him up from his old apartment in Brockville.

Nick doesn't miss a beat and, with a deadpan expression, perfect delivery, and devastating timing says, "Oy, I wonder what Passover and Hanukkah must be like around here."

"Aww, c'mon! Jeez, honey, if only ya just coulda seen the look on your face when we came through the door, you woulda laughed, too! Just thank the fuckin' lord you were holdin' onto that sign in front of you. Conor and Nick thought it was fuckin' hilarious. C'mon. Forget about it."

Adam keeps looking at me with that stupid, lop-sided, dumb grin on his face while trying to stifle yet another laugh.

"You just wait! Next time you bend over in front of me, your fuzzy ass-hole is going to get captured on Kodak film and make it into the next-day edition of the *Ottawa Citizen* inside the *Death Notices Section!*"

"Aww, c'mon now. They didn't get to see as much of ya as I did. And we all went out and had a nice dinner afterwards. What can I do to make it up to ya?"

"I'll have to give that some thought. I will admit though, I was sure your eyes were going to pop out of their sockets and you blocked their view and covered me up with your ski jacket as fast as you could. I suppose I should be grateful for that small, gallant gesture, at least."

"Aww, c'mere, butt-boy. I promise ya I won't bring any more surprise guests over—until the next time!"

He starts to laugh all over again.

"You bastard!"

It's finally Dad's sixty-third birthday and Adam are I are down in Brock Vegas at home on Bethune Street to celebrate with him and Mom. We're about to head over to the Peacock Inn once Mom finishes covering up her new, super-short hair with that Pucci scarf I gave her for Christmas.

"Happy Birthday, Dad."

"Thanks very much, Aaron." He sits back, sighs and says, "I'm not afraid to admit I have been feeling my age lately. I guess this is as good a time as any to let you know that I have put in my letter of resignation for formal retirement in late spring of next year."

"I don't think of you as old at all. You're my Dad. I don't think you'll ever be old to me."

"Nevertheless, son, time marches on and catches up with all of us sooner or later. Your mother and I are thinking of putting the house here up on the market and considering one of those seniors' retirement apartments they're building beside St. Francis Xavier on Church Street where the old Notre Dame Convent is now. We'll have our choice of which apartment if we sign up and get our names onto the list right away. The building is supposed to be done in late 1980. You know, I think I'd like to be able to look over at the stained-glass windows of the church from a balcony and I could go to morning Mass every day."

Hmmm, what does Mom think about this?"

"She's tired and bored herself and wants to travel a bit. We were thinking about going out to Calgary to visit Astrid and Geraint and the grandkids this year, and then maybe on to Banff and Lake Louise to see the Rockies—maybe even as far as Victoria in BC. The house here is getting to be a lot for her to manage, and it's just too big now for the two of us to rattle around in. Time for someone else to love it and take care of it and raise a family here now."

"I understand. But what about Blackjack? "

"Well, son, we have plenty of time now to plan and nothing is certainly going to happen overnight. We're all going through important life-events and changes right now—best to think them through carefully and not act too quickly."

"Yeah, I guess so.

We're all together at The Peacock Inn and Mom is helping herself to a third glass of Pinot Noir. After topping up Dad's and Adam's glasses, she hoists hers up and says, "Cheers, Richie! Happy Birthday!"

"Thanks, Ana, honey, but slow down with that wine until King Yee serves us some food. I'm not carrying you back home after dessert."

"Ohhh, Richie! I was thinking we could go out dancing at the Flying Dutchman after this. Adam, you promised to show me how to do *The Hustle*. You didn't forget now, did you?"

"Uhm, no ma'am, I didn't." Just then Adam leans over to me and whispers, "But I sure as hell was hopin' she would!"

At last I have my opportunity!

"Mom! That's a great idea! I haven't been out there in ages! That big stone fireplace in the lounge there would be perfect on a cold, snowy night like tonight. Let's do that. It'll be fun!" Then I smile and whisper into Adams' ear, "And that's for not telling me about Conor and Nick on Valentine's Day!"

The Bee Gees are blaring out from the speakers on the dance floor. And Adam looks positively mortified while Mom tries to follow his rhythm and dance moves.

"All he needs is a tight-fitting, white polyester suit and platform shoes to match your mother and they could go on *American Bandstand* together," says Dad as he laughs and sits back, watching the two of them try to dance together.

"Mom really makes you laugh at times, doesn't she?"

"That's one of the secrets to a happy marriage!" Dad smiles and comes out with a corny, lame, old line I've heard him say many times before... *happy wife, happy life*. He chuckles, and continues, saying, "You just have to laugh at life sometimes, son. We're all going to wind up dead and buried someday. Might as well enjoy the ride until we get there. Remember that, Aaron."

"Uhh, uhm, Dad, just so you know, I talked to Adam about Mrs. Arendsdorff and the apartment sub-let. We really don't want to get involved with those people at all. Alleyn is pretty creepy, actually. You already know that, Dad. Besides, you haven't seen that place, so you wouldn't know anything about it. It's pretty grand and formal. I don't think it's really Adam's or my style. We'd feel uncomfortable, like we'd have to live up to its elegance all the time and well, it just isn't what Adam and I were thinking of when we eventually move. Besides, it's only a one bedroom. And we were thinking of two, for when you and

Mom and when Adam's mom and Bast come up to visit and maybe stay on weekends. Adam's hoping to eventually get another car once he starts work, too. He really misses not having one. And outside parking in the back of that building is not something he wants to have to cope with in the winter months. Indoor-heated garage parking, two bedrooms and maybe something more modern in a high-rise building close to the College is more along the lines of what we were thinking of."

"Funny you should think of that just now, son. I meant to tell you, they took Alleyn out of Elmgrove a couple of weeks ago. He was in rough shape when they first brought him in. It looked like someone had worked him over pretty badly. His jaw was wired shut and his face badly bruised with stitches to close up a deep laceration on his forehead. His father was convinced that some drug-dealer from Ottawa had come down to their house and attacked him. I haven't seen or heard from either him or Alleyn's mother since they came to Elmgrove to take Alleyn back to Maitland. He was only in there for barely more than forty-eight hours before they came back to have him officially discharged. It was all so strange. I have a sneaking suspicion they won't be bringing him back for any more treatment either. Last time I spoke with Mr. Arendsdorff, he said he was certain Alleyn was going to be better in time, that he and his wife were leaving for Europe for an extended period and that Alleyn would be fine on his own in Maitland with their maid and handyman there. I don't think he wants to have to deal with him and is embarrassed and ashamed that his son would ever be considered a potential candidate for admission into a place like Elmgrove, to be completely honest. That whole episode isn't over yet. And I don't see a happy ending to it either."

"Not much laughter there is there, Dad?"

"No, Aaron, I'm afraid not."

"Thanks so much." I say and lean back in my chair, stretching and rubbing the back of my neck for a moment, and then resting my elbows on the table. It had been a long and hectic morning up to that point. "My assignment for Lynda Naagy-Birdsong is coming up soon, and I just haven't been able to find the Art Nouveau research material on Victor Horta I need at Algonquin. How are you doing with your courses, Nick?"

"Good God! That name, *bird-seed!*"

"Knock it off, Nick! Adam calls her *bird-brain*. Jeez! I've almost called her that a few times myself."

He chuckles and then says, "Well, I figured it was time we got to know each other, uhm, with your clothes on this time, that is, since we're both dating guys who went to school together back in Brockville. We're almost the same age and it's great to be able to talk with someone else who's got at least half a brain, and who's gay, and not in one of my classes, if you know what I mean."

"Yeah, I do. So, how are you doing with your courses? And uhh, don't remind me about Valentine's Day again, or I'll start calling you *Nico* the way Conor does all the time!"

He rolls his eyes, laughs and then responds with, "Well, second year in Urban Planning is turning out to be a formidable challenge. I'll be glad to have a break in a couple of weeks."

"Me, too, actually. I don't know if I'm going to have to work on assignments over the March Break. I hope not though, because I want to spend some time with Adam. He's been so good with me and with trying to get himself set up at home. And he just got official word from

National Health and Welfare he got the job they interviewed him for. He's nervous though because they want him to start French language training in early July. And I know that's really been preying on his mind ever since he got the call from them."

"Well, hell! I'm fluent in French and so is Conor! You be sure to tell him if he ever needs someone to help, we'd be happy to do whatever we can."

"Thanks. I know he'd appreciate that. So, what do you and Conor have planned for Winter Break?"

"Well, his dad isn't doing so well right now. They're thinking about selling the farm outside of Merrickville and maybe moving into Brockville where he can be close to his doctor and get some decent health care. That place has been in his family for four or five generations though, and his older brother still lives right beside it with his family. Conor wants to go down with me to spend a few days with his mom and dad. They're nice people. I really like them very much."

"We're both pretty lucky with the guys we wound up with aren't we, Nick?"

"I'd say they were lucky to wind up with us."

Just then a bell starts to ring in the cafeteria and he has to rush off to make it to his next class.

"Gotta go. I'll give you a call and we'll get together later on in the week, OK?"

"Later, *Nico!* Bye."

"Good afternoon. Is this Mrs. Jason Blaine Blanchard?"

"I haven't been a Mrs. Jason *anything* for many years," says Delphine. "Who is this calling?

"Oh, I am sorry. I should have introduced myself first. I'm Angelica McCarthy from the law firm, Crawley, Crawley, Carruthers, Manafort, Stronach, and Feltmate in Edmonton. I understand you and Mr. Blanchard were once married and have an adult son, Adam. Am I correct in assuming this?"

"My name since the divorce is Bogaert. What's this all about?" Del asks. She is beginning to get irritated and impatient with the woman on the other end of the phone.

"I'm sorry to have to be the one to tell you this, Mrs. Blanchard, errr, Ms. Bogaert, but Adam's father, Mr. Blanchard has had terminal cancer for the past two years and well, sadly, he died the day before yesterday."

"Oh my God! I had no idea. Jason deserted Adam and me and I haven't had any contact with him since our divorce, years ago. We didn't know he was sick! In fact, we didn't even know for sure where he was after he signed the divorce papers, although we suspected it was Edmonton or at least somewhere in Alberta."

"Well, I'm calling you to obtain a phone number to contact your son, Ms. Bogaert. Mr. Blanchard made up a will and filed it with us some time ago now, assigning Adam as executor and sole beneficiary to his estate."

"Ohh, really! Well, I'll tell you right now, neither Adam nor I will be held responsible for any of that sorry bastard's debts! He almost destroyed me when he walked out on us and I damned near lost the house back then. I want nothing to do with him and his miserable, pathetic excuse for a life. And I won't have my son involved in any of his messes, either!"

"You misunderstand, Ms. Bogaert. He left a life insurance policy in Adam's name and there is some money and possessions, like furniture and a car that he left for his son."

Delphine is shaking with emotion at this point and is completely shocked about what this woman is saying to her on the telephone.

"I don't understand! He wanted nothing to do with us when he abandoned us. Why would he do this now? Why? Why?"

"I can't answer that, Ms. Bogaert."

"I'm having trouble taking this all in at the moment."

"Quite understandable under the circumstances, Ms. Bogaert. This must be a big shock for you."

"That's putting it mildly, Miss… what is your name again?"

"McCarthy. That is, Mrs. Angelica McCarthy."

"Well, I want to be the one to break this to Adam, Mrs. McCarthy. Give me your phone number and I'll have him give you a call once I've had a chance to talk with him."

"Don't wait too long please, Ms. Bogaert. Mr. Blanchard made his funeral arrangements over a year ago and he will be cremated within the next couple of days. He didn't specify what he wanted done with his remains, and outside of the man he has been living with—err, that is, I think they are living together—there is no one out here to take his ashes or make any binding legal decisions or handle the details of his estate. Please have him contact us as soon as possible."

Delphine hangs up and then stares at the phone for the longest time.

She is in shock…

How in the hell am I going to break this to Adam? she thinks. All these years and now I have to re-live it. His father—bisexual! I suspected it all along and should have said something to Adam long before now. His father... bisexual and living with another man. This is all just too much right now! A bisexual father and him gay. Oh, God! I thought I'd never have to have this conversation with Adam! Oh, God! What now?

"Heya, Mom," Adam says into the phone from our apartment. "How was Quebec City? Did you and Bast get to see his family and didya have a good time down there?"

"Never mind all that for now. I received a phone call today from Edmonton and there are a few things I have to tell you."

Adam looks over at me at my drafting board and covers the receiver with his hand. "It's my mom calling, Somethin's up. She sounds kinda upset.

"Edmonton, Mom? Who do ya know in Edmonton?"

"Just listen to me here, Adam. This isn't something I can talk to you about over the phone. I'm driving up there tomorrow first-thing and we can talk face-to-face. When are Aaron's classes? And will you be there alone in the morning? This is important, darling."

"Uhm, yes. He'll be over at the College tomorrow and we can talk then. Can't you even give me a clue about what ya wanna talk about?"

"*Not now!* I'll be up there right after nine. Just be there!"

Adam hangs up the phone and frowns. "What was all that about?" I ask.

"Dunno. She's comin' up here tomorrow to talk to me. She said somethin' about gettin' a call from Edmonton. She sounded pretty serious and wouldn't tell me any more than that."

"You think she's OK?"

"Guess I'll find out tomorrow."

"Good God, Adam! This place is tiny. No sofa and just a bed and nowhere to sit?!"

"Ohh, Mom! It's OK for now. Now go sit at Aaron's drafting board or desk and I'll getcha a coffee and you can tell me what this is all about."

"Are these some of the things Aaron does at school?" She picks up Linda Naagy-Birdsong's architecture booklet from last semester and starts to thumb through it.

"Uhm, yeah." Adam points to the maquette on the desk beside the drafting board. "That model there is a student workspace he made last semester. And those pen-and-ink renderings are gonna be part of a store design he's workin' on right now for his Professor Massimo whatshisname. I helped him with that Brockville architecture booklet there in your hands, by the way."

She puts it down and stares at the maquette in silence. Then she turns to face Adam and says quietly, "I had no idea he was so talented."

"I told ya, Mom, he's somethin' and someone real special—to me. Now, what broughtcha all the way up here from Brockville? What's goin' on?"

"I'm not sure where to start, darling."

"I'm listening. Just take your time, Mom."

"Well, uhh, yesterday I got a call from a lawyers' firm in Edmonton about your dad."

"What?!"

"Yes. Exactly my reaction, too. Uhm, uhh, Adam, he died three days ago!"

Adam's mouth is wide open. He stares at his mother, not knowing what to say.

"I might as well start at the beginning and tell you what I know. First off, I don't want you to get angry at me for not telling you about this before now. I always suspected, but I never knew for sure. There were reasons he left you and me years ago that I hoped neither you nor I would ever have to face. And now it's all coming back to force me to re-live the time I was married to him and what others gossiped and hinted to me about after he deserted us. He just wasn't around for us, Adam."

"I know, Mom. I don't really remember him bein' in the house when I was really little, except for the times you and he argued."

"I know that. How do I tell you this? Uhm, he wasn't there much after I got pregnant and had you. And, well, he always kept telling me he felt trapped in a relationship he just wasn't cut out to be in. I never knew for sure, but I always suspected there were others he was with. After all, he lost complete interest in me and was never around. That's why you don't have a lot of memories of him when you were just a little boy. "

"Go on."

"Well, darling, this lawyer woman called me yesterday from Edmonton to get your phone number because she needed to contact you about your father. I'm probably going to blurt this out here and it may be very confusing for you, but I'm upset and her call gave me a real shock. I'll tell you everything I know and then you can decide if you want to contact them."

"OK. Keep talking."

"Seems like your father had a will and has named you as executor of his estate."

"What exactly does that mean, Mom?"

"It means that you are responsible for settling his affairs and are the beneficiary of anything he has left after everything is settled and paid off."

"I haven't got any money to pay off his debts! He screwed you over but good back then. I remember, and he's not gonna do the same to me, now that he's dead."

"I know, Adam, and I told that woman as much. She said he didn't have many outstanding debts and that he left you a life insurance policy and that whatever money is there would more than cover whatever he owed. Also that he had a car and some furniture and personal effects that all belong to you now."

Adam stares at his mom, waiting for her to continue.

"What's the catch here? I know you. What aren't you telling me?"

"Well, darling, I never knew for sure until years later, but to be honest, sex between your father and me was non-existent those last three or four years before he disappeared. God! Oh, how do I tell you this?"

"I'm a grown man, Mom. You can talk to me. Go on."

"Well, Adam, your father was bisexual."

"What?!"

"Bisexual. I didn't know that when we got married. And, thinking back now, I think he married me to hide that from everyone in Brockville, including probably himself."

"Ohh, Mom!"

"I didn't want you to ever have to know that. After all, that was something private and intimate between him and me in our marriage. When he left, you were still just a young teenager. I knew you were gay even back then and didn't want you to think you were the way you were because of him. Ohh! This is all just so complicated!"

"Mom! It's OK."

"You were so angry with him for deserting us and were having your own identity problems. I was just trying the best I could to keep the house and not lose it and keep us going."

Silence from Adam. Then: "I don't know what to say. I just don't."

"Apparently, he's been living with some man for the last few years in Edmonton. That much I got out of the woman who called. But I have no information other than that to give you regarding his, uhm, living arrangements out there. God knows what kind of situation you'll be walking into and dealing with, should you decide to call the lawyer back."

"Have ya got that phone number on ya?"

Delphine is crying at this point. She hands the scrap of paper with the phone number scribbled on it to Adam.

"He's to be cremated in the next day or so. You won't make it out there before then if you decide to go. He made his funeral arrangements when he was diagnosed with terminal cancer a couple of years ago. I'll get you a plane ticket to fly out if you do decide to go. God, what a sad end to a sad story. I'm so sorry, Adam!"

"I don't blame you for not telling me about him, Mom. I just wish I coulda got to know him a bit. I think he and I coulda helped each other. What a waste. Jeezus fuck!"

"He would have been proud of the man you've turned out to be. And I know, whatever the problems there were between him and me, well… he *did* love you. I guess what he left to you should prove that, after all this time."

"Money and stuff, Mom, money and stuff. What's it all about, anyway?"

Later that afternoon, and I'm trying once again to get hold of Adam on the phone… finally, he answers it at the apartment. "Is your mom still up here? I tried calling you when I had some free time over lunch-break and there was no answer. Did you go out with her for lunch?"

"Uhm, no. She needed to get back to Brockville and I just had to get the hell outta here myself for a bit. I laced-on my skates and was out on the Canal. The season's almost done now. Think this might be the last of it 'til next year. The ice was really pretty fuckin' lousy. When are ya comin' home, Aaron?"

"I was going to head over to Wallack's to pick up some stuff for my presentation boards for my store project. You sound *really strange*, Adam. Is everything OK? What did your mom want to talk to you about?"

"C'mon home, baby. I need you, like, right now, Cookie. Fuck Wallack's. Come home. The walls in this place are closin' in on me without you here. Pack your shit up there and get your butt back here with me. I need you here. *Like, right now!*"

"I'm on my way."

"Toss that jacket on the floor and then get your tight, fuckin' little butt over here! I need to feel you, like, right now! I need to feel somethin' real—anything."

His hands are all over me, wildly tugging at my hoodie and tee-shirt and then jerking the zipper on my jeans as he grinds himself into me. I can feel his heart beating and. with one violent motion, he pulls me into his hairy chest, yanks down my pants, and forces me against the wall.

"Lube my dong up! The KY just fell off the top of the armoire there. I hafta be inside you. This day's been unreal. The only thing keepin' me from losin' my mind is the thought of you! Your ass is mine! Now, rub my dick with that shit. I'm gonna ram your ass 'til I bust a load and you're gonna need to be extra wet and juicy down there to take what I'm gonna shove into ya!"

I can feel his urgent need radiating like heat lightning and reach down to grab onto his throbbing cock. The crotch of his pants is moist and sweaty. It feels like a-hundred-and ten degrees down there. I'm biting and sucking his penis right through them and I can hear his soft moans every time I rub his strong inner thighs with my hands that seem to have taken on a life of their own as they work themselves all over his hairy pleasure trail. The tight seam of his pants that rides up his ass crack tells me he's free-balling. And all I can think of is his fuzzy, man-ass-cheeks and furry pube-bush. My mind is obsessed with having his pheromone scent all over me. I pull his zipper down and start to work his cock with my tongue. Wave after wave of his heady, intoxicating and overpowering male essence fills my nostrils up with his fresh sweat and spicy *Adam Blanchard aura.* Then he groans and grabs onto my neck and shoulders and forcefully thrusts his cock deep inside my mouth.

"I just *gotta* know you're all mine and what we have is real. Nothin' between us, nothin' to hide, just you and me. Lick my cock head and suck up that juicy man spunk 'cause it's all for you and no one else!"

His pants wind up in a wrinkled heap on the floor beside him.

There's no time to make it to the bed, so he squats down with me still on my knees and pushes me onto the hard floor on my back. I can feel every inch of him on top of me as his hands move over every part of me, eventually clawing and grabbing onto my butt and hoisting it up off the floor. His lips and tongue work my nipples into hard, sensitive points of hot, burning pleasure. All I can think about is his big cock about to thrust into me.

"Lift your legs up around my shoulders 'cause I wanna see your face when I'm inside ya. I hafta see your big brown eyes when I'm doin' ya, baby. Somethin' real—somethin' honest—somethin' special —just you and me."

The KY that fell off the top of the armoire when he threw me into the wall lies beside him on the floor. He grabs the tube and twists the cap of it off with it held firmly between his teeth. He spits it out and it rolls under the wash stand where the TV is.

"Fuck it! I'll get it later."

The lube is warm on his fingers as he plays with my butt. He works my sphincter muscles with three of his fingers and then urgently exclaims, "No time for foreplay. I just gotta be in you, like, right now!"

Then he rams his massive, throbbing, hard cock deep into me with one continuous, thrusting motion. It feels like it's going deeper and deeper into me and never going to stop.

"You'd better start moving that big thing back and forth because you're rubbing my prostate and I'm going to cum really fast if your cock keeps touching it that way," I whisper breathlessly to him.

"Aww, Fuck! I can't hold back any longer!" he shouts. "Fuck! Fuck! Fuck! Fuckin' Jeezus fuck!"

I can feel his big shaft erupting and shooting his thick, copious cum-load deep inside me. I can feel every muscle contraction of his pulsating cock as he groans and cries out my name.

"Shit, Adam! I'm cumming, too!"

My back is arched up off the floor. I'm shaking and vibrating with jerky, involuntary movements against Adam as he keeps thrusting his big cock into me. He's panting, his chest continues to heave against me while his strong heart beats an irregular pounding rhythm of need and passion that touches my very essence and core-being.

Collapsed and breathless on the floor together, fully-spent and satiated with arms and legs entwined and carelessly-tossed clothing all around us, he sighs and says, "Aaron, honey, Cookie. I love you."

"I love you, too, Adam."

"I needed you and you dropped everything and came right away when I begged ya to. I'll *always* be here for you. *Always. I'd never leave you.*"

Just then I look into his eyes and can see that he is on the verge of crying. Tears are starting to well up and he is blinking to hold them back. He pulls me in tight and close to him and buries his head into my shoulder and exhales deeply. I can feel his hot breath on my neck. Then I feel a single tear drop onto my neck.

"What went on earlier today with your mom!? You were a crazy man with me just now. It was perfect, but I know you. Something happened here today. Is your mom OK? Are you OK? Talk to me. I'd never leave you either. *Never*, Adam. Now what's going on?"

"Ohh, honey! I don't know how or where to begin." Suddenly he starts to cry and his sobs touch something deep inside of me.

"Adam, you once said you'd always be there for me and you'd never let me down. Let me be here for you now. I love you. Just start talking. Doesn't matter how long it takes to get it out. I'm here now and listening. Take your time.

"My dad died."

"What?! I thought your mom and you didn't know where he was."

"Mom and I, well we didn't know for sure. That's why she came up here today, to tell me that."

"I'm not going to interrupt. Just keep talking."

"Well, she told me he was bisexual! And that's why he left her and me years ago."

It's taking everything I have not to ask him questions, but I know he's hurting and has to get this out in his own way and in his own time. All I can do is put my arms around him and hold him.

"He died of cancer and was sick for a long time. He was living with some guy out in Edmonton. And some lawyer woman called Mom yesterday asking her for my phone number 'cause they needed to get in touch with me."

"Go on."

"Well… seems he died and made me executor of his estate. They want me to fly out there to settle his affairs. He's gettin' cremated and I'm not gonna be able to make it there beforehand. He made all his funeral arrangements a while back and didn't want a service."

The tears keep flowing and his shoulders softly shake. And all I can do is to keep holding him.

"Mom says he left a life insurance policy and some money and stuff for me in his will. I don't give a *fuck* about any of that *shit*! So many years wasted. He shoulda been there for me. I coulda been there for him. Jeezus fuck! What a lost opportunity for us to get to know each other."

"Hoist yourself up onto the bed there. I'm going to make us some coffee. It's cold in here. Take that quilt of your mom's and wrap it around yourself. I'll put the water on and be right back."

"Mmmm, the hot cup feels good in my hands," he says when I return with the coffee. "Thanks, baby."

"No problem."

"Mom said it was up to me whether I wanted to go out there. This man he's been livin' with, I'm freakin' out about havin' to meet and deal with him. And then there's havin' to go through all his stuff—some man who is my dad that I don't even hardly know, like, fuck! I just don't know if I wanna do that. Mom left me the name and phone number of this woman from the law firm that has his will. They want me to fly out there and take a week or two to settle his affairs. I'm kinda fucked up over this. Do I go or just say fuck it all and forget about him?"

"How is your mom handling this? She must have been totally shocked when they called her."

"She was real upset and told them she wouldn't pay for any outstanding debts and neither would I. Then they told her about the insurance and money and stuff and said she didn't need to worry about any of that. She had a hard time tellin' me about Dad and their marriage and why he walked out. She never knew for sure about him and other men—at least that's what she said. It was hard for her to talk to me about her life with him. She told me she'd pay for a plane ticket though if I wanted to go. And I have some money your mom and dad gave me for my birthday put away, too."

"Well, you've got a few weeks before you have to start your new job."

"A bit more than that. They want me to start there on April 10th, the week after Easter Monday. That gives me six weeks or so to get everything cleared up there and back home here before I hafta start.

"That's good. If you go, you can start the new job with a clear head. And if you *do* decide to go, don't worry about me here. I'm not going to tell you what to do. You need to figure that one out for yourself. I'll support you in whatever you decide. I love you. And, as you say to me all the time, I'm here for ya."

10 March / April

"It's just somethin' I *gotta* do, Mom. Maybe not so much for him as for me. He was my dad, and even though he's gone now, maybe I can learn some stuff from his life. And maybe that might help me to figure out my own. Do you understand that at all?"

"Not really, no, Adam. You're a grown man yourself now and about to make a new and exciting start in life. I don't know what you think you could possibly learn from how he lived his."

"Maybe how *not* to live mine. I dunno. That might be all I discover. Besides, I think it's kinda my duty as his son to make sure his affairs are settled. It's a matter of respect, and him bein' family and my dad and all. Dontcha think he woulda done that for me if the situation were the other way around?"

"I really don't know. But if that's how you feel, I'll get a plane ticket for you here in Brockville and have it transferred up there so you can pick it up from a travel agency. When do you want to go, darling?"

"I'm thinkin' in the next couple of days. I called that McCarthy lady and she told me I could stay at Dad's place 'til everything gets settled. It'd just be me there. That man Dad was with… well, he has his own house and only ever came over to stay when Dad wanted him to."

"I don't want to hear about any of that. If you have to go, then go. Wrap everything up quickly though and get back here to us before Easter, ready to start your new job. Promise me that, darling, please."

"I will, I promise."

It's Tuesday, March 7th, 1978, and Adam has his duffle bag and knapsack packed. He's waiting for Conor to pick him up to take him out to Uplands Airport to catch his Canadian Pacific Airlines flight direct to Edmonton for early that evening.

"Are ya sure you don't wanna come out to the airport with Conor and me to say g'bye there?"

I shake my head no. "I'm kind of like my mom that way. I'm not good with goodbyes."

You're gettin' more and more like your mom every day."

"That's a horrible thing to say!"

Adam laughs, pulls me close, and says, "You know, the next couple of weeks are gonna be hell without ya. I left a couple of my shirts in the laundry basket in the bathroom. You can wear 'em and pretend I'm here with ya while I'm gone. Does that work for ya?"

"Call me when you get there and let me know you're OK. "

"I will, baby."

"And remember, I'll be down in Brock Vegas with Mom and Dad over winter break."

"I will, baby."

"And remember, I'll be seeing Cala and Charlie and Rob and Bryson when I'm there."

"I will, baby."

"And remember, call me the second you know you're coming home."

"I will, baby."

And remember, I love you."

Just then, Conor honks his horn outside and Adam chuckles and says, "I will, baby. Oh, Jeez—meant to say I love you, too!"

The big Canadian Pacific Airlines Douglas DC-8 jet with distinctive red and orange markings along the aluminium fuselage and the big C logo on the tail fin is out on the tarmac. Luggage and food trays are being loaded into the cargo hold as the plane's turbines rotate with a high-pitched whine inside the massive jet engines on each wing.

Hmmm, Aaron would laugh if he knew our colours were on the plane, Adam thinks and smiles to himself. *Jeezus fuck! I wish he woulda come with me to say g'bye here. I love that crazy, perverted little bastard.*

He hands his boarding pass over to the flight attendant and heads through the doors and across the frozen tarmac to board the non-stop flight from Ottawa to Edmonton.

Five hours and crossing three time zones—Eastern Daylight, Central Daylight, and Mountain Daylight... since we just turned the clocks ahead an hour, he should be on the ground in Edmonton by nine o'clock their time.

As he settles into his seat and adjusts and snaps the seat-belt buckle in preparation for take-off, Adam thinks, *There better be a damn decent meal on board, and I could sure as hell could use a beer once we get up in the air.*

Halfway into the flight, the monotonous drone of the jet engines change octave as the pilots force an ascent to a higher altitude to avoid wicked turbulence over western Manitoba. Eventually, Saskatchewan lies hidden below the thick cloud cover as darkness envelopes the DC-8 with the sinking sun disappearing into the western horizon and the distinct purple outlines of the mountains in the far distance. It's turning out to be one long, stressful, and unnerving flight.

The final descent into Edmonton International Airport is rough.

Strong gusts pummel the wings of the big jet as the lights of Edmonton below start to poke through the heavy clouds. The pilots struggle to hold a straight trajectory as they begin the plane's final descent and approach. The blue lights of the runway flash and seem to mock Adam as he watches the ground quickly rise up to meet him.

It's a scary touchdown with one head-jerking, sickening thud, then a stomach-turning, sudden bounce and then another slightly less violent thud as the reverse thrusters start to scream.

There are a few tense moments while the pilots struggle to correct a sideways skid from the crosswinds and then the plane gradually slows, just before the end of the airstrip. Finally, the big DC-8 starts to turn and taxi off the runway back toward the terminal. Most of the debarking passengers are deathly pale as they head down the mobile stairway onto the tarmac and into the bleak, bitterly cold Alberta night.

Luckily, Adam's duffle bag is one of the first to come down the carousel. With his backpack slung over his shoulder and duffle bag firmly in hand, he strides through the airport's noisy and overly-bright, fluorescent-flooded main concourse and through the sliding exit doors. Taxis with steamed-up windows idle away, their heavy exhaust fumes adding to the nauseous stench of jet fuel and hydraulic fluid that the Chinook winds coming off the Rockies relentlessly blow like piercing needles assaulting his exhausted face.

Welcome to Edmonton, Blanchard, he thinks. There is a grimace on his face as he shrugs and hails a cab.

"117 Londonderry Square, North West Edmonton. It's supposed to be around where the Namo/Clareview Shopping Centre is."

Adam sits back in the cab, hoping the man his father was with left the key in the mailbox like that woman from the lawyers' office said he would. *Otherwise I'm gonna be fucked for a place to stay tonight,* he thinks.

Twenty minutes later the cab driver pulls into a townhouse development. "Ya better just wait here for me, sir for a minute while I go check for a key in the mailbox."

Fortunately there's a key there so Adam pays the cab fare and stares back at the front door.

Well, ya made it this far, Blanchard. No turnin' back now.

The place is freezing cold and smells faintly of cat urine. He flicks on the light in the entry, wrestles his boots and ski jacket off, dumps his knapsack and duffle bag, and starts to survey the place.

It's very compact inside with just a sparsely-furnished living/dining room and small galley kitchen on the main floor. The kitchen overlooks a tiny backyard with a six-foot wooden privacy fence and a gate that opens up to a single-car parking spot behind the unit. In one corner of the yard there's a Taoist yin-yang symbol hanging on the fence banging against it in the wind.

Better go see if his car is out there.

On with the boots again and then out the sliding doors and through the piled-up snow. Adam stops dead in his tracks at the depressing sight of a huge mountain of snow and ice under which is what he assumes is a car. *Jeezus fuck! Looks like it hasn't been moved in like, weeks and weeks. Too tired to think about that now. I'll figure out where that stinkin' cat piss smell is comin' from inside and find a shovel in the morning. Sure as hell hope he's got some clean sheets and a decent bed upstairs. Just need to find a thermostat to crank up the heat and get a good night's sleep.*

Once upstairs, Adam looks for his dad's bedroom. He eventually finds a linen closet and searches to find fresh sheets for Jason's bed. *Hmmm, brand-new orange sheets and towels in here, still in the plastic.*

Hanging above the bed in Jason Blanchard's bedroom is a large, elegant black-and-white canvas. To Adam, it looks like Japanese calligraphy with character symbols masterfully hand-painted onto a piece of fine linen, tightly wrapped around a cedar wooden stretcher.

In small subtle black script below the characters are the words *wise sky* and *small forest*.

Adam stares at the artwork and thinks, *just who the hell is this man who was my father, anyway?*

The next day, Adam is sitting in the reception area of Crawley, Crawley, Carruthers, Manafort, and Feltmate, waiting for Mrs. McCarthy.

"Good morning Mr. Blanchard," she says as she sweeps in, carelessly tossing her lynx fur coat and Louis Vuitton briefcase over onto the surface of her assistant's desk. "Thank you sooo much for coming out so soon. I trust you had a good flight and that Mr. Kobayashi left a key for you to be able to access your father's condo."

"Uhm, yes, ma'am, he did."

"Oh, please, come into my office and do have a seat. And call me Angelica. I've known your dad and Riku for many years, and it's nice to *finally* get to meet the son your father always went on about." She sits down and smiles across the desk at him.

Adam is totally shocked by this revelation.

"Uhm, Angelica, I haven't seen or heard from him since I was fifteen or sixteen. This is all kinda weird to me. Why did he name me as his executor and what's he been doin' out here since he walked out on my mom and me years ago?"

"Well, Adam, all I can say about that is that he's been working since I first met him as a Property Manager for Riku Kobayashi, who has a small restaurant and several apartment buildings and condominium and retail store rental units here in Edmonton and Calgary. He and Riku were, uhh, close for many years. Riku is devastated over his death and was there night and day for him during this past year. I have a phone number for him and he'd like to meet you, if you are at all interested to make contact. I understand he has been looking after your father's cat ever since he was admitted into Hospital in December."

"My dad had a cat?!"

"Yes. He named it Adam, by the way." Just then Angelica flashes one of her Colgate smiles at Adam.

Adam's jaw drops at that revelation and he just stares out the window in silence as she continues.

"As I told your mother, there is an insurance policy in your name that he made out for you years ago when you were a baby. We've taken the liberty of contacting the insurance firm and providing them with a death certificate. Once you let me know where you'd like the money from that policy deposited, I will instruct them to pay out the claim."

"Uhm, uhh, how much was the policy for?"

"Seventy-five-thousand dollars, Adam. May I call you Adam?"

"Yes, please, Angelica."

"There is more in his estate, as well."

Adam is in shock. He stares at her as she continues.

"Because he knew he wouldn't be coming back out of the Hospital the last time he was admitted, he put everything in motion then for you to handle his affairs. He was very-organized," Angelica says.

She tells Adam his father has a car that, with the exception of a couple months' outstanding fees for unused parking and inside storage, is fully paid for. They can clear up any outstanding accounts on that from his chequing and savings accounts. Adam needs to look after transferring ownership of the car and taking out a temporary insurance policy on it. He'll need to have the registration and insurance transferred to his name and address if he decides to keep it. Licence plates will need to be done up, as well, for Ontario. His bank received a death certificate from the law firm the day after he died, Angelica explains, and is expecting Adam to call to discuss how he wants to deal with the money in his father's accounts—another thirty-seven thousand or so—more than enough to cover his outstanding debts. His rent is paid-up to the end of March and, since he was renting from Riku, there won't be any problem with that. He saw to it that his credit card was paid off, but Adam will have to cancel it. There are going to be a few small expenses, like ambulance fees and maybe some medications that weren't covered under the private-members' health-care plan he had with Mr. Kobayashi's company, and that the law firm will look after settling those. She says Adam will need numerous copies of his official death certificate for when he has to notify the Canada Customs and Revenue Agency for his final tax assessment and he'll have to cancel his father's provincial health card, driver's licence, and social insurance number.

Then Angelica pushes his wallet across the table at Adam. "They are all in there," she says. "We provide clients going through this with what we refer to as an *Executor Tool Kit*. I can see from the expression on your face you've probably never had to deal with any of these administrative estate details before. Am I correct in assuming that, Adam?"

"Uhm, yes, Angelica. I'm still kinda reeling from the shock of all this. Not sure really where to start with it all, to tell you the truth."

"I understand completely. Most people don't. Usually they're going through a period of intense grief and sadness over their loss, and then they have all of this responsibility thrust upon them. I want you to know that I was extremely fond of your father, and still am of Riku. I am here for you now to answer any questions and help out in any way that I can. I am truly sorry for your loss."

"That's just the thing though. How can ya lose someone you never thought ya had? So many years and no contact with him. Then all of this when it's too late."

"You may wish to speak with his partner, Riku. I don't know how you feel about that, but I know him well and he was devoted to your father. Maybe he can answer some of your questions. That may help you come to terms with of all of this. Here's his phone number. He has a very chic and fashionable little restaurant downtown. My husband and I dine there quite frequently. He's a wonderful man and I know he would very much like to meet you and perhaps get to know you, if you are at all interested."

"Thanks, Angelica. I guess I'd better, if only to pick up Dad's cat."

Once outside of Angelica's office and in the reception area by himself, Adam sits down for a moment and starts to look inside Jason's wallet. He finds a picture of Jason and him from when he was five or six. He recognizes the scene and remembers that they were at the Brockville Memorial Centre trade-fair together, where amusement rides like the Ferris wheel, tilt-a-whirl and carousel were set up in that shot. Jason has his hand on Adam's shoulder. They're standing together smiling and Adam is looking back at the camera. Jason, who towers over Adam in the shot, is looking down at his son with a tender expression on his face.

Jeezus fuck! So many wasted years after he disappeared.

It's finally winter break and I'm back in Brock Vegas with Mom and Dad for a week away from flipped-out Iona and her comedy cast of crazy College calamity cohorts at Algonquin.

"Mom? Dad? I'm glad we're all together here right now because something happened with Adam and I wanted to tell you both about it in person while I'm down here this week."

Mom is the first to sound in. "Oh my God! Tell me he's *still* living with you! Tell me there's nothing wrong!"

"Yes, that's all fine."

"Ohh, thank God for that!"

My dad quietly looks up from his newspaper and asks, "So, son, what's happened with Adam? You have our attention."

"Well, uhm, where do I begin with this? Let's see. I guess, first off, I need to tell you that Adam's dad died of cancer a couple of weeks ago out in Edmonton. Adam's gone out there to settle his estate. His mom got a call from some lawyer firm out there and he flew out a couple of weeks ago because his dad named him executor of his estate."

Mom and Dad stare at each other, not saying a word.

Then Mom suddenly exclaims, "Oh my God! Del must have been stunned to take that call. It's like a ghost coming back to haunt her all these years later! Go on, what else happened?"

Dad sits across the table from me, not saying a word.

"Well, she drove up to Ottawa the next morning to talk to him about the call and tell him some things about her marriage and why his dad walked out on them all those years ago."

"Go on."

"Well, I don't know if I should be saying any of this to the two of you. Please don't say I told you to either Adam or his mom, but she told him about why his dad left and that he was living with someone out there in Alberta for years until he died."

Finally, Dad says something. "A man or a woman, Adam?"

"So you know then! How long have you known about him, Dad?"

"Son, I've known about Jason Blanchard for years. There are no secrets in Brockville. He was a friend to one of the cooks who worked in the kitchens at the Psychiatric Hospital back then. I think his name was *Raju* or *Riijo* or *Reeku* or something like that. He was Japanese.

That friendship went on for two or three years before Jason disappeared, back in the late-sixties. It wasn't like Jason was being discreet about it, either. I used to see that new, flashy, silver grey SST of his back then parked behind the Hospital in the furthest corner of the staff parking lot after-hours in the dark-shadows. It got to be a real subject of gossip and speculation amongst the staff at the time. You remember that, don't you, Ana?"

"Yes, I remember all the gossip."

"So, what else did Adam say?"

"He was really upset and told me he just had to go out there to discover whatever he could about this man he never really knew, who happened to be his father. I've talked to him a couple of times since he arrived in Edmonton. He's met with the lawyer out there and is settling things now. He'll be back here just before Easter."

"We absolutely won't bring any of the intimate things up about Jason and Del with Adam when we see him, I promise you that. And, Ana, you are not calling Del to speak with her about any of this either, I positively forbid it!"

Mom looks over at Dad, nods, purses her lips and quietly looks down at the tabletop.

"Does she know that you know, Aaron?"

"Uhm, yes, I think she does."

"Well, you just keep your lips sealed when you see her and let her come to you if she wants to talk or confide. This is a private matter between her and her son. Adam won't thank you if you upset his mother or try to get mixed up in any of this without him asking you to. You be there for support for him and let the two of them work this all out between themselves… do you understand what I'm telling you here?"

"Yes, Dad."

The façade of Mr. Kobayashi's restaurant is discreet and elegantly understated. A simple black-lacquered, heavy, solid-wooden door with highly-polished, silvered-chrome push and kick plates and hardware leads into the dining space beyond. To the right of the door is the word *Komorebi* inscribed with simple, flowing raised-silver letters on a white enamel plaque surrounded by a pencil-thin, black enamel frame.

The interior of *Komorebi* is like nothing Adam has ever seen before. It is ultra-sophisticated and minimal—carefully-edited and strictly-composed with a conscious aesthetic attempt to limit any use of colour inside, except for strategic, focal points of pale aqua and sky blue, sparingly executed in certain areas where stunning, minimalist white blossom *ikebana* arrangements are artistically staged and placed in order to focus and direct the eye. The restaurant represents a disciplined oriental aesthetic emphasizing black-and-white Japanese calligraphy prints on the walls, *Chiogami Yuzen* paper and ebony-framed wall sconces, natural straw-like tatami style mats on the floor and sliding Shoji screen panels to separate off parts of the restaurant, creating more private and intimate smaller spaces within the main space. There is a quiet serenity and cool elegance to the restaurant. Extremely tall, high-backed privacy booths, rising up almost to the ceiling with pale blue, leather-upholstered seats, aqua-coloured back rests and discreet, warm-white fluorescent lighting fixtures cleverly concealed behind the tops of the seat backs are toward the front of the space. At the back are two large U-shaped, *Teppanyaki* cooking stations where people gather together to watch Shogun-dressed master chefs make an art of cooking right in front of their eyes. Adam takes one of the booths at the front and thinks, *Aaron would be really impressed with this place.*

A stunningly beautiful, young Asian woman dressed in an exquisite deep coral, indigo blue, intense red, and vibrant orange silk kimono embossed with egrets, ibises, and herons approaches him and asks if she can serve him.

"Thanks, I'm here to see Mr. Kobayashi."

"Ahh, you must be Adam." She smiles, bows, and disappears to find Riku.

Adam's eyebrows shoot up involuntarily when Riku approaches. He's not what Adam expected at all. In front of him is a slim, well-proportioned man, almost as tall as Aaron, at just a bit under six feet—most uncommon for a typical Japanese male.

Riku pauses to study Adam. Adam Richard Blanchard, this compellingly handsome young man before him. The adult son of his lover…

He motions for the young woman to serve Sake and bring Mr. Blanchard a Sapporo beer. "I do not think this morning it is too early for alcohol, Yumiko," he tells her and then turns back to Adam.

He moves with graceful poise and is dressed from head-to-foot in black linen. He has thick, straight black hair and a near flawless light-skin complexion. Riku's almost-black eyes are larger and wider than those one would expect on a typical Japanese man—so sensual with long lashes concealing whatever thoughts he must be thinking. There is a gentle, serene, almost androgynous quality to him that fascinates Adam. He looks to be in his early to mid-forties.

Riku looks at Adam and thinks, *you are as tall as he was and you have his eyes.*

"I'm Adam," Adam finally says. "You must be Mr. Kobayashi." Adam starts to get up to take Riku's hand, but Riku motions for him to sit back down with a smile and simple hand gesture.

"Welcome to *Komorebi*. My name is Riku. I would like you to call me that, if you wish to."

"I'm sorta uncomfortable right now. So let's see how this goes, Mr. Kobayashi."

"I understand. This is not easy for me either."

"You're not what I expected."

Riku smiles shyly and replies, "You are precisely how your father described you to me. I see him in your eyes. I would know you anywhere. I am so sorry for your loss, Adam."

"Uhm, uhh, this is all so weird. I just don't know what to say back to you."

"You don't need to say a word. I'm just happy you felt comfortable enough to come and meet me."

"This place is beautiful. The name of this place, uhh, what does it mean?"

"Thank you for saying that it is beautiful. The word *Komorebi* is Japanese and difficult to translate. There are some Japanese words and expressions to describe emotions that do not have equivalent words in English. *Komorebi* is like a dance of light. Think of sky and sunlight shining through the leaves of trees in a forest, and then reflect on how you feel when you see their movement and experience the warmth of the sun on your face. That is the best way I can think of to describe *Komorebi*."

"Wow, that's beautiful. I'll remember that word. Uhh, the reason I am here is Mrs. McCarthy said I should come to meet you and that you wanted to meet me, too. And that you have his cat."

"Ahh, yes, Angelica McCarthy. She has been so supportive and helpful this past year."

"I understand my dad worked for you and she told me he rented his place from you, too?"

"Yes, Adam. Your father was a proud man and insisted on being independent and paying his own way. I never wanted to take anything from him, but he was determined. And renting to an associate provided tax-relief benefits for my company over the years. He was a good Property Manager—and so much more than that—to me."

Riku's expressive eyes open wider, briefly allowing Adam to see the emptiness, sadness, and pain hiding inside.

Adam cannot help but feel some measure of empathy for this man. "I hope you don't mind my sayin' this, but I can tell you're a really nice man, Riku. I can see how my dad, or anyone, for that matter would find you attractive."

"Riku blushes and simply says, "Thank you for calling me Riku."

"I understand he was sick for a long time. And you were with him 'til the end. What kind of cancer did he have? There are so many questions."

"It was prostate cancer. He didn't suffer much until the last."

"Why did he never try to contact me? I woulda come if he'd only just asked. I just don't get that, like, at all."

"He didn't want to interfere with your life and hurt your mother any more than he already had when he walked away from her and their marriage. You were so young—he was so unhappy and conflicted when he made the decision to leave you both back then. He felt your mother would be the best one to take care of you."

As Riku talks, Adam looks around the restaurant until his eyes fall on a large, six-panel hanging screen depicting trees in a forest on one of the walls. "Uhm, Riku, that's beautiful—that screen there."

"It is a copy of one of Japan's national treasures. It represents a sixteenth-century ink on paper screen by the famous Japanese artist Hasagawa Tahaku. You have a good eye for subtle beauty, Adam."

Adam thinks of Aaron as Riku says the words *subtle beauty*. *There'd be no livin' with Aaron if he ever heard that from anyone.* And then he smiles and decides to confide in Riku.

"Uhm, you aughta know, Riku, I'm gay myself."

Riku's eyes open wide. He is silent for several moments before he smiles ruefully and finally speaks.

"Since you have felt comfortable to confide in me, I will do the same with you now, Adam. I want you to know that it was difficult for me with my family back in Japan when it was discovered I was homosexual so many years ago. At that time, my parents felt I had brought shame and dishonour down upon the family. It was then that I came to Canada to start a new life for myself at a young age with very little. As you know, I met your father when I worked in the kitchens at the Psychiatric Hospital in Brockville. He followed me out to Edmonton when my parents died and they left me money to start my restaurant and begin to invest in real estate."

"Uhm, Riku, I have a partner back in Ottawa and his name is Aaron. He's a lot younger than me and goin' to College right now. I love him— as much as I think you probably loved my dad."

"... even when months and days are long, life is short... "

419

"What's that, Riku?"

"Oh, I *am* sorry. That is a Japanese proverb. I was thinking of it when you spoke just now. You know, you were never far from your father's thoughts. We closed down the restaurant here every October 19th to celebrate your birthday… just he and I. And Mrs. Tonner always kept him informed of how you were doing when you started to work for her at the store."

Adam is stunned to hear this.

"I never knew that, Riku!"

"Of course you wouldn't have, Adam. She knew your father very well from the time he was born and promised him when he left Brockville she would watch over you as best she could and keep him informed. I assume she never knew you were gay and still does not know now?"

"Uhm, no. That is, not until after she met Aaron. I think she sorta knew after that."

"We have much to discuss and share. May I come over to spend time with you for the time you are in Edmonton? I would like that and want to help you with whatever you may need during this difficult time, for us both."

"I'd like that. Any time at all. It's your house, after all."

"Interesting, I've never thought of it as mine." Riku says and is silent for a few moments while looking around with a sad expression at the tranquil and spare dining space in the restaurant. "This condo was always a safe and comfortable place for us both. That was how I always thought of it." Then he comes back to the present sober reality, continuing to say, "You will also want to meet little Adam. He resembles you. I can see now why Jason felt compelled to adopt him years ago. Strong, determined, with beautiful eyes, and an abundant, dark sable

Manx coat of fur. Hopefully, you are not as willful and headstrong as your tailless namesake."

"Well, I'd say that Aaron would probably think otherwise," Adam says and smiles to himself.

"Heya, Cookie! I got to meet Riku today."

I'm upstairs on the hallway extension phone. "Who's *Riku*, Adam?"

"He was my dad's lover. He's really somethin'. You'd like him. He's a super-cool guy."

"How are you doing with getting everything settled out there?"

"Well, uhm, Dad's remains from the crematorium are with me now. They're in a beautiful, copper urn that the Funeral Director told me was Japanese and very old. Guess that makes sense now after meetin' Riku. I met with the lawyer, too, and she gave me lots of information and I'm gonna go through what he has here in the house and start to figure out what to keep and what I want to either donate or throw out in the next week or so. I'm gonna head back there after that and take my time comin' home and you can let everyone know I'll be back, just before Easter. You know, I'm really glad I decided to do this."

"I figured you would be. But I didn't want to push you into anything you didn't feel right about. You'll call your mom and let her know, right, Sasq'?"

"We're not gonna have any problems with money and finances, baby. I'm not gonna get into all the details with you over the phone, but my dad saw to it that I'd be well taken care of after he was gone. I feel real good about that."

"He must have loved you."

"Yeah, I think he really did after all."

"I miss you so much," I say to him.

"I miss you, too. Ya know, honey, I haven't had a lot to laugh about since I got out here. I miss you teasin' me and, well, uhm, oh yeahhh! I miss that cute, tight boy-butt of yours, too. I'll be drivin' Dad's car back from Alberta when I leave here. I figure it'll take me a week or so to get back. Are you gonna be in Ottawa or Brock Vegas when I get there?"

"Probably in Ottawa. Depends on whether you get back—on a school day or over a weekend. Mom and Dad say hi, by the way, and that they're very sorry to hear about your dad."

"They're good people. You're lucky to have 'em both."

"Sooo, do I dare ask about this car of your dad's? Hopefully, it's better than that crappy, old Ambassador he left your mom when he disappeared."

"Uhm, uhh, baby, it wasn't always crappy!" Adam says, while sounding a bit defensive and offended. "But as for my Dad's car here, well it's a 1972 Dodge Charger SE Magnum 440 Rallye two-door hardtop coupe. At least, that's what the badges and lettering say on it. I hadta dig it out from under more than two-and-a-half feet of snow to get a decent look at it. It musta been sittin' outside of Dad's place here the whole six weeks or more he was in Hospital. It's kinda slippery-looking, like a shark fin with a power bulge, front hood scoop and a big back spoiler."

Then he tries to pretend like he knows cars and blurts out, "Ya know, it's got a huge, honkin' 440-cubic-inch, 5.7-litre magnum, four-barrel, hemi 280-horsepower V8 motor, a heavy-duty Richard Petty Nascar racing-tuned suspension, and a three-speed 727 torque-flight automatic transmission.

"Oh yeahhh! And it's got *tiny black-and-white houndstooth upholstery* and *cute little coco mats* on the floor!"

I have to bite my tongue not to burst out laughing when he comes out with the words, *tiny houndstooth* and *cute little coco mats!*

"Uhm, uhh, do you even know who Richard Petty is or what any of that actually means?"

Five seconds of an embarrassed pause later and he admits in a little boy voice, "Uhh, nooo, not really. I read it in the owner's manual and off the service repair papers I found in in the glove compartment. It just made me feel kinda butch to be able to say that to ya just now—especially the power bulge thing."

Stifling a smile, I respond with, "Hmmm, thought so. You're not exactly a gear-head or a mechanical genius when it comes to cars. Your Nascar track record with me isn't exactly the greatest, you know."

"Aww, c'mon honey, gimme a break. Honestly though, my dad musta really loved it 'cause it'll look brand new once it's all cleaned-up. He took real good care of it. He musta stored it somewhere heated indoors in the winters until he got too sick this past year, 'cause there's like, no rust on it at all that I can see. It's gonna be a real pig on gas and the trip back in it will probably bankrupt me. Red-line the damn thing and you'll probably see the needle on the gas gauge start to go down. But it's got next to no miles on it, like, only eighteen-thousand or so, and even though it sat behind Dad's place here practically all winter, I was able to get someone to give the battery a boost and it started up just fine for me. I don't think my dad drove it hardly ever at all. I'll get it all tuned-up before I make the trip back home there."

He pauses for a moment, then chuckles and continues with, "Ya know, now that I'm really thinkin' about it, it kinda reminds me of you. I think I'm gonna name it the *Aaron Sex-Mobile*. The dual mufflers on it moan and groan just like you do when I stick my dong in ya. And it throbs and shakes and vibrates just like you when ya cum for me, too!"

Adam then let's loose with one of his obscene, dirty laughs and continues with, "It's got a really big, cushy, padded front-seat that leans right back for me to stretch my legs out. I tested it and you'll be able to play with King Kong while I drive and go free-ballin' anytime ya like. I'll even spray some of my Eau Sauvage cologne on the driver's seat where my furry crotch and fuzzy ass'll be sittin' so ya can feel right at home down there!"

More teasing laughter and then he asks how his old clothes are holding up in the armoire. "They're gonna be wantin' ya to start looking for a real private place for us to play with each other in the Aaron Sex-Mobile. I might even letcha loose on my new trousers and jacket from Craig's in my new wheels on special occasions, if you're extra-special nice to me."

I'm deadly silent on the other end of the phone.

He senses it and realizes he'd better quit while he's ahead. "Aww, c'mon now, baby. I hope ya do know there's nothin' wrong with a little fetish and kink as long as you're not hurtin' yourself or anyone else with it. We all have strange things that make us hot and juicy and get our *wires* up. Hmmmm... izzzn't it." And then he laughs.

"Seriously now, honey, this whole thing you've got with my old pants and jacket doesn't bother me 'cause it's harmless and you really get-off on it and I get *fringe-benefits* from it. I know you love me for more than just my old clothes. It's the sweaty, sexy Sasq' man hunk under those clothes that ya really love."

"God! You are one big, perverted, horny, dirty-minded Sasquatch. The fact is, those are the first clothes I ever saw you wearing when I started to jerk-off and fantasize about you back in Tonner's. You looked so damned confident and manly to me—a real hot-looking, well-hung, hundred-percent, masculine man with a sexy, hard ass and a really big bulge. That's why I remember it and still get-off on that old jacket and pants—especially when you're wearing them with nothing on underneath."

"Aww, I know that and understand. But just so ya know, I'm gonna tease you about it every now and then. Trust me, though. I'd never embarrass ya in front of anyone else and it'll always be our little secret. OK, butt-boy?"

"Dig that hole a little deeper there, Blanchard."

He roars with laughter and delivers the final line of his Adam Blanchard amateur-improv-comedy-act. "Oh, and while I'm thinkin' of our extra-curricular play-time here, start makin' up shopping lists 'cause I'm gonna be takin' lots and lots of long-distance, slow-lane, round-about trips to the grocery store, the hardware store, the drug store, the book store, the convenience store, the department store, and any other damn fuckin' store I can think of with you between my legs, workin' my stick-shift!"

"Adam. Uhh, uhm, actually—all I really wanted to know was what colour it was."

When I say that to him, he starts to choke and almost pass out on the other end of the phone line with raucous laughter.

"Uhm, Sasq' man… ?"

"Yeahhh, baby?"

"Adam… ?"

"What, baby?"

"You'll never make it as a comedian. Better stick with your day job."

"Aww, honey. C'mon now! Laugh! I miss you! But, seriously, about the car, it'll be OK for now and should get us around in the city there just fine. I think though, I'm probably just gonna keep it for a year or so and then maybe trade the Aaron Sex-Mobile in for somethin' newer, somethin' cheaper on gas, once things settle down with findin' a new place for us and startin' my new job and all."

"Trading your Aaron in for something newer after only a year? We're going to have to have a very serious discussion when you get back."

Another guffaw and then he says, "Had to have the last laugh, didn't ya?"

"Always. And I miss you, too! Please don't stay out there too long. I love you! Come home soon."

Several days later, Adam is back at Jason's townhouse waiting for Riku to arrive. An extremely-refined, elegant, and graceful-looking, metallic sky-blue NSU Ro80 German sedan glides up in front. Riku climbs out and starts to walk up to the front door. He pulls a key out to let himself in, then remembers Jason is really gone and that he must now ring the doorbell instead of intruding on Adam's privacy.

The look of sadness on Riku's expressive face over the loss of his lover is evident.

"Heya, Riku! Thanks for waitin' for me to get myself organized before comin' over. I woulda called ya before this, but there's just so much to go through. And I wanted a few days to get my head around everything."

"I understand. Thank you so much for letting me come. I know where Jason keeps tea. Do you mind if I make us tea, or would you rather do that yourself?"

"It must be very strange for you to feel like a guest in this place. I've been thinkin' about that a lot since we met and I think I'd be just as comfortable as you, if you went ahead and just did the things you normally would if my dad were still alive and here now. Is that OK with you?"

"Thank you. We had our rituals and I would like to make tea for us." Riku smiles warmly.

"You know, Riku, I'm sorta shocked at how much my dad and I had in common. First thing I did was go through his books in the upstairs second bedroom. He was really interested in history, wasn't he?"

"He had many interests. He was a complicated, passionate, multi-faceted man who was curious about a great number of things. He loved his books, his cat, you—and me. He loved life."

"I see that now. By the way, I don't blame you for anything he did to my mom and me back when he left her. I've thought about that a lot and I wantcha to know that."

"Thank you. That means a great deal to me to hear you say that. So, have you made any decisions regarding his personal effects here? I assume that Angelica is helping you with all the administrative estate details. Do you have any questions for me regarding anything here that I may be able to help you with?"

"Well, this is gonna sound really weird, but I, like, just *hafta* ask. Like, what's with that really bright, electric-blue and black racing-striped car of his? I've met you and seen what he has in this place, and uhm, uhh, that thing just doesn't seem to sorta fit into the picture of someone who would be with you and live here somehow."

Riku looks at Adam and then breaks out into a huge chuckle. "So funny. Oh, yes, that car. I was appalled when he first bought it. Jason could be a very loud, brash and impulsive man at times. He was like an excited child with his first bicycle when he saw it in the dealer's show-room. No amount of logic or objection from me could dissuade him from having to have that car. At the time, I was convinced he simply wanted it to underscore his independent nature and free spirit as a clear message back to me. You see, he had one of my company vehicles to drive for work. After he acquired that car, I had to forbid him to drive it when representing the company—too outlandish and in such vulgar, questionable taste. And so aggressively loud! Over time, however, its rarity and value increased immeasurably. What is it they say? Oh, yes, it is what they call a *muscle car* and is highly prized and sought after now as an important and desirable collectible that keeps increasing in rarity and value. Oh, the irony of that when I think back now. Over time, it became a source of much good-natured teasing and laughter between he and I. In many ways, Adam, he was a unique and complex man, so full of wonder and passion. That car is very much the essence of who your father was."

Riku then pauses and says quietly, "It will be the laughter I miss most, now that he's gone."

Adam doesn't know what to say to offer any comfort to Riku for his loss and obvious grief. All he can do is reach out to take his hand and give him a moment to compose himself before continuing.

"That's some funny story about the car and my dad. It's just, well, I guess it's just 'cause when ya really look around here, this place is so simple and peaceful. Like, for instance, those clay pot things there on the dining room table."

"You mean the *raku* pottery?"

"Yeah, those—they're just beautiful and so... different."

"I brought those back for him the last time I went to the *Nishijin district* of Kyoto when my parents died. They came from their house and once belonged to my father's parents. You think they are beautiful, do you? It is the unpredictability of the outcome when they are removed from the firing-kiln that generates those intense colours. To me, that is a metaphor for all those who love that life can be so uncertain and yet so beautiful with all of its flaws and imperfections. In Japanese, the words *wabi sabi* describe the magic and perfect beauty of the imperfections where gold has been used to repair visible cracks in the clay."

"You're gonna want those back, Riku. There must be lotsa things around here you would want to keep. Anything you want, I think you should have. I've looked through some of his photograph albums and I want you to have 'em."

"Adam, I want you to have those pieces of *raku*. It would give me great pleasure if you would permit me to gift them to you."

Adam is humbled by this gesture. "I don't now what to say except thanks, Riku." And then he looks over at an elegant minimalist floral arrangement set in an exquisite indigo blue, glazed ceramic vase.

"Those flowers and vines with that one piece of white birch bark there are beautiful, Riku. All together that way, they're so simple and, well, just so refined-looking."

"I will take that as a compliment. They are called *ikebana* and I create them. It is the act of deliberately selecting and sensuously experiencing the touch and texture of each leaf, branch and blossom in order to create something beautiful that makes this a true art form of personal expression and fulfillment. Your father always liked them. I do the ones in *Komorebi* as well."

"Riku, after so many years together, there's gotta be other things that hold memories for you here."

429

"Things, Adam. Things cannot bring back those we have loved and lost. They may generate memories, but one cannot hold memories in one's hand. They are merely material objects after all. There is one item I know he treasured however, and I would be most grateful if you could bring yourself to gift it to me. There is a black-and-white print above his bed that is very special."

"You mean the one with the script writing that says *wise sky* and *small forest?*"

"Yes, that is the one."

"What does that mean. Riku? I've been curious about that ever since I first saw it. That piece is just like, really beautiful."

"Those words are translated from the Japanese. *Riku* is wise sky and *Kobayashi* is small forest. Do you understand why that would be special to me?"

Adam is silent and nods.

"There is also a Cypress bonsai in his room that was another gift from me. It is over a hundred-and-fifty years old—a token symbol and reminder for me of the endurance of love in an ever-changing and fragile world. I would wish for that to be returned to me as well."

Consider it done. No problem. Uhm, I've been thinkin' about Dad's ashes, too, Riku. I have 'em here and I was thinkin', uhh, would you like to have 'em? Seems to me he woulda wanted you to have 'em."

Riku is on the verge of tears. After a few quiet moments of introspection, he says, "Adam, your father and I had intended to fly to Japan together before he became ill. He always wanted to travel back there with me one more time and I regret we never had the opportunity to do so before he died. In a way, he could have a last wish granted if I were to take his ashes back there with me after you have returned to Ottawa."

"I think he really woulda liked and wanted that."

"Now then, Adam—have you decided what to do with his furniture here and the rest of his personal effects?"

"I was thinkin' to maybe take his European and Asian History books and a few of his other things back with me. Not much though. And for sure, not the furniture. I don't know what to do, or who to call to have that taken care of."

"Perhaps I could help you with that. Anything you do not feel you want could be left here and either donated or sold with the money given back to you or charity. Your father loved animals. Perhaps a donation to the animal-shelter here in his name? I can take care of that for you and would be honoured if you were to allow me to help you."

"That sure would be a big help. Wouldya do that for me after I leave?"

"I will, on one condition."

"What's that?"

"That you promise me you will come back to Edmonton with your young man to visit me one day."

"You can count on us for that, Riku. Aaron and I will be there for ya from now on. Ya know, Riku, sometimes it's the people you choose to be with in life who become your *real* family. And trust me, you're like family to me now, in so many ways."

Both Adam and Riku smile at each other, then take a few moments to quietly reflect upon all that has just been expressed so poignantly between them.

Riku is the first one to speak and says, "Good! Now what do you plan to do with Jason's cat?"

"I'm thinkin' since my dad named him after me and all, he should be comin' back home to Ottawa to be with me."

"Oh! I am so glad you said that, Adam! I am allergic to cats!"

Adam laughs at the irony of this revelation. Riku looks over at him and smiles thinking, *you are very much your father's son...*

It's Thursday, April 10th, 1978, just past six-forty-five in the evening.

I'm standing just inside the front door waiting for Adam to pull up in front of our apartment on Argyle. *Jeez, when he told me he was leaving Toronto this morning, I was sure he'd be back by now.* And then I hear a growling, throaty-sounding car from a half-block away. Suddenly, there is Adam out front, hopping out of an outrageous-looking, electric-blue muscle car with bold black racing stripes and a huge, big spoiler on the back, striding across the street to meet me. He's wearing the loudest, brightest, untucked buffalo plaid flannel shirt in the world, along with a padded, quilted sleeveless vest and those tight, man-ass-accentuating jeans that arouse me every time he bends over in them. *Where in the hell did he ever get those worn-out, construction boots from? Does he think he's one of The Village People? Jeez!* I try to pick my jaw up off the floor.

"Good God! Did you mug a colour-blind lesbian in Edmonton for that orange plaid flannel shirt, Adam? And that car—that's it?! That's the car your dad had?!"

"Heya, my sexy, little Cookie-Butt-boy! Sure am glad to be back. Come and meet the *Aaron Sex-Mobile!*"

"It's not a sex-mobile. It's a pimp-mobile!"

Adam is not impressed.

I walk over to get a closer look at it and peer inside to see the back. "Just checking to see if Starsky and Hutch are back there. Where's Huggy Bear, stashed in the trunk? Adam? Do they know you stole their car?!"

Adam is *really* not impressed.

Actually, it looks more like something Malibu Barbie would drive. Does it have matching blue Barbie suitcases in the trunk with thirty-seven changes of clothes in them?" Is there a make-up kit and hair dryer in the glove compartment? How many vanity-mirrors are there on the sun visors? Where's Ken? I wanna meet Ken!"

"Knock it off, Aaron! Ya know, you really can be kinda bitchy at times. It was my dad's car and he loved it and it deserves some respect. Dontcha be makin' fun of my dad's car."

I think that's the first time he's ever used the 'B' word with me and I can't help but laugh. He just gives me one of his reproachful looks.

"You aughta know right now, too—I'm keepin' it. I got to really like it while driving back and it's here to stay."

"What's with that colour? I'm going blind just staring at it. "

"Oh, fuck off, Aaron! With all the masturbating you did back in Brockville before ya met me, it's a wonder ya didn't go blind years ago!'"

We're both laughing now.

"I asked them at the dealership about that colour when I took it in for a tune-up before headin' back. They told me it was a special Richard

Petty blue that he had on all his Nascar race cars. Look at the power bulge on the hood. I think it just got a little bigger now when it was checkin' ya out."

"Very funny. Hah, hah. OK, I guess I'll get used to it. But no fuzzy-dice or any of those damned pine-tree air-fresheners hanging from the rear-view mirror—promise me that, please."

"The only thing fuzzy in it will be what's hangin' between my legs. And that's just for you, honey."

"OK, mister *Saturday Night Live*. I had a weird feeling you were going to want to keep the car, so I went ahead and asked my classmate Lauren Marcato about good repair mechanics in the city. Her uncle runs McNabb's Shell station on Beechwood Avenue in the east end and he's really knowledgeable and good with Mopar repairs. You and he are going to get to be super good buddies, I think, if you keep your dad's car, seeing as though you are totally clueless when it comes to maintenance and repairs. Just keep your wallet open and he'll empty it whenever he needs to. Jeez…"

"What's *Mopar*, baby?"

"Mostly old parts and rust! Actually, it's when you take the words motor and parts and join the words up together. Seriously, they use those letters as a term for Chrysler muscle cars. You'd really better become familiar with this stuff if you're going to keep that thing."

"Never you mind about my dad's 440 Magnum Charger! You won't have to get used to it. I'm gonna keep it and store it away somewhere and just drive it once in a while. We'll rent two parking spots wherever we're gonna move to and I'll buy somethin' newer and more practical for every day. Maybe a Toyota Celica, or a Datsun, or a Mazda, or a Honda—hmmm—yeahh—maybe somethin' Japanese and economical and cool and fun to drive like that, eh? You can choose it. And I'll even letcha pick the colour on that one. Does that work for ya, my sexy, little butt-boy?"

"Can you afford that?"

"Uhh, yeah, I can. But I'll fill ya in on all of that once I getcha back inside to give ya a proper hello."

Later, we lie wrapped around each other and sprawled-out together in the bed and I say to Adam, "That's just about the biggest and hardest eight-inch hello I think I've ever received."

"And it's nice to see that eight still goes into one there with long-division, butt-boy." Then he leans up on one arm, wraps one of his muscular legs across mine to trap me in place and looks intently over at me. "Uhm, Aaron, there's somethin' I kinda, sorta forgot to tell ya about my dad and his place out in Edmonton. And seein' as though Riku is gonna be takin' care of the arrangements from Edmonton, I guess I better letcha in on it now. We're gonna have a visitor comin' to stay with us. And his name is Adam, just like me."

"Jeez, Adam! And you're telling me this *now*? There isn't even enough room for us here as it is! How in the hell do you think we're going to manage, having to cope with someone else in this place? And someone with the same first name as you?!"

"Not someone, honey—something."

I'm staring at him with a raised right eyebrow, waiting for what'll come out of his mouth next.

"Seems my dad had a cat he named after me. Riku was takin' care of him when Dad was in the Hospital and asked if I'd take him now that he's gone. Riku is allergic to cats, and, well, I just couldn't let him put poor little Adam into an animal shelter. Riku really didn't wanna have

435

to do that either, 'cause Dad just loved that cat. I'd never forgive myself if I let that happen. Riku is gonna have Adam flown to Ottawa and I'll go pick him up from the airport when he gets here. I was gonna drive home with him from Edmonton, but, honestly, it woulda been too long a trip and just too hard on both me and little Adam. Are you gonna be OK with this, baby? He's a really nice cat and won't be any trouble at all. I'll take care of him and you won't hardly even know he's around. Please say you'll be OK with me havin' little Adam here."

"Well… as long as you feed him and clean his litterbox and he doesn't get into any of my school work assignments, I guess it'll be OK. You have to promise me, though that when we move, you won't stick his litterbox in the bathroom because I don't want to have to be stepping on cat litter in the middle of the night. And he better be neutered and not be peeing on everything, either."

"I promise. And I think I remember Riku tellin' me he was fixed."

"OK, then. Well, at least *one* of you will be. I'll be able to tell you two Adams apart that way, I suppose."

He grabs me and laughs. "I don't think we're done just yet sayin' hello to each other," he says. "C'mere and show me again how much ya missed me."

The next morning, I'm already off to classes before eight-thirty. Adam is catching up on the local news on TV while finishing a third cup of coffee when the phone rings.

"Hullo."

"Yes, good morning. Would a Monsieur Adam Blanchard be there, please?"

"It's Adam speaking. What can I do for ya?"

"Hello, *Monsieur* Blanchard. My name is Sergeant Jean-Jacques Dufour. I'm the Chief Security Advisor for the Ministry of Health and Welfare for National Headquarters here in Ottawa."

"Yes Sergeant Dufour. Can I help ya with somethin'?"

"It's about the recent competition you were successful in winning and the job offer signed-off by Mrs. Andrea Gauthier in Procurement. We need you to come in to answer a few questions regarding an incident that allegedly occurred last year. A report came in to our attention from an anonymous source connected with the RCMP that claims you were arrested and held-over, pending trial for a crime supposedly committed by you last spring. We must get this cleared up and I want you to come in to where you were interviewed so that we can put this to rest. Are you free this afternoon to come in to discuss this matter with me?"

Adam is stunned, starts to perspire and slowly, hesitantly responds with, "Uhm, yeah, uhh, alright, sure. OK. I wasn't arrested. But sure, no problem. What time wouldya like me to be there?"

Adam shows up at Sergeant Dufour's office a few minutes past two-thirty and comes face-to-face with an imposing, salt-and-pepper-haired, tall, strikingly-handsome gentleman with piercing green eyes who reaches out to shake Adam's hand. He gestures for Adam to sit down at the chair in front of his imposing mahogany desk. Adam has a strange sense of deja-vu when he takes a good look at Sergeant Dufour. "Thank you for coming in on such short notice, Monsieur Blanchard. I called the Ottawa Police Department after we spoke and they corroborated your statement that you were not officially arrested for any crime. There are some police notes and mug shots taken from the incident however by the attending officers that must be clarified before you can be fully-cleared with Security for the job being offered to you. Would you care to

explain and clear-up exactly what happened on the evening in question that was mentioned in this report that came in to our attention?"

Sergeant Dufour leans back in his chair, folds his arms and stares back unblinkingly at Adam.

"Well, Sergeant, if ya know the date and details of what went down that night, ya already know what happened, so there's no point in me denying or tryin' to hide anything that went on."

"Go on."

"OK, well, then—might as well be right up-front with ya from the start here. I'm gay and went into the Club Baths at 1069 Wellington that night to hook-up with someone. There's no way to sugar-coat it. That was the night the Club Baths got raided. You probably remember the newspaper article right after everyone got picked up and hauled into the cop shop that night. They were threatening to name everyone rounded up and publish their names in the paper. And the police were gonna arrest us all and hold us over for bail hearings before a judge the next day. Nothing happened though because somehow the charges all got dropped and the newspaper reporter most likely was told to bury the follow-up story naming people. That's about all I know about it. The thing is though that yes, I was in the wrong place at the wrong time. But I wasn't arrested and charged with anything."

"I appreciate that you've been honest and forthcoming with me. This was actually a test to see how you would handle this and whether you would be honest and up-front about the incident. Many would have lied or tried to hide details of this and as such, could eventually become potential targets for intimidation or extortion. The level of security clearance required for your position is, fortunately, for you, not at the top-secret level. And your exposure to sensitive Crown and Cabinet information would be minimal. As such, I see absolutely no reason to officially deny you your clearance. Might I suggest that in the future however, you be more discreet and circumspect in your private affairs?"

"Uhm, yeah, errr, yes uhm, thanks, Sergeant Dufour. I appreciate that."

Sergeant Dufour gets up and reaches out to shake Adam's hand. "I'll speak quietly to Mrs. Gauthier to let her know that your clearance will be fast-tracked in order for you to start on the date she wants you to. Good luck to you, Adam, uhh, may I call you Adam?"

"Yes, sir."

"The name's Jean-Jacques, Adam. Please, just call me Jean from now on. And a word to the wise for you for the future—no more visits to the Club Baths. There are other ways to find that sort of pleasurable entertainment, if that's what you're looking for. Much safer that way. Consider that as sage advice from a sympathetic and empathic, under-standing, somewhat older and much more experienced uncle." He holds his index finger up to his lips to reinforce the need to be discreet and keep silent. Finally, he gives Adam a little wink and a knowing smile.

"One last thing, Adam."

"Uhh, uhm, yes, errr, Jean, what's that?"

"Do you know the name Jeremey at all? Does that sound familiar to you?"

"Uhh, uhm, yeah, I sorta do, sir."

"Well, I can't disclose details. But I suggest you remember and be extremely wary of that name in the future. He's no friend of yours."

"Uhm, OK, thanks, Jean. I'll remember that."

"Good lad. Now, when you get yourself settled around here, I'll give you a call and we can have coffee or lunch together to get you off on the right foot, OK, Adam?"

"I'd like that, sir, errr, rather, Jean. And thanks a lot!"

As Adam is leaving the office, Sergeant Dufour takes the unclassified file in his hand and starts to feed it into the shredder.

The machine is grinding noisily away and the file disappears into the slot feed at the top. He calls out to his admin assistant and tells her to call Andrea Gauthier to expect Adam in to report for his first day, as per their discussion earlier.

11 April / May

"Hi, Dad."

"Aaron, son. How are you making out with school and did Adam make it back OK from Edmonton yet?"

"School is finishing up this year OK. I just have to finish some working drawings for my retail store project and do a formal presentation of it. Then a couple of other small projects on Colour Theory for Elzbeth Mountebank and I think that should wrap everything up. And yes, Adam got back a few days ago and actually, that's one of the reasons I'm calling you."

"Was he able to wrap everything up with his father's estate and how is he coping with everything?"

"His dad was very generous with him. I don't think Adam is going to have any problems about money or anything like that."

"I wasn't actually referring to that. How is Adam dealing with the knowledge now about his dad's life and the years apart?"

"I think it was good he went out there. He seems happier and maybe even a bit more focused now that he's back. He's just about to start his new job. And I can tell he is starting to think about his future and where he wants to go in life. Does that make any sense to you at all?"

"Having closure and finding answers will do that, son. I'm very happy to hear that. Just remember what I said to you about not getting involved in anything between Adam and his mother.

"Yes, Dad. I remember what you said."

"What goes on between a husband and wife—or a parent and child for that matter, is intimate, private and delicate when it comes down to emotions, motivations and actions. You and I will never know what transpired between Jason and Delphine in their marriage. Nor should we. Jason is gone now. And while he may not have been there for Adam over the years, it is neither for you nor I to judge whether he was right or wrong in his actions. Love, in whatever form it may take is a positive and powerful force in this world. And we all must live our lives as honestly and true to ourselves as we can. I have no doubt that Jason loved his son. And perhaps it may have been for the best that he left to find his own personal happiness, rather than remain and continue to bring sadness and pain to both Delphine and Adam."

"I think I understand what you are saying."

"Aaron, remember when we talked before you left home for College and all of the hurtful things Astrid said to you. I told you at that time to pursue your own happiness and to be true to yourself. I think that is what Jason had to do many years ago when he left Delphine and Adam. That he left some kind of legacy for Adam is a testament to a father's love for their child. I am sure now that will give Adam some peace and hopefully, for Delphine as well, in time. Adam's dad will be there now in spirit with him for the rest of his life. I believe that is how God would want it. God can work in mysterious ways, son. And I think Adam now knows he was loved and hopefully, with that knowledge can now move forward confidently with his life, however he chooses to live it."

"Yes, Dad."

"Oh, and on a completely unrelated matter, Adam's old car, his father's old Ambassador broke through the ice and sank on March 24th, Good Friday at one-twenty-seven in the morning. We didn't win anything on the lottery, son... unfortunately.

Meanwhile, I'm thinking about life and death, and endings and beginnings, and the perfect irony of Adam's old Ambassador choosing to end itself in such a poetic, timely and melodramatic fashion... on *Good Friday* of all the days on the calendar.

"Uhm, I'll let Adam know that, Dad. Thanks, and bye for now."

Monday morning and it's Adam's first day on the job with National Health and Welfare.

He's in the bathroom in front of the mirror wearing only an unbuttoned white dress shirt and pair of sexy, white, open-mesh, fly-front underwear briefs with a razor in his right hand, shaving. All I can see is his hot, shapely man-ass, big bulge, and long, hairy legs as he scrapes the stubble below his beard. His pleasure-trail is teasing me to go in there and rub my hands along it.

Several minutes later, he's sitting on the bed watching me get ready for my classes. I can't help but sneak subtle, furtive glances over at him. He looks just like the pornographic sex god he is: Sockless, a brand-new, navy blue and russet-orange striped silk tie loosened around his neck, his legs spread invitingly, his new grey tweed sports jacket lying casually beside him.

"What's with the glasses?"

"Figured they'd make me look all serious and intelligent there, butt-boy. And they turn into dark sunglasses when I'm outside in the sun"

"Hmmm, don't know about that. They're sure working for me though. You look like a hot, hunky, horny stud Professor out of a really hot and sexy porn film. Certainly better than the ones I have at Algonquin, that's for sure."

He gives me a wink and a dirty laugh and finishes putting on his jacket.

"Uhm, Adam, I'll be in classes most of the day. But I should be back here before you finish work."

"That's OK, baby. Not sure how this first day is gonna go. There's stuff in the fridge for dinner. We'll get caught up then. "

"You're going to be just fine today, Adam."

"Hope so, Cookie-Butt. Talk later, OK?"

"Adam! Welcome to your first day on the job." Andrea Gauthier, one of the two who interviewed him in February for his position at Health and Welfare, smiles warmly and motions for him to sit down in her workstation.

"Today will be just an orientation-session and introduction for you with the other staff and then meeting with HR to get you started off on the right foot. I've scheduled an internal staff meeting for ten this morning with the three current employees who will report to you. There's been a slight change of schedule with respect to your language training. A spot opened up earlier than anticipated and we've placed you in a class starting in late-May. You'll actually be starting with those then instead of later on in June. We'll appoint one of your employees to temporarily take over and act in your position while you are studying at

Asticou. Until then, you'll be sitting with me to interview temps to fill the jobs for which we've received funding for the new fiscal year."

The rest of the day seems like one stressful race from one office to another with Andrea until four-thirty.

"Jeezus fuck! Am really kinda tired here. Hope your day wasn't as confusing as mine," Adam says when we're both back home in the apartment in the evening. He sighs and runs his hand through his hair.

"So, how did your first day go?" I ask him.

"Well, I'm thinkin' the three people who are gonna be workin' for me will be a challenge. I think only one of them knows one end of a pencil from the other. The other two, well, do you remember that Gilda Radner character, Roseanne Roseannadanna from *Saturday Night Live* and that Mrs. Wiggins secretary character offa *The Carol Burnett Show*? Like, I swear one of 'em looks and sounds just like Gilda Radner! And the other was wearin' a girdle so tight, she walked with her ass stuck way out in high heels and in a skirt I don't even think she could sit down in!"

I'm killing myself laughing while Adam bends over and sticks his ass in my face to demonstrate and get a reaction out of me. "Andrea told me I'd be starting language training earlier in May though, so I won't hafta be dealing with them right away. Oh yeah, and I think I'm gonna take a drive out to where this language training centre is in Hull later on. It's called *Asticou*. So how's about you ride along with me and we'll check out your *ass-ta-cutie butt-cheeks* on the way home. Whaddya say?"

"Oh jeez, that's got to be like, the lamest pun you've ever come up with," I groan and roll my eyes at him.

"Never you mind! My dong just got real excited when you said *cum* there, so we're goin' right after supper! And roll your eyes like that at me again and I'll have to hold ya down and discipline ya. That's really disrespectful, ya know!" Then he laughs and starts to tickle me.

I'm laughing while struggling to fight him off, and then say, "Not tonight, Adam. There's a brand new show starting on TV called *Dallas* with Larry Hagman and Patrick Duffy in it. It's a brand new TV show about oil and Texas and power and wealth and I think just this one time I'd like to stay home and watch it. Patrick Duffy is really hunky and kind of reminds me of you. You go on ahead and check out *Asticou* though, OK?"

"Nope! Not without you along for the ride. We can maybe do it over the weekend then."

Saturday morning finally arrives...

Adam is sitting over by my desk, excitedly waving this glossy brochure about. "Aaron, uhm, Conor and Nick were tellin' me about a new condominium building almost all finished now, close to them in the McKellar Park area. That's just on the other side of Westboro. It's close to the Lincoln Fields Shopping Centre and Bayshore. I think we should go on over and maybe have a look at it. Conor got a sales brochure for me to check out and I kinda like it."

"I think the sooner we can get out of here, the less likely we're going to wind up killing each other. Let me see that brochure. Hmmm, four floors with dark, brownish-red brick and huge, big balconies with brown-tinted-glass railings facing onto National Capital Commission parkland along the Parkway and the Ottawa River. The view would be amazing from the back."

"I'd need a car for sure to get back and forth to the Campus," I tell him, "and I refuse to drive that screaming neon thing of your dad's on the Queensway or have anyone see me park it in the student parking lot at Algonquin."

Adam gives me a stubborn and reproachful look and says, "You're never gettin' your hands on the keys to that car, you! It's mine, baby! It was my dad's and he loved it. And I love it, too. Get used to it 'cause the Aaron Sex-Mobile's here to stay!"

I've given up on trying to be logical and reasonable with him about that damned car. "All right, Adam," but we're just going to have to get *something* more practical eventually for daily use."

"We'll go and check out smaller cars today," he says. "Now... no more talk about my dad's car!"

"OK, Adam. I give up. But there's no urgent need for another car right away. I'm almost done my semester and we have all summer to figure that one out. Besides, I want to get my bike out soon and ride up and down the Canal and along the Western Parkway out to Bayshore. You can rent or buy one, too, and I'll follow right behind you and stare at your hot, sexy, fuzzy man-ass butt-cheeks and long, furry legs while you pedal."

Adam's mouth is agape and I've managed to render him speechless and totally catch him off-guard once again. *God! I just love doing that to him!*

Then I smile and say, "OK, I guess I'll just have to get used to the car. Oh, by the way, if it's the Aaron Sex-Mobile, when does it get to see some action and earn the title?"

Adam lets loose with a huge laugh and says, "Well, honey, I was hopin' you were gonna bring that subject up sooner or later. Ya wanna take a ride out to Asticou with me right now, and after that check out those condos?!" Next thing I know, he's got his car keys in his hand and is out the door in a flash, bounding down the front steps of the apartment building, hopping into his car, revving it aggressively, staring back, and impatiently waiting for me to hop in with him!

Yup, faster than a speeding bullet, for sure...

Ten minutes later and the Aaron Sex-Mobile is rumbling down the Parkway with Adam's big dick out of his jeans, sticking straight up and demanding my attention. He spreads his long legs and grabs my head and starts to urgently push it down into his delicious and spicy *Adam Blanchard pube-forest*. He gives me a suggestive, dirty laugh and then says, "I think we're gonna take the scenic route along the Parkway and you can play with King Kong on the way."

"Is there a cum-towel under the front-seat?"

"Uhm, yeahhh. I've still got my old cum-towel under the seat and I also stole your cute, sexy little Superman bikini briefs. I've been usin' 'em to rub one out with in the car ever since I got back from Edmonton."

"So *that's* where they went to!"

"Yep, ya got me doing sexy, kinky, fetish things with your clothes now, too."

"Just make sure they're freshly-laundered and back in my armoire when you're done with them."

"Well, to quote you, all things are negotiable."

One ejaculation and fifteen minutes later, Mr. King Kong dong and his amazing sex-mobile pulls up in front of the condo building. He kills the engine and we sit in Adam's steamed-up Charger surveying the building.

"So, whaddya think?"

"About what, Sasq'? Your cock or the condo?"

"Ha, ha, ha. Like, who's the goddamn fuckin' comedian now, eh?" he says and starts to grope and tickle me in the front-seat.

"Well, I kinda like the building. What do you think?"

"Well, it'll be close for me to take an OC Transpo express bus back and forth downtown where I'm gonna be for work. Let's call the developer and come back and check 'em out. Whaddya say?"

"Well, I guess one more trip along the Parkway won't hurt."

"And one trip out to Asticou now with me givin' ya a hand-job on the way won't hurt either!"

A couple of days later and Adam is on the phone with the Sales Agent for the condo building. He took down the phone number from the brochure and is talking away *at* him… "Hullo. My name is Adam Blanchard and I'd like to make an appointment with one of your sales people to come and look at one of the *Sussex* model two-bedroom units you're sellin' at 727 Richmond Road."

"Oh, I *am* sorry, Mr. Blanchard. That particular model sold out over six months ago. It's the most popular floorplan in the building."

"You mean to tell me they're all paid-for and occupied right now?"

"Well, there's one unit that the new owners have not moved into yet on the top floor. They're an older, retired couple and one of them has recently taken ill, along with some mobility issues. I believe they're considering holding-off on the move for now and may be interested in renting it out with the possibility of selling it at some point in the future, if health issues continue to persist and become more serious for them."

"You wouldn't happen to have their name and phone number handy there, wouldya?"

"I can't give that information out over the phone without their permission, Mr. Blanchard. But I could give them a call to let them know you may be interested in speaking with them about their unit. Would you like me to do that?"

"Yes, please." Adam gives him his phone number and hangs up.

Three phone calls and two weeks later, Adam and I have a key from the owners and are checking out the condo.

"So, whaddya think?" says Adam.

"It's nice. Everything is really white and bright and clean and fresh and spacious. I like that the kitchen opens up to the living and dining rooms with that long counter bar, along with the recessed pot-lights right above it. It's good for privacy that the two bedrooms are separated on either side. That huge walk-in closet in the main bedroom is perfect with the three-way illuminated mirror and all those shelves, drawers, racks and built-ins. And the bleached, white-stained hardwood floors are just beautiful. It'd be good to have a full-size washer and drier right in the place instead of having to do laundry in a common room or laundromat. And that view from the balcony through those big sliding-doors reminds me of looking out over the St. Lawrence River back in Brockville. That dining room chandelier has got to go though. Maybe replace it with some cool track-lighting along that long wall. I could see one of those beautiful, bright-coloured, quilted wall-hangings of your mom's on that wall hanging like a piece of artwork there. Do you think she'd do one of those for us?"

"Maybe, honey. We can ask her, for sure. I think she'd be real flattered."

"So, what do you think?"

"Well, I like that we have a one-year option to buy it, if we want, and that we wouldn't have to go through any real estate agents either. We'd be saving a whole helluva lot of money on realtor fees if we didn't hafta do that. It's bright and I really like that wide-open living/dining room space, too. We can shove a great big sectional sofa and TV/stereo system in there and still have lots and lotsa room! It'll be good to have a decent-sized kitchen with new appliances and those white Corian countertops with the matching Corian double sinks. There are two bathrooms, so I won't be waitin' for you to stop starin' at yourself in the mirror every morning. And an option for an extra parking space in the garage. Well, I think it could work out just fine. And it'd be nice to be so close to Conor and Nick."

He is rewarded with his mention of my staring at myself in the bathroom mirror with an irritated look and a melodramatic eye-roll. "Remember what I told ya about rolling your eyes at me there butt-boy!" he says and then laughs.

Several days later, and I'm working from home at my desk when Adam comes into the apartment after work, late in the afternoon. I gesture over to the envelope sitting on top of the TV and say, "Uhm, uhh, hey, Sasq'! When I was home this morning finishing up my water-colour rendering for Massimo, a courier came and delivered an envelope for you. It's over on the TV there."

"Hmmm, wasn't expectin' anything. Did ya see a return address label on the envelope?"

"It says it's from *Komorebi* in Edmonton."

"Ahh, it's from Riku then. Ya know, I'm gonna take you out there some day real soon. You just gotta meet Riku and see that restaurant of his, you'll love it. It's fuckin' beautiful! And you and Riku will really like each other, too. I just know it."

Adam is examining the envelope and reading the address on it and thinking, *Jeezus, sure as hell hope there's nothin' wrong with little Adam and that Riku's not havin' any trouble with the airline tryin' to get him shipped back here.*

Inside the courier packet is a simple, buff-coloured envelope that has Adam's name on it in elegant script lettering. There is a sheet of exquisite, traditional Japanese stationary paper inside the envelope that reads:

"Dearest Adam,

It was so good to have the honour of meeting Jason's son. He would be so proud of how you've grown to become the fine young man you are.

I have just returned from Kyoto and gave much thought to my years with your father when I was there.

As I told you when we met, your father was a proud man—very headstrong and independent. I see those same qualities in you. You and he are so very much alike, in so many ways.

I am reminded of a Haiku when I think of you and your father.

"... Kites tangle
In summer twilight
Father and son... "

Adam, I am a very wealthy man today because of your father's love, encouragement and support over the years.
I want to do the right thing by him for his son.

The money he gave to me over the years was something I never spent. I opened up a bank account, invested it and let it accumulate to collect interest for him in the event that, should something ever happen to me, he would be well taken care of.

He never knew that.

I have no need of this money and I believe he would want me to give it to you. That is something I want to do now.

I hope you will accept this in memory of your father... a man who loved you very much.

With my very best wishes to you for your future happiness,

(Your friend always) Riku Kobayashi—Riku"

Adam is dumbfounded and starts to cry as he sits down on my drafting stool and just stares at the certified cashier's cheque in his hand for one-hundred and ninety-seven-thousand dollars, made out to Mr. Adam Richard Blanchard.

"Adam! What's wrong?! Did something happen to little Adam?! What does that letter say? Why are you crying? Ohh, Adam, what can I do?!"

Adam hands me the cheque and the note from Riku and then simply says, "Here... read what Riku wrote and then look at the cheque."

"Hiya, Mom. Can I come down to see ya tomorrow? There's somethin' I wanna talk to you about concerning Edmonton now that I've been back for a while now. It's really kinda important."

"Of course, darling. I'll be here all weekend. Will Aaron be coming with you? Should I plan for lunch or dinner for you two?"

"No, Mom. What I wanna talk to you about is just between you and me, OK?"

"Nothing wrong between you two, I hope?"

"Nah, Mom. Nothin' like that. I'll see ya in the morning."

The next morning, Adam pulls up in front of his mom's house back in Brockville. Delphine is watching from the master bedroom window above the garage as Adam parks his dad's car in front and strides up the paved concrete path to the front door.

"Hey, Mom."

"Sooo, that screaming bright blue, neon thing was the car Jason left you?"

"Uhm, yeahhh. And dontcha be givin' me a hard time about it either. I've already heard it *all* from Aaron. And you shouldn't talk yourself, given that your car is like, bright lime-green, for God's sake!"

"Hmmm, just like Jason to have been driving something as impractical and attention-grabbing as that. Oh well, I won't speak ill of the dead. Come on into the kitchen. I have a pot of coffee on. Would you like some breakfast, darling? What can I make you?"

"Nothing, Mom. Thanks, that's fine. I have somethin' important to discuss with you."

"OK, Adam. I'm listening."

"Uhm, well, Mom, seems that Dad left me a whole lot of money—you should have this."

He hands an envelope over to Delphine with a certified cashier's cheque inside for twenty-five-thousand dollars.

"I don't understand, darling. What is this, Adam?"

"Well, he left me a really big life insurance policy. And with the money invested just before he died, well, we're both gonna not hafta worry much about money from now on.

Delphine is speechless.

"It's comin' at a good time for me. With the new job and decidin' about a new place to move to and all, well, this is gonna make things a lot better in the long run. I'm thinkin' about maybe buyin' this place we just rented with an option to buy up in Ottawa and maybe even taking some part-time courses at Ottawa University to eventually get a degree. I've always wanted to study history. And Ottawa U has some great Professors and part-time courses. Now that I'm permanently in the government, a university degree will really help if I wanna advance in my career. And with Aaron doin' so well now, well, I think we're both gonna do just great together in the future.

Delphine keeps staring at the cheque and back at Adam. "This is all too much, Adam! Your father left this for *you*. I can't take this. It just wouldn't feel right to me if I accepted it."

"Mom, think of it as me paying you back for the money you spent on my education in Kingston and Dad's share of what he left you with to pay off his debts and the mortgage on this place when he took off. I'm tellin' ya right now, there was a lot more than that in his estate. And you're gonna take it 'cause it's mine now and I wantcha to have it. You're my mom, and I love you, and I'm not gonna take no for an answer."

After a long pause, Delphine finally says, "Adam, Bast and I have been talking about marriage. How would you feel about having him as part of the family?"

"I want you to be as happy as I am. You deserve that—as well as what's in your hand right now. Now go on ahead and plan some fantastic honeymoon somewhere with Bast and prove to me that *happily-ever-after* isn't just some stupid thing they say in fairy tales, and bedtime stories, and in those really dumb Harlequin romance novels ya stash away in your night table drawers!"

"We'll discuss the money situation in greater detail when I've gotten over the shock of this and we've both had a chance to think and plan rationally and sensibly. What I will do for now is plan that holiday in France that Bast and I were wanting to go on once we got married. His parents were from the west coast of France in Normandy, close to *Caen*, in a little village called *Bénouville*. They fled France during World War Two and Bast has always wanted to go back there to see where they lived."

"I know that place! There was a famous battle there during the Normandy Invasion in World War Two. And there is a really beautiful chateau there. Aaron and I were talkin' about that place a while back. It's in one of his books on architecture and was designed by some eighteenth-century French Architect called LeDoux—I think he said he was named Claude Nicholas LeDoux. Aaron told me he really wanted to go see that place someday. I think he said it was a Maternity Hospital now or somethin' like that. It's even got a little chapel they rent out for couples wantin' to get married there."

Delphine looks at Adam and smiles. "I think with you and your history, and Aaron and his architecture, the both of you are going to be together for a long, long time. You're obviously very well-matched. I'm so happy."

"Thanks, Mom. I think so, too."

The much-anticipated and long-awaited message confirmation from Riku finally arrives with respect to Adam junior—the cat—much anticipated I should say by Adam senior—the one who isn't neutered.

"Sorry, baby, but I've had to put the kitty litter box in the bathroom here 'til we move. But it's in the far corner and you won't be steppin' in it or anything once little Adam's here."

Jeez, I swear he's just like a first-time father with that cat. He's already bought five different coloured collars for it and matching food and water bowls and a scratching post and the damned thing isn't even through the front door yet.

"Remember what I told you, Adam. I'm not allowed to have pets in this place. It's in my lease. So for the rest of the time we're here, you're just going to have to be extremely careful about not letting him roam the hallways here."

"Aww, honey, it's OK. We're only gonna be here for a little while longer. And just look at this cute orange harness and sun goggles I got for him to protect his little kitty eyes."

Oh, God!

Several days later, Adam is out at Uplands Airport awaiting the arrival of his namesake. Finally, an animal cage is brought to him in the cargo hold pick-up area and Adam junior and Adam senior are reunited.

"Heya, little buddy! I'll getcha outta that cage and into the plastic travel crate I bought for ya in just a sec'. Here, I got a cute little orange collar with your name tag and license on it. We'll put that on first and then head on home.

Adam junior gets to sit in the front-seat heading home from the airport. On the way, Adam tells his new pal that he's got to be a good boy for Aaron.

"He likes dogs and has never had a cat before, little Adam. And you just gotta stay away from his school assignments and not poop or pee anywhere you're not supposed to. You got that, little buddy?"

Adam junior stares balefully back at Adam senior and promptly coughs up a hairball on the *black-and-white-tiny-houndstooth upholstery fabric* front-seat!

"So, this is Adam, eh?" I say as the plastic crate with an oversized bath towel over it is smuggled into the apartment. Well, he *is* kind of cute. His fur is beautiful and he has really nice eyes."

I bend down to get a closer look and a paw comes out with claws fully extended. All I hear is a loud *meeeeeow* as little Adam tries to eviscerate me.

"Just remember what I said to you, Adam. He has to stay away from my drafting board and my assignments and he is *not* sleeping on the bed with us. You got him his own little kitty canopy bed there and that's where he's going to sleep… that's non-negotiable. And the first time he draws blood from me, he goes right back to Riku, and he can serve him up as an entrée with some *wasabi* in his restaurant. You got that?"

"Uhm, yeah, honey. He'll be just fine once he gets settled. Now dontcha be hurtin' his feelings now. You won't hardly even know he's around, I promise."

The next morning I look over at my drafting board and see two tiny little cat stools on top of my drafting assignment for Gaelen that is due later that day. In addition, the pungent smell of cat urine seems to be mysteriously emanating from the red Bokhara rug in front of the fireplace.

"Adam! He's left two turds on my assignment and he's peed on my rug!"

"Aww, Aaron, I'm sorry. I'll clean it up. Is your drafting gonna be OK, I hope?"

"When I get home after class, big Adam, you let little Adam know he and I are going to have a serious discussion with some ground rules set up around here. You got that?"

"Uhm, yes, Aaron."

Later on that afternoon, I open the door to the apartment after class and can see Adam sitting cross-legged on the floor with little Adam in his lap, purring away loudly.

"Now, Adam. We discussed this already, little buddy and I thought we came to a mutual understanding and agreement. You just can't be poopin' and peein' on Aaron's stuff. I thought we clearly understood this when I brought ya back home from the airport."

I can't help but smile and chuckle quietly. "Adam, he's a cat! Do you really think he understands what you are telling him right now?"

"Uhm, yeah, honey. I know he understands. He's a *smart* little Adam!"

"Well then, let's see if he understands this: Little Adam, one more gift for me on my drafting board and you're up for adoption. You got that, cat?"

Adam junior lazily stretches out and yawns as Adam senior continues to scratch the back of his neck.

12 July / Epilogue

It's Monday morning, July 7th, 1978.

"Hey, honey?"

"Yes, Adam?" I'm sitting at the counter bar in the kitchen in the new condo, wearing my bathrobe and finishing my first cup of coffee before the day begins.

"Do ya know where my second brown shoe went to? I wanna wear 'em with my blue pants when I head on in to *Asticou* for language training this mornin'."

"Uhh, nope, sorry, Adam, no idea."

Two minutes later, Adam has another question.

"Hey, honey?"

"Yes, Adam?"

"None of my socks match in the drawer. It's like, I've got one of each. Where'd all the other ones go to?"

"Must be in the wash. Or maybe little Adam was playing with them... I don't know."

"Hey, honey?!"

"Yes, Adam?"

"Where's all my damned underwear? There isn't like, any in the drawer here!"

"Must all be in the laundry then—with the socks."

"Dammit! I'll have to go free-ballin' today then. Shit!"

Another couple of minutes pass and then Adam yells out from the bedroom..

"Aaron, baby?!"

"Yes, Adam?"

"My employee pass to get into the building, have ya seen it, honey?"

"I think I saw it under some of my stuff over there on the coffee table."

He bends down to scoop it up off the table while I sneak a stealthy glance at his sexy butt and smile.

Then thirty seconds after that, Adam continues to search around the living room and then stomps back into the bedroom.

"Aaron, where in the fuckin' hell is my goddamn wallet?!"

"Last time I saw it, it was on the dresser under one of your orange bath towels in there."

"Jeezus fuck! Am gonna hafta take the car today to make it in to class! The bus'll never get me over to Asticou on time."

Another minute passes.

"Honey?"

"Yes, Adam?"

"Where the fuck are my goddamn car keys?!"

"Right here on the counter where you left them yesterday. I can see that Superman fob tag thingie just under the corner of the newspaper here."

"Shit, man, gotta rush or I'm gonna be really late! Will talk to you later, OK?"

"OK, Sasq'."

He pulls me into a head-lock, ruffles my hair and gives me a quick kiss. He heads out the door and down in the elevator to the parking garage.

The Aaron Sex-Mobile is sitting there just waiting for him... with a flat, deflated left rear tire.

Just then a lightbulb starts to go off. It dawns on him that someone maybe doesn't want him going in to *Asticou* today. First the shoes, then the socks, then the wallet, and then, like, absolutely no underwear at all in the drawer and having to go full commando—all too coincidental. King Kong is starting to twitch inside his pants as he stands there, pondering the possibilities.

He slowly smiles to himself and then heads back upstairs to find me still sitting at the counter, calmly pretending to read the newspaper.

He gives me a suspicious, questioning look and then says, "Uhm, uhh, Aaron, you're readin' the editorial section of the newspaper upside down there, baby. Uhh, honey, Cookie, baby, my car has a flat tire. I just don't get it. It's almost like it kinda doesn't want me to leave today. And now I just don't know how the fuck I'm gonna make it out to Asticou with no goddamn wheels this morning. Uhm, uhh, you wouldn't happen to know anything about that now, wouldya, baby?"

"Adam, what day is today?" I reply while putting down the newspaper and giving him a sly little smile.

"Dunno. What day is it?"

"It's one year to the day since you first picked me up in your old Ambassador back in Brockville and introduced me to your big King Kong dong."

He stares at me, dumbfounded.

"Oh, shit, Aaron! I completely forgot!"

"That's OK. I didn't. Uhh, I think you and King Kong and I are going to be spending the day in bed together today. Happy anniversary, Sasq' man!"

"Aww, Happy Anniversary, Cookie! What a year it's been, eh?"

His pants are off in record time and on the floor as he heads boned-up and bare-assed into the bedroom. He turns around, gives me one of his suggestive grins, then laughs and growls. "Get you're tight little buns in here right now, ya horny, kinky, perverted, sexy little twink!"

"You mean *your* little twink, don't you!?"

"Only if you have a pump to inflate the flat tire on my car, *kid*!"

I'm laughing my head off and say to him, "Love you, Adam. And don't call me *kid!*"

He grins and chuckles, then says, "Love you, too, baby. Now get your tight, sexy, little Cookie-Boy butt-cheeks in here."

The End

List of Characters

1. Aaron Richard Christie (Main Character)

2. Adam Richard Blanchard (Main Character)

3. Richard Christie *'Richie'* (Aaron's Father)

4. Ariane Christie *'Ana'* (Aaron's Mother)

5. Astrid Christie (Aaron's Sister)

6. Geraint (Astrid's Husband)

7. Old Gerry (Brockville) Prentice ESSO Gas Station

8. King Yee (Brockville) The Peacock Inn

9. Mrs. Tonner (Brockville) Tonner's Pharmacy

10. Louie (Brockville) El Paso Restaurant

11. Monsignor Cranston (Brockville) St. Francis Xavier Church

12. Delphine Bogaert (Blanchard) *'Del'* (Adam's Mother)

13. Sebastien Forestier *'Bast'* (Del's Boyfriend)

14. Jason Blaine Blanchard (Edmonton) Adam's Father

15. Wendy Yaegar (Brockville)

16. John Yaegar (Brockville)

17. Jimmy Yaegar (Brockville)

18. Cala Cuthbertson (Brockville) Aaron's Friend

19. Charlie Rieder (Cala's Boyfriend)

20. Cora-Leanne Cuthbertson (Brockville) Cala's Sister

21. Corinne Cuthbertson (Kingston) Cala's Sister

22. Tina-Louise (Kingston) Corinne's Friend

23. Fat Carlo (Brockville) the Shopping Centre – Radio Shack
    Friend of Geraint

24. Mr. and Mrs. Nicholson (Brockville) Landlords for Adam on
    Pearl Street West

25. Miss Janice Delahaye (Brockville) Bethune Street neighbor

26. Mrs. Larocque (Brockville) Cedar Street

27. Angelica (Brockville) Evangeline's Dress Shoppe

28. Eveline (Brockville) Evangeline's Dress Shoppe

29. Kitty (Brockville) The Woolbox

30. Old Joseph (Brockville) Craig's Mens' and Ladies' Wear Store

31. Mrs. Craig (Brockville) Shopper at Tonner's Pharmacy

32. Mr. and Mrs. Elasse (Brockville) Symington's Home Hardware

33. Mat Elasse (Brockville) Symington's Home Hardware –
    Mr. and Mrs.'s Great Nephew

34. Zakary - aka 'Trick' (Brockville) Disk Jockey/Radio Announcer at
    The 401 Inn

35. Mr. Saladino (Brockville) High School Teacher

36. Mr. Berenson (Brockville) Assistant Football Coach

37. John the Waiter (Ottawa) The Lord Elgin Hotel – Pick's Place

38. André the Waiter (Ottawa) The Lord Elgin Hotel – Pick's Place

39. Marisol (Ottawa) Leasing Agent for the Landlord on
    Argyle Avenue

40. Marianna (Ottawa) Colonial Furniture sales clerk

41. Alleyn Arendsdorff (Aaron's Classmate at Algonquin)

42. Jeremey Kessler (Alleyn's friend)

43. 'Mother' (Alleyn's Boss from the Hudson Bay Company)

44. Dexter von Kellner *'Dex'* (Anchor for an Evening Sports Broadcast Network)

45. Lorita Schaible (Aaron's Classmate at Algonquin)

46. Melora Holt (Aaron's Classmate at Algonquin)

47. Jakobe Erikschöenn *Jako* (Aaron's Classmate at Algonquin)

48. Connie Caserta (Aaron's Classmate at Algonquin)

49. Lauren Marcato (Aaron's Classmate at Algonquin)

50. Yolanda Vargas (Aaron's Classmate at Algonquin)

51. Cliff Horton (Brockville) Aaron's friend

52. Robert Galanos (Brockville) Aaron's Friend

53. Gemma (Kemptville) Robert's Sister at The Rideau View Inn

54. Bryson Steyn (Kingston) Robert's Boyfriend

55. Conor Rekford (Merrickville) Adam's Friend

56. Nicolas Marulli (Nick) *'Nico'* (Ottawa) Conor's Boyfriend

57. Jean-Louis-Pierre-Francois (Hull) Doorman/Bouncer at Sac's Nightclub

58. Mrs. Andrea Gauthier (Ottawa) Department of Health and Welfare

59. Hilary (Ottawa) Interviewer from Department of Health and Welfare

60. Angelica McCarthy (Edmonton) Jason's Lawyer

61. Yumiko (Edmonton) Waitress from *Komorebi*

62. Riku Kobayashi (Edmonton) Jason Blanchard's lover

63. Sergeant Jean-Jacques Dufour (Ottawa) Department of Health and Welfare – Chief Security Head

64. Iona Ouspenskaya (Ottawa) Algonquin College – Department Head of Interior Design at Algonquin College

65. Elzbeth Mountebank *'Ela'* (Ottawa) Algonquin College – Instructor

66. Lynda Naagy-Birdsong (Ottawa) Algonquin College – Instructor

67. Massimo Visconti-Ciccone (Ottawa) Algonquin College – Professor

68. Gaelen Goderich (Ottawa) Algonquin College – Professor

69. Evan Copland (Ottawa) Algonquin College – Professor

The Pets

1. *Brock Vegas Blackjack 'Blackjack'* (the Christie's Labrador Retriever)

2. *Melissa Etheridge 'Melissa'* (Cora-Leanne's' Miniature Poodle)

3. *Marlene Dietrich 'Dietrich'* (Alleyn's Purebred Afghan Hound)

4. *'Little Adam'* (Jason's Manx breed Cat from Edmonton)

CPSIA information can be obtained
at www.ICGtesting.com
Printed in the USA
BVHW070220260621
610173BV00001B/1

9 781525 597756